The Riddle of Ra

D.P. Scott

ISBN-13: 978-0993684142
ISBN-10: 0993684149

DEDICATION

For my daughters, Brittney and Alexandra

AUTHOR'S NOTE

This is a work of fiction, although the places and ancient sites are real. Any resemblance to persons, living or dead, is completely coincidental.

CHAPTER ONE

It was a bleak, cold February evening. The pounding rain, threatening to turn into snow, almost completely obscured the ambulance driver's vision, as he cursed and tried to focus on the slippery road. Close to his destination, he confirmed his arrival by radio, turned off the siren, veered to the right, and parked under the protective canopy. An awaiting orderly flew to the back of the vehicle and yanking the doors open, he assisted the paramedics with the stretcher. Rushing through the hospital's automatic sliding glass doors, they took the patient into a cubicle equipped with resuscitation equipment.

The six member medical team arrived in the room at exactly the same time as the patient and instantly set to work, working quickly and in silence, completely in tune with one another. The paramedic, who had been giving chest compressions en route, was immediately replaced with one of the team members and the patient was bagged by another as the anesthetist readied the intubation equipment. Cutting the patient's shirt along its seam so as not to disturb the already running intravenous, the garment was quickly removed and anterior and lateral electronic leads were applied to the chest. Chest compressions were halted for a moment to check for cardiac rhythm and when none was noted the defibrillator was booted to 150 joules.

"Clear!" said Dr. Davon Marshall, notifying the team to move away from the patient and the metal bed frame. She quickly glanced up to check that the team was standing back before pushing the SHOCK button. The patient responded by spasmodically jerking on the stretcher. Looking at the ECG monitor Dr. Marshall saw the line was flat. "No response, continue compressions," she calmly said, while she waited for the defibrillator to reboot. She was the team leader and it was her job to run the code. "Martha, has she had Epinephrine?" The answer was affirmative. "Give another dose in three minutes. Stop compressions and clear!" The patient was shocked, but again there was no response.

"Davon, I need a second," called the anesthetist, who was in the process of intubating the patient. He inserted the plastic tube down her windpipe and taped it in place against her cheek. "Done," he said as he attached the tube to the ventilator and moved away from the bed.

"Martha, prepare Amiodarone 300 mg diluted in dextrose, and clear!" Davon shocked the patient again.

The ECG monitor beeped and the team glanced up to see some cardiac rhythm, but it only lasted for a brief moment before again returning to a flat line. The patient was not responding to treatment.

Davon considered her options. Although she was running the code procedure by the book, there was one more thing she could try. "Continue compressions, give the Amiodarone and increase the dose of Epinephrine to 5 mg." The higher dose of Epinephrine increased the chance of brain damage, but she needed to jumpstart the patient's heart. The nurse picked up the prepared syringes and gave the drugs. Davon waited for her to finish. "Stop compressions and clear!" There was no cardiac response from the shock. Davon paused and looked at the long green flat line, running across the ECG monitor. There was nothing more they could do. "I think we have to call it," she said, checking her watch for the time of death.

Leaving the room with the anesthetist, Davon heaved a sigh. "Damn it, Tom. I hate to lose a patient."

"You can't save everyone, Davon," said Tom. His eyes scanned the brilliant and beautiful physician walking beside him. She was slim, blonde, blue-eyed and utterly gorgeous, and yet she was down to earth

2

and hard working. He desperately wanted to date her.

Oblivious to his desires, Davon stepped around a gurney and continued towards the nursing station. "I know," she answered, wondering why she always found death so hard to accept. "It's just that she was so young."

"You think seventy-six is young?" questioned Tom.

Davon smiled at him. "I do. My dad is seventy-six."

"Really?" he exclaimed in surprise. "Your parents had you kind of late in life, didn't they?" He was thirty-four years of age and had assumed Davon was in her late twenties, but even if she was older than him, he didn't care, he was determined to find a way to get her into a relationship. Tom was used to women chasing him and found Davon to be an enigma. She seemed to have no interest in him whatsoever, no matter what he said or how hard he flirted.

"My mom is younger than my dad," replied Davon, not willing to elaborate any further about her private life. She stopped at the nursing station and called out to one of the nurses. "The cardiac arrest in room five didn't make it, Beth. Please call me if any next of kin arrives."

Another nurse charting at the desk looked up. "There's a man in room twelve waiting for you, Dr. Marshall."

"Thanks, Sylvia. I'll head there now."

"Wait. Why don't we grab a cup of coffee first?" Tom leaned against the counter and looked expectantly at Davon. "I don't remember you taking a lunch break, you must be starving. I'll even pay," he said with a wink, moving closer and lightly brushing his arm against hers.

Davon sidestepped away and signed a form Beth pushed towards her. "I wish I could, but I don't have time. As it is I only have five minutes for a quick assessment of the patient in room twelve because I have a meeting with Dr. Scott at three," she explained, turning to leave.

Tom stared at her in disbelief. "The head of the department!" he questioned with raised eyebrows. "What does he want to see you about?"

The tone of his statement made her cringe—a haughty side of his personality Davon didn't like. "I guess I will find out," she politely replied. As she headed down the hall, she wished she had told Tom it was none of his damn business. Letting out a small chuckle, she knew she would never say that to anyone.

The man waiting in room twelve looked like a business professional. He was well dressed in a black suit, white shirt and funky brown and black striped tie. As he casually leaned against the wall, watching the doorway, he fiddled with his black leather briefcase.

"Can I help you?" asked Davon, approaching him with a smile.

"Are you Dr. Davon Laura Marshall?" He squinted his eyes and looked her up and down as though he was assessing her.

Davon was taken aback at the use of her middle name. No one at the hospital knew her middle name, except for payroll. "Yes, I'm Dr. Marshall and may I ask who you are? You don't look as though you are here for medical attention." She stood near the foot of the stretcher and waited for his explanation. When he shifted his position and walked around her to shut the door, Davon moved towards the head of the stretcher and the call button in case she needed to ring for help. Something just didn't feel right.

"I'm Maxwell," he said with authority, quickly flashing a government identity badge. "We need to talk."

"About what?" Davon's thoughts suddenly jolted back to the day she had made a ruckus at the consulate in New York.

Maxwell completely ignored her question. "Dr. Marshall, you were employed by Prince Abdul Sanduu from February 12th to the beginning of November of last year, is that correct?" He looked her directly in the eye, waiting for confirmation.

4

"Yes," Davon answered, clearing her throat. Her thoughts galloped in a million directions. Should she ask to have a lawyer present before answering any more questions? Was he from the IRS? Four days ago the three hundred and fifty thousand dollars she had earned while working for Prince Abdul was transferred to her account at the Bank of America. She didn't think she had to pay tax on the money, but if he was from the IRS...

"And you knew the Prince personally?"

Her ears perked up and she glared at him, instantly switching into doctor mode. It was clear Maxwell was not from the IRS and even if he did work for some branch of the government, he had no business asking about her private life. "I'm not sure where you are going with these questions. I think we are done here." Davon moved towards the door.

"I hope you are not thinking about leaving, Dr. Marshall," he replied as though he was issuing a threat. "We have a few important things to discuss."

Davon hesitated for a moment and turned back to look at him and as she did so her pager went off. Glancing at her watch, she realized she was late for her appointment with Dr. Scott. Walking towards the wall phone, just inches from where she was standing, she reached for it.

Maxwell instantly moved in and cupped his hand over hers. "Please don't touch the phone. As I said, we have a few things to discuss." His voice became low and intimidating, and his manner threatening.

Throwing off his hand, Davon spun around and faced him. "Don't threaten me, whoever you are! I have rights as a US citizen and as far as I know, I am still in the States. Now, you can leave the hospital quietly or I can have you thrown out! It's your choice," she angrily barked. She felt the blood careening in her head and her heart nervously pounding, but she wasn't about to let anyone bully her.

Maxwell laughed under his breath and stared her down. Quite

5

the drama queen, he thought. "Look, I'm going to come straight to the point. We know you know Prince Abdul Sanduu and that you were with him the night before he disappeared. We, I should say the US government needs your help, today, right now. Give me ten minutes, Dr. Marshall. This is very important."

"And why is the government suddenly interested in my relationship with the Prince?" snapped Davon, just as her pager went off again. Frustrated, she looked at the message. "I have to get this. I'm late for a meeting. Give me one minute and then you will have my complete attention." She picked up the phone and dialed the extension. This time Maxwell did not intervene. After she told Dr. Scott's receptionist she would be tied up for another ten minutes, she hung up the receiver and glared at him. "You now have nine minutes to explain!"

Davon ran her fingers through her hair and smoothed out the wrinkles in her scrubs as she took the elevator to the twenty-second floor. It was a futile attempt to tidy her person before the meeting with the director of her department. Rushing off the elevator, she hurried towards the large glass double doors and swinging one open, she entered the spacious office, greeting Dr. Scott's secretary.

"Go right in Dr. Marshall, he is waiting for you," she pleasantly instructed.

Davon knocked before entering. "Good afternoon, Dr. Scott. I'm sorry I'm late."

"Not a problem. Have a seat," he replied, sitting down on a brown leather couch across from her. "I wanted to welcome you back and say thank you for picking up the shifts in Emergency and ICU. Have you been getting enough work?"

"Plenty, thank you. Most of the shifts have been in Emergency, but I have four shifts in ICU next week."

"Well, I wanted to let you know that I have talked with Mark

6

Halls and as always he gives me accolades about your work. So it gives me great pleasure to offer you your old job back with a twenty thousand dollar raise." Dr. Scott leaned forward with a Cheshire cat grin.

"I can't thank you enough," said Davon, squirming in her seat. "But I am not actually in a position to take a fulltime job, right now, that is."

Dr. Scott sat back and rubbed his chin. "Has Massachusetts General offered you a position?"

"No, they haven't," she instantly replied, not really wanting to say anymore, but realizing she needed to give him some sort of explanation so that he would hold the job until she returned. "I am going to be taking a bit of time off..."

"Again?" questioned Dr. Scott, wondering if Dr. Marshall had some mental stress issues. His friendly manner evaporated and his eyes became hard.

She could clearly see there was no point in trying to explain, yet for some reason she kept talking. "You see, I was in the middle of my travels when I had to unexpectedly come home. I have been waiting for things to settle down and now that they have, I thought I would go back and finish my trip." He stared at her and offered no input as though he was waiting for more information, so she tried to embellish the story. "The issue was actually very urgent that made me return to Boston," she said with a serious frown. "I don't want to go into details as they are upsetting, however I want you to know that the minute I come back from this trip, I will be more than ready to take the position."

"And when may I ask are you leaving?"

"Next week, right after I finish the scheduled shifts in ICU."

It was obvious he was miffed. "Well then," he muttered, standing up. "I hope you have a better trip this time and that the position is still vacant when you return. Good day, Dr. Marshall."

Realizing she had been dismissed, she did not offer him her hand. She bit her lip as she passed the receptionist's desk, quietly mumbling a goodbye. At the elevator, she roughly punched the down button. Why does this always happen to me, she asked herself? Such rotten timing! I get offered back my dream job and I can't take it! Walking into the elevator, she leaned her head against the shiny brass wall and closed her eyes as it zoomed back down to Emergency.

The second the elevator doors opened, her pager went off. Davon looked at it and then walked over to the nursing station's counter.

"The relatives of your cardiac arrest are waiting for you in room sixteen," said Beth, as she slid the patient's chart across the counter. "You need to finish up the paperwork."

"Right," replied Davon. Still feeling frustrated and unhappy about her meeting with Dr. Scott, she grabbed the chart and immediately headed off.

When Davon walked into room sixteen, she was surprised to see so many people. There were at least eight adults and almost that many children. It instantly brought back memories of her time at the palace where the whole family would attend a medical appointment.

An elderly man stood when she entered. "I am Alfred Steel. Are you the doctor who attended to my wife?"

"Hello Mr. Steel, I'm Dr. Marshall," said Davon, taking his hand. "I'm so sorry that we were unable to save her. Her heart just wasn't strong enough."

A woman with red and puffy eyes came and stood beside Mr. Steel. "I don't understand," she said with a sob. "Mom never had any heart problems."

"Unfortunately, she did. Her heart problem may not have been diagnosed," Davon explained. She was not about to tell them that Mrs. Steel was actually clinically dead when she arrived at Emergency. "We did everything we could. I'm very sorry for your loss." Davon turned

8

back to face Mr. Steel. "Would you like to see her?" He silently nodded.

"We all do," said the daughter.

"Give me a minute and I will have the nurse make the arrangements," said Davon as she turned to leave. Going back to the nursing station, Davon looked for Beth. "There is quite a crowd wanting to see the body. You are going to have to move it into a larger room."

"I'll take care of it. You need to go and see stretcher number four—right side abdominal pain," said Beth, as she scooted down the hall.

CHAPTER TWO

Davon sat at the dinner table with her parents, Pete and Anne, half listening to their conversation, while she rehashed the meeting she had with Maxwell. He had told her a very convoluted, but convincing story, and then asked her to return to Cairo to look for Abdul. Maxwell explained she would be working undercover for the US government and emphasized the fact that it was a job only she could do. Although she had agreed to the project at the time, she was now having second thoughts as she recalled her last few months of employment in the Middle East.

She had taken a trip to Cairo with Prince Abdul to attend a charity event and during the auction portion, someone tried to assassinate the Prince. Because Abdul refused to go to the hospital for treatment, Davon gave him sedation and then sutured his wounds at the hotel. They were supposed to return to the palace the next morning, but Abdul encouraged her to return without him, promising he would join her the following day. However, the next day came and went and Abdul did not return. Frantic with worry, Davon attempted to find out what happened, but because she was the physician to the Prince's nineteen wives and children and no one, except perhaps Mr. Bedon, the Prince's valet, had any inkling about her involvement with Abdul, it put her in a delicate position, making it difficult to ask questions. Mr. Bedon returned to the palace without the Prince and quickly took hold of the reins, immediately taking away Davon's access to the outside world. When Davon began to fear for her life, she knew she had to escape. It was only by the skin of her teeth that she was able to get away.

"It's just three months since I've been home," she whispered, feeling frightened about leaving the security of the United States. Trying to defend her decision to return to Cairo, she considered Maxwell's promise of CIA protection while she was in Egypt. I'm just not sure about this, she thought, as she unconsciously pushed a piece of broccoli to the side of her plate.

"Davon, why are you picking at your food?" asked her mother, looking at her daughter with concern. "This is the reason you're so thin. You have to eat more, especially when you are working twelve hour shifts at the hospital! No wonder you are exhausted at the end of the day."

Davon looked up from her plate and smiled. "Mom, I find it difficult to eat a big meal this late at night," she remarked, wondering if now was the time to broach the subject of the trip. "I appreciate you holding dinner for me, but I actually would be just as happy with a bowl of fruit and yogurt. Besides, I'm sure you and Dad would rather eat earlier."

"We often eat this late," Anne casually replied as though it was no big deal. "More potatoes, Pete?" She picked up the bowl and offered it to him.

"Mom, it's almost ten-thirty at night. I know you and Dad eat at five o'clock. I grew up in this house, remember?" she exclaimed, glancing at her father. "Dad, say something. Don't you want dinner at your usual time?"

"As long as I get food, you will hear no complaints from me. I learned long ago never to argue with your mother," said Pete, scooping more potatoes onto his plate.

"Honey," Anne said. "Are you working tomorrow night?"

"No, I'm off until Tuesday."

Anne looked at her and grinned. "I was toying with the idea of having a dinner party tomorrow night. What do you think? You could invite Matt's mom and his sister-in-law."

"That's a nice idea, Mom, but tomorrow is not a great day for me. I'm busy all day and probably won't be home for dinner."

Anne put down her fork and pondered. "Alright then, maybe I should plan the party for next Saturday. Would that work?"

Davon winced. Next Saturday she would be leaving for Cairo. She had to say something, but couldn't tell them the truth. She took a deep breath and then looked her parents in the eye. "I have decided to take a holiday. I'm going to go to Europe for awhile," she said with determination, the lie surprisingly, rolling easily off her tongue.

"With whom, Davon? I hope you're not going off on your own again," said Pete, leaning forward with concern.

Anne looked horrified. "When did you get a new passport? You need a passport to go to Europe!" she shouted, becoming upset at this little snippet of information.

"I got a new passport a couple of weeks after I got back. And this trip is not a big deal. I'm taking a tour," explained Davon. She paused for a second and then added, "With a group of people."

"We know what a tour is, Davon. Don't get smart," said her father. As a retired intelligence officer, he was never one to mince words.

Davon sighed. "Look, I really appreciate you taking me in, but it is time for me to get my own place." She was grateful they had taken her in when she had unexpectedly returned in November, especially because their house was so close to the hospital, but noticed her parents treated her more like a child when she was living under their roof. "I met with Dr. Scott today and he offered me my old job back, so, once I get home and settled, I'll be moving."

"That's wonderful news about the job," said Anne, trying to

compose herself. "Why then are you talking about going away?"

"Well, before I leap back in to a fulltime position, I thought it would be best to take some time and get my head around everything that has happened." Davon could feel the warmth in her cheeks and prayed her face wasn't beet red.

Pete patted her hand. "You have been through a lot, Davon, and going on a little holiday before starting the job might be a good idea."

"I disagree," said Anne. Narrowing her eyes, she looked at her daughter. "I have a very strong feeling you are up to something, Davon Laura Marshall." Anne always called her children by their full name when she was angry.

"Mom, I don't understand why you never trust me." Davon tried to look shocked, chastising herself because she should have known her mother would see through the lie.

"It works two ways, Davon. I can trust you when you can trust me enough to tell the truth. I can't believe how different you are from your sister when the two of you grew up in the same house. Meg is more like me and I am sorry to say you are just like your father! You and Pete live in secretive worlds."

"What are you saying, Anne? I worked at the Pentagon for bloody sake! Of course I had secrets from you, top secret secrets from everyone!" cried Pete, raising his voice.

Anne frowned and looked at him. "I'm not blaming you. I realize it was part of your job, but Davon? Your daughter is up to something. I feel it in my bones!"

It was interesting that her mother wanted to be told the truth because Davon knew there was no way she could deal with it. The one person she wished she could level with was her father. He had worked at a high-level job at the Pentagon his whole career and although he never talked much about it, Davon was positive that some time in his thirty-five years or so, he did undercover work. She was positive her dad would be a wealth of information, but Maxwell had warned her not to say anything to anybody. Besides, Davon thought, justifying her reason to keep quiet, if Pete got wind about the real reason of her trip, she knew he would try to stop her. Davon stood up and forced a laugh. "Oh Mom, I love you, but honestly you worry too much. Whatever you feel in your bones is probably the beginnings of arthritis. I am just taking a European vacation and that is all," she said with sincerity, stifling a yawn. "Is there any chance I can get out of doing the dishes? I'm pretty tired tonight."

"I'll help your mother," said Pete. "Go on and get to bed."

Bending over, Davon gave her mother a kiss on the cheek. "Thanks for dinner," she said, vacating the room as quickly as she could.

Davon had just pulled out the suitcase from under the bed when her cell phone rang. She glanced at the caller ID. "Hi Matt."

"Hey, guess who called me tonight? Shawn McLeary. He's coming to town with his fiancée and he wants to get together tomorrow for a beer followed by supper. Are you up to it?" asked Matt enthusiastically.

Davon remembered Shawn, one of Matt's childhood friends. "Gee, I can't, Matt. I have some things I need to do tomorrow."

"Can you try to get your errands done in the morning? I said we would meet them around four-thirty."

"I wish I could, honestly, but I'm busy all day tomorrow." She sounded a touch evasive, which was unusual for her. Although she contemplated telling him she was going away, she was in no mood tonight to deal with the backlash she knew he would give her. It would probably be best to tell him in person.

There was a moment of silence before Matt finally said, "So what exactly are you saying? We always spend the weekend together when you're off. Are you really that busy or are you mad at me for something?"

Davon winced. "Matt, come on...I'm not mad at you. I have just had a horrendous couple of shifts at the hospital and I have a list of things I need to get done tomorrow. I was planning to come over to your place on Sunday and spend the night, if that's okay." She heard him breathing hard and pictured him trying to calm down.

"Alright, if anything changes, let me know. When you get here, I have something I want to tell you. How was your shift today?"

"Exhausting and I lost a patient."

"Oh, so, that is why you're depressed," he said as though the statement summed up the total reason for Davon's aloofness. "Do you want to talk about it?"

"No," she instantly replied. "I know it is part of the job, but it still bugs me."

"Well, I'm glad you aren't one of those cold blooded doctors who don't give a damn. You sound tired. Why don't you try to relax with a hot bath before you go to bed?"

"That's exactly what I am going to do. Say hi to Shawn for me and I will see you on Sunday. Night, Matt." Placing the phone on the bedside table, she plopped down beside the suitcase. How was she going to tell him she was going away? It was one thing to fib to her parents, but Matt? She would have to rehearse the lie because he could read her like a book.

Davon did up the top button on the collar of her coat and peered out from under the black umbrella she was holding, giving the Granary Burying Ground behind her a sideways glance. The cemetery was old—three hundred and fifty-seven years in fact—and contained the remains of close to 5000 people, including Paul Revere, and three signers of the Declaration of Independence. She shivered unconsciously when she saw

15

there was no one in sight. It was getting dark and raining hard, and the wind, which was starting to pick up in strength, was threatening to blow her umbrella inside out.

"Sorry I'm late."

Davon jumped and spun around. "My God, you scared me!"

"I didn't mean to," answered Maxwell, shaking his head at her antics.

"That's hard to believe when you have picked the creepiest place to meet—right in front of a graveyard. Do we really need this type of cloak and dagger secrecy? "

Maxwell rolled his eyes and refused to even consider the question. "Let's make this quick. Here's your plane ticket, and this," he said, handing her a fat envelope, "has ten thousand US in cash and a Visa card for expenses. Use the money for bribes. Your contact in Cairo will meet you at the airport. He will be holding a sign with your initials, D.M. Don't go with anyone else."

"And what if he is not there?" she asked, putting the ticket and envelope into her purse.

"He'll be there," Maxwell replied with confidence. "Once you're in Egypt, just act like a tourist. You won't be able to get a hold of me, but your contact will be able to get a message to his contact if there are any problems. We have already talked about your assignment. Find Prince Abdul and then we will do the rest. Any questions?"

"Yes, I have questions!" said Davon in a frantic whisper. She wished she could wipe the amused stare off his face. "You haven't said anything about how I am supposed to go about finding Abdul. Where do I start? Are there any rules I need to follow?"

Maxwell gave a low indifferent chuckle. "Just follow your nose. And rules? It's Egypt, Dr. Marshall, do whatever you need to do. Good luck." With that remark, he turned and walked into the cemetery, vanishing behind a large tombstone.

The first thing Matt noticed, as he was waiting for the light to change, was the bright yellow rubber boots the blonde woman was wearing. She was balancing her umbrella on her shoulder, the way Davon always did, and was in deep conversation with a man wearing a dark grey trench coat and black fedora. "That can't be Davon," he said, knowing she had the exact same yellow boots. The woman's face was partially blocked by the umbrella. "That can't be Davon," he repeated as though he was trying to convince himself. The light changed to green and he stared at the couple as he went by, looking back through the rear view mirror. He wondered if he should do a circle around the block.

Davon watched Maxwell disappear. Slinging her bag onto her shoulder, she jogged across the street, cutting through a small parking lot to get to her car. Clicking open the door, she jumped inside the jeep and heaved a long slow sigh. "What am I getting myself into?" she asked herself as she locked the door, giving a quick look around before opening the envelope. The ticket was a one way business class fare to Cairo with her legal name correctly spelled. The Visa card was in her name and there was a large wad of fifties, hundreds and five hundred dollar bills. As she fanned through the money, she gritted her teeth and muttered, "I leave next Saturday." Stuffing the ticket and envelope back into her purse, she started the car. As she made a right hand turn to get out of the parking lot, her cell phone rang. Glancing down at it, she saw Matt's name flash onto the screen.

CHAPTER THREE

The man took the brandy snifter from his butler and made himself comfortable on the white leather sofa strategically placed in front of a roaring fire. He smiled as he took a sip of the limited edition cognac, reaching down to pet the Siamese cat, nuzzling his leg. When his cell phone vibrated, he casually pulled it from his pocket.

"Yes."

"It's Maxwell, checking in."

"Did she take the bait?"

"Affirmative. She leaves Saturday, February 14th."

"How appropriate, Valentine's Day. Do you still believe she will be able to find the missing person?"

"I do. She is naive, but smart, and you know who her father is. If the missing person surfaces for anyone, it will be for her."

"Let me know when you get any further information." As he ended the call, he held up his glass and swirled the golden liquor before relishing in another sip. Things were definitely looking up.

CHAPTER FOUR

Matt rushed around the black wrought iron railing, dashed down the stone stairs and pulled open the door to the well-known Cheers pub, made famous by the eighties sitcom "Cheers". Entering the establishment, he quickly scanned the room, looking for his friend, Shawn, who had insisted on the meeting place so that he could show the landmark to his fiancée.

"Over here, Matt!" yelled Shawn, waving from a corner. Matt approached the booth and let out a hearty laugh when Shawn stood up and gave him a bear hug. "It is good to see you, Man. This is Haley, my fiancée," he said, turning to introduce a pretty, petite brunette. From the way Shawn looked at her, it was obvious to Matt that his friend was in love.

"Hey Matt, I'm glad to finally meet you." Haley stuck out her hand and gave Matt a firm handshake. "Shawn talks about you constantly and it is nice to put a face to the name."

"Well then, you definitely have the advantage because I know very little about you. When did you two meet?" asked Matt, sitting down at the same time as Shawn.

"We met about a year ago at work and from the moment I set eyes on her, I was totally mesmerized," said Shawn with a grin. "Where's Davon? Is she coming?" He stuck up three fingers at a passing waiter. "Three drafts, please."

Matt shifted uncomfortably and looked down. "No, unfortunately she's tied up tonight."

"Is everything okay between you guys?" questioned Shawn, detecting the sudden change in his friend's demeanour.

"I guess," said Matt with a shrug. "Does Haley know about Davon's trip to the Middle East?" He looked from Shawn to Haley.

"Shawn told me. I hope that's okay," she said, glancing at her fiancé. "I can't imagine going through something like that." She paused for a moment and then suddenly asked, "Did she really go onto the internet and take a job as the physician to some prince's harem?"

Matt exhaled loudly. "Yes, as unbelievable as it sounds. However, I'm partly to blame. The reason she took the job was because I broke up with her. Davon said she wanted to get as far away from me as possible," he quietly admitted. "I don't know all of the details as she refuses to talk about them, but after being at the palace for eight months, she barely escaped with her life. And now that she's home, it's been difficult for her to forget what happened and get back to a normal routine. The whole thing is totally bizarre to me," he said, shaking his head, "but Davon is a trooper and I know she will get through it. It will just take time."

"It's great you and Davon are back together again. Shawn has nothing, but praise for her. She sounds like a wonderful person and I'm sure things will work out over the long haul. As you said, time is a great healer," Haley offered encouragingly, discretely nudging Shawn.

Picking up on her cue, Shawn quickly changed the subject. They talked about work, the wedding and mutual friends. Soon the three of them were laughing and joking. When Haley excused herself to go to the ladies room, Shawn waited until she was out of hearing range.

"I don't want to cause you any more grief, but do you want to talk about what's bothering you? Every time Davon's name comes up, you look as though you are going to cry."

"Is it that obvious?" asked Matt. Crossing his arms, he tried to decide if it would help to vent the issue.

Shawn leaned forward. "Look, we've been friends since grade school. I think it might help to let it out. Tell me what's going on before Haley gets back. I'm worried about you Man."

"It's probably nothing," said Matt. He paused to gather his thoughts in the noisy bar. The after work crowd was letting off steam, enjoying food and drink in the iconic Boston setting. "I wanted to get together with Davon today and spoke with her last night. She told me she was tied up all day. Then on the way over to the pub, I think I saw her talking with a weird-looking guy in front of the Granary Burial Ground. It was pouring with rain and her umbrella was blocking her face, but I could see some blonde hair and recognized her yellow rubber boots."

Shawn looked as though he was going to burst out laughing. "You recognized Davon by her rubber boots as she was conversing with some man by the Granary Burial Ground?"

"I am not joking, Shawn. I know it was Davon," snapped Matt.

"Okay," Shawn calmly replied, sensing Matt's stress. "What made the guy look weird?"

"He was wearing a trench coat and a fedora." Matt shook his head. "Come on, who wears a fedora?"

"Old men wear fedoras. Was he old?"

"No, he looked around thirty-five or so. I don't know what Davon was doing with him?" Matt let out an exasperated moan. "You know I feel badly about breaking up with her last year, but no matter how hard I try, she just won't let me back in. She doesn't seem to trust me."

"First off, you don't know for sure the woman was Davon. And of course she trusts you. Just remember it's still early days. You can't expect things to go back to the way they were after all that has happened. Give her some time, Matt, she will come around."

"I hope so because I want to ask her to marry me. It was her birthday on January 9th and I went to the jewellery store planning to buy her an engagement ring, but I just couldn't do it. My gut instinct told me she would say no, so I bought her a diamond necklace instead."

"How did she like the gift?"

"She seemed happy about it, almost relieved it wasn't a ring," answered Matt, feeling disheartened. "But, enough about me, how do you feel about getting married? Haley seems like a great girl."

"She is. I'm happy to be tying the knot with someone like her." Shawn noticed Haley heading towards them. "And now that Haley is back," he suddenly blurted out just as his fiancée was about to settle into her seat. "We have something to ask you. Will you be my best man?"

Matt laughed. He was glad to have something cheery to think about. "Yes, I'd be honored."

CHAPTER FIVE

It was still raining when Davon pulled into the hospital parking lot. Reaching into the back seat, she grabbed the umbrella and then started to make her way towards the covered entranceway. Two paramedics were taking a patient on a stretcher through the sliding glass doors and as Davon stepped to the side, she glanced at the bundled person, quickly determining he had been in an automobile accident. Following the stretcher down the hallway, she skirted around to the back of the nursing station.

"What are you doing here, Davon?" asked one of the nurses as she rushed into the station and grabbed a chart.

"I'm looking for Tom. Is he on the floor?"

"Yeah, stretcher five," she replied, dashing off again.

Davon placed her coat and umbrella on one of the chairs and headed off. "Need help?" she asked as she pushed aside the curtain.

Tom was examining the eyes of a semi-conscious female while a nurse, who was sitting next to the bedside, was attempting to start an IV. "That would be great," replied Tom, casting a glance in her direction. "Ava, let Dr. Marshall start the IV. I need you to get me a vial of Decadron."

Davon washed her hands and put on disposable gloves before switching places with Ava. "What's wrong with her?" she asked as she settled into the vacated chair.

"I'm not sure. She collapsed at work. It looks like she has some cerebral swelling, but I can't see any evidence of head trauma. I'm waiting for her husband to get here so he can give me some medical history."

Davon pulled the tourniquet tight and gently patted the vein to pump it up. "No wonder Ava was having trouble starting the IV, her veins are small." She swabbed the site and pushed the needle forward. "Good," she said when she saw a return of blood. Securing the catheter in place, she hooked up the IV line and stood to adjust the flow of the intravenous fluid. "Tom, I came to see you tonight because I wanted to ask you for a favor. Could you possibly take my ICU shift on Friday?"

Tom looked up at her and grinned sheepishly. "Oh, so you didn't come to get me for coffee? Well then, I'm not sure if I can help."

"Please Tom, I wouldn't ask if it wasn't for an important reason," pleaded Davon. She bit her lower lip and waited for an answer. It was going to be difficult to get a replacement for her shift if Tom could not do it.

"A shift in ICU will cost you dinner, Davon."

Relieved, Davon smiled happily. "Alright, I'll take you for dinner, if you'll take my shift."

"Then it is a deal. How about taking me to Toni's tomorrow night?" Tom suggested, wanting her to commit to a date, sooner than later. He was excited about the prospect of being alone with her.

"Oh, sorry, I kind of have plans for Sunday," said Davon as she thought about Matt. "Would Monday work?"

Tom didn't get a chance to respond because Ava pushed her way around the curtain. "The husband has arrived and is waiting for you at the desk. Here is the vial of Decadron you requested. What dose would you like me to give her?"

"Hang on one second, Ava," said Tom, moving Davon outside of the curtain and towards the doctor's lounge. "On Monday, I'm going to New York for a couple of days. Can you get out of whatever you are doing on Sunday night?" he asked, looking hopeful.

Davon was conflicted. If she did not take him for dinner on Sunday, it would have to wait until she got back from Cairo. She was positive that wouldn't sit well with Tom. "Tomorrow will be fine. I will meet you at Toni's at six o'clock."

He gave her a radiant smile. "Can I pick you up?"

"No, thanks, I'd rather meet you," she politely told him, thinking the last thing she wanted to do was give him the impression it was a date. "Thanks so much Tom, I really appreciate you doing this for me. I hope the rest of your shift goes well."

CHAPTER SIX

Davon put her clothes in the dryer, turned it on and then returned to her bedroom. She had slept in, showered and was now starting to organize her outfits for the trip. Picking up her cell phone from the bedside table, she thought about Matt. She needed to let him know she would not be coming over to his house until later this evening. "He's going to flip out," she muttered, feeling nervous about calling him. "A text will be easier." Quickly typing a plausible explanation for being late, she fired it off, however seconds later her cell phone rang.

"Oh brother," she sighed, debating whether or not to answer it. She let the call go to voice mail, but when it started ringing for a second time, she reluctantly picked up. "Hi Matt, is everything okay? I'm just on my way out."

"No, everything is not okay! What do you mean you can't get over here until around nine tonight. I booked us a game of tennis at the racket club this afternoon. You bailed yesterday and now you're bailing today!"

Davon was irritated. She didn't have time for this. "As I said in the text, something came up. Sorry."

"What came up? I want to know!" he loudly barked.

The question startled her and for a moment, she was unsure if she should lie, but since Matt was already furious, she decided she might as well tell him a soft version of the truth. "Actually, the reason I can't make it over until later is because Tom is doing me a big favor and I agreed to pay him back by taking him to dinner tonight."

She heard Matt swear. "Why didn't you say anything yesterday?"

"Because it was only arranged last night. Tom wants to go to Toni's and I don't want to drive all the way over to your house and then all the way back over here. We're meeting at six o'clock and I figured we should be finished by eight, so I should be at your house by nine."

Matt swore again, this time under his breath. "Tom is a nice guy, but he's interested in you. Maybe I should come."

"Stop it! I hate it when you get jealously protective. And Tom is not interested in me. He is dating some nurse from one of the surgical wards and I think it's serious. Look, I really need to get going. Can we talk about this later?"

"Fine, see you later."

Davon put the phone down on top of the dresser and let out a groan. "How am I going to explain Cairo?"

CHAPTER SEVEN

Tom pulled open the door to the small, but chic Italian restaurant, flashed a smile at Davon, who was waiting in the lounge, and sauntered up to her. "You are a heavenly sight for weary eyes, Davon," he said, eyeing her up and down. "Beauty and brains! Such a rare combination!"

"Oh Tom, quit goofing around. Our table is ready. Come on." Taking her wine glass, she led him to a corner booth set for two. "How was the rest of your shift last night?" she asked, sitting down on the well-padded red imitation leather seat.

As Tom settled across from her, he quickly scanned the restaurant, hoping to see someone from the hospital. Only blocks from Boston General, the chef owned and operated establishment catered mainly to yuppies and was often frequented by hospital staff. "Busy, but no more than usual. I'm glad I'm off the rest of the week," he replied robotically, disappointed there was no one to see him with Davon.

"You do remember you're working for me on Friday," mentioned Davon as she opened the menu.

"Yeah, I remember. I wish the shift was in Emerg though because ICU is completely full. They are even using the overflow room. You're going to be swamped tomorrow."

"Great!" she replied with a sigh. "What was wrong with the young woman, the one you were examining when I barged in on you?"

"Don't know yet. We're waiting on the brain scan, which she hopefully had today. Her husband said she had been complaining of headaches and had been exhibiting odd behavior for a couple of months—forgetting things, driving to the wrong place, pulling into the neighbor's driveway. I suspect the problem is a tumor. The telltale sign is that her left pupil is slightly dilated."

"How old is she?" asked Davon, glancing up at him.

"I think around twenty-six or twenty-seven. I don't recall her exact age, but she is young."

"Well, let's hope if it is a tumor that it's operable!" said Davon as the server arrived to take their order.

"Do you want to share the pizza special, Davon?"

"Good idea." She looked at the waitress. "Could we have one pizza special and I would also like to order a green salad please. Tom, what would you like to drink?"

"How about a decanter of the red wine you're drinking?"

Davon nodded. "And a decanter of the house red, please." Picking up the menus from the table, she handed them to the server.

When the waitress left the table, Tom leaned forward and grinned. "I can't tell you how happy I am to finally get you alone. I have wanted to go out on a date with you for the longest time."

"This is not a date, Tom," replied Davon, quickly correcting him. "It's payback for doing my shift on Friday."

"Oh come on, can't you humor me. You don't always have to be so politically correct," he moaned. "I thought you could come back to my place after we finish eating. My condo has an amazing view of the bay and..."

Davon wondered how she was going to get through the meal. Although Tom was harmless, he could be incredibly irritating at times. "You know that's not going to happen, so don't even bother asking. I'm taking you to dinner because you're doing me a favor, period!"

"Alright then, since I'm doing you a favor, maybe you can do a favor for me."

"If you need me to pick up a shift for you—no problem. However just so you know, I'm going to be away for a while," she informed him.

"You'll be back by the end of March, won't you?"

"Most likely, why?" she replied, eyeing him suspiciously.

"Because I've got two tickets and I would like you, Dr. Marshall," he said, pausing dramatically, "to accompany me to the hospital's annual Spring Ball." He held up his hand to silence her when he realized she was going to refuse. "Before you say no to my request, just remember it is a fund raiser for the children's ward and is actually a lot of fun."

Davon shook her head. "Tom, how many times do we have to go through this? I think you're a great guy and I enjoy working with you, but I'm dating Matt. You know that."

"It wouldn't be a date, just a favor. I don't want to go alone."

"What happened to the nurse you were dating?" she asked, trying to be patient. She didn't think he would back out on his promise to do the Friday shift, but one could never be sure.

This time Tom shook his head. "It didn't work out. After the second date, she wanted to get married. Although she did not actually come out and say it until the fifth date, she started leaving hints around my apartment, like wedding magazines and honeymoon travel brochures. And you won't believe this, but she left about two hundred messages on my phone after I told her the relationship was over. She told me I was going to regret breaking up with her and one day I would realize it was the biggest mistake of my life."

"It just might be your biggest mistake," laughed Davon.

Tom ignored the comment. "Anyway, will you come to the ball with me as a friend?"

"Oh Tom, I really can't. For one, Matt wouldn't like it. And secondly, it's a formal affair and I don't own a ball gown." For a few seconds Davon was lost in thought as she recalled the beautiful gown she had worn when she had accompanied Abdul to the charity event in Cairo. She wondered what happened to the dress. It was probably in one of the palace's storage lockers with all of her other clothes. They're only things, she told herself, sighing. Oh well, she really had no regrets, except leaving before she could settle things with Abdul. She had been backed into a corner, fearing for her life and had no choice, but to leave the Middle East. At least she had been paid for her services, and the two Persian carpets she selected in Dubai had been sent to her parent's house in Boston. She was glad Lamna had insisted she send them to the US.

Davon was brought back to the present with Tom's hand waving. "You're not listening to a word I'm saying!"

"Sorry, I just remembered something I forgot to do. But, I'm listening now," she answered, trying to control her wandering thoughts.

"Can you ask Matt? I mean, can you say we're just friends, helping to raise funds for the children's ward."

Davon's frown softened. "Alright, I'll ask him. But in the meantime, please look around for another date."

The decanter of wine arrived with their food. As they ate, the conversation turned back to issues at the hospital. "What did Dr. Scott want to see you about?"

"Oh nothing," replied Davon, hesitating for a moment before saying, "He offered me back my old job."

"Good for you! When is your starting date?"

"We didn't firm up the details because I'm not sure how long I will be away. I told him I wanted to take a bit of time off before I commit to a fulltime position."

"Knowing Scottie, I'm sure he took that well!" Tom let out a snort. "Where are you going anyway? Is Matt going with you?"

Davon used her well-prepared answer. "I'm taking a tour of Europe. The tour is only two weeks, but I'm planning to go back to some of the countries—ones I really like. And Matt might come if he can get away. His business is booming right now, so he'll have to wait and see."

"Well," said Tom, his eyes sparkling. "I have vacation time. Why don't I come on the tour with you? As a friend," he added, when he noticed her exasperated expression. "It's no fun going to Europe by yourself—drinking wine alone at outdoor cafes, having no one to share the amazing sights, eating every meal by yourself. What do you think?"

Davon all but threw up her hands. "Tom! If you do not stop hitting on me, I am going to get up right now and leave you to finish off the pizza by yourself!"

"Okay, okay, I'm sorry," he cooed. "It is just that I'm enthralled by you, Davon Marshall and I want to give you a chance to get to know me."

"I do know you!" she replied through gritted teeth.

"Not the real me, you only know the doctor me," he protested, trying to think of something that would wear her down and make her see the light. He knew without a doubt, they were a match.

Davon stiffened. "I'm only going to say this once Tom, so listen carefully. I like you very much and I love working with you because you are a really good doctor. We can be friends, but there can be nothing more. You're a great looking guy and you have a wonderful personality and I know there is an amazing woman out there for you, but it is not me." Tom's manner cooled. He wasn't used to defeat. When he leaned back in his seat, Davon leaned forward. "Please, let's forget all of this and just be friends. I don't want to lose our friendship."

It took a few seconds for Tom to come around. "Well, I got that message loud and clear," he said, stuffing a piece of pizza into his mouth. "I will be your friend, Davon, but mark my words—one day you will regret you gave up on me."

"I'm sure I will," said Davon, thinking it was ironic because Tom was repeating, almost verbatim, the words the surgical nurse had said to him.

The check came to the table and Davon paid with her credit card, using the portable ATM machine. She finished entering her information and as she handed the machine back to the server, she suddenly spied Matt coming through the front door of the restaurant.

"Unbelievable!" she whispered under her breath, looking annoyed.

"What's unbelievable?" asked Tom.

Davon gave him an amused stare. He had caught her in a moment of irritation and she didn't want him to know it was about Matt. "The cost of the meal, of course, unbelievably reasonable," she replied, trying to cover up the blunder. Lifting up her hand, she waved. "Matt, over here," she called in a casual tone as if to say she was expecting him. She waited until Matt approached the table and then said, "Tom, you remember Matt."

Tom stuck out his hand. "Hey Matt, good to see you." As he shook Matt's hand, he frowned, mystified that Davon hadn't chosen to mention her boyfriend was coming to the restaurant.

"Yeah, good to see you too," Matt muttered politely. He then turned his attention to Davon. "I was driving by and suddenly remembered you saying you were having dinner here tonight. I thought I might join you."

Liar, thought Davon, through her half smile. She gave Matt the eye, letting him know she was angry. "Oh sorry, we've already finished the meal. I even paid the bill, but if you want to order something..."

"No, that's alright," said Matt, interrupting her. "I'll have something at home. Are you ready to go then?" he asked abruptly. When Davon nodded, he grabbed her jacket, which was hanging on a hook nearby and helped her into it.

Making small talk, the three of them left the restaurant, parting once they were out of the door. Matt linked arms with Davon and insisted on walking her to her car. She marched towards the vehicle almost pulling him along beside her.

"You're not saying anything, so I'm guessing you're mad I drove over here." Matt knew he was in trouble.

Davon stopped moving and looked at him. "You bet I'm mad. You drove all the way over here to check up on me! I told you I would come to the house after I finished dinner. The fact is you don't trust me, Matt!"

Matt tried desperately to make amends. "Davon, it's not like that. I was worried you might be too tired to drive all the way over to the house, so I thought I'd come and pick you up. We can drop your car off at your parents..."

"And how am I supposed to get home tomorrow! I have to work on Tuesday!" yelled Davon.

"Yeah that might be a problem," Matt agreed, nodding thoughtfully. "You have to understand. I really needed to see you tonight because I have something to tell you."

Her temper had flared and although Davon still glared at him, she spoke in a softer tone. "What is it?"

"Well, next weekend is Valentine's Day and you are going to kill me when I tell you this," he said, a bit concerned about how she was going to take the news, "but I took a peek at your schedule and I know you only have four shifts booked in ICU, which means...we are going to the Water Street Bed and Breakfast in Charleston for the weekend."

"Oh Matt!" exclaimed Davon, pulling away. She started to walk again, slightly ahead of him. Reaching her vehicle, she clicked open the doors. "It's cold. Why don't you jump inside and I'll drive you to your car."

Matt moved in front of her. "Wait, are you upset because I looked at your schedule or are you telling me you don't want to go to Charleston?"

"Just get into the car and I will explain," she said with a depressing sigh. Once they were both inside the jeep, Davon turned and looked at him. "I love the fact that you want to take me to Charleston, a place you know I adore, but I can't go this weekend because...because I am going to Europe on Saturday. I'm taking a vacation."

"What! Davon, please tell me this is not true," roared Matt, shaking his head. He aggressively ran his fingers through his short sandy brown hair as he tried to process the statement. "You booked a vacation without me! Are you going with someone else?" He felt pangs of jealousy raging inside as he recalled Davon talking to the man at the Granary Burying Ground.

Davon reached out for his hand and he hesitated for a long moment before he took it. "It is nothing like that," she calmly told him. "I'm going alone. I love you, Matt, but you cannot expect me to fall back into this relationship as though nothing happened. Please, I need a bit more time to figure things out." She knew if she explained some sort of rationale for the trip, he would calm down. "Since I've been home, I am just not myself and rushing back to work hasn't helped, even though I thought it would. The biggest problem is I feel a barrier between us. I know you feel it too, Matt, and although it is probably all my fault, I sincerely believe to get back to normal, I need to take some alone time.

That's the reason I decided to go away for a couple of weeks."

Matt stared at her. He wanted to believe her, but... "Why didn't you discuss it with me before you booked the trip?"

"I hope you aren't implying that I need your permission to take a vacation!" snapped Davon, suddenly becoming angry again.

"No Davon, I'm not saying that, but I don't understand why you need to get away or what you need to figure out," exclaimed Matt. "It's not rocket science. I love you and you love me and we are meant to be together. You said it yourself at least a million times before I stupidly ended our relationship. Forgive me, Davon. The reason I broke up with you last year was because I was feeling pressure. I knew you wanted to get married and it was overwhelming. All I could think about was how was I going to support you, when I was struggling to support my mom, Tina and the kids."

Davon huffed. "First of all, I'm a physician. You don't need to support me. And secondly, your dad and brother died three years ago and you're still supporting your brother's wife and kids. Why doesn't Tina get a job? After all, the kids are both in school. Of course, you have to take care of your mom, but Tina?" Davon shook her head in annoyance.

Matt slowly nodded. "I hear you. I always thought Tina was lazy. She graduated from high school and basically has never worked a day in her life." He let out a heartless laugh. "That's not quite true. I remember she did work for about a week as a receptionist at the company. I think Dad let her go. Obviously, Allen married her for her looks and not her work ethic!"

"Hey, I have an idea," interrupted Davon. "Why don't you offer Tina Stephanie's maternity position at the company? It would help you out because you won't have to worry about finding a replacement and it would be the gentle nudge she needs to get back into the workforce."

"I don't know, Davon," he said, not the least bit convinced.

"Just ask her. It would only be for a few months and it will be good for her. Tina's self-esteem must be really low. I can't imagine what it feels like to be young and fit and a parasite on your brother-in-law."

"You're probably right. I'll ask her tomorrow." Although he was not certain about recruiting Tina for the position, he was trying to make peace. "Look, it's already eight-thirty, do you still want to come over and spend the night?" he cautiously asked, deciding to let the discussion about the trip drop. He knew there was no sense in continuing the argument because it would only lead to Davon going home to her parent's house. Someone had to take the highroad, even though he still could not believe she booked a European vacation without him.

Davon started the vehicle and then leaned over and kissed his cheek. "You know I do!" she said, hoping Matt would not bring up the subject of the trip again tonight.

CHAPTER EIGHT

Waking to the sound of running water, Davon glanced at the clock on the bedside table. "It's only five-thirty, Matt! Do you really have to get up this early?" she hollered into the bathroom.

"Sorry Honey, I have a meeting at seven o'clock with the Weyburn client," Matt called from the shower. "I forgot to tell you last night."

Davon flipped onto her side and pulled the covers over her head. She had a slight headache, probably from the wine. Groaning loudly, she counted her lucky stars she didn't have to work today. *I never would have made it through the shift,* she told herself as she thought about the upcoming trip to Cairo. She swore quietly. "Maybe I shouldn't go."

At her first meeting with Maxwell, Davon had been shocked to discover how much information the government had on Abdul. Apparently, they had been monitoring his movements for years because as president of OPEC, Abdul had a great influence not only on the price of oil, but on the production rates, which had a direct link to the US economy. Maxwell had told her since the disappearance of Abdul in Cairo, there had been a major upheaval in the world's oil industry, causing chaos in the US markets. "We know something happened to Abdul because he hasn't surfaced since we lost his tail at the charity event in Cairo. The person now running the Sanduu Corporation is his twin brother Adin, a man, who refuses to work with the US government," he had explained with conviction. When the statement did not seem to persuade Davon to jump on board, Maxwell had quickly added, "Not only will you be serving your country, doing this job will give you closure. Don't you want to find out what happened to Abdul?"

Of course, Davon wanted to find out! The memory of leaving the wounded Prince in Cairo, a man she had been totally besotted with, in the care of Mr. Bedon—the assassin's accomplice—had haunted her every waking moment. "I have to go," she whispered into the pillow, "because nothing will be right with Matt until I find out if I am supposed to be with Abdul!"

"Are you talking to me?" asked Matt, coming into the bedroom with a towel wrapped around his waist.

Davon threw back the covers. "You know I like to talk to myself," she said with a chuckle, sitting up. "I am, however, trying to break the habit." She smiled at him and took in his buff physique. Matt was just over six feet tall and had a body like Adonis. "Are you sure you don't have time to come back to bed?"

"I wish! Weyburn is a big client, who doesn't like to be kept waiting and I have to meet him at the building site. How about giving me a rain-check? I'll pick up lunch and try to get home by one o'clock."

"I really don't have time to hang around," said Davon, straightening the duvet cover. "I should go home and start packing."

Matt reached up and angrily grabbed his flannel shirt off the hanger. "So, you're still planning on taking the trip on your own." He took a deep breath and then turned to look at her. "Is there any chance I can get you to change your mind?"

"Please Matt, I'd rather not discuss it anymore," she said firmly, meeting his gaze.

Not wanting to start another argument, he resentfully let the matter drop. "I know you don't like to stay here when you're working because my place is so far away from the hospital, but will you stay Thursday and Friday night? I'll drive you to the airport on Saturday morning."

Davon felt tears forming in the corners of her eyes. "Alright, I will stay here and thanks for being so understanding...about everything, Matt. You really are a great person! I'll get my packing done today and then I can drive over after work on Thursday."

Matt finished dressing. Trying to hold it together, he bent over and gave her a loving kiss goodbye. "Well then, I guess we have a date for Thursday. I hope your shifts aren't too hectic this week. Give me a call tomorrow, if you can." With those parting words, he left Davon sitting on the edge of his king-sized bed, contemplating how she got herself into such a mess.

CHAPTER NINE

As Tom had predicted, ICU was exceptionally busy the following week. The unit was completely full and five patients had to be housed in the overflow room. When Davon finished her shift on Thursday, she was extremely tired. Taking the stairs, she took a quick detour to the hospital cafeteria to buy a coffee before heading to Matt's house. Grabbing the takeout cup, she exited the building and made her way to the parking lot.

It was dark and raining lightly when she got into the car. Davon sat there, seizing a moment to clear her head. She shrugged her shoulders up and down and rubbed a tight spot on her neck. Sighing, she took a sip of the steaming coffee, and then winced— it tasted like day-old sludge. "Gross," she said, taking another sip. "I should probably toss it, but I need to be awake and engaging when I get to Matt's house." Starting up the jeep, she drove towards the main road and inched her way into the traffic as she continued to sip on the strong brew. It was just after 8:00 pm, but the traffic was heavy and it took her almost an hour to get to the townhouse.

Davon parked on the street directly in front of the house and then noticed Matt's truck was not in the driveway. "That's strange," she said as she popped open the trunk and got out of the vehicle.

Retrieving her suitcase, she walked to the entranceway and

fumbled for her keys. Matt's home was one unit of a block of colonial townhouses he had renovated. They were three stories high, made of gorgeous old red brick and were situated in a good part of town. When the owner had run out of renovation funds, Matt had had the foresight to ask for one of the corner townhouses in lieu of payment. The owner had whole-heartedly agreed and Matt had been able to move in three months before the entire project was finished.

As she stepped inside the doorway, her cell phone started ringing. She glanced at the name of the caller before she answered. "Hi Matt, I just got here. Where are you?"

"I can't talk long," he whispered. "I'm at another meeting with Mr. Weyburn and his lawyer. You know how he is paying me to build him an office building and a huge house. Well, now he is getting a divorce and he doesn't want his wife to get a thing. It's a bit complicated because he wants the work to continue, which is good for me, but his lawyer has to work the numbers. I could be here for a while. There are eggs in the fridge if you want to make yourself an omelet. I won't be able to get home for dinner. Sorry."

"Don't worry about me. I'll find something to eat. Hang in there," she replied, disconnecting.

Davon was in bed, but still wide-awake when Matt crept into the ensuite bathroom. "How did it go with Mr. Weyburn?"

"I was trying to be quiet. Did I wake you up?"

"No, I had some coffee near the end of my shift. So, what happened?" she asked, propping herself up with pillows.

Matt looked completely drained when he walked over and sat on the edge of the bed. "The lawyer may have found a loophole, I don't know. The whole thing is crazy because Weyburn is loaded and yet he doesn't want to give his wife a dime. Apparently, she was cheating on him with one of their employees and now he is out for blood. I still don't understand why I have to be involved. The whole damn scenario has been going on all week. I just want to build, not get caught up in the client's personal life!"

"I know it's horrible, but things will work out. Try to mentally distance yourself from the situation and that is probably all you can do," she suggested, giving him a nudge. "Go get cleaned up and come to bed. We can talk more about it tomorrow."

When Matt climbed into bed, Davon reached for him and pulled him close. He responded by embracing her as though he never wanted to let go. Both of them were seeking solace and escape, yet ironically, their needs for comfort were for radically different reasons.

Early the next morning, Davon got up a few minutes after Matt. While he was in the shower, she went downstairs, put on coffee and then made pancakes.

"This is nice," said Matt, kissing her when he came into the kitchen. "Are you sure you have to leave tomorrow? You could cancel your trip, stay here and take care of me."

Although she could tell he was joking, it was what he didn't say that irritated her. She knew he was still angry about the trip, but regardless, she was going anyway. "Matt, please don't try to make me feel guilty for going," she replied sternly. "You know this is something I need to do."

"Sorry Hon, I promise to not say another word about the you-know-what, but if you're leaving tomorrow, we should try to make the best of today."

Davon turned towards the stove so he could not see her face. She had the feeling he might suggest she meet him for lunch and that was the last thing she wanted to do. She had added several items to her list and needed to go over to her parent's place to retrieve some of them. "I have errands to do this morning and then I'm going to my parent's house, which should take a good chunk of the day. I just realized I forgot my bathing suit," she said, convincingly. She did not want him grilling her as to why she was going back home, when she told him last night she was totally packed. "I'll come back and meet you here tonight. What time do you think you'll be done?"

"Too bad you can't meet me for lunch," he said, pulling a long face. "I might be a bit late because I have another stupid meeting with Weyburn at three o'clock. He wants to rendezvous at Kelly's bar. I just hope he doesn't expect me to be his drinking buddy and listen to his problems all night." Matt poured syrup on the pancakes Davon put in front of him and took a bite. "Mmm, this is good. I'd suggest you meet us there, but I know if Weyburn gets your ear, we will never get away."

"By the time I drive over to my parents, listen to them yell at me again about the trip, and then get back over here, it will probably be at least four or five. You might be finished by then."

"Okay, why don't we plan to be back at the house by six o'clock at the latest? I'll just stand up at ten to six and tell Weyburn I have another pressing meeting. "

"Perfect," said Davon, smiling.

Glancing out the bedroom window, Davon watched Matt pull away from the curb. She turned back to the list of items she decided she needed for the trip. Adding a Swiss army knife to the bottom of the list, she jumped into the shower. She wondered if it would be wise to call Ted about Maxwell before she left. Although Ted was stationed at the US Embassy in Dubai and had helped get her out of the Middle East three months ago, she wasn't sure if he would be able to retrieve any information on Maxwell. She figured the Embassy was linked to the State Department, but she was not positive if Ted was at a high enough clearance level to access information about agents working for the CIA. "It might not be a smart move to call him," she mumbled, getting out of the shower and toweling off. "Ted would probably start asking me a bunch of questions, ones Maxwell would not want me to answer and if I do tell Ted the truth, I would be tipping off the State Department about a CIA directive." She plopped down onto the bed, thinking hard. In many ways, she hated being secretive, even though her mother thought the opposite was true. "Whatever," she said, "In this particular circumstance, I really have no option. Uncovering the dirt on Maxwell, with less than twenty-four hours left before the trip, isn't going to happen." Pulling her damp hair into a ponytail, she grabbed her clothes, selecting a bright turquoise t-shirt and skinny jeans.

It was only seven-thirty, but it would take over an hour to drive to her parent's house. Davon hoped her father would be at the indoor golf court, a place he frequented on a regular basis, because she needed to scrounge through his workshop in the basement.

CHAPTER TEN

"What are you looking for?" asked Anne, coming halfway down the basement stairs. She squinted her eyes and looked at her daughter.

Davon tried to appear innocent. "I'm just getting a few things for the trip. It's kind of an outdoor tour and I forgot some stuff when I packed on Monday. Go and make the tea, Mom, and I'll be up in a second," she replied, light heartedly.

"If you tell me what you're looking for, I can help you find it."

"I have already found most of the stuff I want. I was just seeing if Dad had a map of Europe," Davon said nonchalantly.

"His maps are in the file boxes on the book shelf," Anne told her, reaching the bottom of the stairs.

Davon held up a red one. "I found them, Mom. It will just take a sec to locate the map I need."

"Alright then," Anne replied, turning around. "I'll make the tea."

Davon let out a sigh of relief as she pulled the map of Egypt and her dad's GPS monitor out from behind her back. She replaced the file box onto the bookshelf and started to head for the stairs, suddenly stopping in mid-stride. Returning to the bookshelf, she searched one of the boxes for a European map. If her mom mentioned anything to her father, and he went to check his indexed maps, it would look odd if she had not borrowed a map of Europe. Grabbing one, she shoved the monitor and maps into her pocket alongside the Swiss army knife, miniature tool kit and hair trigger alarm and then turned to the stairs, jogging up them two at a time.

A floral china teapot, two mugs and a plate of oatmeal cookies were already sitting on the kitchen table when Davon came into the room. Making her way to her usual spot, she sat down, smiling pleasantly as her mother removed her apron and joined her.

"This is nice, Honey. I cannot remember the last time we shared a cup of tea."

"I know, Mom. It is crazy how busy I have been at work, but it's great because they have welcomed me back with open arms."

Anne smiled. "How could they not welcome you back? You're the best doctor they have."

It was a remark designed to please and Davon wondered what her mother was planning. "Mom, there are thousands of really good doctors at Boston General and although I appreciate the comment, I still have a lot to learn."

"Well, Dad and I are very proud of you," she touted, making direct eye contact.

Here it comes, thought Davon, wincing. She is going to bring up the trip. "Is Dad at the golf court? I was hoping to be able to say goodbye again before I take off," she spouted, trying to ward off the subject.

"I think his virtual game started at seven, so he should be home by lunchtime. I have no idea why he gets so much enjoyment playing golf with a computer." Anne shook her head. "Why don't you stay for lunch?"

"I wish I could, but I promised Matt I would meet him. So," she said, taking a sip of tea as she stood, "I probably should take off."

"Wait a minute, you haven't even had a cookie and I wanted to talk to you about something," said Anne, looking wounded.

Realizing she was not going to be able to get away from listening to her mother's unwelcome advice, Davon slumped down into the chair and reached for one of the smaller cookies.

Anne leaned close. "Your father and I talked last night and well, I was going to phone you today because we thought I could join your tour. It's lonely going on a vacation by yourself," she said, getting more and more excited as she spoke. "So, I already started packing and just need to get my passport out of the safety deposit box and if it is too late to get on your flight tomorrow, I will jump on another one and meet you." She looked at Davon triumphantly, expecting her to be thrilled.

"Hang on, Mom," said Davon, rendered almost speechless by her mother's idea. "That's..." She wanted to say absolutely ridiculous, but knew she had to let her mother down softly to prevent an altercation, "is a great idea, but, you know what would even be better, if you, Meg and I went on a vacation together. We should definitely plan something for the future. The problem with this trip is I have already made arrangements to meet someone," she blurted out, racking her brain for the answer to her mother's next question, which would be "Who are you meeting?"

Anne appeared dumbstruck. "Are you meeting a man?" she asked. Leaning back into the chair, she crossed her arms and lifted a cynical eyebrow.

"Actually, I'm getting together with one of the female physicians from my class," Davon quickly replied not rising to the bait. "Anita Collier landed a job in Munich at one of the teaching hospitals there. She recently emailed me about the European tour and because I knew I needed to get away and think about things, I decided to go for it."

"Well," said Anne with a pouty sigh. "I don't understand why you keep everything to yourself. Why didn't you tell us about Anita the other day when you mentioned the trip?"

Davon shrugged. "I'm not sure, Mom. We were talking about

other stuff and it just didn't come up. You have to realize I have been through a lot and I'm sorry to tell you this, but I feel constant pressure from you and Matt to return to the Davon I used to be. I need time to think and figure out what I want to do with the rest of my life and I have come to the realization that I can't do it in Boston. I love you and we will definitely plan a trip with Meg when I get home," she said, standing. "I probably should get going."

Anne rose from the chair and walked over to her daughter. "I love you too, Honey, and I'm sorry if you are feeling pressure from me. The only thing I want is for you to be happy. Have a wonderful trip and although I can't promise I won't worry, I'll try not to fuss too much while you are gone."

After they embraced, Anne saw her to the door.

The lie sat uncomfortably as she maneuvered through heavy traffic. Davon already felt remorseful about the stories she had been telling her parents and now she had fabricated another one about a fictitious friend in Europe! The quote: 'Oh! What a tangled web we weave...' crossed her mind. Her life certainly was becoming a tangled web of deception. Davon sighed and pushed the conversation she had with her mother out of her head, promising herself she would not participate in any more discussions about the trip. "The best recourse is silence," she muttered, wondering how she was going to get through the evening with Matt. Determined to focus on the assignment at hand, she thought about the few purchases she had to make and what she was going to pick up for dinner.

It was close to 3:00 pm when Davon struggled up the walkway to the townhouse, packages and groceries in tow. She went around to the back entrance, which gave direct access to the kitchen. Hauling her bags through the door, she put the groceries away and then after glancing at the time, ran up the stairs to the bedroom. Matt would be home around 6:00 pm and she wanted to have her packing completed and her clothes ready for the morning. The last thing she wanted was for him to inspect the contents of her luggage.

She emptied out her suitcase and then systematically repacked, placing heavier objects at the bottom of the bag. She considered the outfits she was taking. All of the clothes were relatively nice, however, she only had one dress—a rather simple style made from a stretchy navy fabric and one pair of blue jeans. She had brought yoga pants, black T-shirts and had pulled together several summery top and pant combos. A pair of black sandals and a pair of newly purchased sneakers snaked around the sides of the case. Satisfied she had not forgotten anything, she placed her dark woolen pants and heavy sweater on a corner chair, zipped up the suitcase and positioned her black lined raincoat on top of it.

Going down to the kitchen, she put on music and opened the fridge. The frozen lasagna she had purchased from a deli was beginning to thaw. Placing it onto the counter, she pulled out some garden greens and began to make a salad. The lasagna would take fifty minutes to bake, so Davon would put it in the oven just after five-thirty. She estimated that would give Matt enough time to get home and shower before supper.

It was 7:35 pm when her cell phone rang. "Is there any chance you'll be able to get away soon? The lasagna is getting cold," she said the second she answered it.

"I'm on my way to the car. Weyburn is unbelievable! But, I don't want to spoil our last night together talking about him. I'll be home in fifteen minutes. See you then."

By the time Davon reheated the lasagna, Matt was sailing through the front door. "I made it!" he called, rushing over to give her a kiss. "How was your day?"

"Good. I think I have everything I need for tomorrow." Davon handed him a glass of wine as they made their way into the living room. "You look tired, Matt. I know the meeting with Weyburn was frustrating, but was it successful?" she asked, sitting down on the sofa beside him.

"I guess. Weyburn certainly likes me. He gave me a down payment to start working on the office building, but has put a hold on the house plans until his divorce agreement is finalized, which is fine by me because I really don't have the man power to do both projects at the same time," he said with a shrug. "Did your parents hassle you about the trip this morning?"

"No, not really."

"I know I promised not to say anything, but I was thinking about your trip and you going home to get your bathing suit," he said, pausing for a second when he saw the fury building in her eyes. Although he realized he should probably drop the subject, for some reason he couldn't help himself from continuing. "Isn't it the wrong time to go to Europe? I mean, it's winter there too and probably pretty chilly. I can't see it being bathing suit weather."

Davon let out a long drawn out sigh and glared at him, furious that once again he found the need to challenge her decision. "How many times must I tell you? I don't want to discuss it," she replied, abruptly standing. She was tired of everyone, judging her every move. "I need to get the lasagna." Stomping into the kitchen, she removed it from the oven and placed it onto a hotplate in the middle of the table.

Cautiously joining her in the dining room, Matt sat down in his chair. He watched her slap a large serving onto his plate. "It looks delicious, Davon. Thank you," he said, quietly, taking a tentative bite. The mood had become decidedly frosty.

"It might be a little overcooked on the top, but I bet the inside is just fine," she mentioned as she took her seat. She was still steaming about the bathing suit comment and was angry with herself for slipping up! She had thought about the weather in Egypt, but had not even considered Europe! Why had she said she needed to go home for her bathing suit, she asked herself, feeling incredibly foolish as they ate in silence for a few minutes.

"Can you please pass the salad?" asked Matt, bringing Davon back to the here and now.

She handed him the bowl and tried to breathe. There was no point in fighting with him tonight, she told herself, wanting to leave Boston this time on a peaceful note. "Did you get a chance to ask Tina about the job?"

"No, I completely forgot. She usually goes over to Mom's house on Saturday mornings. Maybe I'll drop in and talk to her after I drive you to the airport."

She knew he could not run the business alone. "You need to hire someone for the position as soon as possible. Stephanie is seven months pregnant and sometimes things can go wrong in the last trimester," she lectured. His procrastination bothered her.

"This is why we're a great team," he replied, trying to sound positive. "I like it when you look out for me." He toyed with is food, struggling to find the right words to ask about her plans for the future. He did not want to upset her again. "Do you have any idea about what you might do when you get back? Are you going to continue living with your parents?"

"Actually, I already told them I'm moving out. It was nice that they took me in and their house is certainly near the hospital, but I can't stay there any longer. You know what my parents are like," she said, sounding more like her old self. "They are constantly breathing down my neck and watching my every move. Although I love them to bits, I need my own space."

With a pleading glance, Matt lifted his glass. "Well, you could always move in with me. After all, we did talk about living together a while back," he suggested, hopefully. When Davon's smile faded, he became nervous. "I know I live too far away from the hospital, but I can sell this place. We can buy a house together, one closer to the hospital."

"Matt, not yet," she replied in barely a whisper.

This time his face fell. He reached out and took her hand. "I want to marry you. I love you with all of my heart. What can I do to make you forgive me for breaking up with you last year?"

"I have forgiven you. I forgave you a long time ago," she said, squeezing his hand. "You rescued me in Dubai. I know you love me and I love you."

"But..." he said, reading her uneasy expression.

"But," she continued, not really wanting to have a conversation about their relationship, "I'm not totally convinced we are meant to be together."

Matt tried to control his frustration. "Davon, you know that isn't true. We will get over this hump. I promise I will wait as long as it takes for you to get through whatever you're going through."

"Listen to me. I don't want you wasting your time waiting for me. You need to live your life to the fullest extent, like I plan to live mine. If we are meant to be together in the future, we'll be together. You are an amazing man and I love you, truly, I do, but at this moment in time, I cannot promise you anything. Tomorrow, I think it might be best to part as friends."

Matt stood so quickly, he almost knocked his chair to the floor. "Part as friends!" He was incredulous! "What about last night? Didn't that mean anything? Does it have something to do with Tom? Are you going to Europe with him?"

"Don't be ridiculous!" said Davon, raising her voice. "I'm not going to Europe with anyone. This is part of the problem. You have always been jealous of me!" She exhaled loudly. "The whole thing is bizarre, because when I wanted to get married, remember, you were the one who broke up with me!"

"So, this is payback!"

Davon stood and faced him. "I think I should go."

"No, please, I'm sorry. I don't know what has gotten into me. Let's go into the living room and discuss this as adults," he said gently, trying to usher her towards the sofa. "I guess I'm afraid because I feel like I am losing you." He sat down on the couch, but instead of sitting beside him, Davon chose a chair directly across from him.

"I'm sorry if you feel that way because really, you are my best friend. You have shared so many of my most happy times. Although the breakup was one of the worst moments of my entire life, in a roundabout way, it became one of the best parts of my life because I grew from it. Suddenly, I had to become my own person. Matt, you are solid, responsible, loving and caring and I do love you, however, you pushed me out of the nest and now that I have seen some of the world, I can't fly back, at least not yet. Do you understand what I am trying to tell you?"

"I understand. But, please, I beg you, don't give up on us," he pleaded.

"I am not giving up on us. I just can't totally commit to a relationship right now." Davon rose and walked over to him. "My flight leaves really early tomorrow morning. How about if we stop talking about this subject and call a truce?" she suggested, ruffling his hair. "Come and help me do the dishes before we go to bed. I have to tell you what my mother said when I went home this morning. You won't believe it."

CHAPTER ELEVEN

Matt broke the uncomfortable silence as they approached the airport. "I would really like to take you to the gate, Davon. I don't care how much it costs to park the car."

"We have already discussed it. Please drop me off at the international departures. You know I hate long goodbyes," she said with a definite briskness in her voice. There was no way she wanted Matt hanging around while she got her boarding ticket to Cairo at Turkish Airlines. She listened to him huff. "Matt, we finally worked through things last night, please don't ruin our goodbye. I love you. I really do, but I need a bit of time. I thought you understood." Davon could almost cut the tension in the air. "I will be back in two weeks. Throw yourself into work and before you can turn around I will be home."

"Fine," he replied curtly, flicking the indicator to change lanes so that he could go up the ramp to the international departures. "In case you forgot, you haven't given me your return date. Do you get home on the 28th?"

"Here. Stop the car here." Matt swerved to the curb. "This is great," said Davon, opening her door. "I'll email you my return flight itinerary. I'm already late." She jumped out of the car, opened the back door and pulled her suitcase off the backseat.

Matt met her at the curb. "Are you sure you don't want to level with me, Davon? I have a bad feeling in my gut. And..."

Davon stiffened and pursed her lips. "I need to do this, Matt. Please don't question me."

"Okay, I won't say anything else, but promise me you will find a way to let me know you're safe."

"I will," she quickly replied, anxious to get away from his persistent grilling, which made her feel uncomfortable. She gave him a hug and a peck on his cheek. "Thanks, Matt, for always being there." Turning, she quickly walked through the opening sliding glass doors and did not look back.

CHAPTER TWELVE

Davon glanced at the other passengers as she gathered her things in preparation to deplane. She had changed planes in London and although she had not slept the first leg of the trip, she managed to get a couple of hours of shut-eye from London to Cairo. She was surprised at how rested she felt.

Standing up, she tied her jacket around her waist, slipped a scarf over her hair like some of the other female passengers, and got out her travel visa and passport. The line moved slowly, but soon she was making her way through a crowded hallway towards baggage. Her first impression of the Cairo airport was that it was in dire need of a renovation. She had been here once before, but had arrived on the Prince's private jet and had bypassed regular security. Not entering the airport, she didn't realize how dismal the building really was. The pinky white floor and wall tiles, many badly chipped, looked as though they were from the seventies. Welcome to the real world, Davon thought to herself. Following the signs, she nudged and slowly inched her way towards her destination. Although the halls were of ample width, they were packed with people, all trying to be the first to get through immigration. After waiting in the wrong lineup for almost an hour, Davon finally got close enough to see a less busy booth with a flashing sign that said 'Foreigners'. Squeezing into that lineup, she glanced behind her and noticed she seemed to be the only Caucasian in the vicinity. As she approached the booth, she fiddled with her scarf, pulling it further down her forehead and glanced at the soldiers situated by the exit doors, all with semi-automatic machine guns slung over their shoulders.

"Nationality?" abruptly asked the male customs official dressed in military attire.

"American," answered Davon, handing him her travel visa and passport.

"What is the reason for your visit?"

"Tourist," replied Davon, maintaining an expressionless face.

He quickly looked at her passport, at the computer and then for a long lingering moment at her. Then with a loud thud, he stamped her visa and gave her a brief grin. "Welcome to Egypt, Ms. Marshall," he said, sliding her documents across the counter.

"Thank you." Davon took the passport and carefully placed her visa inside. Moving cautiously around the soldiers to exit the restricted area, she set off to find her luggage.

"Thank goodness my luggage didn't get lost," she said when she spied her grey suitcase with its bright orange tag coming down the ramp. Grabbing it, she placed it onto one of the available pushcarts and started to make her way through the frosted automated glass doors.

Surprised at the number of people on the other side of security, Davon scanned the signs that almost every man seemed to be holding up and looked for one with the letters: D.M. There were none. Forced by the exiting crowd to continually move forward, she soon found herself among the waiting group of sign holders. Slowly pushing her cart, she glanced from side to side looking for a sign with her initials. Suddenly, she caught a glimpse of a young stocky man in a chauffeur's uniform holding a sign with D.D.M.

"Excuse me," said Davon, approaching him. "Do you mean just

D.M? I am looking for someone with a sign that says D.M. and you have an extra "D". Do you mean D.M?" she asked again, wondering if the extra "D" stood for doctor.

"Yes, D.M," replied the chauffeur in poor English. "You come, please." He immediately took possession of her luggage cart and began to forge his way through the crowd, indicating for Davon to follow, which she did.

Davon stared at the chauffeur's back and analyzed the situation as they walked across the airport foyer. "You would think my contact would speak better English, but he is cute and looks strong enough," she said under her breath. It was then that she felt a light tap on her shoulder.

"Excuse me Miss," whispered an elderly man dressed in native clothing. "You must come with me." He whisked out a tattered piece of paper with D. M. roughly scratched on the surface, showed her, and then quickly stuck it way as if he was afraid someone else would see.

Davon slowed her pace, but kept an eye on the chauffeur. "Really, you are my contact?" She looked at him sideways, confusion and doubt on her face. He was short, very short in fact, looked to be at least seventy, and appeared to be of Indian decent not Arabic. "That fellow there," she said, pointing at the chauffeur, who was in the process of exiting the airport. "He also has a sign with D.M."

Aware of her ambivalence, the elderly gentleman pulled out a black and white photocopied picture of Davon and showed it to her. "Is that your luggage?" he inquired, watching the chauffeur pop the trunk of a shiny black limousine.

"Yes," replied Davon, now convinced she was going off with the wrong man. She dashed out the door. "Stop," she cried, jogging towards the car. "I am sorry, but there seems to be a mistake. You see, this gentleman is the person I was to meet." She pointed to the man coming towards the car and then tried to take her suitcase from the chauffeur, but he held on to it tightly.

Coming to the rescue her contact quickly explained to the

59

chauffeur in Arabic that there had been a misunderstanding. He then turned to Davon. "The driver wants to be paid because he is worried he has now missed the person he was supposed to pickup. If you have some American money you should give him a few dollars for your suitcase."

"Is five enough?" asked Davon, fumbling in her purse.

"Plenty," he said with a nod. She handed the money to her contact, who handed it to the driver in exchange for her suitcase. "This way, Dr. Marshall, I am afraid my vehicle is in the car park and it is a bit of a walk. By the way, my name is Baboo. I am pleased to make your acquaintance." They briefly shook hands and then walked side by side, passing several construction sites. "I was asked to make a reservation for you at the Hilton Hotel. I believe you stayed there on your last visit to Cairo."

"Yes, I did," replied Davon, moving around a large hole in the sidewalk.

"Now, I have not been briefed on your assignment, but I do know we are looking for a member of the Royal Family," Baboo said, his voice becoming a whisper. "Perhaps, you can fill me in when we get to the car." They walked for another five minutes towards a fenced car park that held hundreds of vehicles. It was extremely warm and the sidewalk running alongside the busy road was dusty and dirty. "Not much further," said Baboo, pointing to an old navy blue Vauxhall that was in dire need of a paint job. "It does not look like much, but it runs well."

Baboo opened the passenger door and Davon got inside. The black leather seat was extremely hot and Davon could feel the heat through her pant legs. She rolled down her window while she waited for her contact to put the suitcase in the trunk and tried to think of a polite opening. I am afraid this is not going to work. I expected someone a bit younger—a James Bond type of guy, more like Maxwell. I mean if I knew martial arts and could handle a gun, I could deal with the bad guys myself. You see, I need some help...and believe me, this is not about your age, but I presume that this type of work might be a bit difficult for you. She grimaced, not wanting to offend as she thought about her arthritic father, who she figured was just a few years older. Davon groaned. "How am I going to let this man down lightly?" she asked herself as she came to a realization. "Of course, he is just picking me up. Baboo may be helping with the case, but he is most likely taking me to my contact." She unconsciously let out a huge sigh of relief as Baboo got into the driver's seat.

"I apologize about the car, but times have been rather slow, not much work these days. It may look better if we rent a limousine before I take you to the Hilton. What do you think?" asked Baboo.

Davon turned and looked at him. "Before we do anything I think we should discuss our roles. You mentioned that you haven't been briefed on the case. Does that mean you are taking me to someone who has a plan of how to get started?" Although Baboo seemed like a nice person, Davon was hopeful he was just a driver.

"I am afraid you and I will have to develop a plan. When I accepted the contract, I was given your picture, told to write the initials D.M. on a sign and meet you at the airport. My contact said the case was about a missing person from the Royal Family and told me you would be staying at the Hilton. I was given half of my fee and it was implied that you would be paying the remainder when the job is done."

Davon frowned. "So you are my contact." She bit her lip when Baboo nodded his head in confirmation. "I don't mean to sound rude, but what are your qualifications for the job. I'm concerned because I think this job might be dangerous and...

"You are worried that I am too old. Is that it?" asked Baboo, interrupting her.

"Well, frankly, yes," answered Davon, feeling very uncomfortable. "I don't mean old in the sense of the word, but maybe you are just a bit senior for this type of case."

Baboo turned the key in the ignition and the old car, with a belch of black smoke, roared to life. "Well, Dr. Marshall, do not be concerned. I am seventy-two years old, but in very good health. I have a black belt in kung fu, a tenth degree black belt in judo, and am a master at knife throwing. I do yoga every day and have been in the investigative business my whole life. I speak seven languages and am completely trustworthy. Believe me, and I say this with confidence—you are in good hands. Now, if you have the funds I suggest we rent a Lexus for our trip to the Hilton. Since it is frowned upon for an unmarried woman to be traveling with a man, who is unrelated, I will be a family friend escorting you around Cairo." Baboo looked at her and smiled. "You see, that is where my age comes in handy. If your contact was younger, there would be gossip and trouble."

After spending nine months in the woman's quarters at the palace, Davon completely understood the significance of what Baboo was telling her. "Alright, you have convinced me that you are the right man for the job. Now, I will tell you what I know and then we can come up with a plan together."

Baboo drove up the ramp to the entrance of the Hilton and stopped the dark grey Lexus at the tall glass sliding doors. He turned around to speak to Davon who was sitting in the back seat. "Call me only on the secure cell phone I gave you. Do not use the hotel phone, it could be tapped."

"Got it," replied Davon as the doorman opened the door to the vehicle. She exited the car and had a fleeting second of deja vu. The sounds and smells she experienced four months ago were exactly the same and she could see Abdul with his unimposing allure, talking and laughing with the hotel manager and Bedon—horrible Bedon—yelling at the bellmen to get the bags. Taking a moment to compose herself, she took a deep breath and walked into the foyer, letting Baboo and the doorman sort out her luggage.

She was surprised when the desk clerk greeted her by name. "Dr. Marshall, welcome back. We have your suite ready for you. The same one you had the last time you stayed with us."

Davon knew that particular suite had cost several thousand per night. "Oh, thank you, but since I am traveling alone today, I would prefer a smaller suite, something a bit cozier. My last suite was very beautiful, but it was so large I felt a bit nervous being there alone." She gave the clerk a warm smile.

"Of course, Dr. Marshall. We have a lovely corner suite on the seventh floor, which overlooks the Nile. It is only nine hundred square feet. Will that suite be suitable?"

"Yes," said Davon, handing him her passport and credit card. She didn't dare ask the price. "Would it be possible to set up a meeting tomorrow morning with the hotel manager?"

The clerk returned her items and placed the room card onto the countertop. "The manager is in his office now if you would like to see him right away."

Davon hesitated. She did not want to miss the opportunity to speak with the manager, but she was feeling a bit tired from the flight and knew she needed to be in top form for the meeting. "I would prefer to see him tomorrow, if that works."

"He will only be at the hotel in the morning. I can set up an appointment at 9:00 am for you." Davon nodded and the clerk entered the appointment time into the computer. "His office is on the tenth floor, room 1006. Here is his business card with the time and date. Would you like a wakeup call, Dr. Marshall?"

"Yes, eight o'clock please."

When Davon turned around a female clerk greeted her. "Welcome back to the Hilton, Dr. Marshall. I will be showing you to your room. Your bag has already been delivered. Please come this way. She did not take Davon to the private elevator, but instead walked to the end of the lobby towards a grouping of six elevators.

The clerk pressed the button for the seventh floor and then turned to look at Davon. "Would you like me to make arrangements for a tour? I can ask for the guide you had on your last visit."

"Unfortunately, this is strictly a business trip," replied Davon, feeling remorse because she would have liked nothing better than to go back to the Egyptian Museum.

"I see," said the clerk as they exited the elevator and started to walk down a beautifully decorated corridor.

Her suite was at the end of the hall and when the clerk opened the door, Davon was thrilled with the view. She was on the opposite side of the hotel from her last stay, but the view of the Nile was still superb. She tipped the clerk and after the young woman departed, Davon immediately stripped down in preparation for a long hot shower while enjoying the stunning scenery from the bedroom window.

CHAPTER THIRTEEN

The early morning sun promised a hot day. As Davon ate breakfast on her suite's large balcony, she watched several flat bottom boats maneuver along the scenic Nile. Coming from the dead of winter, she relished in the heat, enjoying the luxurious surroundings of the hotel as she nervously rehearsed the story she planned to tell the hotel manager. Although Baboo had come up with the idea, it was going to be up to her to carry it out.

Taking a final sip of coffee, she stood and gripped the balcony's handrail, gazing at the beautiful scenery below. The hotel's large lush tropical garden, full of exotic flowers, exploded in a riot of color. Davon's eyes were drawn to the flaming orange and yellow birds of paradise—the only flower she was able to identify, and then traveled to the wide and busy pedestrian walkway, which hugged the edge of the River Nile. Early morning shoppers, hurrying home with their packages in tow, mixed with tourists enjoying a leisurely stroll along the river. "Where are you Abdul?" she softly whispered. "They told me you are still in Egypt and somehow I feel your presence. Is it my imagination because I'm at the Hilton where we spent our last night together or are you really here?" She felt herself becoming emotional as she recalled the night of the charity event, the assassination attempt on Abdul's life and the resulting bullet wounds—the ones she had cleaned and sutured at this very hotel. And that was the last time she had seen him. Wiping a single tear off her cheek, she glanced at her watch and realizing it was close to the time for her appointment, she turned her back on the beauty of Cairo and braced herself for the task ahead.

"Come in, Dr. Marshall. Welcome back to the Hilton, please have a seat," said the hotel manager, offering her a black leather chair. "I apologize for your suite. I just found out you are on the seventh floor and..."

Davon smiled. "Oh, please do not concern yourself. I am very happy with my accommodations. The suite I stayed in last time was very beautiful, but it was much too large for a single person," she said as she sat down, straightening out a crease in the leg of her pantsuit.

"So, if you are not here about your suite, what can I do for you?" he inquired, appearing perplexed.

"I am here about a very sensitive confidential matter, one I hope you can help me with," she said, clearing her throat. "It is regarding my last visit." She leaned forward and looked him directly in the eye. "I need to know who Mr. Bedon contacted the day I checked out. The date was Friday, September 25th."

The hotel manager adjusted his glasses. "Of course, I will need to check our phone records to see if we have anything, but frankly, Dr. Marshall, I am a bit surprised at your request. Mr. Bedon is Prince Abdul's personal assistant and all of my dealings are usually with him."

"Exactly, and have you spoken to Mr. Bedon since our last visit?"

"No, I have not."

"That is because we are investigating him for wrongful doings. I have been sent by Prince Abdul to find out what Mr. Bedon is up to," she said with a sense of authority.

"I see," he replied not readily offering any information. He shifted several times in his seat, looked at the top of his desk and exhaled slowly all the while trying to avoid eye contact. It was clear he was uncomfortable dealing with a woman.

"Well," said Davon, standing. "If you are unwilling to co-operate, I understand, but it will be in my report to Prince Abdul. Good day."

"Please, Dr. Marshall, if you could wait one moment, I can make a phone call."

Davon perched on the edge of the chair and watched him pick up the phone. She had no idea what he was saying as the conversation was in Arabic.

Putting down the receiver, he looked at her. "We keep detailed records of all phone calls as clients more often than not use the same services on each visit and we want to be able to put their calls through quickly. On the morning of your departure, we have a record of putting a call through to Strike Bodyguard Service for Mr. Bedon. I am not sure if that is helpful, but it is all I have."

Davon jotted down the name and asked for the phone number and address. As she stood to leave, she placed a five hundred dollar bill on his desk. "This is thank you from Prince Abdul. Should you remember anything else, please leave a message for me in my room."

As she left the office and walked down the hallway, she managed to hide her jubilance until the elevator doors closed. Feeling extremely pleased with herself, she pulled out the secure cell phone from her purse in order to call Baboo and then remembering the hotel elevator cameras, discretely put it back into her purse. It will be better to call him from my suite, she thought, chastising herself. Think like a spy, Davon! After all, you're working for the CIA.

Securing the door to her room, she sat on the sofa and dialed Baboo's number. "Baboo," she said quietly, "the plan worked. Bedon contacted the Strike Bodyguard Service the day I left Cairo."

"And what else?"

"That was all the information I could get out of the hotel manager. I wanted to ask if the Prince checked out on the 25th, but the way my story went, I figured I should know what day he left the hotel. Anyway, I think we need to pay a visit to Strike Bodyguard Service."

"I agree. I will be there to pick you up in twenty minutes."

The grey Lexus pulled up to the front of the hotel and the bellman opened the back door for Davon. Davon got inside and waited until Baboo was driving down the ramp before she scooted forward in her seat and addressed him. "Thanks for coming so quickly. I have been concocting a story for the bodyguard service and want to run it by you before we get there. But I need to ask if there are many bodyguard services in Cairo?"

"Yes, there are quite a few bodyguard services. We have many rich sheiks, who require protection."

"Is Strike Bodyguard Service a popular choice?"

"Yes, and Ace Bodyguard Service is another widely used company."

Davon went over her plan and Baboo made one suggestion. "I think it may be better if you tell them you are looking for bodyguards for your employer. No one with money would make their own arrangements for protection."

"How could I be so stupid! Thank goodness I have you, Baboo," she exclaimed, just as they pulled up in front of an older one story building with 'Strike Bodyguard Services' on a large sign above the entranceway.

Baboo turned around and looked at her. "You are supposed to be an important person and we need to make an impression. Please let me open the car and building door for you."

Davon got out of the vehicle and walked with determination

towards the building while Baboo locked the car. Taking a sideways glance at a large man, who was standing near the entrance, she halted in front of the shiny metal door and waited for Baboo. The man kept one eye on her as he watched Baboo approach and Davon, positive there was going to be trouble, wondered if she should tell the guy to back off. However, before she could utter a word, Baboo was standing beside her. Moving around her, Baboo reached for the door's wide metal handle. This was exactly what the man was waiting for. Like a bolt of lightning, he stuck out an arm, blocking their way.

"No women," the employee said in heavily accented English. Extremely muscular, he stood almost two feet above Baboo.

"Please move back, Dr. Marshall," said Baboo calmly, waiting until she stepped out of range. Smiling at the obstruction, Baboo proceeded to explain in Arabic why they needed to enter the premises.

The employee's reply was curt with a lot of hand and arm motioning and even though Davon could not understand what was being said, she knew the man had no intention of allowing them to enter. Baboo quickly retorted and then again attempted to reach for the door handle, which the employee appeared to deem as a threat. Raising a fist, he shot a quick punch in Baboo's direction. "No!" shouted Davon wincing, horrified that a person who was three times the size and half the age of Baboo would even consider attacking him. However, although she did not realize it at the time, she had no reason to be concerned, for after a sudden whirl of activity Baboo was again standing beside her while the employee was ten feet away on the pavement, holding his head.

As though nothing had happened, Baboo casually opened the door. "After you, Dr. Marshall," he said with a twinkle in his eye.

"Impressive," she replied with a wide grin. The room they entered was large, but poorly lit. On the far right, they could see a boxing ring with two scantily dressed fighters going at it and about fifteen men standing around, enjoying the spectacle. "Excuse me," called Davon. "Is there anyone here who speaks English?"

An older, cleanly shaven man walked quickly towards them. "I am sorry, but women are not allowed here. You must leave."

Davon stood her ground. "I am in need of several bodyguards for my employer, a famous celebrity. I heard you were one of the best services, but I guess I will have to go to Ace Bodyguards," she informed him as she started to turn around.

"Please wait. Now, I understand why you are here." The man nodded thoughtfully. "Today, we will make an exception. I am Raol, the owner. Please come this way." He took them into a grungy makeshift office and cleared a stool for Davon to sit on. "How many bodyguards do you need, Miss?"

"My employer is the star in a movie, which is being filmed in Cairo. She will probably require four or five bodyguards. Is that possible?"

"Yes, of course."

"Good. You were recommended to me by a business acquaintance, Mr. Bedon." She watched his eyes light up in recognition of the name.

"Mr. Bedon, yes he is a client of ours."

"So you are doing business with him now?" she asked casually, hoping to glean more information.

He nodded enthusiastically. "We have a long-term contract with him. May I offer you tea?"

Davon smiled sweetly, wondering how many germs were breeding in the place. "No thank you. I just have a few more questions. If you have a long-term contract with Mr. Bedon, then I presume another long-term contract would not be a problem," she said, hinting to the fact that her contract would be another cash cow. Her eyes locked with his and she tried to analyze his body language. "Do you travel out of Cairo? Mr. Bedon mentioned something..."

"Yes, my bodyguards travel within Egypt and to other countries, no problem."

Davon hoped Abdul was still in the vicinity, but nothing is ever simple, she said to herself, trying to think of a way to pull more information out of the owner. "Yes, I remember, Mr. Bedon said they were moving to...ah...what was the name of the place? I am sorry I cannot seem to recall," she said, scrunching up her forehead as she pushed a strand of hair behind her ear. "I have talked to several people about recommendations for bodyguards and I should have written the information down. I know Mr. Bedon said they were moving and that he was very happy about your help because..."

The owner rose to the bait. "Mr. Bedon did thank me for the help we gave him in organizing the move to Luxor. I arranged the private plane and the transportation to the palace. I would be happy to make similar arrangements for your employer if the need comes up."

"Fantastic," said Davon, standing up. "I think that is all the information I need. I will discuss this with my employer and I will get back to you within the week. And please, my visit here is to be confidential. We do not want the press leaking any news prior to the big announcement about the movie."

"I understand," replied the owner, handing her a business card. "I am looking forward to hearing from you."

Raol saw them to the door and as they exited the premises, Davon caught a glimpse of the bodyguard Baboo leveled, keeping his distance, but glaring malevolently. "Quite the place," she muttered to herself as Baboo opened the back door to the vehicle.

"Good work, Davon," said Baboo, slipping into the driver's seat and pulling away from the curb. "There are hourly flights to Luxor. I suggest we book a flight for later today. Do you have any preference for time?"

Davon thought for a moment. If what Raol said was true, then going to Luxor was the next logical step, but there were still too many unanswered questions. Four months had passed since she had last seen

71

Abdul. If Bedon had taken him to Luxor, would he still be there now? She shook her head, trying to rid herself of the worst-case scenario—that Bedon had succeeded in killing him. "Book an evening flight, Baboo, and is it possible for you to put out some feelers to find out where Abdul might have been taken? I presume it would be a palace owned by the Sanduu family."

"Yes, I can definitely look into it. My understanding is the Sanduu family owns many properties in Egypt."

"Thank you," Davon replied absent-mindedly, already imagining the prospect of seeing Abdul again. She squeezed her eyes shut and recalled the last time she saw the Prince, remembering him in bed, nude from the waist up, trying desperately not to moan in pain while she changed the dressing of his bullet wound. He was a very sexy man, tall, dark, handsome— the perfect male specimen! Even in doctor mode, where she professionally attended to him, she had found herself distracted by his muscular physique and dark bedroom eyes. The car braked for a light and Davon was quickly brought back to the present. If they did discover the whereabouts of Abdul, she knew Bedon would use his power to prevent her from seeing him. Bedon hated her with a passion! "Baboo, I'm wondering if it is wise to use my real name. I've told you about my history with Mr. Bedon and I'm positive he will have spies in the area, especially if Abdul is indeed a hostage. When we check into the hotel in Luxor, they are going to ask for my passport. The last thing I need is for Bedon to find out I'm in the vicinity."

"Do you speak any other languages?" Baboo asked, looking at her through the rear view mirror.

"I'm fluent in French."

"Then I suggest we go to my friend and get you a French passport with a new name. It will not protect you from being physically recognized, but it will help thwart name recognition."

Baboo took her to a rundown apartment building where they had to walk up four flights of stairs. "We do not use real names here," he advised before knocking three times on the door, waiting and then knocking three more times. Someone peered through the peephole and then slowly opened it.

"Welcome, my friend," said a wrinkly old man in perfect English. "Who is this?"

"A friend in need of a passport."

"Come in, come in," the man replied, ushering them inside a tiny, dark apartment set up like a photo lab. "Can you pay in US dollars?"

"Yes," they answered together as they followed him down a short hallway into a cramped living space.

"She requires a French passport, today," said Baboo.

The old man's squinty black eyes suddenly turned on her. "What name will you use?" his croaky voice asked.

"Michelle Girard," she replied without hesitation. It was her French great grandmother's name on her mother's side of the family, a name she remembered from the family tree.

"Write the name on this piece of paper," he commanded, offering her a pen. Davon printed the name in large bold letters. He waited for her to finish and then pointed to a white backdrop in the corner of the room. "Stand in front of the screen and do not smile." After she got into place, he quickly took two head shots and then without a further word, vanished into a back room.

Davon moved beside Baboo. "How much is this going to cost?"

"Three hundred and fifty dollars. I hope you have the exact cash on hand."

Davon opened her purse and pulled out her wallet. Extracting three one hundred dollar bills and a fifty, she put them on the table.

73

"Next time, Baboo, give me the heads up. I'm lucky I had the right amount."

It was going to take an hour for the passport. While they waited, Davon and Baboo sat beside one another on uncomfortable wooden chairs quietly discussing their plans for Luxor. It was decided Baboo would meet with his contacts in town to try to uncover the whereabouts of the Prince. Davon's job was to plan ways of making contact with Abdul, once they found him.

Her thoughts whirled as she struggled with the task she was assigned. "I can't come up with anything. If I know Bedon, he will have bodyguards everywhere. No one will be able to come within a mile of Abdul."

"Do you know anything about the Prince's routine? His likes, his interests, when he takes his meals? Does he exercise daily, take walks? Anything you can remember about him will be useful. I know we believe he is being held hostage, but is there any possibility he is hiding out?"

Davon shook her head. "Absolutely not!" She did not want to go into details about her last few days with Abdul or let Baboo know the Prince had proposed to her the night before he disappeared. "Abdul is not that sort of man. He is family focused and would never go months without seeing his children. In fact, his eldest son died a few weeks after his disappearance and Abdul did not attend the funeral," she explained with sadness in her voice. "I can assure you Abdul is being held somewhere against his will." She paused for a moment, trying to think of something relevant. "All I can tell you is Abdul is responsible, very social and business focused. I really don't know about his personal routines." She remembered Abdul telling her he had breakfast at seven-thirty in the morning, but for some reason she chose not to mention it.

"Well, keep thinking about it. Once we discover his location, I am sure some sort of opportunity will present itself," replied Baboo just as the old man walked back into the room, holding out her forged passport.

In the car, Davon fingered her authentic looking French passport and thought about Abdul. The possibility of a future with him came and went as it had for months now, but she quickly brushed it aside. "Focus on the reality of the situation!" she whispered. "You can't change the fact that he has nineteen wives!" Although she realized a relationship with the Prince was futile, for some reason she still pined for him. Looking down at the cream-colored pantsuit she was wearing, she suddenly felt depressed. None of the outfits she brought from Boston were elegant and Abdul always dressed to the nines. She quickly debated about going to see Cheri, the owner of 'Cheri's Creations' where she had bought some extremely beautiful clothes on her last visit to Cairo— clothing she had to leave at the palace near Dubai last November when she had barely escaped with her life. Pushing up the sleeve of her jacket, she glanced at the time. Considering she had to return to the hotel, pack and then get to the airport, she wondered if it was even possible. "Baboo," she called, "Do we have twenty minutes for a visit to a clothing store called Cheri's Creations? If I get a chance to meet with the Prince, I should improve my wardrobe." Of course, Davon wanted to look her best if an opportunity to meet Abdul arose. What she did not seem to realize, was even if the only clothing she had was a burlap sack, she still would be a jaw-dropping beauty. With an aristocratic nose, pouty lips, high cheek bones, silky ivory complexion and willowy shape, she looked more like a runway model, getting ready for a shoot than the lead investigator of a missing person, who's primary objective is not to stand out but to blend into the shadows.

Baboo typed the name of the store into the GPS. "The store is not far from here. But, since it is almost one thirty and the last flight to Luxor is around six pm, we should try to be at the airport by four-fifteen at the very latest."

"I'll only need twenty minutes," said Davon. She hoped the boutique was open today.

When they arrived at the store Davon was pleased to see the 'OPEN' sign in the window. "I'll be finished by two o'clock. Do you want to wait?"

"There is something I need to pick up and I think I should go and get it now. I will be back here at two," replied Baboo.

"Okay," answered Davon as she jumped out of the car. Dashing inside the store, she hurried towards the sales counter. Expecting to see Cheri, she was surprised to see a young woman ringing up the purchases of another customer. She glanced up the stairs to the second floor and still not seeing Cheri, moved around a rack of evening gowns towards a display of elegant, but short dresses. She pushed past the groupings of red, blue, and white and then took her time scanning through the black ones, finally settling on a size four Oscar de la Renta with spaghetti straps. It was simple yet chic with fine black sequin imbedded in the material, which when turned towards the window shimmered in the sunlight.

The clerk finished with her customer and headed towards Davon. "I am Clare. May I help you find a gown, Madame?"

"I was actually looking for Cheri. Is she in the store today?"

"No, I am sorry. She is in Paris on a buying trip. But if there is something you need, I am more than capable of helping you."

Although Davon felt disappointed, she smiled. "I do need your help. I have to catch a flight and only have twenty minutes to get a little black dress—maybe this one, a linen pantsuit, preferably black and a pair of jeans. Last year Cheri helped me find some amazing clothes and..."

"Well then, you will be in our records," said Clare. Scooting around the counter she pulled out a red leather-bound book. "What was the name?"

"Davon Marshall."

Flipping through a few pages, Clare smiled. "Yes, I have you. Size four, shoe size seven. I have the list of things you have purchased in the past and I know what designer clothes fit you well. If you would like to go into the dressing room, I will pull some pieces together for you." She pointed to the dressing room on the main floor and nodding, Davon walked towards it.

By the time Davon was undressed, Clare had several outfits hanging on the back of the door. The first piece of clothing she tried on was the Oscar de la Renta dress. It fit her beautifully and she loved it. Opening the door to the fitting room, she showed Clare. "What do you think? I like it."

"The dress looks very nice. But, it should be worn with a higher heel."

Davon let out a small chuckle, realizing that Clare's fashion sense was very similar to Cheri's. "I didn't bring a pair of black dress shoes with a higher heel. Do you have something in the store in my size?"

"Let me take a look." She returned minutes later with a stylish pair of black stilettos. "These just came in from Italy. Try them on."

The shoes fit like a glove and looked fantastic with the dress. "I'll take the dress and the shoes." Davon looked at her watch and saw she only had another twelve minutes. "If you could start ringing up these purchases, I'll try on the pantsuit and jeans." She noticed the pantsuit was identical to the blue one she purchased last year. Clare had included a teal silk shirt and Davon was thrilled at how it accented her blue eyes. Removing the pants, she tried on the jeans. "I'll take everything," she called as she exited the dressing room. She handed Clare her personal Visa and as she waited for the purchases to be wrapped, she noticed Baboo pulling up in front of the store. "Could you please give my best to Cheri when you see her?"

"Yes, certainly, Miss Marshall. Thank you for shopping at Cheri's Creations."

When Davon reached the door, she saw a box of brown wigs, sitting on one of the display tables. "Are these for sale?" she asked, turning back to look at Clare. Although Davon had never worn a wig before, she figured it might be a smart move to work as a brunette for her undercover operations.

"They are for the mannequins, however, I could sell you one."

Davon selected a shoulder length wig and returned to the sales counter. "I'll take this one," she confirmed, adding when she detected Clare's surprise at the purchase, "I think it's fun to change your look sometimes."

"Yes. Thank you again for coming in. Good day, Miss Marshall."

Happy with her purchases, Davon handed the bags to Baboo, who put them into the trunk before assisting her into the backseat of the vehicle.

CHAPTER FOURTEEN

They arrived at the airport with plenty of time to spare and after checking in, Davon and Baboo found a quiet corner to continue the discussion about their strategy. Baboo had talked to several of his contacts in Cairo and had discovered some valuable information. The Sanduu Corporation owned two properties in Luxor. A house on acreage on the outskirts of town and a large, heavily guarded compound near the city's center, situated besides the Sofitel Winter Palace. Baboo's contact assured him the house was rarely used and if the Sanduu family came to Luxor, they always stayed at the compound.

"I have made reservations for us on the top floor of the Sofitel Winter Palace on the side that overlooks the Sanduu compound. You are booked under your alias. Please refer to me as your assistant while we are staying at the hotel. I have brought surveillance equipment and I plan to monitor the compound day and night. Tomorrow morning, I have a meeting with a contact in Luxor. Your job will be to help me operate and monitor the video equipment and to scan the internet for leads. How does that sound?" asked Baboo.

Davon nodded. "Fine, I want to be of help in any way I can. I just wish I spoke Arabic so I could do some ground reconnaissance with you. I really want to get involved."

"Many people speak English in Egypt," noted Baboo. "The

problem is the private investigation business is male dominated. I am sorry to say my contacts in Luxor would refuse to talk with you, unless you handed them a big bribe, whereas they will exchange information with me for free. That being said, the same situation like the Hilton or Strike Bodyguard Service could occur where I will need you to be involved," he said, trying to reassure her.

They heard their flight number called and as it was considered improper for them to sit together, Davon flew business class while Baboo sat in the economy section for the one-hour flight.

It was dark when they arrived at the hotel, but the grounds and building were well lit with lights in the trees and strategically placed spotlights around the building. Davon smiled when she saw the Victorian architecture of the beautiful Sofitel Winter Palace. The hotel, built in 1905 had had many famous guests, Howard Carter—the man who discovered the tomb of King Tutankhamun, and Agatha Christie—the author who wrote "Death on the Nile" during her stay. As Davon walked up the grand u-shaped staircase to the entranceway, her thoughts turned to Matt, knowing with his construction acumen, he would have love it. "I hope he has a chance to come here one day," she said quietly, turning around to look for Baboo, who was having the rented Lexus valet parked.

"Are you ready to go in?" asked Baboo.

The bellman opened the door for them and they entered the building. The foyer reminded Davon of her apartment at the royal palace, where she had lived for eight months in the lap of luxury. The Persian rugs carpeting the marble floor, the large white marble pillars supporting an opulent ceiling and the thick decadent plaster mouldings were all perfect examples of early twentieth century architecture. She took her time walking towards the wide white marble reception desk, enjoying the regal atmosphere.

Four smiling clerks looked at her, expectantly. "Good evening, Madame," said one of them. "Are you checking in?"

"Yes, Michelle Girard and Baboo Bhat, my assistant," she said with authority.

"Of course. Passports and a credit card, please," said the clerk, searching the computer for the reservation.

Davon swore under her breath. She had forgotten the Visa cards she had were in her real name. "Ah, I don't travel with a credit card. I will be paying cash for the rooms."

"That will be fine, Madame, however we still need a credit card as a deposit," the clerk replied, making eye contact.

"Baboo, do you have a credit card?" she asked without turning around.

"Yes, Ms. Girard, I do," he replied, putting his card onto the counter.

Concerned about Baboo's card limit, Davon put two five hundred US dollar bills on top of it. "Please apply this to my account."

The clerk took the money and the card. "Madame, the reservation specifically asks for a room on the right hand side of the hotel, yet we have many suites with outstanding views of the Nile and the Valley of the Kings. Should I change the reservation?"

"Baboo?" Davon questioned.

Baboo stepped forward. "My room is to be on the right hand side of the hotel, top floor please. Ms. Girard will have a suite with views of the Nile," he said, quickly stepping back behind her.

The clerk made the changes, gave them the room keys and organized a bellman to take up their luggage. Baboo took his suitcases from the luggage trolley and left to find his room while Davon followed the bellman to the elevator. The bellman took her to a large Victorian suite filled with antique furnishing and exquisite French doors, opening out onto a good-sized balcony. After tipping him, Davon took a quick look around and then ventured outside. Although it was dark, she could still make out the water, but had trouble seeing the West Bank of the Nile.

She was outside when the phone rang. "Yes, Baboo, thank you so much for helping me out at reception. I totally forgot the credit cards were in my real name."

"The thought did not cross my mind either, but no worries, we made it through. I wanted to let you know that my room has a perfect view of the back of the Sanduu compound where the car entrance is located. The infrared binoculars work extremely well and I am positive we will have no surveillance issues. I will come to your suite right after my meeting tomorrow morning, probably sometime around noon. We can discuss our strategy again, once I gather some more information."

"Okay, see you tomorrow at noon." Davon hung up the receiver and glanced at the clock on the bedside table. It was almost nine pm and it had been a very busy day, yet she did not feel the least bit tired.

Grabbing her computer and notebook, she sat on the sofa in the bedroom and looked at the vast list of Egyptian properties owned by the Sanduu family. There were seven in the general vicinity—two in Luxor. The other properties were spread out along the Nile and included an island. Davon ran her finger along the map and tried to determine distances. Five of the properties were accessible by boat, she figured, however they had to first determine whether Abdul was in Luxor before they branched out. Baboo's contact had said the most likely place to find him was at the compound near the Winter Palace because of its high surrounding walls and tight ground security. She googled the Sanduu family and read about their holdings and involvement with OPEC. Abdul was the conference president and had been so for many years. Most of the other information on the site was general in nature.

Closing the screen, she sighed as she turned her thoughts to Baboo's rendezvous with his Luxor contact. "Damn it, I hate being a woman sometimes!" She quickly decided that instead of twiddling her thumbs in the room, waiting for him, she would explore the Luxor Temple in the morning. It was located near the hotel and she knew there would be no problem getting back before noon. With the decision for a morning tour made, it was time for bed.

CHAPTER FIFTEEN

In the morning, Davon took the hotel shuttle to the Luxor Temple. Built in 1400 BC near the River Nile, it was once considered the holy of holies where the principle god Amun dwelt in its sanctuary. As she walked towards the temple, she was impressed with the giant sitting statues of Ramesses II, which flanked either side of the entranceway. Moving in the direction of the statues, she paused for a moment, examining the decorative seventy-five foot granite obelisk standing in front of the first pylon. The brochure said there had been a second obelisk, but it had been removed and gifted to France in 1833. Glancing up at the towering, but plain non-descript brick pylons, she stopped to scrutinize the statues and then entered the temple. The size of the temple was not huge, measuring only 850 by 200 feet, but because most of the inner walls had not survived, it somehow seemed larger. Exploring the open courtyards, Davon spent over an hour inspecting the colonnades and individual decorative columns as well as examining several colorful reliefs, while reading about the layout and the functions of each chamber. "Amazing," she whispered to herself, wishing she could understand the meaning of the hieroglyphics carved into the columns and existing walls.

As she made her way around a group of German tourists, who were heading in the opposite direction, she paused to observe an interesting phenomenon, which was developing on an open portion of the temple's grounds. A small twister about five feet in height was spinning madly, gathering dust and sand as it moved back and forth for several minutes in the same location. Racking her brain, Davon recalled a whirlwind was a violently rotating column of air caused by ground surface air much hotter than the air above it. She was thoroughly enjoying the spectacle, when all of a sudden the twister turned and began to make a beeline towards her. Concerned for her safety, she jumped behind a column, pressing her back into the hard stone base. She felt the rushing force of the twirling mass as it flew passed and observed it heading across the temple's grounds and then out to sea. Remaining beside the column, she watched the whirlwind until she could no longer see it. Then shaking her head in disbelief, she glanced at her watch. It was time to return to the hotel for her meeting with Baboo.

Davon arrived back at the hotel just before noon and ordered room service. When there was no sign of her partner by one o'clock, she reluctantly sat down at the table on the balcony and anxiously ate her meal, not really tasting the food. She wondered what was taking him so long and hoped Baboo had not run into trouble. Covering up his meal, she pushed the trolley into the suite and in an attempt to stop thinking about the worst-case scenario, she opened her computer, but unable to concentrate on the information on the screen, she quickly shut it down. There was no point in trying to distract herself. She needed to move. For four worrisome hours, she paced, and now convinced that Baboo had indeed run into some sort of difficulty, she decided to try to call Maxwell, using the cell phone number he had given her in Boston. In hindsight, she should have insisted on Maxwell giving her the emergency contact number of the CIA agent in Egypt instead of relying on Baboo to contact the agent if she got into trouble.

"Why didn't Maxwell think about a situation where Baboo gets into trouble!" she shouted. Davon reached for the phone, but just as she was about to dial, the doorbell rang. Racing to the door, she yanked it open. "You're late! I was so worried!" she said with relief as she ushered Baboo inside the suite.

She steered him towards one of the high-backed antique chairs in the living area. Baboo sat down and let out a long sigh. "I am sorry I took so long, but it takes a lot of work to get people to open up here. Were you anxiously waiting at the hotel all day?"

"Not all day," Davon admitted. "I went to the Luxor Temple this morning."

"And how did you like it?"

"Considering it is not one of the best preserved temples, I still thought it was quite amazing and the giant sitting statues of Ramesses II were fabulous. Something quite interesting happened when I was visiting the site," she said, launching into an explanation of the unusual twister phenomenon.

Baboo leaned forward and smiled. "We call twisters, whirlwinds of happiness," he informed her.

"Whirlwinds of happiness?" she echoed, wrinkling her brow as she thought about the devastating effects of a tornado.

Baboo laughed loudly. "It is considered lucky when a small twister comes near a person because it gathers up all of your troubles and takes them far away."

"Wouldn't it be nice if that were true," Davon replied with a smile, wondering how such a strange superstition came to be. "But enough about my morning. What happened? Why did your meeting take so long?"

"The whole ordeal was very time-consuming. I should have called you to let you know I was going to be late. I was however able to speak with a few people, but no one knows if Abdul is at the compound."

Davon let out a moan. "So, what are we going to do?"

"I have an idea," Baboo said, pulling a photograph out of his pocket. It was of a woman, probably in her mid-forties, wearing a headscarf. "This is a picture of the compound's cook. Her name is Marium. Like most women, she goes to the public market every morning to buy the daily produce. I was thinking that maybe you could speak to her at the market tomorrow and ask her a few questions. There is one problem," he said, pausing for a second, "Marium is always accompanied by a bodyguard."

"Why would a cook need a bodyguard?" asked Davon, unable to come up with a reason.

"Most likely because they do not want her talking to anyone. I have been told she speaks English. Would you be comfortable casually asking her if Prince is at the compound?"

"Do you really think she will tell me?"

"She might, if you offer her a substantial bribe of three hundred US dollars for the information."

Davon thought for a moment and then nodded. "Okay, it sounds like the best option we have so far," she eagerly replied. "I better wear the brown wig and a headscarf so I'll blend into the crowd."

"A dark wig is probably a very good idea," said Baboo as he pulled some electronics out of his bag. "This is an earpiece transmitter. By using this device, we will be able to communicate with each other. You just need to turn it on, and put it in your right ear. If you talk in a slightly lower than regular voice, I will be able to hear you well. Should we try it out?"

Davon took the earpiece, turned it on and walked into the bedroom. Shutting the door, she inserted it into her ear. "Hi, can you hear me?" she said in a whisper.

"Yes, can you hear me?"

"Affirmative," said Davon, feeling a rush of excitement. She thought about her father and wondered if he had ever in his years at the Pentagon worked as a spy. Returning to the living room, Davon put her earpiece on the table and sat down to voice some concerns. "What if Marium refuses to talk to me? I can't very well chase her around the market, Baboo."

"Approach her gently and remember that money talks in this part of the world. Her wage is probably less than a dollar a day. You will have to pretend you are shopping and maybe start with a question about produce or some women's issue. The only thing you need to keep in mind is that the bodyguard will be keeping an eye on her."

"Good advice," muttered Davon, already planning some opening statements.

Baboo shrugged. "Well, that is almost all I have to tell you except I also found out that one of the male employees at the compound was recently fired. I do not know the reason, but I heard he is now working at the Valley of the Kings giving tours of King Tutankhamen tomb."

"I'm listening," said Davon, leaning forward with interest.

"After we attempt to see Marium, we may want to pay him a visit. I will have to feel out the situation and decide on the spot whether you will approach him as a tourist or I will single him out on my own. However, I must warn you that this particular assignment could be dangerous. If you would rather not go..."

Davon's heart rate quickened. "Stop right there, Baboo. I definitely want to go!"

"Alright, then that is the plan for tomorrow, but now I have reconnaissance to do." Standing up, Baboo headed towards the door.

"I thought I would have dinner around seven o'clock. Would you like to join me," Davon asked, now feeling quite excited at the thought of playing a part in the investigation.

"Thank you, but no. I will order room service and eat while I am watching the compound."

"Can I help?"

"No, Davon, relax tonight, you need to be in prime form tomorrow morning. We will leave the hotel just before eight. Study

Marium's photo, so you will be able to immediately recognize her. "

After Baboo left, Davon decided to visit the gym before dinner. Doing up her runners, she glanced at the clothes, hanging in the wardrobe. It will be best to wear my black pants and black raincoat to the market, she thought, knowing the majority of women here tended to outfit themselves in dark clothing. The problem was she did not have a black headscarf. Not wanting to attract attention to herself by wearing a colored headscarf, she grabbed some money from her wallet, deciding to hit the small clothing store in the hotel on the way to the gym.

Early the next morning, with a basket on her arm, and dressed in a black T-shirt, black pants, black raincoat and black headscarf over her brown wig, Davon left Baboo at the car and headed slowly towards the large produce market. She made her way down the narrow aisles blending in as well as possible amongst the other women, who were selecting produce from overloaded tables of fresh garden vegetables and local fruit. Pretending to shop, Davon picked up and examined pieces of fruit while she scanned the crowd for Marium.

"Can you see her?" asked Baboo through the earpiece after ten minutes had lapsed.

"Not yet," Davon said quietly. Using some Egyptian pounds, she stopped and purchased a cantaloupe from one of the vendors. Putting the fruit in her basket, she proceeded down the aisle, looking up every few moments from the fragrant mounds of oranges, lemons and limes. Scooting around a rather large woman, Davon glanced over at the next table and suddenly saw her target. "Have her in my sight," she whispered. Exiting the aisle she was in, she quickly moved two aisles over and slowly inched her way towards Marium, where the target was inspecting some lettuce. When she was directly across from her, Davon picked up a head of lettuce and casually said, "Such beautiful weather we are having."

Marium looked up momentarily. "Yes," she replied in English, immediately looking back down at the pile of lettuce. She selected one, examined it and then put it down and selected another.

"You are Marium, aren't you?" At that remark, Marium snapped her head up and they made eye contact. Davon saw terror in her eyes. "Don't be afraid," Davon whispered. "I am a friend, who is here to offer you three hundred US dollars."

Marium narrowed her eyes, swallowed and then returned her gaze to the lettuce. "And why do I have such a friend?"

Davon waited until another woman walked past them. "I need information. I want to know if Prince Abdul Sanduu is staying at the compound." When Marium remained silent, Davon added, "Three hundred US dollars are yours if you can tell me." She pulled the money out from her pocket and showed it to Marium.

"I do not know the answer to your question, but my husband is the assistant to the assistant of Prince Adin. He will know."

"Can I meet with him?" Davon quickly asked. She looked behind Marium and noticed her bodyguard watching them. Averting her eyes to the lettuce, she waited for Marium's response.

"Meet me here tomorrow morning and I will bring you an answer," Marium said quietly. Dropping the lettuce she was holding, she spun around, leaving Davon alone at the table.

Davon waited for a few minutes and then made her way back to the car. "Did you hear?" she asked Baboo, once she was safely inside.

"I did not hear all of her answer."

"She said she doesn't know if Abdul is at the compound, but her husband is the assistant to the assistant of Prince Adin. She told me to find her here tomorrow morning and she will let me know if her husband will meet with me."

"Good. It sounds promising."

"I hope so. If her husband doesn't know anything, we'll have hit

90

a brick wall."

"We still may get a lead from the fired employee. He might be disgruntled enough to talk. I am heading to the Valley of the Kings right now," said Baboo as he pulled away from the curb.

Davon let herself fall back into the seat and then turned to look out the window. She stared at the reddish golden sand of the West Bank and thought about the place where so many of the Egyptian pharaohs were buried. "I read up on the Valley of the Kings last night. Did you know sixty-five tombs have been discovered there? They are not all tombs of pharaohs, some are tombs of nobles, and many are classified as unknown, but the most famous discovery is the tomb of Tutankhamun. I googled it because I wanted to be able to ask your man a few legitimate questions about Tut before I hit him with questions about the whereabouts of Abdul. Do you have a description of the ex-employee?" she asked, thinking they needed to make sure they approached the right man.

"He is Egyptian, in his thirties, about 5'8" in height, has a slim build, and wears glasses," said Baboo as he made a right hand turn onto a bridge, crossing the River Nile. "I would like to do a stakeout near the tomb and observe him for a bit before he is approached. And I should probably do this on my own, Davon," he said, listening to a small groan in reply. "I know you want to help, but the best thing you can do when we get there is to be a tourist. Let's split up when we enter the site and then rendezvous in forty-five minutes at the tomb."

"Really Baboo?" exclaimed Davon, getting the feeling he was trying to protect her from danger. "I am being paid to do this job just like you."

"Remember we are a team. However, no one is going to take notice of me, sitting on a rock, watching the action. You on the other hand..."

"Okay, now I understand what you mean," replied Davon. "I'll explore a couple of the other tombs and then meet up with you at the specified time."

They left the plains and greenery alongside of the Nile and headed into the desert. It was beginning to get hot and Davon could see the heat waves rising from the golden colored sand. Looking down at her outfit, she frowned. It was going to be uncomfortably warm exploring the Valley of the Kings dressed in black. She removed her headscarf, wig and coat and placed them onto the seat, feeling a jolt as the car left the pavement and moved onto a semi-steep well-trodden dirt road. The road led upwards to the rolling Theban hills and would take them through an ancient, once well-guarded pass and then directly to the royal burial complex.

She could hear the car straining as they approached the summit. Davon stared at the sun glistening on the peak of al-Qurn, an iconic pyramid-shaped hill that was once thought to protect and guard the royal necropolis and then turned her gaze to the treeless, barren, rock-scattered excavation site below. "Wow, the Valley of the Kings doesn't look like much," she said, pressing her nose against the window as they began their descent. She studied the plain, bordering on ugly, desert valley as they drove down the dusty road and into an almost empty parking lot. "It makes you wonder why this place was chosen as the royal burial site."

Baboo pulled into a space beside an oversized van and turned off the ignition. "My understanding is that it had to do with the type of rock. The valley is made up of limestone and shale and these types of rock make it easier for tunneling."

"Maybe so, but remember, in those days they were still working with hand tools. I can't imagine how many slaves died building the tombs," she exclaimed as she started to get out of the vehicle.

"Do not take anything of value with you. I have heard there are pickpockets in the area," cautioned Baboo as they watched three loaded tour buses make their way into the parking lot.

Davon removed the bag from her shoulder, extracted several bills from her wallet and then discretely stuffed the bag under the backseat. "I will just take some bribe money," she said quietly, putting the bills into her pocket."

As they walked towards the entry kiosk, they made plans to rendezvous in forty-five minutes. Once through the turn-stall gate, they parted ways. Davon immediately headed to the tomb of Thutmose III, hoping to see as much as she could before the rendezvous time. However, when she arrived, her initial excitement of being the first in line turned to disappointment when the guide at the entranceway explained she had to wait.

"We only allow groups of three or more to enter the tomb," said the guide, blocking her way.

Frustrated, Davon took a step back and prepared to wait, thinking she would stay for ten minutes before moving to another tomb, however well before the ten-minute limit, a group of four tourists appeared at the entranceway.

The tour guide waved his hand to get everyone's attention. "I will now give you some information about the tomb before we enter as it is sometimes difficult to speak once inside. Thutmose III was the sixth pharaoh of the eighteenth dynasty. His tomb was discovered in 1898 by Victor Loret. It is built thirty meters below the ground and is considered a Middle Kingdom tomb because it has a tunnel with a ninety-degree turn. You will find the complete funerary text on the walls of the oval-shaped burial chamber, which is supported by two pillars and has a ceiling decorated with stars. The burial chamber is large and holds a beautiful red quartzite sarcophagus. Once we arrive in the burial chamber, you will have approximately eight minutes to inspect the tomb. Please follow me," instructed the guide, closing the door after the five tourists entered the gloomy passageway.

Directly behind the guide, Davon carefully inched her way down the steeply inclined dimly lit corridor. It was four feet wide and only five and a half feet high in some sections, which required them to crouch awkwardly as they continued downward towards the burial chamber. A piece of wooden planking had been placed on the ground with narrow strips of board nailed to it. This served as foot holds so one did not slip. Although occasionally there was a handrail, they were few and far between one another. The earthen walls smelled unpleasantly damp and

Davon grimaced when she had to touch them to steady herself. She began to think about bacteria and viruses that thrived in musty closed-off spaces, but before she could get carried away with her reservations of being underground, they arrived at their destination.

The burial chamber was spacious and held only one object—a red quartzite sarcophagus placed in the center of the room. Making her way around the coffin, Davon examined the detailed carved reliefs on each side and then turned her attention to the decorative walls. The wall paintings were rudimentary scenes of simple black figures against a creamy colored background. Borders of red and pink highlighted some of the areas. Although the scenes were almost child-like in their character, the images were astonishingly bright, considering they were painted 3500 years ago. She was marvelling at the vibrant blue ceiling dotted with golden yellow stars, when the guide's voice jolted her back into reality.

"It is time to leave. Another group is waiting to see the tomb," the guide yelled loudly, indicating they needed to move towards the tunnel.

Exiting the tomb was just as grueling as entering and the second she came out of the narrow space Davon inhaled and exhaled several times, enjoying the sweet, albeit very warm fresh air. The crowds had thickened dramatically in the ten minutes or so she was underground and looking at her watch, Davon decided she had time to explore one more tomb before setting out to find Baboo.

Her second choice was the tomb of Ramesses III, one of the largest in the valley. Locating the tomb on the map, she set off uphill, finding it in the center of a massive mound of rock and sand. Its entranceway, which ran about twenty feet into the mound, was constructed of new concrete and looked clean and inviting. Following a group of tourists through the newly constructed brass gates and into the first chamber, she was pleasantly surprised at the obviously refurbished wide concrete staircase, high ceilings and colorful reliefs covering the walls. Tall images of the pharaoh, the gods, and everyday scenes of working villagers filled every available space. She briefly joined a tour group, but then quickly set off on her own to see as much as she could before leaving to meet Baboo. The background of all of the reliefs were creamy white, similar to the tomb of Thutmose III, however the detailed paintings in this tomb were not just done in black, but in bold colors of red, gold, green and blue. She examined the reliefs and after spending as much time as she dared, she quickly made her way to the burial chamber to inspect Ramesses's stone sarcophagus. The topless coffin was made of reddish colored rock and featured beautifully carved reliefs and hieroglyphics. Making one quick loop around, Davon realized it was time to get to the rendezvous place. She made her way out of the tomb, hurried down the hill, and scanned the area for Baboo.

Stunned at the hundreds of tourists now milling about, Davon ventured towards the tomb of King Tut. Standing on her tiptoes, she looked over the crowd for her partner.

Baboo saw her first. "Davon, over here," he called, waving.

She made her way through the throngs of tourists to the opposite side of the pathway, directly across from King Tut's tomb. "Is that the target?" she asked, discretely pointing to a man, who fit the description Baboo had given.

"That's him working the tomb alright. The problem is Tut's tomb seems to be one of the busiest and I do not think we will be able to get near him until the end of the day. It looks like we might have a long wait," said Baboo, looking comfortable sitting atop a large rectangular stone block. "Were you able to explore any tombs?"

Davon nodded. "I saw the tombs of King Thutmose III and Ramesses III. They were both absolutely amazing," she replied excitedly. "Wow, for some reason I didn't expect the Valley of the Kings to be so busy." She leaned against the stone block and eyed the target. "I have a suggestion. Why don't we go on a tour of King Tut's tomb and then try to corner him once we are in the burial chamber."

"I do not think that is a good idea because I am not a big fan of closed-in spaces. It might be best if we wait until the end of the day."

"That's crazy, Baboo, we can't wait until six o'clock. It's not even noon and it is already close to forty degrees. Look, I'll go on the tour and you can wait for me here."

Baboo inhaled deeply and then let out a long drawn out sigh as he weighed the risks. "I am not sure you will be safe. The target looks like a bad character."

"I don't think you need to worry, Baboo. I will be with an entire group of tourists," she reminded him, glancing over at the crowd lining up for the next tour of the tomb. She had found the encounter with Marium to be exhilarating and was looking forward to another spy-like reconnaissance. "How should I approach him?" she asked as though the decision had already been made.

"Please be very careful," advised Baboo. "In the burial chamber give him a glimpse of the bribe, which should not be more than one hundred dollars and then tell him it is for some needed information. Ask him to give you a few minutes after you exit the tomb. I want to be there for the meeting."

"That's simple," said Davon. Not anticipating any issues, she turned and made her way towards the end of the line.

The target was already in the middle of his lecture when she nudged her way to the forefront of the group. "Although it is the most famous, King Tutankhamun's tomb is one of the smallest. He died about the age of seventeen. Scholars believe that because he died at such a young age, his rightful tomb was not ready, so it is thought he was buried in the tomb built for his advisor Ay, who actually claimed power following his death. We will now begin the tour. Only fifteen people per tour please," he said, as he indicated for the tourists at the front of the group to begin entering the tunnel.

As the guide counted out the numbers, Davon squirmed her way forward, getting through the doorway as number fourteen. Shutting the door after the fifteenth person entered, the guide followed the tourists down the steep corridor. The tunnel was horribly similar to that of King Thutmose, yet much narrower in width. The lighting was poor, Davon was unable to see around the heavyset man in front of her and she had no idea how many meters down they needed to travel. Although she did not suffer from claustrophobia, she felt as though there wasn't enough air to breathe every time she was forced to crouch down because of the low ceiling height. Concentrating on remaining calm, she was relieved when the group finally reached the open space of the tomb. As they gathered around the sarcophagus, the tourists appeared to be enthralled with the wall paintings. Davon heard many comments of appreciation. She too took notice of how incredibly beautiful and detailed the reliefs were, but knew she needed to focus on the job at hand. With her eye on the target, she somehow managed to wiggle next to him.

Leaning into his ear, she whispered, "I have one hundred US dollars for some information I know you possess. Are you interested in meeting with me once we exit the tomb?" She discreetly pulled out a hundred dollar bill and showed it to him.

The guide pointed to his ear and feigned hearing problems. Motioning to an area outside of the doorway, he indicated for her to follow. They turned right and walked several paces down an unlit passageway into a small poorly lit chamber. "This was one of the many storage rooms," said the guide, as if offering an apology for the undecorated, musty smelling room. "What were you saying to me?" he asked, stepping closer. He licked his lips in a sexual way and gazed into her eyes.

Feeling apprehensive, Davon pushed herself against the cold earthen wall, trying to put space between them. Becoming aware of the silence of the room and lack of noise filtering in from the burial chamber, she regretted her decision to come with him. Nevertheless, she told herself, I'm here now, so I'll make the offer and then get back to the group. "I said I will pay you one hundred US dollars for some information, but I want to discuss it with you once we exit the tomb."

"That will not be possible," the target quickly replied, shaking his head. "As you can see I am a very busy tour guide. Ask me what you want to know now." Davon hesitated for only a second, wondering what she should do, but it was too long for him. "I do not have time for this! I have to get to my next group," he muttered, turning towards the doorway.

"Alright," said Davon. "I know your last job was at the Sanduu compound." He remained unmoving, but the slight widening of his eyes gave him away and he appeared somewhat fearful. "Do not worry. I'm not here from the authorities. All I want to know is if you saw Prince Adin's twin brother, Abdul, at the compound in Luxor."

"Adin Sanduu's twin brother?" he repeated for confirmation.

"That is correct. Have you seen Abdul Sanduu at the compound in Luxor over the last few months?"

"Yes, I saw him many times with his brother," he said convincingly.

Davon became excited and letting down her guard she asked for details. "When, when was the last time you saw him? Do you know if he is being held against his will?"

"A week, yes, a week ago and is he being held? I do not know. He seemed to be free enough to come and go."

"Is there any way I could get into the compound to speak with the Prince?"

The guide let out a shrill laugh. "Not unless you want to die. No one can sneak into the compound. It is very heavily guarded. Plus, you are a woman. Why do you want to speak with him?"

Davon huffed in annoyance. "That's none of your business." She pulled the hundred dollar bill from her pocket and offered it to him. "Thank you for the information."

"You are welcome," he replied indifferently, snatching the bill from her. "Shall we return to the group?"

When he moved back to allow her to walk ahead of him, she had a fleeting moment of unease, but brushed it away. That was pretty easy, she thought, pleased with the little bit of information she had gotten. She had only just turned into the passageway when from the corner of her eye she caught a flicker of movement. Without a moment to react, something solid struck the back of her head and before she could even cry out, she felt herself dizzily staggering towards the grimy dirty wall. Reaching out towards nothingness, she struggled to blink the blurriness away. This is not happening, she said to herself as her knees buckled. Suddenly, everything became a spinning whirl of blackness.

CHAPTER SIXTEEN

There were at least fifty people surrounding Tutankhamun's tomb when Davon's tour group exited the tunnel. Jumping onto one of the large granite blocks on the edge of the pathway, Baboo looked for Davon. He watched the target move to the side of the entranceway and assist several of the individuals from the tour group out of the tomb, noticing most of the group press money into the guide's hand as they exited. Finally, the last person was helped out. Without the least bit of concern for the fifty other tourists waiting to go into the tomb, the target shut the door, bolted it, hung a 'TOMB CLOSED' sign on the post and then scurried around the back of the entranceway, quickly vacating the area. Complaining loudly, the crowd eventually started to disperse, leaving an aghast Baboo to rush across the busy walkway to reach the tomb's door.

"Oh, are you the new guide? My family has been waiting in line to see King Tutankhamun's tomb," said a woman dressed in fashionable Western clothing. As she came near, Baboo noticed several other tourists behind her, moving closer to hear his reply.

"No, I am sorry," he apologized. "There are air quality problems in the tomb and I am only here to check out the ventilation system."

She looked at him skeptically. "Well then, when will it be fixed? We're only here today and this was the one tomb we really wanted to see."

"It will be fixed in a few hours. Please come back then," Baboo replied, loudly. Turning his back to her, he waited for the gathered group to move away before removing the bolt. Pulling open the solid wooden door, he gazed down into the completely dark space. "Davon, Davon, are you in the tomb?" he called. He waited for a minute and then called again, positive he heard some movement deep within the tunnel.

"Baboo?" moaned Davon. Pushing herself into a sitting position, she tried to recall what had happened. "You don't need to come down, I'm okay," she yelled, remembering his fear of small spaces. "But, can you turn on the lights? I can't see anything." She ran her hand over the lump on the back of her skull and swore.

"I am looking for a switch. The target bolted the door and then ran. I am concerned he might return and lock the two of us in the tomb. Are you sure you are okay? Can you make it out on your own?" Baboo found a hand switch near the ceiling and flicked it on. Some old-fashioned florescent light tubes sputtered and then came to life, exchanging the darkness for a dim grey gloom.

Davon stumbled to her feet and again rubbed the goose egg on the back of her head. "I'm coming up now. You stay there and guard the door," she shouted, moving as quickly as she was able. Passing the burial chamber, she limped towards the tunnel and started to make her way upward. The air smelled rank and although she was breathing heavily, it felt as though she couldn't get enough oxygen. "I'm almost there," she kept repeating softly, trying to spurn herself onward.

A hand suddenly reached out and grabbed her wrist, pulling her up the last bit of way. "Are you alright, Davon? Come into the light and let me look at you."

The brightness of the sunlight was almost too much to bear. "I lost my sunglasses down there," she said, placing her hand in front of her face to block the glare.

"Take mine," said Baboo, thrusting them onto her nose. "Can

you make it to the car? I need to take you to the hospital."

"I'm fine. I just need to sit down for a minute and I don't need to go to the hospital," she advised him as he escorted her to a nearby granite block. Sitting down on the rock, she smiled grimly at his serious expression. "Really, I'm okay. The guy hit me on the head for what reason I don't know and I must have passed out."

"How did it happen with all those people down there?" he asked with an incredulous look.

"It was totally my fault. I whispered to him what you told me to say and he pretended he couldn't hear. Then he motioned for me to follow him to one of the storage rooms and when I explained there that I wanted to have the discussion on ground, he told me he was too busy and I believed him. I did get some information out of him," she said, giving Baboo the details of what the target told her.

"And you paid him?"

"Yes, that is what is so weird," she replied. "Wait a minute!" Standing up, she reached into her pocket and pulled the inside fabric out. "I had three one hundred dollar bills in my pocket when I got here. I gave him one hundred for the information. He must have seen the other bills because I distinctly remember pushing the two other hundreds to the bottom of my pocket after I paid him."

Baboo grimaced. "I should not have let you deal with him."

"You couldn't have known this was going to happen and as I said I'm okay, but I think I'm ready to head back to the hotel," she said, stumbling to her feet. "I honestly feel like I have had enough adventure for one day."

They rode most of the way back to the Sofitel Winter Palace in silence. As they neared the hotel, Davon looked at him. "Are you going to do reconnaissance again tonight?"

"Yes, I need to do reconnaissance every night. If some clandestine occurrence is about to take place, it usually happens under the cover of darkness. At the moment, the compound seems a little bit too quiet, so in my humble opinion, I would say that neither of the Sanduu Princes are presently in residence there."

"Can I help you tonight?"

Baboo parked by the front steps of the hotel. "Give me a call once you have freshened up. If you are feeling up to it later, your help is most welcome. However, do not forget you have a meeting with Marium early tomorrow morning."

"I haven't forgotten the meeting with Marium," replied Davon as she exited the car after the bellman opened the door.

CHAPTER SEVENTEEN

Davon groaned when she looked at her reflection in the bathroom mirror. There was grime smeared down the right side of her face and bits of dirt entangled in her hair. Using a hand mirror, she took a peek at the bump on the back of her head. It was about two inches in circumference and tender, but luckily, the skin had not broken. Stripping down, she got into the shower and lathering up, she let the hot water pound at her shoulders, back and aching right hip, all the while thinking about how desperate the target must have been to attack her for an extra two hundred dollars. "It was my fault," she said getting out of the shower. "In retrospect, I should have stuffed his money into another pocket before I broached him."

After drying off, she donned the hotel robe and headed for the living room phone. "Yes, I need a bucket of ice and do you have a quick laundry service? I need my clothes laundered and returned this evening."

"Of course, Miss Girard, I will send someone up with the ice and to pick up your laundry," said the front desk clerk.

"Thank you. Now, could you please connect me to my assistant's suite?" There was only one ring before Baboo answered. "Hi Baboo, I'm feeling much better and would like to help out tonight. What time would you like me to come?"

"Why don't you come after dark, around six-thirty or seven. We can order dinner and I will show you the ropes."

"Great, see you then," replied Davon, hanging up the phone.

Davon held the bag of ice to her head while she checked her emails. After deleting many of the work related ones, she read the email from her parents. She quickly sent off a brief reply, which said relatively nothing except that she was having a great time. Taking a deep breath, she clicked on the email from Matt. As she suspected it was a letter of apology and understanding, wishing her the best trip ever. Her heart sank and feelings of guilt surfaced. Matt was a fantastic person, yet something had changed in the nine months she had been away, and the passion she had once felt for him was gone. She knew she still loved him, but in a more platonic way and although she had desperately tried to recapture the feelings of the former soul-soaring romance, she had been unable. She was well aware he would marry her in a heartbeat. Gritting her teeth, she shook her head. She would only marry a man who was her soulmate and if she should never find him, then so be it! "How ironic," she hooted, "if Matt had not broken up with me last year, I wouldn't have taken the job in the Middle East and we most likely would have been engaged or married by now." Letting out a sigh, she leaned back into the chair. "Obviously, I was never meant to marry Matt." Her thoughts then turned to Prince Abdul. Although she did not want to believe it, she knew it was Abdul, who was responsible for the change of heart. She smiled as she recalled their chance encounter, the searing glance that had ravished her whole being, and the intensity of their first meeting, where she advised him about the health problems of his teenage daughter. Contrary to her assumptions about a man born with a silver spoon in his mouth, she found Abdul to be loving, caring, generous and down to earth. Her heart throbbed as she remembered the evening he had taken her by helicopter to dinner in Dubai...and then the trip to Cairo. "Stop it!" she said to her reflection in the windowpane. "You may never find Abdul and if you do, you cannot forget he has nineteen wives! Why can't you admit the reason you so illogically agreed to return to Cairo to find him wasn't because you wanted to work for the CIA, it was because you think you're in love with him. Face it Davon, until you get over Abdul, a life with anyone else will never work." Davon hung her head in misery and wondered what she was doing in Egypt, pretending she was a spy. "But, that is exactly why I need to find him, to prove to myself the feelings I have are purely infatuation," she blurted out. "I know it's ridiculous to pine after a man I have spent less than forty-eight hours with, let alone a man who is married nineteen times over, yet for some reason I can't seem to get him out of my mind."

Refusing to dwell on the depressing dilemma, she reread Matt's email. She really could not respond, not the way she was feeling and she didn't want to lie to him about a tour she wasn't on. Standing up, she stretched and then made her way onto the balcony. It was almost six o'clock and the red sun was just about to dip behind the flaming red western hills. The red and orange hues sparkled on the River Nile and made the smooth calm water appear as though it was on fire. Several feluccas with tall white sailing masts completed the tranquil scene. They were heading towards a large rustic dock already filled with at least a dozen riverboats and turning together in total synchronization, the long wooden sailboats expertly steered towards the dock and into the berths awaiting them. Davon unconsciously observed the uncanny sailing maneuver and once again thought about her whereabouts and the fact that she could have been severely injured or killed inside the tomb. She bit her lip and regretted her involvement in the investigation. "What was I thinking?" she quietly muttered, chastising herself for coming to Egypt. She gripped the railing and stared at the sun's bright red outline behind the rolling hills just seconds before it vanished. Taking one last glimpse at the breathtaking view, now scattered with increasing shadows, Davon stepped inside.

"Please come in," said Baboo, greeting her at the doorway. "How are you feeling? You still look a little pale."

"I'm fine. I'm just feeling a bit discouraged. You know, wondering what I'm doing here, thinking about the meaning of life," she replied, slumping down onto the sofa.

Baboo sat down beside her. "I guess those feelings are normal when you are on your chosen path and run into a horrendous obstruction in the road."

Davon realized what he said was true. No one had forced her to come to Egypt. "I did choose to come here to look for Abdul, although I probably should have said no when I was asked," she explained. "The problem is I didn't realize the potential danger of the project. I just leapt right in. I'm not trained for this type of work. I'm a doctor, not a private investigator."

Baboo nodded his head as he listened. "The road of life is never easy, it is a continuous struggle with twists and turns, however, when you come to a fork in the path, if you always remember to use your seven chakras as a guide, the pathway you choose will be an amazing journey."

"How do you use your chakras as a guide?" she asked, wanting to understand.

"You pause and breathe. Then you ask yourself the question and listen to what your body tells you. Your brain gives you logic, it helps you choose the smartest path, your heart gives you righteousness, it helps you choose the purest way and your gut gives you instinct, which helps you remember the lessons of the past."

Davon smiled. "That's really beautiful, Baboo. I apologize for feeling sorry for myself. Being locked in King Tut's tomb must have affected me more than I thought."

"No apology is necessary. I would have been extremely shaken up if I had been hit on the head and left underground. You are incredibly brave."

"Thank you," replied Davon, feeling embarrassed at the compliment after she had been so morose. "Are you hungry? I can order dinner."

Baboo handed her the room service menu. "Dinner would be welcome. I would like the vegetarian meal on the first page, please."

Davon called down to the kitchen, ordered their meals and then glanced at the large amount of equipment Baboo had placed on the balcony table. "Goodness, what is all that?" she asked, pointing.

"It is video surveillance equipment. Some of it is mine and some of it is borrowed from one of my contacts. I am trying to do twenty-four hour surveillance, but with my meetings and the cleaning staff coming into the suite, I am averaging about eighteen hours per day. When I leave the suite, I have to dismantle the equipment and pack it away. The last thing I need is a report of suspicious behaviour going to the Luxor police."

"Have you seen anything unusual?" asked Davon, peering out at the compound's ominous looking twenty-foot wall, which surrounded several large buildings.

"Not really and I have spent hours looking at the footage. As I told you, I suspect the Princes are not at the compound."

"Well, hopefully Marium's husband will have some good news," said Davon. "What can I do to help?"

Baboo gave her a weary smile. "I could use another set of eyes to help to go through the footage. I don't want to get bleary-eyed and miss something."

"I would be more than happy to do that for you," answered Davon.

CHAPTER EIGHTEEN

In the morning on the way to the public market, Davon moved to the edge of her seat. "Baboo, if Marium says her husband won't or can't see me, what should I say?"

"Don't worry. If she turns up for the rendezvous this morning, her husband will have agreed to meet with you."

Baboo parked near the entranceway of the marketplace. Davon adjusted her earpiece as she waited for him to open the door. Getting out of the vehicle, she did not look back. As she scanned the almost all female crowd, she casually strolled through the stalls and then towards the overly stacked vegetable tables where she had spoken to Marium the day before. The place seemed busier than yesterday. Because most of the shoppers were wearing headscarves and long raincoats, it was difficult to locate her target. Davon walked up and down the aisles for at least ten minutes, pretending to inspect the perfectly ripe tomatoes, cantaloupes and watermelon, all the while looking for Marium. She could not see her or the bodyguard anywhere and grew concerned. "I can't find her, Baboo and I am in the exact same place as yesterday," she murmured quietly into the headpiece.

"You have not been there long. Keep moving around so you do not attract attention and Marium will probably find you.

Moments later, just as Baboo had predicted, Davon felt someone put something into her hand.

"Don't turn around," whispered a female voice.

Davon froze in place and leaned inward towards a table stacked three feet high with romaine lettuce. Out of the corner of her eye, she caught a quick glimpse of Marium hurrying away. Stuffing the piece of paper into her pocket, she turned and moved in the opposite direction, heading back to the car. Once inside the vehicle, she pulled out the folded piece of paper.

Baboo started the car and moved into the traffic. "What happened?"

"I couldn't find her, but she obviously saw me because she passed by and shoved a note into my hand. It says her husband will meet me at the Karnak Temple tonight at midnight. The code word is 'scarab'."

Baboo's eyes met hers in the rear view mirror. "I am very concerned about the meeting place and the time they selected. Women should not be wandering around at night in this part of the world, especially at the Temple of Karnak and Marium is well aware of that. It might be a plot to draw you out and I do not want a repeat of King Tut's tomb. I don't think it is wise for you to go."

"I have to take the risk, Baboo, because we have little else to go on. Besides, you will be with me," she said with confidence. She watched him shake his head.

"The man will be spooked if he sees two of us waiting, however, I suppose I could impersonate you."

Davon laughed. "Believe me, up close and personal, you cannot pass as a woman. I know I had a little meltdown at the hotel last night, but I'm okay now. Trust me. I can do this, Baboo. I will meet him at the temple and you can hide nearby in case anything happens."

"I still do not think it is a good idea, but since there is little time to figure out an alternative, we will have to go with it," he replied, pausing for a moment before adding, "I will hide as close as possible in the shadows and park the car nearby in case we have to leave in a hurry. But, promise me right here and now that if I yell 'get out', you will run to the car as fast as you can."

"I promise," she pledged as they returned to the hotel to rest up for the midnight rendezvous.

CHAPTER NINETEEN

The night seemed overly eerie as they drove to Karnak Temple, a ten-minute car ride from the hotel. Although not quite full, the moon was high in the sky and bright, creating shadows in abundance. Baboo, on the alert for others, slowed the vehicle as they approached the temple. He scanned the area for a good place to hide the car, selecting a spot near a grove of palm trees.

Davon looked intently at the semi-lit sphinxes, flanking each side of the entranceway to the temple. "How utterly beautiful, they have the head of a ram and the body of a lion and there has to be at least forty of them!" she exclaimed excitedly. "I can hardly wait to see them up close! Did you know they were made for Ramesses II?"

Baboo turned around and looked at her. "Originally, this was called the avenue of sphinxes because they ran all the way from the Temple of Luxor to Karnak Temple, but Davon," he calmly said, "we are heading into a potentially very dangerous situation. We need to focus on the circumstances and have our wits about us." His lecturing continued in a serious tone as he glanced at his watch. "It is five minutes to twelve. On your way to the entranceway, duck down and skirt around the sphinxes and do not stand directly under the spotlights, but to the side, partially in the shadows. Be in enough light, so that he can see you, but not in enough so that he can take a shot or throw a knife, if that is his intention. Now, I will be hiding behind the fifth sphinx, on this side, in case you run into trouble."

Dressed in black yoga pants, a black sweater and with a black headscarf covering her hair, Davon blended well into the shadows. Ducking down as Baboo advised, she wove her way to the entranceway, standing erect in partial shadow at the foot of the great temple. Her initial elation at the sight of the sphinxes had vanished and now she felt uncomfortable in the eerie unearthly silence. She shifted her weight uneasily as she listened for the sound of footsteps. At least fifteen tortuous minutes passed and just as Davon thought the meeting was a hoax, Baboo alerted her to an intruder through her earpiece.

"Someone is approaching on your right. Move back into the shadows because I am positive he has seen you."

Davon did as she was told and waited until her contact moved into the light.

"What is the code word?" the contact whispered.

"Scarab," replied Davon, maintaining her position.

"Show me the money."

Davon pulled out three one hundred dollar bills and dangled them in front of him for only a second before putting them back into her pocket. "All the money is here, but you have to answer a few questions first."

The contact moved closer and slouched against the wall. "I had to walk here from Luxor," he said with a long exhale as if to explain his tardiness. "What do you want to know?" He stood directly in the spotlight and Davon was close enough that she could see small beads of sweat upon his brow.

"Is Prince Abdul staying at the compound in Luxor?"

"No."

Davon sighed. "Has he been there? Is Prince Adin there?"

"They were both here about one month ago, but then they moved to the palace in Morocco."

"Morocco? He is in Morocco?" asked Davon with surprise.

"At the moment, but they are coming back to Luxor in a few..."

"In a few what?" she questioned as she watched his head slump forward to his chest and his body in almost slow motion slide down the sandstone wall of the temple and onto the sandy desert floor. "Sir, are you alright?" she yelled, flipping him over. His face was covered in blood and it spurted out freely, coloring the golden yellow sand, bright red. "Oh My God! He's been shot!" she muttered in revulsion, instantly locating the bullet entrance hole just above his left eye.

"Get out!" yelled Baboo, "Now!"

Davon instinctively reached for the man's carotid artery, which was slowly fading. There was nothing she could do to save him. When she heard the crack of sandstone behind her, she unconsciously ducked. "Shit! Now they're shooting at me!" She quickly yanked back her hand and in doing so, knocked the victim's arm forward, exposing his left wrist. She froze in midstep. There on his wrist she saw a large tattoo of the 'All-Seeing Eye'.

"What are you doing?" screamed Baboo into her earpiece when he saw her hovering over the victim. "Get to the car!"

Davon needed no further coaxing when another shot shattered the tip of the sandstone brick behind her. Leaping off the stone landing, she began to weave her way back through the line of sphinxes, sprinting as quickly as she could to the waiting vehicle. With the motor running, Baboo had the passenger door open. The second Davon jumped into the car, Baboo stepped on the gas and sped away.

"Oh My God!" she said, turning around to see if anyone was behind them. "Who was it? Did you see anything?"

"I saw nothing until I heard you say he was shot and then I saw two shadows running across the parking lot. They must have followed him, assuming he was giving away trade secrets. I am driving to the airport and then back to the hotel just in case they are following us. They have to have a vehicle, but I did not hear or see it."

"They had a silencer on the gun. I actually didn't realize he was shot until I flipped him over. Oh, why did this have to happen?" moaned Davon. "The guy was just a simple man trying to make a few extra dollars, it's not fair."

"You don't know the whole story. Your simple man was probably up to no good long before you came along," replied Baboo. "But it is unfortunate that this occurred because now we will have to keep a low profile for the next few days. In fact, I am going to get a different colored car tomorrow. Did you get any information from him?"

"He said Abdul and Adin are in Morocco, but they are returning to the Luxor compound in the next few something. I hope he meant days. He said the word 'few' and was then shot. It was a bullet to the head, so incredibly horrible!" She let out a gasp. "Baboo, I want to find a way to give the three hundred dollars to Marium. It's the least I can do."

Baboo sighed. "I am afraid that is impossible. Think about it, Davon. She knows her husband was meeting you at Karnak Temple and that you were going to give him money for the information. So, if he was alive when you left him, you would have given the money to him. If the money suddenly surfaces now, Marium is going to tie you to the murder."

"And what will happen when the money is not found on him? She still might tell the police about our meeting."

"I do not think so. You see, her husband could have been killed for the money after he met you. Marium will keep her mouth shut because she does not know the truth. You see, everyone knows to keep silent in this country for fear of being charged with the crime. Marium will not say anything."

"I still feel responsible for his death. Who would have killed

115

him?" She asked, reliving the event and the fact there was nothing she could have done to save him. "Baboo, I did notice something weird about him, though, and it might have some meaning. He had a tattoo of the 'All-Seeing Eye' on his left wrist."

"Ah, the eye of Ra, the Egyptian sun god," said Baboo.

"Yes. The Sanduu logo is a statue of Ra. I saw it when I googled the Sanduu holdings. I wonder if it has any connection."

"We need to look into it." They arrived at the airport and Baboo went down the ramp, circled around and then started to exit.

As he drove to the hotel, Davon removed her scarf and brown wig and combed out her blonde hair with her fingers. "So what do we do now? Just wait?"

"That is what the Private Eye business is, a waiting game. You must be patient. We will find Prince Abdul, trust me."

CHAPTER TWENTY

The next four days were spent doing reconnaissance in Baboo's suite. Davon and Baboo took turns watching the car entrance to the compound with binoculars during the day, and then at night, a video camera was set up for fourteen hours to film the entranceway. Every morning, Davon ordered brunch in the room and someone, usually her, watched the tape while eating breakfast.

"This is boring, Baboo," said Davon, taking a sip of coffee. "I don't know how you do this for a living. Nothing is going on at the Sanduu compound. It is the same thing night after night. She pressed the fast forward button, but kept her eyes glued to the screen. About an hour into the viewing, she noticed something. "Hang on a second," she cried, pausing the video. "Come and see this." She turned towards Baboo, who was using binoculars to watch the compound.

He put down the binoculars and moved towards the television. "Backup the video, stop and now press forward," he instructed, sitting down in a chair beside Davon.

The video showed a dark colored limousine driving up to the car entranceway at 2:12 am. When the vehicle stopped, a male passenger got out of the car to talk with one of the security guards. "Can you zoom in closer?" asked Davon, leaning forward. "I need to get a look at his face." Baboo paused the machine and zoomed in. "Yes!" exclaimed Davon.

"That is definitely one of the brothers, but I don't know which one," she said, exhaling slowly. "So, what is our next move?"

"Well, I can find my contact in Luxor and see what he has heard on the street about the return of the Sanduu Princes or I can get a hold of the paying contact and tell him we believe Prince Abdul is at the Sanduu compound in Luxor."

Davon thought for a moment. "My contact in Boston said I was to actually see Abdul and be able to say without a doubt that we have found him. The man on the video could be his twin brother, Adin." The statement was true, but deep inside Davon desperately hoped to be able to speak with Abdul. She wanted to meet with him, not just for her own selfish needs, but felt it was crucial to give him the heads up before she sent in the CIA to rescue him. However, would it even be possible to sneak into the compound? She considered what the fired Sanduu employee had said about the tight security at the complex. "Go and see what the word is on the street, Baboo, and I will stay here and keep an eye on the place while you're gone. If Abdul is there, we have to find some way to get into the compound. Is there any way you can feel out your contacts for ideas, because I'm drawing a total blank."

It was almost seven o'clock when Davon heard Baboo's key in the door. He came through the doorway smiling and Davon had the feeling he was up to something. "What is it? What did you find out?" she eagerly asked.

"Sorry, I am late, but I had to wait for my contact to go out and talk to some people. The good news is, there is going to be a party tonight at the Sanduu compound. Apparently, it has been in the works for a few days. I do not know what type of party it is, but food is being ordered in large amounts."

"Fantastic!" Davon was elated. "Great work, Baboo. Now, how do we get an invitation?"

They moved into the living room and sat down. "Again, Davon, I have to warn you that crashing the party could be dangerous."

Davon looked him in the eye. "I realize getting into the event could be risky, but please know if Abdul is actually there, he will protect us from harm."

"I applaud you for your faith. However, do not forget Abdul is supposedly a hostage. How is he going to protect us if he cannot protect himself?" asked Baboo with a sigh.

"I know it sounds crazy," she said, "but I have a gut feeling everything will be okay. It is almost as though things are falling into place. We started with nothing and now look where we are, so close, so very close! We can pull this off, Baboo. Let's go to the party!"

"I do not think you understand the gravity of the situation," said Baboo, amazed at her bravery. "The event could be a male affair or it could be a couple's party, but regardless of the type, as an Indian, I would never be invited, nor do I have the clothing to attend. We have to think of another way."

Davon was repulsed at the thought of discrimination. "Really, Baboo, they would discriminate against you?"

"It is not a matter of discrimination," he reassured her. "The party is for rich Arab sheiks and there is no way I can pass as one of them."

"Then I will go to the event by myself. I have the clothes and I am sure I will be able to get in somehow," she said with determination. She watched Baboo purse his lips in disagreement. "Work with me, Baboo," she pleaded, "Please help me come up with an idea."

"I am concerned about your safety."

"Look, it is already seven-thirty. We have no other choice and as I said, Abdul will protect me."

Baboo's eyes narrowed. "Then, the first thing we need to determine is what kind of function is being held. I suggest you go and get ready for the party, while I stay here and watch for the guests to arrive. If I see females attending, we can order the hotel limousine and send you over."

Davon smiled at her victory. "Any suggestions as to how I can get inside?"

"If attendance is by invitation only, it could be tricky. You show up and if you are asked for an invitation, look through your purse, and pretend you dropped it somewhere," advised Baboo, looking distraught. "The biggest issue is that you will be arriving without a date, which is unusual in this part of the world. You will have to make up some kind of excuse for him. Would you be comfortable flirting with the bodyguards to get in, because that might be necessary?"

"Very comfortable," replied Davon, trying to project a confidence she did not feel.

Without mincing words, Baboo described the downside of dropping into an event, unescorted and uninvited. "All I can tell you is to trust your gut instinct. If you are feeling unsafe, feign illness. Egyptians have a distaste for sickness. That might be your best chance of getting out the door. Are you still positive you want to go ahead with the plan?" When Davon nodded, he continued, "Alright. Go and get ready and I will phone you the second I see anything."

Davon ordered room service and then jumped into the shower. She was excitedly nervous. She had never crashed a party before and this event, she knew, was no simple house party! As she washed her hair, she tried to think of a reason why she would be arriving at the function on her own. It was a man's domain in this part of the world and women just did not go to parties unescorted. She planned to wear the black dress she had bought at Cheri's and would be going as a blonde. Her rationale was that Abdul would immediately recognize her, however, she thought cringing, so would Mr. Bedon.

Toweling off, Davon slipped on her housecoat and hearing the doorbell, answered it, letting in the bellman with her meal. She snacked as she dried her hair and practiced her alibi in the mirror. "My date is parking the car. He asked me to check in," she said with a smile. "My date had an emergency he had to attend to. He will be coming to the party as soon as he can." She flopped onto the chair in front of the mirror feeling disillusioned, worried security would not let her enter. "I think I need to use a sexier voice." She stood up and vocalized her alibis again, in a softer, sweeter tone, all the while trying to look innocent and helpless.

Finishing off her meal in her housecoat, she put on her makeup and then slipped into her dress and new black shoes. She was almost ready when the phone rang.

"The guests have started to arrive and it is definitely a fancy affair. I have seen more women than men, but as you know, I can only see who gets out of the left side of the vehicle. None of the women are wearing headscarves and there are many Caucasians, so you are in good company. Are you ready to go?"

"I guess," Davon replied, sounding slightly unsure.

"Your earpiece will not work in the compound, so take the cell phone and text me DD if you are fine and XX if you are in trouble. If you run into trouble I will do everything in my power to get help," said Baboo, picking up on the uncertainty in her voice. "Remember, if you are at all uncomfortable with this project, you do not have to do it."

Davon bit her lower lip and sighed. "It's alright, Baboo, I want to do it. It will be worth it if I can get to Abdul."

CHAPTER TWENTY-ONE

Davon took several deep breaths as she concentrated on the wording of her alibi while she waited in the hotel entranceway for the limousine. Although outwardly she appeared calm, inside panic threatened. The horror of being locked in Tut's tomb and witnessing the murder of a contact was still a little too fresh in her mind. I cannot think about anything else, but getting into the compound, she silently told herself just as she heard a female voice call her name.

"Ms. Girard, are you attending the party at the Sanduu estate?" a desk clerk asked, holding something out. "I think you need your passport to attend. All the other people going to the event asked for their passports." The clerk handed her the document and then smiled.

"Thank you so much, I completely forgot," replied Davon with gratitude. She clutched the passport, thankful the document was a forgery, and walked down the stairs to get into the awaiting limo with no idea of why she would need it. "Oh no!" she suddenly moaned, realizing the passport was probably required to match her name with the name on the guest list. "Help!" she mumbled as the limousine zoomed away from the hotel, making a turn at the main street onto the compound's driveway.

They stopped behind another vehicle and Davon watched as two women, dressed in stunning evening gowns got out of the car. She waited to see their escorts, but the women appeared to be alone. This is not the way things are done here, she thought, wondering what was going on, but before she had time to debate the issue, her limousine pulled up in front of the entranceway and her door was opened.

"Welcome Miss, please go through the gates to the reception area," the guard said in broken English.

Nervously clutching her evening bag, Davon wondered if she should try to tag along with the two women ahead of her. One was a brunette, the other a redhead and they were absolutely gorgeous. Davon wondered what their excuses for dates were going to be.

The women immediately walked towards the reception desk as though they knew the routine and Davon saw them handing the man at the desk their passports and cell phones. Moving casually towards the table, she listened and noticed the man jotted down their passport numbers and then gave the documents back to the women, but put their cell phones into a box. "What escort service sent you?" he asked, writing down the responses.

Davon instantly paled. "Oh My God, I'm a hooker," she said under her breath, feeling quite faint. Unsure if she was going to be able to pull off this task, she saw the man wiggle his index finger at her, indicating she was to approach the table.

"You are new," he exclaimed. Looking her up and down, he appeared pleased with what he saw. "Passport and cell phone please."

Davon felt her stomach lurch as she handed him the items he requested, craning her neck to see what other escort services were on the list.

"What escort service sent you?"

"Pricey," she answered with a French accent, praying the name was right because she was having trouble reading upside down.

"What, Pricey is in France now," snapped the woman, standing behind Davon.

Davon turned around and smiled at her. She was a stunning blonde in a long shimmering silver gown, which seemed a bit out of date. "Oui, for some time now," she answered, ignoring the woman's sneer. Taking back her passport, Davon was directed towards a lovely reception room where she could hear soft music playing.

As she entered the room, she stared with admiration at the architecture. It was a very large space with rounded arches and alcoves on each corner. The walls were painted light green and the soft white molded ceiling held twelve massive chandeliers. Tables, overflowing with food and drink, had been set up along one wall and most of the women were gathered there in groups, chatting.

Determined to fit in with the group, Davon inched her way over, stopping beside the woman she spoke to at reception. "What a lovely dress, it really suits you. I don't know what I was thinking wearing this short frock. I'm Michelle," she said with a nervous laugh.

"I'm Susan. It's obviously your first time, so the agency should have told you what to wear. Why didn't you ask?"

"Stupid, I know," replied Davon, shaking her head. "Susan, can I ask you about the procedure? What should I expect?"

This time Susan laughed. "We hang around here until the men arrive. If someone likes you, you go with them. It is as simple as that and if they are happy with you, you may even get some money or a piece of jewelry," she replied, pointing to a diamond bracelet on her wrist. "I got this last time. Pretty nice, isn't it?"

Davon fought the urge to roll her eyes. "Yeah, wow." The thought of having sex with a stranger made her feel sick to her stomach and the only thing circling around and around her brain was how to ask Susan if she had a condom to spare. She listened to the woman natter on about all of her escapades, boasting about this gift and that, and as she talked, Davon realized she was just a piece of eye candy—pretty to look at but nothing upstairs. Before the opportunity arose to ask about a condom, a man made his way into the middle of the room, clapping his hands to get everyone's attention.

"Girls, be quiet and please line up along the wall. The men will be arriving shortly."

The women excitedly lined up in front of the tables and Davon could see they were all vying to get into the best position to stand out. Following Susan to the end of the row, she stood behind her, trying to hide. She felt nauseatingly apprehensive and wondered if she should immediately feign sickness. Being part of this event was not going to help her find Abdul and she knew it. The man clapped his hands again to silence the women and although a hush overcame the group, Davon could still hear whispering. I have to get out of here, she thought, squatting down somewhat as she backed up into the table, directly behind her. Glancing around, she observed bodyguards standing in front of the exit. It's now or never, she told herself. Carefully, she proceeded to slowly slide along the side of the table, deciding to approach the bodyguard, who had checked her in, and explain that she had the flu.

She had moved only slightly when a door across the room opened. A small group of men walked along the opposite wall, some of them, but not all, slowing their gait to look at the women. The central figure of the group, however, kept his eyes to the floor as he marched forward. Davon immediately recognized him, positive he was Abdul. She pushed around Susan, who let out a huff, and leaned forward to get a better look. It was his gait and his inability to ogle the girls that gave him away. One of the attendants looked as though he was trying to draw Abdul's attention to the girls by repeatedly blocking his way while pointing them out, but Abdul would have no part of it. Davon needed to do something quickly to get his attention and without a second thought, she moved back to where she had been standing and swept a tray of champagne glasses onto the floor. The loud crash caused the group of men to stop in their tracks and all eyes, the women as well, to turn upon her.

"Excusez-Moi," she blurted out overly loudly. She looked directly towards Abdul and willed him to see her. They linked eyes for

125

only a brief second, but she was positive he recognized her. Then without another glance, Abdul exited through a door to his right and was gone.

"What was that all about, Michelle? Are you trying to get us into trouble?" spat Susan, turning on her.

"Sorry, it was an accident. I bumped into the table," Davon mumbled, surprised that not one of the thirty or so women, even asked if she was okay.

Susan gave her a disgusted look, shook her head and then stormed down the line, squeezing into the middle. "It was an accident," she said, imitating Davon's accent to the young woman beside her.

When two workmen appeared to clean up the mess, the organizer asked the women to move to the other side of the room. Dawdling behind the group, Davon scanned the area for the door where Abdul had exited. She counted at least three doors and thought she saw a fourth before she had to move back into the lineup, where both of the women on either side of her, instantly stepped away. Man, they're ostracizing me, she said to herself in honest disbelief. Just as she was about to attempt an apology, she heard male voices and saw about fifty men, entering the room. The women immediately went to work, seeking out the richest and most powerful males, while Davon ducked behind one of the decorative columns determined to find the place where Abdul had exited. She went inside a small alcove, which contained a door, but when she turned the knob, she discovered it was locked.

"Damn it!" she swore in frustration, jumping when a hand reached out and tapped her on the shoulder. She spun around.

"Hello," said an over-weight, balding man. Smiling, he held out a champagne glass and offered it to her.

"Yeah, I don't think so," squeaked Davon under her breath. "Sorry, do you know where the restroom is? I'm feeling a bit nauseous. I think I'm going to throw-up."

"Yes, yes. You come with me. Yes?"

"Oh please, he doesn't speak English," she complained to no one in particular. Glancing into the reception room, she noticed two or more men surrounding each one of the women. "What were they thinking? They should have brought in more women. Go over there," she said, pointing to Susan. "She likes you. She will go with you." She made dramatic hand gestures and somehow he seemed to understand. Shrugging, he happily went off to approach Susan. "Thank God," said Davon. She gave an involuntary shudder and then quickly moved towards the next alcove.

The door it contained was also locked. Leaning her ear against it, she tried to hear if someone was inside the room, but all she heard was silence. "Come on! I need some luck here," she said softly as she moved as unobtrusively as possible in the direction of the next doorway. On route, she took a moment to glance towards the activity in the reception room. The last thing she wanted was to be surprised again.

She was standing in front of the fourth and last doorway in the vicinity, when out of the corner of her eye, she saw a well-built man, drawing near. He was looking at her with curiosity and she knew he was wondering what she was doing. Davon turned and faced him. "Can you please tell me where the restroom is? I'm not feeling well."

"I can show you a bathroom on the way. You have been requested. Come with me, right now," he sternly demanded, not showing any hint of concern about her wellbeing.

She understood from the tone of his voice that he would not accept any excuses and suddenly envisioned walking into a room with a fat, old man, lying naked in bed. The thought actually did make her feel physically ill. Oh My God, I don't think I can do this, she said to herself, as she was steered towards a staircase. As they walked up the stairs, she noticed a gun in a hip holster and wondered if the guard would use it if she tried to flee. Rolling her neck as though she was stretching, she leaned forward and tried to discretely look at the inside of his left wrist for an 'All-Seeing Eye' tattoo, thinking it might be a type of branding Adin used for his men. If this guy was from Strike Bodyguard Service, she might be able to use the fact that she knew his boss to make some sort of deal, so that she could leave the compound. When the attempt to see the tattoo failed, she faked a fall.

"Sorry, I caught my heel," she said innocently, reaching out to him to help her stand. When he did so, she glanced at his wrist, saw the tattoo and instantly broke out into a sweat. The guy definitely works for Adin, she told herself, wondering if Mr. Bedon had recognized her when she arrived and had sent for her. They turned and started to walk down a long hallway and Davon lagged behind, pretending to look at the mosaics on the walls. Racking her brain, she tried to figure out a way to get away from him. "I really have to go to the bathroom," she blurted out, stopping in midstride.

"There is a bathroom here," he tartly replied. They had stopped in front of dark mahogany French doors where he quickly knocked twice. When a large burly man opened one side, her escort motioned for her to enter. "The bathroom is in the foyer to the right," he told her, turning to leave. Not knowing what to do, Davon cautiously walked through the doorway. As she entered, the burly guard exited and closed the door behind him. She heard a key turn in the lock.

Davon felt her heart beginning to race. She scanned the foyer and then cautiously peeked around the curtains into the room. Realizing there was no one there, she felt relieved. "I might be locked in a room, but at least I'm alone," she said softly, wondering if there was some way out. She moved towards the window and then stopped dead in her tracks. A side door, which she assumed was the door to a closet, was slowly starting to open. Grabbing a glass paperweight from a table, she prepared to attack because there was no way she was having sex with anyone tonight! She moved quietly towards a sidewall holding the paperweight high, ready to strike if necessary, as she watched a dark headed male enter the room. He walked past her, not noticing her body pressed between a bookcase and the wall. For a second, he appeared confused, but then as if he sensed her presence, he slowly turned around and looked at her.

Davon placed the paperweight onto the shelf and let out a huge sigh of relief. "Abdul, you're actually here!" she happily exclaimed.

"Davon!" he cried, rushing towards her. He swept her into his arms and held her tight. "I could not believe my eyes when I saw you in the receiving room. How did you come to be here?"

She felt her heart melting at his touch. "I came to rescue you because I was afraid Bedon and Adin were going to harm you. Have they hurt you?" she asked, noticing that although he appeared thinner, he looked well.

Abdul paid no attention to her question as he led her to one of the expensive looking leather sofas positioned in the middle of the room. "I cannot believe you are here, but now I am worried about your safety. How did you even get into the compound?"

"I snuck in with the prostitutes, before I realized that was what they were. If you hadn't come downstairs, I would have been in a really bad predicament."

"Yes," said Abdul with a nod, "you would have. I feel embarrassed that you had to witness it."

It was hard to sit so close to him and be professional. She reminded herself that he was a married man nineteen times over and struggled to ignore the tingling sensation running down her spine. "I know how the story goes and I can only say I'm glad you're not involved," she assured him. "But, you haven't answered my question about Adin. Has he hurt you?"

"Adin is my twin brother. I hope he would never hurt me." He put his arm around her and pulled her towards him.

She didn't resist and letting down her guard, she gave him a tender kiss on the side of his cheek, quickly berating herself when strong feelings of lust overpowered her. Moving a few inches away, she tried to avoid looking into his eyes. "But he is keeping you here as a hostage, isn't he?" she asked, lifting the side of his shirt to look at his old bullet wound, the one she had sutured closed in Cairo. She needed to distract herself. "Stay still, Abdul, I need to have a look at your wound."

"Yes, I am a hostage, but so far he has treated me fairly well, although..."

"Although what? Are you in danger?" She stopped what she was doing and looked at him.

He met her gaze with tenderness. "You don't need to bother yourself with my problems."

Davon pursed her lips. "Abdul, remember, you once promised you would treat me like an equal. I want to know what is going on. You have no idea what I have gone through to get here!"

Abdul nodded and looked at her lovingly. "I understand. You put yourself in danger to help me and I love you for it. You are the bravest woman I have ever known. But please, let's not spoil the few moments we have with my problems." He hoped she would let the matter drop because he needed to protect her from his dangerous and unstable brother, but seeing the expression on her face, he realized there would be no rest until he answered the question. "How does my wound look?" he asked, hoping to switch the subject.

"Your wound has healed beautifully," she replied, sitting up straight. She smiled when he took her hand and kissed it. "Answer the question. Are you in danger?"

Abdul shrugged. The beautiful woman before him was going to get to the root of the situation whether he liked it or not. "I want to say no, however the real answer is I am nervous because something horrible has happened to my brother. He has changed. He is angry and violent and we have almost come to blows several times. He said he will not release me until I hand over the statue of Ra and with the statue, the control of the Sanduu holdings and OPEC."

Davon was confused. "What does a statue have to do with the control of your business?"

Abdul leaned back and frowned as though the weight of the world was upon him. "I do not even know where to begin."

"Then start at the beginning," she suggested, trying to be encouraging.

"Ra is the sun god and symbolizes protection and power. Most of the statues of Ra have the body of a man and the head of a falcon, as does ours." Davon nodded as she listened, well aware of the history of Ra. "Our statue of Ra has been in the family for three generations. It is a long standing tradition that the person who owns the statue has control, not only of the Sanduu Corporation, but of the entire oil cartel."

"I still don't totally understand why ownership of a statue gives you power, but speaking of Ra, I saw two men from the compound with tattoos of the 'All-Seeing Eye' on their inner left wrists."

"Adin is always taking things too far!" huffed Abdul. Standing up he went to the kitchen area and opened the fridge. "What would you like to drink?" Davon joined him and selected a bottle of flavored water. They returned to the sofa and he continued his story. "Every March there is a meeting of all of the oil barons. The person who holds the statue of Ra is automatically the president. The statue is mainly symbolic, but being the president is a very powerful position, which gives you the final say in the regulation of oil prices and market distribution. It is a position many desire. Our family has held the presidency for thirty-six years, but it was not always so. I do not know how my grandfather obtained the statue of Ra, but I do know it was not always owned by our family. Now, Adin wants to take over because he thinks I am not ruthless enough to hold on to the power of the organization. He tells me others are seeking the statue and he wants to know where I am hiding it."

"What will happen at the meeting in March if you don't show up with the statue?" asked Davon with concern.

Abdul shook his head. "It is going to be a big problem for Adin, especially if he does not take me to Vienna. However, I'm trapped here and Adin has shutdown all of my contact with my men. I can't get to the statue."

"What about Bedon?" interrupted Davon. "Doesn't he know where the statue is?"

"Bedon is dead. Another example of Adin's ruthlessness!" he said bitterly.

Davon was surprised. "Well, I can't say that I'm sorry. How did it happen?"

"He made the mistake of deceiving Adin, trying to get more money, I suppose. It probably had to do with the location of the statue. However, Bedon did not know where the statue was. When I found out about his death in Morocco, I told them I did not want to know the details. All this deception makes me sick."

Davon realized she had to tell him the truth about why she was here. "Abdul, I am working with the CIA. They told me to notify them when I found you. They are going to organize a rescue."

Abdul gave a hearty laugh. "And why is the CIA concerned about me?"

"I don't know," she answered, feeling confused by the question. "This guy came to see me in Boston and..."

"What were you doing in Boston?"

"Oh boy," sighed Davon, "I have a lot to tell you. How much time do we have?"

"All night."

"Good, because it may take that long to explain everything that has happened."

CHAPTER TWENTY-TWO

Going through the last four months systematically, Davon started by describing in detail her last month at the palace and how she escaped. When she reluctantly told Abdul about the death of Hepbet, he cried, and she had to hold him for almost an hour before he was able to come to terms with the death of his eldest son. Finally, she was able to get to the end of the saga, explaining how an agent from the CIA paid her a visit at the hospital, which led her to Cairo, Baboo and the discovery that he was at the compound in Luxor. She even told him about the murder of Adin's man at Karnak Temple.

"It is not the CIA who is looking for me, Davon. You were duped. It is one of the big US oil companies trying to locate the statue of Ra. I did not believe him, but Adin is right. It seems it is not only my brother, who is vying for power. If a US oil company is interested in the statue, there must be a problem with oil distribution or price," he said, pondering for a moment. "I don't even know what a barrel of oil is going for. Adin will not let me near a computer or newspaper."

"Oh," replied Davon, putting two and two together. "Now the whole thing is beginning to make sense. The price of oil is falling dramatically. I think it is somewhere around forty or fifty dollars a barrel."

Abdul's eyes widened. "This is disastrous! I have to get the statue and find a way to get to the meeting!"

"I can organize a rescue."

"No," replied Abdul, shaking his head. "The compound is too well fortified."

"So what can we do?"

"Hmm," said Abdul, looking thoughtful. He stroked his chin and remained silent for a few seconds. "I can tell you where the statue of Ra is located and you can get in touch with one of my men." He then shook his head, changing his mind. "No, I cannot involve you. It is much too dangerous. Never mind, I will think of something."

Davon took both of his hands in hers and looked at him. "I'm the only chance you have! Let me help you, Abdul, I want to help."

"You do not understand whom you are up against. My brother's men will not hesitate to kill you."

"I'm not afraid," she told him, suddenly feeling a sense of courage she did not know she possessed. "Please let me help you."

Abdul imagined the worst. "I don't know. If anything happens to you I will never forgive myself." He glanced at his watch and then pursed his lips for a long time as though he was hesitant to tell her anything else. "The meeting is on March 2nd in Vienna, Austria. It is usually held at the Hotel Sacher Wien."

"That's next week! Wait, let me memorize the facts. Is the hotel name two words?" Abdul spelt it out for her. "Okay, continue."

"Usually it is an all day affair. I am sure Adin will let me attend because I am the only one who knows the password to the computer program to open the meeting. He has tried many times to get the password out of me, but I have refused to tell him. Without the password and the statue, there is going to be an issue with the other participants. I am betting he will take me to the meeting, thinking I will somehow manage to get the statue to Vienna and he will be right if you can organize a way to get it there. But, listen to me, Davon, you are to only contact my man. Let him take care of securing the statue and getting it to Vienna. I want you to go back to Boston. I will find you, God willing, after this whole affair is over. Do you understand?"

"Yes, Abdul. Which one of your men should I contact?"

"Jafar Rahin. I do not have my cell phone and therefore no phone number, but have your man try to locate him."

"My man, Baboo, is supposedly working for the US oil company. How can I trust him?"

"What you do is offer him more money to switch sides and he will come around," said Abdul. Davon shook her head because she was not convinced. "You must let your man help you. There is no way you can find Jafar on your own."

"You don't seem to understand. Baboo is a loyal, decent person. I cannot see him switching sides. I'll do my best to try to persuade him, but it's not going to be easy. Now where do I tell Jafar he can find the statue?"

Abdul exhaled noisily. "It is almost humorous because Adin brought me to the right location, he just does not know it."

"The statue is at the compound?"

"No, it is near the water on the Sanduu..." Before he could finish the sentence, there was a knock on the door. Abdul put his finger to his lips and without another word he was on his feet, running into the foyer. Davon heard angry words and then two bodyguards entered the room. "I am afraid you have to leave, Miss. Thank you for your time," said Abdul. He kept his back to the guards and removed the watch from his wrist. Pointing to the back of it, he pressed it into Davon's hand as she stood.

Davon grabbed her handbag from the table and gave him one last encouraging look as she left with the men. Everything will be fine, she told herself, positive that Abdul's man, Jafar, would have an idea where the statue was being kept. She slipped the watch around her wrist and followed the guards back down to the reception room, trying to imprint on her brain the information Abdul had told her. The whole situation was surreal and Davon had a hard time understanding how two identical twins could be like night and day. Although she had only briefly met Adin, she knew enough about his antics to know he was a cruel and ruthless man, so unlike the soft spoken and loving Abdul. She was pleased she had found Abdul well and hoped the situation would not change before she could find the statue and rescue him.

When they entered the reception room, it was almost empty. Selecting her phone from the box at the door, Davon exited the compound and walked towards the waiting limousines. As she started to scan the cars, wondering which one was from the hotel, she heard Baboo's voice.

"Ms Girard, your limousine."

Davon walked quickly, keeping her pace measured so as not to attract undue attention from the guards. When she arrived at the vehicle, she stood at the door, waiting for Baboo to open it for her. She did not say a word until they were both safely inside. "Thanks for coming to get me, Baboo. How long did you have to wait?"

"Four hours. I got here around midnight and was getting worried because you did not text me."

"I couldn't text you because they took everyone's cell phones."

"Well, I am just glad that you are safe. Were you able to contact Prince Abdul?"

Davon was not sure if this was the time to tell Baboo exactly what happened. She needed to feel out his loyalty before she could tell him the actual truth. "It was a very stressful affair and some interesting things occurred, but I'm really too exhausted to talk about it now. Can we meet for brunch tomorrow and discuss it then?"

"Of course, as I said, I am just glad you are okay."

They got back to the hotel within minutes and after Baboo let Davon out of the car, she said a quick goodnight and then dashed to her room.

Lying in bed, Davon reminisced about her meeting with Abdul. It was wonderful seeing him again, but it bothered her tremendously that he was being held against his will. Although he had assured her that his brother would probably release him in due time, it was clear Abdul was afraid of what Adin might do. She was sure Adin had a hand in the death of Abdul's son Hepbet, so why, she wondered, had he not yet killed Abdul. The reason, she figured, had to be linked to the statue and computer code. Abdul was smart to refuse to tell his brother the whereabouts of the statue or the code needed to open up the meeting. Digging her teeth into her lower lip, she sighed. Abdul was right; she needed Baboo's help to find Jafar.

Her thoughts turned to Maxwell and she questioned if Abdul was correct about him being employed by a US oil company. If true, why would Maxwell put on a charade about being with the CIA? Nothing seemed to make sense. She flipped to her right side and watched the sunlight expanding along the wall. Thinking back about her first meeting with Maxwell, she realized she had not really had a good look at his badge. He had merely flashed it at her and said the government needed her assistance. She was the one who had made the assumption. "What an idiot I am! I have to be more careful about the people I trust. But, the real question is what is a US oil company or the US government really after—Abdul or the statue?" She drummed her fingers on the sheet and tried to think of every possibility. Abdul had mentioned his group not only had a major influence over the price of oil, they regulated the price worldwide, and that Adin, acting as president in Abdul's absence, was obviously letting the price of oil slide. Davon grimly recalled a headline in the papers about the falling price of oil. She wished she had discussed this fact further with Abdul because maybe it was the US government trying to locate him to discuss some options. She groaned, thinking this was the second time in less than a year that she needed advice and had no one to turn to.

She fell into a fitful sleep and felt horrible when the alarm went off at 8:00 am. Pushing the hair out of her eyes, Davon sat up. "I need coffee," she mumbled, barely able to keep her eyes open as she felt her way to the kitchenette and the coffee pot. She filled the machine with water, placed the coffee pouch in the holder, turned on the machine and then went to take a shower. As she washed her hair, she wondered how she was going to convince Baboo to work for Abdul.

CHAPTER TWENTY-THREE

Davon practiced her persuasive skills as she waited for Baboo to arrive. When the doorbell rang, she took a deep breath and answered it. "Come on in, Baboo and have a seat. I've ordered brunch. It should be here in about twenty minutes." They walked into the living room and sat down across from each other on matching sofas.

"So," he said, "you mentioned you had an interesting evening last night."

Davon swallowed hard. "When we met, Baboo, you said you had been paid for half of this job and that I was responsible to give you the final payment." Baboo nodded. "Would you say we are at or over the halfway mark? I mean, I don't even know what you get paid, but you have been working non-stop for nine, almost ten days."

"I was paid one thousand US dollars," he replied.

"Okay, one hundred dollars a day times ten is a thousand dollars, so I think you are now working for me, correct?" In her mind, a hundred dollars per day in Egypt seemed like a fair price.

Baboo adjusted himself in his seat and then looked her in the eye. "Is there something you would like to tell me, Davon? I have a feeling something is not quite right."

"Everything is fine," she said. Shifting into doctor mode, she met his gaze. "I need you to switch your allegiance to me. I will pay you two hundred dollars a day plus expenses, but you must cut all ties to whoever originally hired you. If you cannot agree to this arrangement, I understand, but our business relationship will be over."

"I see," said Baboo, pausing for a moment to digest the offer. "Then, I assume you did meet with Prince Abdul last night and uncovered some important information that for some reason you do not want our employer to get a hold of."

Davon made sure her facial expression remained neutral. "Baboo, please, consider my offer. Can I ask if you even know the name of the company or institution that hired you?"

"I am usually not privy to who is paying the bills. I always work through a middleman. However, the problem is if I switch sides and withhold information from my contact and he finds out, I will never get another job from him or anyone else in the business. They will blacklist me."

"What if you cancel your contract? I will offer you a bonus of ten thousand dollars to switch allegiance," she said assuredly, convinced that finding Abdul's man and getting the statue to Vienna was probably worth at least that much.

Ten thousand dollars was more money than Baboo made in a year. He knew if he turned down the offer, it would leave Davon alone and in a potentially dangerous situation. Even though he did not know all of the details of the assignment, he knew enough about working as a private investigator in Egypt to realize she could not do this by herself. "I will find some way to cancel my present contract and will agree to your terms if you promise to be completely honest with me. I have a feeling you are treading in treacherous water and for us to stay alive, I need to know all of the background information."

Davon stood and stuck out her hand. "Good, then it's a deal. Make the call and cancel your contract before I tell you anything and then you won't be lying when you say we have hit a brick wall."

"You are a very good negotiator, Dr. Marshal," he said, shaking her hand to cement the deal. Pulling out his cell phone, Baboo dialed the number. He spoke in Arabic, but Davon heard the words 'Luxor' and 'Morocco'.

When Baboo disconnected, she cornered him. "What did you say?"

"I told him we are in Luxor and uncovered information that the target was at the Sanduu palace in Morocco. I asked if we should proceed there. He said we are not to proceed as they already have a man in place in Morocco. He thanked me for the information and terminated my contract."

"I guess it's good news because now you are available to help me, but does that mean my contract is also cancelled?" she asked, wondering about her responsibility to Maxwell's group. "What about the credit card they gave me?"

"I presume your contract is also terminated and they are most likely cancelling the credit card as we speak. You would be wise to keep the expense money they gave you as pay. In this type of business it is hard to submit a bill for work after the job is done because it is usually ignored and not paid."

Davon made a rough calculation of the cash she had on hand. "I have given out a few bribes, but after paying the hotel bill I will have about seven thousand dollars left. If I give you five thousand as an initial payment, that will leave me enough to purchase a couple of plane tickets," she said, thinking about Vienna. She did not mention the fact that Abdul had instructed her to return to Boston once they found Jafar. She was going to Vienna, come hell or high water. "Thank goodness, I brought my personal credit card."

"We can talk about my payment later. Depending on where we have to go from here, you probably should be paying in cash as credit card purchases are an easy way to track someone's whereabouts." Baboo saw Davon frown. "I hope you do have a backer. You are not funding this job on your own, are you?"

141

"No, of course not. I will definitely be reimbursed," she answered, not concerned in the least about money. It was the thought of her movements being tracked that gave her cause for worry.

Breakfast arrived and as they ate Davon filled Baboo in on the details of her meeting with Abdul. He nodded as he listened, asking several questions about the man he was supposed to locate. "I will put out feelers, but do you remember Abdul saying anything about what country his man might be in?"

"No and I didn't even think to ask. Maybe you could contact the Sanduu headquarters in Dubai and ask them about him?"

"Your suggestion is a logical one. However, you do not want a report going to Adin saying someone is asking questions about Jafar Rahin. I will go through the usual channels first and hope Jafar is not in hiding. If I were Adin, trying to find the statue, I would have taps on every one of my brother's men. I hope Adin has not already gotten to Jafar."

Davon looked at him attentively. "We only have five days to round up Jafar, find the statue and whisk it to Vienna. Tell me, what do you need me to do?"

CHAPTER TWENTY-FOUR

While Baboo tried to locate Jafar, Davon searched the internet for information after inspecting Abdul's Rolex watch for clues. On the back of the watch was an inscription in hieroglyphics, which with the internet's help she interpreted as 'To a loving son'. There was also a detailed etching of the Egyptian goddess, Isis, with several etched stars above her head.

"How is Isis related to the location of the statue of Ra?" Davon asked herself as she googled pictures of the goddess and locations of her temples. Scanning through several pictures, Davon couldn't help but notice how Isis resembled Cleopatra with her jet-black hair, elaborate headdress and sceptre. She read about three existing temples of Isis: one was in Pompeii, Italy, another was in Ephesus, Turkey, and a third was in Egypt on the island of Philae. The statue has to be on Philae, she thought excitedly, cursing when she read further down in the article that Philae Island was submerged in Lake Nasser in 1902 when they created the Aswan dam. "Give me a break!" she yelled just as Baboo entered the suite.

"It sounds like you are having a frustrating day," he said, walking towards her. "So have I. I made phone calls and talked to all my sources. At this point, Jafar Rahin is nowhere to be found. He is not in Egypt or the United Arab Emirates and his family is gone too. He is in hiding and finding him may be next to impossible."

"Were you able to find a way to get in touch with the Sanduu Corporation?"

"One of my contacts has a cousin who works as a secretary for the corporation in Kuwait. She discretely looked into the system and was able to get me a home address, but when I got someone to check it out, the apartment was vacant."

Davon groaned. "Well, I guess we will have to try to find the statue on our own with nothing to go on!" she shouted, pointing at the computer. "According to Google there are three existing temples dedicated to Isis, but Philae Temple—the only one in Egypt—is under several feet of water! Abdul said the statue was in the area and near the water. I am pretty sure he said near the water, not in the water!"

Baboo appeared baffled. "The temple is under water?"

"When they created the Aswan Dam, Philae Temple was not important enough to relocate. It is submerged in Lake Nasser," she explained. Leaning back in her chair, she looked defeated.

"I remember reading about one temple being moved to higher ground," said Baboo. "I believe it was Abu Simbel."

"You are correct. Abu Simbel Temple was moved, but it is a monument to Ramesses II and Nefertari, not Isis." Davon stood up, stretched and then glanced at her watch. "It's dinner time. Why don't we go to the Indian restaurant down the street and try to figure out what we are going to do next."

As they ate their meal, Davon brainstormed. "Abdul told me it would be impossible to rescue him, but, I think we should attempt to see him again. We need to find out where the statue is being kept. You could drive me to the gate and I could tell the guards that he asked me to return on this particular date."

Baboo disagreed. "No, it is much too dangerous. You would be putting yourself on their radar and what happens if you run into Adin? He could lock you up and never tell Abdul that you were there, he could let you go and put a tail on you or he could kill you."

"Okay, then how about this," she persisted. "Why don't we scope out the marketplace for Marium. I know she may still be away, grieving for her husband, but she will have to go back to work sometime. And when she does return to the marketplace, I will slip her a five hundred dollar bill and a note for Abdul."

"Another very dangerous suggestion. First of all, you have no idea what Marium will do when she sees you and secondly, she has no way of getting a note to Abdul unless she bribes one of his guards. And then there is the problem of how to get Abdul's answer. Trust me, plans that depend on people you do not know, never work."

Davon bit her lip. "Well, what do you suggest? We need more information and we are out of options and almost out of time."

Baboo put a forkful of rice into his mouth and chewed thoughtfully before he spoke. "I think we should wait another day or two. I will keep making the rounds to see if anything has come up about Jafar and you keep searching for information on the internet."

"I have read almost everything on the internet about the Sanduu Corporation, its holdings and about temples dedicated to Isis and I haven't found anything that will help us find the statue of Ra," she tried to explain to him. She took a deep breath. "You know what's funny? For some reason I have this gut feeling Abdul was trying to tell me the statue is in a place dedicated to Isis. Philae is under water, but there are the remains of two other temples in Pompeii and Ephesus," she said, pausing to think for a second, "however, that doesn't make sense because Abdul said his brother was looking in the right location for the statue of Ra, which means it has to be somewhere around here. I don't know, Baboo," she said, rubbing her forehead.

"I suggest we keep at it for another couple of days. If absolutely nothing comes up, we will be forced to go to plan B."

"And what is plan B?" asked Davon with a quizzical look.

"Breaking Abdul out of the compound."

"Even though Abdul said that would be an impossible venture!"

Baboo looked at her with a serious expression. "I do not think it is impossible to break him out of the compound, but if it comes down to that, I guarantee someone will get hurt."

Finishing their meal, Davon paid the bill. They left the restaurant and walked down the poorly lit street in silence, each one deep in thought. Just as they were nearing the long hotel driveway, a lone vehicle passed by, illuminating them and the entranceway.

"If you really think it might be possible to break Abdul out of the compound, maybe we should just bite the bullet and start hiring some people right now."

"Getting the people to attempt the job will not be a problem. It is the fact that someone could get hurt or killed, which causes me to hesitate," said Baboo as another vehicle approached them. The car suddenly veered to their side of the street and stopped, its overly bright headlights almost blinding them. The driver's door opened and a muscular man rushed towards Davon. He lifted her up and shoved her against the trunk of a nearby tree, locking his hand around her throat.

"What are you still doing in Luxor, Whore?" he asked. Davon recognized him as the bodyguard who had taken her to Abdul's suite.

When she did not reply, he sneered and grabbed her breast. This time Davon responded by kneeing him in the groin. He swore, and just as he pulled back his fist to strike, Baboo kicked him hard in the back of the knees. When he fell to the ground, Baboo punched him in the head until he collapsed.

"He's one of Adin's bodyguards," gasped Davon as she stared at the lifeless figure on the ground.

"He will only be out for an hour or two. We have to get out of here," said Baboo, dashing to the attacker's car. Turning off the motor, he pulled the keys from the ignition and threw them into an adjacent bush. "Let's get back to the hotel."

They jogged down the driveway towards the hotel's grand entranceway, slowing to walk up one side of the u-shaped staircase. Davon let out a sigh of relief when she looked through the window and saw the doorman in the lobby. "I don't think the porter saw anything, however he's heading this way," she said, signalling to Baboo to move back. She smiled when the attendant opened the door for them.

Entering the hotel, Davon immediately started towards the elevator, but Baboo stopped her. "We need to check out of the hotel and go somewhere else. It was obvious that you were heading here," he whispered.

"You're right," she replied, walking quickly to the reception desk. "Hello, we would like to check out, please."

The reception clerk appeared surprised. "Of course, Ms. Girard. I am sorry to tell you that you must also pay for tonight as check out is normally at noon."

Davon nodded wholeheartedly. "I understand. I will be paying in US dollars," she said, reaching for her wallet.

After Davon settled the bill, Baboo checked the entranceway for Adin's bodyguard before they made their way to the elevator. When the door closed, Baboo turned to her and lowered his voice. "Get packed and I will meet you at the service elevator on your floor. It is at the back of the east wing. We cannot chance using the one in the lobby."

"Where are we going to go?"

"I have a friend who will take us in."

CHAPTER TWENTY-FIVE

The service elevator took them to the back of the hotel. Exiting the building, Davon waited with the bags while Baboo went to get the rental vehicle. With the headlights off, Baboo pulled up beside her and quietly loaded the suitcases into the backseat. There appeared to be no one in the area, but as far as Baboo was concerned they still needed to be careful.

Davon got into the front seat and Baboo turned out of the loading bay. He had to drive through the parking lot, around the building and down the long driveway, which was the only way to and from the hotel. As they passed the now abandoned BMW, they noticed Adin's bodyguard was no longer lying on the ground.

"He is gone, Baboo. Do you think he has walked back to the compound?"

"It is hard to say. It depends on how badly he was hurt. He may be in the hotel, right now, asking about you." Baboo turned left onto the main street and flicked on the car's headlights. "My friend lives outside of the city. He has a very small house with an attached barn. It is very rustic. Are you up to staying there?"

"Don't worry about me, Baboo, as long as we are safe I'm up to anything. So, we are going to hide out for a few days and then decide about Plan B?" she asked, wanting to know what he was thinking.

Baboo chuckled to himself. Davon was a remarkable person and he was pleased that he was working for her. "Plan B has to be our last resort and since it looks like we are not going to find Jafar, you and I have to try to figure out where the statue is hidden. It will be a challenge, but I believe it can be done. I know you worked for the Prince. Did you meet anyone while you were at the palace who might know the location of the statue?"

Davon instantly thought about Raja. Abdul's wives would not know anything because Abdul never talked to them about business, but Raja—she was certainly in the know about how the palace operated, but the statue? "Probably not," she said, hesitating, "let me think about it."

They drove out of town away from the city's streetlights, which were few, and onto a road that took them towards the desert. A noticeable jolt let Davon know they had left the pavement. She felt the sedan beginning to struggle and bump along the rocky terrain. "It's pretty dark out here. Are we still on some sort of road?" she questioned, peering out the front window to see if she could find any vehicle tracks.

"I am not sure if it is considered a road. It is most likely one of the ancient trading routes. There are no paved roads to the village we are going to, but we are heading in the right direction. There should be a small community just over that incline. Can you see any lights?"

"No, I can't even see an incline, just desert and sky. But, look at the stars! They are so incredibly bright and beautiful. I feel as though I could almost reach out and touch them." She pressed her forehead against the side window and gazed at the dazzling stars, sparkling like diamonds in the night sky.

"It is amazing how vivid the heavens appear when you are in the desert," commented Baboo, steering around a large boulder.

"Oh, there's something over there," said Davon, pointing to the right. "I see lights."

"That is what we are looking for." He drove towards the lights and a few minutes later, they were driving down a narrow lane with a

149

steep embankment on one side and red mud lean-tos on the other. The shacks were connected with uneven mud walls, but each home appeared to have its own metal roof, sloping towards the street. "Just to prepare you, Davon, although my friends have little, they are kind and generous, and are always willing to share. They have been very good to me over the years. I plan to help them out with the money I am earning from you."

He pulled up beside the last shack in the row, which seemed a touch bigger than any of the others and turned off the motor. Davon put on her headscarf as she got out of the car, noticing a narrow stream on the far side of the lane and beyond that, a few isolated structures.

"Baboo," said a man, coming out of a small doorway. He took a quick look down the street. "I thought I heard a car. Why are you here so late?" He detected Davon, looked at her in surprise and then back at Baboo.

"This is my niece, Davon, the daughter of my American cousin. She is traveling around Egypt and I was here on business, so she met me in Luxor. But unfortunately," he whispered, "I ran into a bit of a problem and that is why we are here."

"Come in, come in, I will call Nasa," the man said, motioning for them to follow him inside.

Davon pulled her headscarf tighter and ducked through the doorway. She was amazed at the openness of the room. It was about fifteen feet across with an eight-foot ceiling. Tribal rugs completely covered the dirt floor. She removed her shoes at the doorway, as did Baboo, and waited until the host returned with his wife. Dressed in traditional clothing and with a headscarf hastily tied around her hair, Nasa smiled at Davon, waiting for an introduction.

"This is Davon, Baboo's American niece, his cousin's child. Please meet my wife, Nasa. I am Fatar. Welcome to our home."

"Welcome, Davon. Please sit and I will bring tea," said Nasa.

"May I help you?" Davon asked.

"If you like. Come with me," she replied.

Davon followed her into the cooking room, a tiny area with open shelves. A low rudimentary fireplace made from red bricks and vented by a blackened metal hood flue sat against an outer wall. The heat from the small fire warmed the room. "You both speak English so well, I'm surprised."

Nasa giggled. "Fatar and I took English in school and still go to English class today. We work in the tourism business and must be able to communicate with our customers." She poured water into a black iron kettle and placed it onto a grill over top of the open fire. Fatar said you are visiting our country."

"Yes, I was in Cairo and flew here to meet Uncle Baboo," she replied, continuing with Baboo's fabrication.

"We have known Baboo for many years, yet we did not know he had any relatives, especially ones in the United States," said Nasa, turning to look at her.

Davon didn't flinch. "Well, I guess it was a bit of surprise when I called and said I wanted to visit. He has not seen my mother since she was a child. May I take the cups into the sitting room?" she asked, hoping to change the subject.

"Please, if you do not mind. The cups are here." Nasa removed four cups from a shelf above a small table. She also took down a brown teapot, placed it on the table and then filled it with a pinch of loose tea. "I am sorry, Davon, I have no milk. I used the last drop to make bread for dinner. I will ask Fatar to borrow some from the neighbor," she said, looking dismayed.

"There is no need on our account. Both Uncle Baboo and I drink our tea black."

"Are you sure?"

"Yes, please don't worry."

Nasa went out the back door and returned with a small loaf of bread. She cut thin slices and smothered them with honey, placing them onto a bright red tray. "Can you manage the tray and the cups? I will bring the tea as soon as the kettle boils."

Davon took the cups into the sitting room. Baboo and Fatar were sitting cross-legged on the floor, deep in discussion. Heading towards the only furniture in the room—a plain wooden chair beside a narrow bench—she set the cups on the bench and then returned to the kitchen for the tray. She could hear the kettle whistling and waited for Nasa to pour the hot water into the teapot. Picking up the tray at the same time as Nasa picked up the teapot, the two of them came back into the sitting room together.

"Fatar, please get the small table so that we can have tea! Must I do everything?"

Fatar jumped up and ran into the kitchen returning with a small round coffee table, which sat about ten inches off the ground. He placed it in front of Baboo and then plopped down beside him. Nasa put the teapot on the table and then went to get the teacups, placing one in front of each person. Taking the tray from Davon, she put it on the table and then motioned for Davon to sit.

"So Davon, Baboo tells me that you have just arrived. What are your plans? I can organize some city tours, perhaps a Nile cruise. There are so many beautiful and ancient sites to see," said Fatar, grinning.

Davon flushed. "I am really excited to see it all, but it depends on Uncle Baboo as he has been working in Luxor and..."

Baboo came to her rescue. "I was just telling Fatar about my investigation." He turned and looked at him. "As I was saying, the people I am investigating unfortunately saw me with Davon, which put me as well as Davon on their radar. The word on the street is that they are looking for me with a young blonde woman. I brought her here because I think it is too dangerous for Davon to be wandering around

Luxor."

"They will be spending the night, Nasa," said Fatar, making eye contact with his wife.

Nasa put down the tea she was pouring. "Of course you must stay the night."

Baboo glanced at Davon and bid her to remain silent. "In the morning, I would like to do a bit more digging for information. I hope I can pick up the trail I lost. Is it possible to leave my niece here for a few hours tomorrow before we leave the city?"

"Yes. I will be home tomorrow morning. She can stay with me," said Nasa.

"Thank you," replied Davon and Baboo together.

Nasa showed Davon a small storage room just off of the kitchen. It had a wooden floor and several shelves, holding dishes, pots and pans and other cooking paraphernalia as well as blankets and pillows carefully folded near the back. "It is not much, but it will give you some privacy."

"Thank you, this will be fine," replied Davon, grateful when Nasa pulled a thick area rug from the living room and put it on the pantry's floor.

Getting onto her hands and knees, Nasa patted the carpet into the corners and then reached for the pillow and blankets. "I hope you will be warm enough. Winter nights can be chilly in the desert. Maybe I should get some straw from the barn."

"What do you need straw for?" asked Fatar coming into the kitchen.

Nasa glanced up at him. "I want to stuff it in the crack along the outside wall. I can feel a draught."

"I just settled Baboo in the barn alongside Tete." Fatar threw back his head and let out a hearty laugh. "But I will return and get some straw for Davon." He spun on his heels and headed back out the door.

Davon smiled at Nasa, who was giggling. "Who is Tete?" she asked, wanting to get in on the joke.

"Tete is our loyal donkey. She is not always friendly, especially when she has to give up her bed. However, I am sure Baboo will win her over." Nasa stood and handed Davon a small flashlight. "I will take you to the woman's toilet before you retire. It is not far from our home, but do not go there on your own."

"Thank you," replied Davon, knowing female and male communal toilets were separated in Middle Eastern countries and that women always traveled in pairs as a safety precaution.

Fatar returned with the straw and while he plugged the crack along the wall of Davon's sleeping area, Nasa and Davon went to the communal bathroom. They followed a well-worn path to the women's toilet, which was about two hundred feet from the houses, using their flashlights to illuminate the way. It was built in front of a small embankment for privacy and had the same red mud walls and metal roof as the lean-to shacks. A single bulb hung from the ceiling, providing light. When Davon entered, she was surprised to find two large metal sinks with running water.

"Running water? How fantastic, Nasa."

"Yes," she exclaimed excitedly. "This is a recent addition. Fatar headed the group who designed the system. Now mothers can bathe their children here instead of in the dirty stream."

The elementary plumbing brought only cold water to the sinks and did not include the toilet area, which actually had no hardware at all. The toilets were two separated holes in the ground with planking on either side for the placement of feet. Nasa offered Davon several tissues just as she was about to go behind one of the flimsy curtains to relieve herself, explaining that they had to bring their own toilet paper.

Once in the dimly lit stall, Davon strategized how to utilize the toilet. She had used outhouses in the past, but only ones with built-up seats covering the hole. Realizing she had to squat with her feet on either side of the gap, she got into position.

"Do you need more tissue?" asked Nasa from the other stall.

"No thank you, I'm finished," replied Davon, pushing the curtain to the side. She went to the sink to wash her hands and cringed when the water coming out of the tap was a dirty brown. Although she had planned to brush her teeth, she decided it would be safer to use some of the boiled water from the kettle. Wiping her hands on her pants, for lack of a towel, she waited for Nasa to join her.

Shortly after, Nasa came out of the stall and went to the sink to wash her hands and face. Finishing, she looked at Davon. "So, we are ready for bed. Because electricity is very expensive, everyone in our community retires early. However, we are up at first light to begin our work. Shall we go home?"

When they returned to the lean-to, Davon thanked Nasa for her hospitality and after donning a sweater, she brushed her teeth with her finger and snuggled under the covers inside her cubbyhole. More comfortable than she had anticipated, she instantly fell into a deep sleep.

CHAPTER TWENTY-SIX

Davon turned over and stretched, trying to remember where she was. It was very dark in the pantry and she had no idea of the time. Sitting up, she yawned and listened to the conversation coming from the other side of the door. They were speaking in Arabic. The conversation ended and she heard the outside door open and close. Standing up, Davon pushed the door open a crack and peered into the kitchen. She could see Nasa tending to the fire. Pushing the door fully open, she stepped out of the pantry.

"Good morning, Nasa," she said cheerfully.

"Good morning, Davon. How did you sleep?"

"Very well, thank you. I didn't realize how tired I was. Is Uncle Baboo up yet?"

Nasa grinned. "You slept in. Baboo and Fatar have both left for work."

"Oh," said Davon, glancing at her watch. It was 6:30 am.

"Let me put on the kettle for tea and then I will escort you to the bathroom," said Nasa, placing the blackened kettle onto the fire grate.

It was a beautiful sunny day. Davon walked beside Nasa up the small incline towards the communal toilet, enjoying the view she had missed last night. "I didn't realize you can see Luxor and the Nile from here. What a perfect place to live."

"Fatar and I are blessed to live outside of the city."

Davon stopped and pointed. "Is that the Temple of Karnak?"

"Of course," Nasa said happily, turning to look at her with an expression of surprise. "You know the temples of Luxor. How sad that you will be leaving the city today. I wish you could have visited them. I have lived and worked around these temples my whole life and they are not just structures, they are part of our being."

"I promise I will return to see them one day, Nasa," replied Davon, smiling. She had slipped up mentioning Karnak and recognized she had to be careful about what she said to her hostess. Letting out a sigh, she wondered if Nasa might know anything about the temples of Isis. Maybe there was a temple or ruin in the vicinity that was not well known? "The temple I really wanted to see on this trip was the Temple of Isis. It is crazy because I didn't realize the one on Philae Island is under water from the Aswan Dam. Is there another temple to Isis in the area?" When Nasa shook her head, Davon was disheartened.

"I am sure in ancient days there were many temples to Isis, but the only surviving one in Egypt is the temple originating on the Island of Philae. When the dam was created, this temple was not deemed valuable enough to save and when the area was flooded, it was doomed for an underwater existence," Nasa explained.

"I read about Philae Temple on the internet. I cannot believe they didn't try to save such an amazing piece of history!"

"Yes," said Nasa, nodding. "During the initial phases of the dam, this was the case, but, seventy years later just before the completion of the high dam, UNESCO resurrected the temple from the lake and relocated it to the nearby island of Agilkia."

"What?" cried Davon. Her eyes widened with excitement. "The temple was moved!"

Nasa was taken aback at her sudden exhilaration. "Yes, it was removed piece by piece and put back together exactly as it had been originally created. I believe it was sponsored in part by the Sanduu family, who owns Agilkia Island."

Davon could barely contain herself. "That is wonderful news. With some luck, maybe Uncle Baboo can take me there before we have to return to Cairo."

After freshening up, they headed back to the house for breakfast. Davon asked about the reliefs of Isis at Philae Temple, how to get to Agilkia Island and the distance from Luxor to the island. She found Nasa to be a wealth of information and was thrilled when Nasa told her about another temple, which contained two reliefs of Isis.

They stopped to collect some eggs from the chicken coup before going into the kitchen. "So, let me get this straight. There are twelve reliefs of Isis at Philae Temple and two reliefs at the Temple of Horus in Edfu?" questioned Davon.

"Yes. I hope Baboo will be able to take you to see all of them. They are spectacular." While Nasa organized the meal, Davon took the cups from the shelf and poured the tea. "Baboo said he would be back before noon and asked for you to be packed and ready to go. However, you are more than welcome to stay longer, Davon. It is very nice having another woman in the house."

"I have enjoyed being here and appreciate the offer, but it is up to Uncle Baboo. I'm just following his schedule," replied Davon, removing her headscarf. "Nasa, I noticed Fatar has a cell phone. Is there internet in the community? I would like to check something on my computer."

"I am afraid not. But, we do have many internet cafes in Luxor and there is internet at the airport."

"Alright then, I guess I will have to wait until we fly out," Davon told her just as the sounds of a vehicle filtered into the room. She located her scarf and quickly covered her hair as Nasa opened the door and welcomed Baboo into the house.

"Did you find the person you were looking for, Uncle Baboo?"

Baboo shook his head as he stepped into the living room. "Dead end. We will have to seriously consider plan..." He stopped in midsentence and looked at his hostess. Giving Nasa a smile, he addressed her. "I hope Davon was not too much trouble."

"Not at all. I have enjoyed her company. How was your meeting?"

"It was not as good as I hoped. We may have to stay in the area for a few more days."

Nasa beamed. "Wonderful!"

Davon willed Baboo to look at her. "Uncle Baboo, Nasa told me something very interesting today. The temple of Isis from the Island of Philae was rescued from its underwater grave and was moved to a nearby island called Agilkia. I was wondering if it is at all possible to go and see the temple."

Baboo turned his gaze to Nasa. "Hmm. How far is Agilkia Island from Luxor, Nasa?"

"It is about one hundred nautical miles along the River Nile. I can get Fatar to organize a boat to take you there, but you must stop in Edfu, midway, to see the Temple of Horus. It is magnificent!" she touted, for Davon's sake.

Baboo looked puzzled and Davon was not sure if he was just acting or really not convinced they should go to the island. "Apparently, the Temple of Isis was saved by UNESCO and a local family. What was the name of the family, Nasa?"

"It was reconstructed by the Sanduu family. Have you heard of them, Baboo? They own real estate in Luxor as well as the Island of Agilkia."

"The name does sound familiar. Well Davon, if you would like to see this temple let's have Fatar make some arrangements." When Nasa pulled a cell phone from her pocket, he said, "Could you ask him to arrange the felucca for tonight?"

Nasa laughed at the suggestion. "Feluccas are sailing boats and they only sail as far as the Esna locks. For this journey you will need a private river boat."

At the dock, Baboo handed the car keys to Fatar. "Are you sure you do not mind returning the rental car?"

"Please do not worry. My friend works at the airport and it will be good to see him. I will have him drive me home after his shift. Will we see you when you return to Luxor?"

"I am not sure, Fatar, but I will be in touch. Thank you for all you have done," said Baboo, giving him a slap on the back.

Davon moved forward. "Thank you and please thank Nasa again for me. I enjoyed meeting both of you very much."

"I have told the captain to take good care of you, Davon. Safe travels," he said with a wave. Fatar stood by the car and watched them walk across the gangplank and onto the flat-bottomed boat.

Davon looked at the other twenty-five vessels tied to the rickety wooden wharf as she stepped aboard, noticing that every docked boat had another two or three crafts tethered to their starboard side. The boat Fatar had organized was small compared to the other riverboats and it looked as though it was in need of repair. She hoped it was a fit vessel, not relishing the idea of being dumped in the River Nile—a river she knew was full of African crocodiles. She glanced at the brilliant full moon above the male crew of eight lined up along the deck railing. Dressed in pristine white shirts and pants, they stood staring straight ahead seeing nothing.

"Welcome to the Pharaoh," the Captain said to Baboo, completely ignoring Davon. "The boy will show you to your cabins below. We will leave at first light to reach the locks before noon." He paused and then pointed to a solid looking wooden table and chairs. "Meals are served on deck at your pleasure. Please let the boy know if you would like to have tea or coffee before you retire."

Baboo glanced at Davon. "Nothing for me," she replied, boldly staring at the Captain.

Her attention was quickly directed to a boy of about eight or nine years of age madly struggling with their luggage. With Davon's carry-on and Baboo's camera strung about his neck, he noisily manipulated the three medium-sized suitcases by dragging them one at a time over several obstructions. Davon was aghast that no other crew member offered to help. Stopping in front of Davon, the boy gave her a big grin and then motioned eagerly for her and Baboo to follow. "Come please," he said with a heavy accent.

When Davon reached out to help with one of the suitcases, Baboo stopped her. "It is his job, Davon, let him do it."

Davon frowned, but turned and followed the boy down a narrow poorly lit corridor as he bumped and wrestled with the luggage. He stopped almost at the end of the hall in front of a tattered wooden door. "For you," he said, grinning. As he opened the door, Davon pointed to her suitcase and the carry-on around his neck. Carefully bracing Baboo's luggage against the wall in the hallway, he placed Davon's possessions in the cabin and then turned to the door right across from it. "For you," the boy said to Baboo.

After the boy put Baboo's suitcases in his room, Davon pulled an American dollar bill from her pocket, handed it to the boy and said thank you in Farsi. She laughed at his excitement as she watched him dance his way back towards the deck. "For a moment I didn't think the little guy was going to make it carrying our luggage," she said, glancing into her cabin. It appeared to be a decent size with a double bed, small desk and easy chair in one corner. There were heavy brown drapes pulled across one wall and Davon trusted there was a window behind them. "I was hoping to get to an internet cafe before we came on board because I want to research Agilkia Island," she said, speaking softly.

"Fatar gave me this," said Baboo, pulling a brochure from his jacket pocket. He offered it to her.

Davon looked at the picture of the Temple of Isis on the island of Agilkia and then opened the pamphlet. "Great. It gives us some basic information about the temple, so that's a start, but I would still like to get a copy of the floor plan and look at some in depth pictures of the temple on the internet." Her voice became hardly audible. "I mean who knows where the statue is hidden. It could be anywhere and I think because we have so little time, it makes sense to know the Temple inside and out before we even get there." Davon flipped over the pamphlet and looked at a picture of the town, Aswan, and a diagram, which pinpointed where the riverboat docked, showing the overland route one took before taking a smaller boat to Agilkia Island. "Aswan looks pretty tiny, Baboo. I'm not sure it will have an internet cafe."

"The boat is scheduled to stop at Edfu tomorrow, a fairly large touristy town, which is situated before Aswan. I planned to ask the Captain to skip the stop, but if you want internet..."

Davon pondered. "Although we are cutting it close, if we only make a quick stop at Edfu, get to an internet cafe and find a couple of detailed books of Philae Temple, I think we will have enough time. I want to arrive at Agilkia Island knowing everything I possibly can about the Temple of Isis, so we can quickly find the statue and get it to Vienna," she answered. "Just a side note, I read that Edfu has one of the best preserved temples in Egypt—it's the Temple of Horus."

"Was that not the temple Nasa mentioned this morning?"

"Yes, we talked about the temple, but she was not aware I knew about it. You see, Horus is the son of Isis. And when I was googling temples to Isis, the Temple of Horus came up because it has a relief and a column with an elaborate carving of Isis."

"You do not think the relief or column of Isis has anything to do with the statue of Ra, do you?"

"Maybe, who knows? The Temple of Horus is near the water and Abdul said 'it is near the water' before he pointed to the picture of Isis on the back of his watch. But, when Nasa said the Island of Agilkia is owned by the Sanduu family, I nearly flipped. I believe the statue is on Agilkia Island. " They heard someone coming. "Let the captain stop at Edfu so we can get to an internet cafe and pick up some brochures on Philae Temple. See you at breakfast," said Davon as she ducked into her cabin, closing the door.

CHAPTER TWENTY-SEVEN

Early the next morning, Davon awoke to the rhythmic vibrations of the boat's motor starting up. Getting out of bed, she pulled back the curtains and smiled. Through her large porthole, she could see the first rays of sunlight peeking over the rolling desert hills. The boat was moving towards the middle of the Nile and Davon noticed the other riverboats, docked alongside for the night, were also on their way upriver.

After a shower in her very tiny private bathroom, she threw on her jeans and a long sleeved shirt. Covering her hair with a navy scarf, she yanked open the door to her cabin and proceeded towards the deck.

"Morning Baboo," she said cheerfully, sitting down beside him at the breakfast table. "How did you sleep?"

"Wonderfully," he replied, pointing to the starboard side of the vessel. "Look!"

Davon crouched down to peer under the canopy. "Oh, how incredible!" she exclaimed, quickly walking to the railing to get a better view. On the west side of the Nile at least thirty hot air balloons filled the sky. They were every color of the rainbow. "What a fantastic way to see the Valley of the Kings." She enjoyed the scene for several minutes before returning to the table.

"Coffee?" The little cabin boy from the previous night grinned at her. His hair hung in disorder about his face, giving him an impish appearance as he precariously held a tray with a coffee urn and two cups.

"Yes, thank you," replied Davon. She watched him place the tray in the center of the table and then pour some of the steaming brown liquid into the cups, placing one in front of her and the other in front of Baboo. "What's your name?" she asked as she took a sip of the pleasantly smelling brew.

He looked quizzically at her, processing the question, then beamed. "I am Abis!" he said as though she should already know. He gave her a smile and then dashed off when another crewmember called his name, leaving Davon to chuckle.

Baboo laughed with her. "I spoke with the Captain this morning and he said it may take a few hours to get through the Esna Locks. As you can see, all of the riverboats docked last night in Luxor are heading that way and although the locks can accommodate several vessels at one time, it is done by a queuing system. We may not get to Edfu until late this afternoon."

"Well, I'm sure the Captain will do the best he can to get us there quickly. In the meantime, let's enjoy the scenery and try to relax a bit because I have a feeling things are going to get very hectic over the next few days." She took a sip of coffee, gazing around Baboo to take in the hot air balloons above and the lush greenery on either side of the river. She could see healthy palm trees and thick papyrus growing along the shoreline. The greenery traveled inland for about a quarter of a mile and then abruptly stopped. After that, all that could be seen was the arid unforgiving desert. Davon understood why the River Nile was called the 'River of Life' because without this primary water source, life in Egypt would be nonexistent.

When they reached the locks, Davon saw two larger riverboats in the queue ahead of them. She was astonished to find both vessels surrounded by bright blue flotillas. "What's going on there?" she asked a crewmember as she watched the men on the flotillas throwing bagged items up to the tourists, who were hanging over the railings of the riverboat's decks.

"No English," said the boy, shaking his head.

Baboo asked him in Arabic and then translated. "The colorful dinghies hold local vendors selling their wares. The vendors throw up items in clear plastic bags to interested customers and if he or she agrees to buy, they settle on a price and then the customer throws down the money in the bag."

"Wow, it certainly is an inventive way to make a living," replied Davon, pointing to the vessel in front of them. "It seems like there is a lot of interest in buying merchandise on that boat." They watched at least forty bags flying up to customers as the riverboat waited for its turn to enter the lock. "I guess the flotillas will be heading our way next."

"The boy said the Captain will not allow the vendors near our boat because there was a problem last year," replied Baboo just as several of the flotillas ventured nearby. The men in the dinghies held up their wares and tried to get Davon's attention, which caused an instant commotion onboard.

There was much yelling and Davon and Baboo watched as three crewmembers angrily waved the blue dinghies away from the ship. The vendors, eyeing the beautiful blonde potential customer, hoped she would encourage them to come closer. However, once they realized this was not to be, they anxiously paddled towards the next ship waiting in the queue to get the better of their rival sellers. A loud siren suddenly pierced the air and the vessel next in line slowly proceeded towards the first lock. Davon checked the time as their boat followed the first boat into the long rectangular metal box. She recalled the River Nile was one of the few rivers flowing south to north, and noted with astonishment that they were traveling uphill.

Once the ships were inside the box, the metal gate swung shut and gallons of water began pouring in from large diameter pipes, filling the lock to the water level of the proceeding one. This procedure lifted the boats to the next level and it was repeated twice. When the front gate opened for the second time, the riverboats exited into a higher section of the River Nile. Looking at her watch, Davon estimated the whole episode had taken less than thirty-five minutes.

CHAPTER TWENTY-EIGHT

It was one-fifty pm when their boat docked at Edfu, the fourth boat tied up alongside of three other riverboats. On the deck and ready to disembark, Davon and Baboo watched the docking operation with interest. They saw the crew securing the boat to another and wondered how they were going to get to the dock, which was now three vessels away.

Abis, the cabin boy joined them at the railing. "Follow please," he said with authority. Taking them onto the deck of the next moored vessel and through its lounging cabin, he skirted around the tourists, checking often to see that Davon and Baboo were following. Making his way to the portside deck, he led them onto the next riverboat, repeating this course of action two more times until they stepped onto the rickety dock.

"Thank you, Abis, for coming to our rescue because..." Davon said, stopping in mid-sentence. She noticed thirty or more nineteenth century, two-person horse-drawn buggies, lined up at the pier directly in front of them. "My goodness, it seems like we have stepped back in time," she exclaimed, concerned that this was going to be their mode of transportation, as she could see no automobiles in sight.

The eight year old glanced at her and smiled. "No worry, I get you best price. We take buggy to temple." Before Davon could say another word, Abis ran to one of the shabby black buggies and called to the driver.

"Did he say we, Baboo? I hope Abis isn't planning to come with us. I do not want to have to watch out for him and I do not want to go to the temple," protested Davon.

Baboo laughed. "I am sure Abis is perfectly capable of taking care of himself. The Captain told me he was raised here in Edfu." They noticed the lad waving. "I think he is trying to get our attention. Let's see what he has arranged."

They walked to where Abis was standing with the driver. "Four American dollars and he take us to Temple Horus and wait to take us back to boat. Okay?" His grin was endearing, but Davon already had an agenda.

"Abis, we are not going to the Temple of Horus. We just want to buy some books on Philae Temple and go to an internet cafe," replied Davon, pointing to herself and Baboo. "You can go back to the boat."

The boy looked as though he was about to cry. "I help you. This place no safe for tourists. Please, I help you," he pleaded.

Davon melted. Although she was positive she would regret the decision, she found herself nodding. "Alright, you can come, but you have to promise to stay with us. We need to find a bookstore or kiosk selling books on Philae Temple and an internet cafe and then we have to get back to the boat so that we can leave for Agilkia Island before it gets dark. Do you understand?"

"Yes," he said happily, "I tell driver go fast." Jumping into action, he helped the driver put a stool in place so Davon and Baboo could get into the cab. Once they were settled, he scooped up the stool and adroitly climbed a narrow stirrup ladder to sit alongside the driver for the ride. The driver flicked his whip and the horse took off at a trot, turning left towards the main town's square.

Almost completely built of beige sandstone bricks, the low-rise buildings and narrow roads of the town blended well into their desert surroundings. The driver skillfully directed the horse and buggy around vehicles, donkey carts and crowds of people, walking in the streets and squares. They passed a large spice market and for a moment the scent of curry, cinnamon and cumin filled the air. Davon turned to look at the colorful variety of freshly ground seasonings piled high in wicker baskets and then observed the customers, mostly local women and young girls, wearing burkas. In Cairo and Luxor, she had noticed the majority of women wore long scarves and full-length raincoats, and therefore assumed that in Edfu, the religious traditions were stronger. Pushing a stray piece of hair behind her ear, she pulled her scarf down and tightened it.

The driver stopped the buggy at the entranceway of a courtyard. Thinking they had arrived at the main square, Davon peeked around the side of the buggy's canopy. Frustrated, she called out, "Abis, I told you we do not have time to visit the Temple of Horus," she said, trying to control her anger as she eyed the incredibly beautiful structure.

"But Missy, is wonder world!" replied Abis, jumping down from his seat. He pulled out the stool and placed it on the ground for Davon, and then looked up at her.

"You mean it is a world wonder," she said, correcting him. "And yes, it is spectacular." Davon knew the Temple of Horus was the second largest in Egypt and one of the best preserved, and although she had seen pictures, she was unprepared for its astonishing beauty. She gazed at the two giant golden sandstone pylons, standing over 100 feet high, rising from the desert sand and dominating the landscape. Directly in front of them on either side of the entranceway stood perfectly preserved matching sandstone seven-foot statues of the falcon god, Horus, wearing the double crown of Egypt. "Unbelievably spectacular," she muttered quietly under her breath.

Baboo was also amazed. "It appears to be very well preserved," he said. He then motioned Davon's attention towards a large number of kiosks selling books and paraphernalia. "We can most likely find a booklet on Philae Temple at one of those booths. And since we are here, we should probably take a look at the carvings of Isis as they could have some significance."

Davon glanced at her watch and then looked at the temple, torn between desperately wanting to explore the unbelievably beautiful site yet worried about wasting precious time. "I asked Nasa about the background of this temple when she mentioned there was a relief and a column here dedicated to Isis. Horus is the son of Isis, but it is a bit confusing because Horus and Ra are both depicted as falcons and hawks and both have all-seeing eyes. The two statues at the entranceway obviously represent Horus as a falcon, but they might give us an idea as to what we are looking for. I guess we could take a few minutes to compare the relief sculpture and carving of Isis to the picture on the back of Abdul's watch. It might help in the long run."

"So, let's get going," said Baboo, encouraging her to get out of the buggy.

"Okay, Abis," she called, stepping out and onto the stool. "We are ready to go to the temple, but we need to be quick and please, make sure the driver waits for us."

"Yes," he replied, running towards them.

They quickly made their way to the kiosks and Davon bought a booklet on the Temple of Horus and two booklets on the Temple of Philae while Baboo paid their entrance fees. Glancing through the first pamphlet as they walked towards the temple, Davon found a poor rendition of the column to Isis and showed it to Abis. "Do you know where this column is located?" When Abis nodded, she asked, "Can you take us there?"

Abis gleefully led them towards the entrance and when they reached the perfectly preserved falcon statues, Davon paused to inspect them.

"We do not have much time, Davon," said Baboo, waiting to follow her through the grand entranceway.

"Sorry," she answered, quickly glancing up at the giant reliefs on the front of the pylons as she stepped through the massive entryway. "The booklet says the temple was finished around 57 BC. There are several chambers and carved reliefs including many ceilings decorated with astronomical figures," she told him. Davon was awestruck as they hurried behind Abis, now thankful that the young boy had brought them here. She slowed her gait as she tried to take in the spectacular structure and then suddenly noticed Abis disappearing behind a column. "Abis, wait for us!" she called, dashing after him.

Once inside, they found themselves in a large paved courtyard with a surrounding colonnade. There were thirty-two columns with paired capitals or pilasters of various forms. Davon was amazed that every capital appeared to be unique and tried to glance at the reliefs on the columns as Abis power walked quickly across the courtyard and into the next hall. Lagging slightly behind, she entered the second hall and was stunned to see it held even larger and more beautiful columns.

Abis jogged to the rear of the room and turned, giving them a glowing smile. "Here, this one you like. I know. This one."

Davon and Baboo approached the column, scanning the surroundings to see if anything else in the vicinity might hold a clue. Reaching into her pocket, she pulled out Abdul's watch and turned it over. She showed Baboo. "Very similar, except what she is holding is just a touch different. Right here, do you see what I mean? On the watch it looks like a lotus staff and on the carving, it looks like a...a long rattle."

"Yes, I see," said Baboo taking out his camera. He took several close ups and then some pictures of the room. "Okay, let's go now and have a look at the relief. Is there a picture in the book?"

Davon quickly flipped through the booklet. "It's in the Birth House," she replied, then skimmed the page and shook her head. "Damn, it says this relief is probably of Hathor, the wife of Horus, Horus and their son Ihy and not of Horus as a boy with his parents," she complained. "Oh well, let's take a look." Davon showed the picture to Abis, who was watching her with interest. "Can you show us the Birth

House and this relief, Abis?"

"Yes," he said with a knowing grin, spreading his arms wide. "I know temple like home."

Davon and Baboo chuckled as they followed their young guide through a maze of different sized rooms, ending up in another open courtyard with several severely damaged columns. The remains of one side of a partial wall held the relief they were looking for.

"Thank you, Abis. You do know this temple well," said Davon as she drew near, examining the piece. "It's hard to say, Baboo. The facial features look almost the same, but she is not wearing robes and her headdress is totally different. I really need to access the internet so I can research Philae Temple and Isis."

"I take you internet cafe in Edfu, in Aswan. Where you want, Missy," exclaimed Abis.

Baboo, who had just started to snap some pictures of the relief, looked up. "Are you sure there is an internet cafe in Aswan, Abis?"

"I sure. You want internet cafe in Aswan?"

"Yes, in Aswan. Go and tell the driver we are ready to go, Abis. We need to hurry back to the boat." The boy turned and ran out of the courtyard, leaving them alone. "Take another quick look around, Davon, because we have to get going. I am not sure how long the journey is to Aswan, but the Captain will not take us there tonight unless we can arrive before it gets dark."

"I'm ready to leave," she replied, sticking Abdul's watch back into her pocket.

They made it back to the dock just before three o'clock. Davon paid the driver and then gave Abis an American ten dollar bill as they hurried through the lobbies of the riverboats to get to their vessel. "Run ahead and tell the Captain we would like to leave right away for Aswan," she said, pressing the bill into his hand. Abis looked at the bill, smiled, and then took off like a bolt of lightning. "Baboo, have you told the Captain we will be disembarking when we get to Aswan?"

"Yes, I have, but since the boat will remain in port overnight, I suggest we sleep on board and disembark in the morning. We can get Abis to take us to an internet cafe this evening and while you are online, you can sign us up for a guided tour of Philae Temple tomorrow."

Davon agreed. "The booklet on Philae said the island is only open from noon to four pm. The tours are sixty minutes long because they don't want people damaging the site and everyone must be accompanied by a guide. How are we going to really explore the temple and island if we have someone hovering over our shoulder?"

"This is off season, so there should not be many tourists. After the general tour, we can give the guide some money if he will let us stay longer to revisit the temple on our own." He looked around and then lowered his voice as they boarded their boat. "The problem will be returning to the island if we do not find anything before four o'clock."

"Well," whispered Davon, "I hope we do find something because time is running out!"

CHAPTER TWENTY-NINE

It was dusk when their vessel pulled into the boat slip at Aswan. Baboo walked over to Davon, who was standing on the deck watching the activities. "I just spoke with the Captain and he asked if we could settle the bill tonight after dinner. He wants to leave at ten o'clock tomorrow morning because he has a party of four to pick up in Edfu in the afternoon."

"Okay, I'll get the money ready. I know we talked about taking a taxi around Aswan, but maybe we should rent a car. It's about a fifteen minute drive to the bay where we need to take the motorboat to Agilkia Island and from the look of this booklet," she said, holding it up, "there is nothing there. I mean no hotels or restaurants. I think I would feel more comfortable having a vehicle since we're on a time crunch. I don't want to trust a cabbie to wait for us."

Baboo threw his head back and laughed. "Very good idea. Are you sure you are a doctor? You seem pretty good at the private investigator's game."

Davon smiled back at him. "At school I excelled in logical thinking. Believe me it helps when you're trying to figure out a diagnosis."

"Ready?" asked Abis, racing across the deck to join them.

"Yes, we are ready," replied Davon. "How far away is the internet cafe?"

"Not far. Please come."

The internet cafe was literally across the street from the dock. Abis took them inside and organized the use of a computer. Davon paid the one hour fee and settled in a chair beside Baboo. As she clicked on Google, she could feel Abis's breath against her neck and knew he was leaning forward trying to look at the screen. Although she figured he most likely could not read English, she did not want to take any chances.

"Abis, please leave us and come back in an hour to take us back to the boat," she said softly, turning around to look at him.

"Yes, okay, I come again. One hour I be here," he answered, reluctantly leaving.

She ignored the disappointed look upon his face and waited until she heard the door to the cafe click closed. "He is a sweet kid, but a little too attentive," she said, grinning at Baboo.

The first thing she did was organize a private tour of Philae Temple. Then, she arranged for a rental car, with pickup at the docks and return to the airport.

"Can you check on flight times to Cairo? I think it would be a good idea to know how quickly we can get out of Aswan," Baboo suggested, glancing at his watch.

Davon checked the information. "There's only one flight from Aswan to Cairo tomorrow night. It leaves at 11:50 pm. Should I book our seats?"

"Hmm," replied Baboo. "I think it might be best to wait until after we make the trip to Philae. After all, there is a chance that the statue is not on Agilkia Island."

Davon moved away from the keyboard. "The statue has to be there. All of the clues point in that direction and there is no other temple to Isis in the vicinity. Let's see if there are any pictures of the reliefs on the internet." She googled temples to Isis and then clicked on Philae Temple.

As they read the information, they compared the detailed floor plan with the one in the booklet. Davon made notes and drew diagrams. Most of the information on the internet was generic, encouraging the reader to book a tour of the temple.

"The Prince has money, so I am sure he would have built a waterproof compartment in a wall to contain the statue. If there are twelve reliefs of Isis at Philae Temple," said Baboo, letting out a whistle, "it is going to be an enormous task because the temple is large, well preserved and I am sure the walls are meters thick. It is interesting though," he continued, "that we think the statue might be on the island. Why is it not in a safety deposit box somewhere?"

Davon lowered her voice to a whisper. "The statue was in a safety deposit box. But, Abdul told me his brother was acting suspiciously and he was worried Adin would try to impersonate him at the bank, explaining to the manager that he lost his key. Luckily, Abdul had the foresight to take the statue and hide it. Unfortunately, he did not think his brother would kidnap him," explained Davon, thinking about the incident at the palace when Adin did impersonate Abdul. She chose not to relate the story to Baboo. On a need to know basis, she reminded herself.

After scanning many websites, they found only one with a picture of a relief. There was no description on the site and it was difficult to determine exactly where the relief was located at Philae Temple. Davon blew up the image and compared it to the etching on the back of Abdul's watch. Although it was difficult to tell because the computer picture was fuzzy, they didn't think the relief matched the etching.

Davon noted the time and feeling frustrated, shutdown the computer. "The meeting in Vienna is in three days and if we don't find the statue at Philae Temple tomorrow, we're hooped."

177

"Do not get discouraged yet because there are still eleven other reliefs of Isis on the island. I suggest we drive to the bay right after we disembark tomorrow morning and try to bribe the guide to take us to the island before noon. Maybe you could say you are doing your thesis on the goddess Isis and need more time to explore the island."

"That might work!" said Davon as they heard the door to the cafe open.

"I here," said a familiar voice behind them. "It is one hour and time for dinner."

On the deck of the boat, Davon and Baboo picked at their food. Davon had memorized the floor plan of Philae and was mentally walking through the temple, trying to visualize the reliefs of Isis, while Baboo was thinking about the equipment they would need to retrieve the statue if they found its location.

When the server left after offering them coffee, Davon pulled an envelope from her pocket. "This is the cash to pay for the boat trip," she said, sliding it towards Baboo.

"Thank you. I will take it to the Captain. After we get the car tomorrow morning, we need to make a quick stop at a hardware shop. I have to buy something."

"What do you need?" Davon asked, quietly.

"A crowbar, in case we have to move some rock."

"For some reason, I figured it was going to be easy to retrieve the you-know-what once we found the location," she whispered. "I envisioned pushing on the relief of Isis and the thing we are looking for magically appears." She stopped talking when the server began clearing dishes from the table. "We can talk more about it in the morning. I'm going to read my booklet once again and then go to bed. See you tomorrow." Standing, she gave Baboo a knowing nod before heading off to her cabin.

CHAPTER THIRTY

Early the next day, they disembarked and headed towards an upper road, running parallel to the dock. Two rental car attendants, wearing bright red jackets stamped with the rental car logo, stood beside a parked vehicle. With their luggage in tow, Davon and Baboo approached them. The attendants quickly loaded the luggage into the trunk. One offered Baboo the keys, the other opened the passenger door for Davon.

"Thank you," Davon said in Farsi as she jumped inside the dark blue Ford. Turning around, she noticed Baboo talking with the attendant. Probably asking for directions, she thought as she opened the empty glove compartment looking for a map of the town.

Five minutes later, Baboo was in the car, starting the vehicle. "I asked them how to get to Philae Bay, to the airport and where to find a general hardware store. I said I was looking for a bolt for my camera pod."

"I presume you are hoping that a store selling bolts has a crowbar?"

"It should. There is a shop in the middle of town," he informed her, moving into the traffic. "Once we get there, stay in the car. I do not want you attracting attention. The last thing we need is people talking about a beautiful blonde tourist buying a crowbar."

Davon smiled, knowing he was only trying to protect her, as she repositioned her white silk scarf, tucking in her exposed hair. "Okay. I'll try to keep out of sight."

Situated on the main street in town, the general hardware store was easy to find. Baboo parked in front of it and turned off the motor. Pulling the keys out of the ignition, he handed them to Davon. "Lock the doors while I am in the shop. I will be as quick as I can."

Davon did as she was told and clicked the lock button the second he was out of the vehicle. She glanced out the window and looked up and down the street, seeing only men loitering about. "That is weird. You would think some women would be doing their morning shopping by now," she muttered to herself, wondering where all of the women were. But just as the words came out of her mouth, she saw two burkas come around a corner and then two more heading towards the vehicle. She noticed that all of the women were wearing niqabs or face veils and their bodies were completely covered from head to toe. When there was a tap on the window, she jumped. It was Baboo holding a brown parcel. Clicking the open button, she let him into the car.

"They had three different sizes. I bought the smallest one, figuring it would fit nicely into my backpack. I hope it is not too small," he said as he put the package into the back seat and then started the motor. He passed a mule cart and then turned left at the intersection. "If you go straight, this road eventually leads to the airport, but to get to Philae Temple, we have to make the first right after a large camel pen. Keep your eyes open because there are no street signs."

"Alright," replied Davon, looking out her window. "I was thinking, Baboo, we should have a code word if one of us discovers a place where the statue might be hidden. I'm suggesting this in case the guide is hovering about. How about something like 'sandstone grey' so the guide thinks we are talking about the color of the stone blocks?"

"Sounds good," said Baboo, nodding. "However, I am hoping we will have some time on our own to explore the island. If we do find

181

the location of the statue, but we cannot get to it because of the guide, I want you to distract him by leading him away from the area. I will go after the statue."

"I can do that," said Davon, assuredly. "I just hope the statue is hidden at Philae Temple because...There's the camel pen, Baboo."

Baboo passed the pen and made a right turn onto a narrow dirt road. The stench of the one hundred or so animals permeated the car. "Oh, the smell is bad," he said, rolling down his window after they had gone some distance. Fresh warm air rushed inside, replacing the foul odor.

They started down an incline and a panoramic view of the Nile spread before them. "That must be Agilkia Island," Davon said, pointing. "You can see the temple. Wow, it looks huge!"

Proceeding down the hill, they approached a large empty parking lot with a few shanty outbuildings. There was a newly built dock on the innermost part of the bay and three older model motorboats tied up to it, but there appeared to be no one in the vicinity.

Baboo parked in one of the marked parking stalls. "There does not seem to be anyone around."

"I'm sure someone will be here shortly," said Davon, getting out of the car. Baboo followed her as she wandered towards the water. She looked down the river and was surprised to see ten brightly painted rowboats pulled up onto the sand. "Do you think they use these rowboats to take tourists to Agilkia Island?"

"No, they are fishing boats. You can see some netting in the second one."

"Oh, you're right," she replied, thinking Baboo didn't miss a thing. "It would be so easy to just take one and row over. The island isn't far away. You could probably swim across," she said, dipping her hand into the water.

"I would not advise that, have you forgotten about the Nile crocodiles. They are vicious, protected by the government and in large numbers all along the River Nile."

Davon smiled at his reply and then looked at her watch. "It's almost ten thirty, so we have an hour and a half to kill. Why don't we sit on the bench over there and plan out some possible scenarios," she suggested, walking towards the dock.

CHAPTER THIRTY-ONE

Within the hour a group of four tourists arrived by private car. When they sauntered down to the dock, Davon became aware of a personal guide accompanying them. By making small talk, she discovered they were from Britain and had won a trip to see the wonders of Egypt, which started in Cairo and continued on to Luxor, the location where their River Nile cruise began. They told her they were nearing the end of the tour and after Philae they would fly to see the Abu Simbel Temple and then home. Davon was relieved, knowing they probably would not want to spend more than their allotted hour on the island. The boat driver for the group of four arrived and began to ready one of the motorboats.

Glancing towards the parking lot, Davon became concerned when she didn't see another guide or boat driver. "Excuse me and sorry for asking, but the tour guide we booked has not arrived. Is there any way we could go to the island with you?"

The Brits looked at their escort, who was shaking his head. "I am sorry. These boats only take six occupants. You will have to wait for the guide you booked." He turned his back to her and began to direct his charges into the boat. The Brits shrugged and then pleasantly waved as the boat pulled away from the dock.

"Good grief, Baboo! Where is the guide I booked? It's after

twelve o'clock."

"That might be him," replied Baboo, noticing a dilapidated car pulling into the parking lot.

Davon took a deep breath and tried to calm herself as she watched a disheveled middle-aged man rushing towards them.

"Hello, hello. Are you the Marshall group?"

"Yes, I hope you're the guide I booked as we are anxious to get to the Philae Temple," said Davon impatiently, picking up her bag and slinging it over her shoulder.

"Of course. I am Amir. We will go now. Please, this is our boat." He showed them to a vessel that had seen better days and made his way towards the driver's seat. After they were settled, he started the motor, pushed off, and headed towards the island.

The journey took no more than seven minutes. Davon's foul mood quickly changed as they approached the temple. The sun, the water and the loveliness of the surroundings had a positive effect. She was amazed at the beauty and the size of the structure, as it loomed overhead and felt optimistic that they would indeed find the statue here. However, when the driver threw a line to an older man waiting on the dock, and Baboo looked at her and mouthed the word 'guard', her spirits again fell. Great, she cursed silently. A flat roofed ochre colored hut, typical of the Nile region and near the water's edge, caught her eye as she exited the craft. It looked as though the guard lived on the island. How are we going to avoid another set of eyes, she wondered, annoyed at the situation. Making her way across the rickety wharf, she stepped onto the shore and mentally ran through her prepared speech as she watched Baboo and Amir, draw near.

"Now," said Amir, with a smile. "We only have one hour at the Temple of Philae, so I suggest two options: I can give you a detailed tour of the temple, which will take the complete hour or I can give you an overview and let you spend the hour viewing the site on your own. What would you like to do?"

Davon returned the smile. "First of all, Amir, thank you so much for bringing us here. It has been my lifelong dream to come to the Temple of Philae." She paused and made eye contact. "You see, I am an American university student, sponsored by the University of Cairo because I am doing my thesis on the goddess Isis. So, you could say I have studied the history of this temple in depth. Baboo," she continued, pointing towards him, "is the photographer I hired to take some pictures of the reliefs. The problem, of course, is the allotted time of one hour, as you can probably understand. Cairo University gave me the impression that I could spend as much time on the island as I needed." She paused again and tried to appear hopeful.

Amir responded with a look of confusion. "This is the first I have heard of this. Do you have any papers to show me?"

"I am so sorry my papers are at the hotel. I didn't think I needed to bring them," she said apologetically, giving him a look of concern. "I guess if I spend more time on the island I am using up your time, Amir," she said, biting her lip as though she was trying to think of some type of compensation. Fingering the one hundred dollar American bill in her pocket, she pulled it out. "I would like to pay you for your time. Will this do?" she asked, offering it to him.

"Yes, thank you," replied Amir, trying to stifle his glee as he took the money. "However," he said as he pocketed the funds, "I might suggest you also offer the island guard a few dollars as he is well aware of the time limits at the temple."

Davon pulled out a twenty dollar bill. "I cannot thank you enough for helping me. Would you be able to give this to the guard? I am anxious to start exploring the temple."

Amir nodded and took the bill. "I will wait here for you. If you have questions please feel free to ask."

"Thank you, Amir," she said as she turned with Baboo and began to walk up the hill towards the temple.

Once they were out of earshot, Baboo looked at her. "Well done,

Davon. Now, where is our first stop?"

"The first reliefs are on several of the columns in a river-facing structure. Right there," she answered, pointing to a small stone temple about twenty feet away. They entered and found the four reliefs of Isis on each one of the corner pillars. Although each relief had minor differences, none matched the image on the back of Abdul's watch. While Davon spent time examining each relief, Baboo looked at the stone block walls to see if there was any evidence of a hidden compartment.

"Should I take pictures of the reliefs?" he asked.

"No, don't bother because I have a feeling this isn't the right place. It's too open. Let's carry on and come back if we need to," said Davon, as she started to exit the building. She quickly glanced at the booklet of Philae Temple and then stuffed it back into her pocket. "The next relief is in the principle court dedicated to Isis for the birth of Horus and it should be in that structure over there," she noted, making her way towards it.

The sound of voices distracted them and Davon and Baboo glanced in the direction of the intrusion. "It appears the other group is heading towards the Birth House," said Baboo, "so we should go to the next place on your list."

With a sigh, Davon pulled out the booklet again. "There are three reliefs in the main hall, which is the largest structure on the island. That's where the other group just came from. But the main hall no longer has a roof," she said, lowering her voice. "And I cannot see Abdul hiding the statue where there is no protection from the elements. We should probably look at the covered reliefs first. What do you think?"

"I would say your assumption is a good one but, let's take a minute to go through this again, so we do not waste time. There are a total of twelve reliefs of Isis at Philae Temple. We saw four in the double colonnade, there are three in the main hall and how many in the Birth House?"

"Two of the reliefs are in the Birth House and the other three are scattered about in smaller temples at the back of the property."

"Well, since we have to pass by the main hall on the way to the smaller temples we might as well have a quick look at the reliefs there."

"Right." Davon walked quickly up a small incline towards two large pylons. She stopped at the opening and gazed upward at the massive granite blocks while she waited for Baboo. "Here are the first two reliefs from the main hall and they do not appear to match the watch," she said when he reached her. Venturing inside they found the third relief on the back wall. It was slightly damaged, however it was an extremely beautiful image of Isis with her husband Osiris. Davon peered at the back of the watch and then looked at the relief. "This one is exquisite and more similar than the others to the etching on the watch, yet it is still not exactly the same." She pointed out the similarities and differences to Baboo and then frowned. "Okay, our next stop is the priest's temple. We have to go out this way, veer to the right and then proceed towards the water."

The priest's temple was made of small slabs of stone and had an adjoining side building that almost touched the water's edge. The two simply adorned pylons flanking the entranceway were less significant than the pylons from the main hall. The building had retained its stone roof and had a height of about ten feet. Davon ducked through the opening and strained to see the inside of the dim interior. When her eyes adjusted to the light, she noticed a plain stone altar at the back of the room and above it a relief of Isis.

"Baboo, do you have the flashlight? I'm having trouble seeing this relief." Flicking on the flashlight, he gave it to her, letting her shine it on the elaborately painted carving. "Wow, this relief is amazing. It has actually retained its original colors. How beautiful, but unfortunately it's not a match either!"

"Shine the light on the legs of the altar," said Baboo. "I can see a carving."

Davon shone the light towards the altar and a miniature relief of the falcon god was illuminated. "Baboo, this could be it! It is a relief of Ra!" she said excitedly, almost dropping the flashlight.

Baboo squatted down and examined the stone leg. "The leg is only about four inches thick. I do not think it is wide enough to hold a secret compartment."

"But look here," said Davon, shining the light towards the base where the leg became much thicker. "It seems like the mortar along this line has been recently replaced." She quickly pulled her Swiss army knife out from her pocket and began to madly scrape at the plaster. "Darn it!" she exclaimed, when the knife easily pried away the substance between the rocks. "It's just decomposing mortar." She stood up, feeling frustrated.

"Can I have the flashlight for a minute, please?" Baboo shone the light up and down each wall, looking for a sign of recent construction or repair. "This is not the right location. I think we need to find the relief of Isis that matches the watch and then if it accompanies a relief of the falcon god, we may be on to something."

"I agree. Let's move on to the next one," she said, trying to hide her frustration and concern that Agilkia Island might be the wrong location. "We need to find another priest's temple on the other side of the island."

As they climbed the crest of the hill, they looked across the water and caught a glimpse of the other tour group standing on the mainland dock. Baboo glanced at his watch. "We have been here for almost an hour and a half. I hope there are no more tour groups coming to the island today." Looking down the hill, he spied a structure similar in size to the one they had just visited. "Is that the other priest's temple," he asked Davon, who was busy reading the notes she had jotted down on the Philae Temple booklet.

"Yes, that's it. However, I just realized one of the smaller temples has two reliefs of Isis. I'm sure the one we just came from only had the one, but I got distracted looking for the hidden compartment. We might have to go back."

"I looked at the other reliefs," replied Baboo. "There was only one relief of Isis in the temple we just came from."

"Thank goodness you're on the ball, Baboo. So, there will be two reliefs in this temple," said Davon, as she looked down the hillside.

Where they were standing, they could see no pathway to the temple. Without any time to lose, Davon took off, quickly sidestepping down the steep embankment. The sandy ground with tuffs of long grass, was dry and unstable. With each step, small rocky debris slid down the hill, accumulating on a flat out-cropping close to the side of the temple. Carefully and closely following Davon, Baboo put enough distance between them so that the rocks he displaced would not hit her. When they reached the second priest's temple, they realized it was a mirror image of the last.

As they approached the entranceway, Baboo came to a sudden stop. Sticking out his arm, he blocked Davon's way. "Crocodile to your left," he quietly warned.

Basking in the sun and very close to the entranceway of the temple was a ten-foot scaly brown crocodile, an ambush predator, which was capable of taking down almost any animal within its range. As an agile predator, the Nile crocodile was able to patiently wait for hours, even days for prey to come within attack range.

Davon looked at the creature and let out a squeaky moan. "Oh no, I think we have a problem. This priest's temple is built exactly the same as the last one and there is only one way in and out. What are we going to do? Should we try to scare him away?" she frightfully suggested.

"We can, but I am worried once we are inside he might come back and trap us there," Baboo replied, pausing to think for a moment. "If I can get him to leave, would you be willing to run inside to check the reliefs while I keep watch?"

"Maybe," she gulped. "I just hope there isn't another crocodile inside the temple."

Taking the flashlight from Baboo, she put down her bag and mentally prepared herself to dash into the temple when the crocodile moved away. Baboo gathered some good-sized rocks and strategically rolled the first one towards the creature, hitting him on the side of the snout. The crocodile responded by opening one eye, but quickly closed it, remaining unfazed and unmoving.

"Can you see anyone in the vicinity?" whispered Baboo, readying his next line of attack.

Davon quickly glanced to the right and left and then up the hill. "No, it's all clear."

"Sorry, Mr. Crocodile, but you are in the way," said Baboo as he lobbed a medium-sized rock right onto the top of the creature's head.

They heard a thud when the rock made contact. The crocodile opened his eyes, raised his head and began to madly swing it about, growling and hissing an angry warning to the perpetrator. Davon and Baboo instantly recoiled and prepared to run if the creature advanced towards them, but whether he was just too old or very tired, once the tantrum was over the crocodile turned sixty degrees and slithered into the water.

"Oh My God!" whispered Davon, her heart racing. "That was terrifying! Okay, keep a lookout, I'm on my way." Running towards the entranceway, she abruptly stopped to shine the flashlight around the interior. "No crocodiles in here," she called as she entered the temple.

Once inside, Davon noticed a definite musty smell to the air. Pulling her scarf across her nose and mouth, she used the flashlight to look around. This temple was more decorative than the last and had colorful reliefs on every wall. The altar situated in the center of the room also had carvings. Davon peered closely at the legs of the altar, recognizing the carvings to be of Sobek, the crocodile god. "How appropriate," she murmured, turning her attention to the walls. The two reliefs of Isis were on the back wall, separated by a brick outcropping. Davon quickly checked to see if they matched the image on the back of Abdul's watch, sighing when she realized they did not. Hastily scanning

191

the remaining walls, she discovered more illustrations of Sobek, a male figure with the head of a crocodile.

"I'm coming out," she shouted, waiting at the entranceway for a response before she exited.

"He is at the edge of the water and I can see his snout. When you exit, run up the hill," advised Baboo. "I have a rock in hand if he moves."

Davon exited the temple at full speed. Halfway up the hillside, she stopped and then turned around. "There were two reliefs of Isis but, of course, no match," she said to Baboo when he joined her with their belongings. "There were also some amazing carvings of Sobek, the crocodile god, which I thought was appropriate, considering our entry sentinel."

Baboo chuckled and then looked again at the time. "It is two-twenty. The two reliefs in the Birth House are the only ones left; hopefully one of them will match the watch etching."

They hiked up the hill and were just about to enter a side door to the principle court, where they would make their way to the Birth House, when Davon thought she heard someone calling her name.

"Miss Marshall," shouted Amir from the bottom of the hill. "May I have a word?"

Stopping in midstride, Davon grimaced at Baboo and then slowly turned around. "Yes Amir, what is it?"

"I just wanted to see how things are going and ask if you had any questions," he said, approaching them.

Davon smiled sweetly. "Everything is going very well, thank you and no, so far I do not have any questions. We have been finding our way around and have taken some amazing pictures of the reliefs, but I still have a few more photos I would like to get." She somehow managed to keep her dismay in check as she watched Amir move around her and then make his way towards the entranceway.

"Have you been in the principle court yet?" he asked. Stepping through the entrance room doorway, Amir directed her attention to a small stone altar adjacent to a sidewall. "As your thesis is on Isis, I just wanted to point out an altar to her that is often overlooked because it is small and for the most part unadorned."

Davon and Baboo followed him into the room and stared at an altar made from a solid piece of rock. A large stone slab top overhung the base by at least ten inches. Davon stood facing the altar, trying to keep her anxiety at bay. They were wasting precious time! She blocked out the drivel Amir was going on and on about and hoped this was not the beginning of a guided tour. As her eyes adjusted to the murky light, she suddenly noticed a small symbol on the front of the altar. She could hardly contain her excitement.

"Excuse me, Amir, but is the altar made of sandstone grey stone?" she asked, shooting Baboo an anxious glance. Walking towards the altar, she patted the symbol, which she could now clearly distinguish as a sun disk atop of a falcon head.

"Yes, yes," answered Amir, becoming animated. "All of the stone for the temple was taken from the same quarry."

"Interesting," Davon said quietly. "Baboo, could you please take some pictures of the altar." She moved towards Amir. "You asked if we have been in the principle court already and the answer is yes. I just wanted to return for a few more photos of the Birth House. But, I do have a question for you about the priest's temples. If you could come with me, I will show you which one," she said, quickly concocting a story to get him out of the room. They left the principle court and Davon took him to one side of the hill, where she then pointed. "How is it possible for the colors of the reliefs in that priest's temple to be so vivid?" she asked. "I have never seen such amazing colors in an above ground building. Being so close to the water, one would think the paint on the reliefs would disintegrate."

"I understand your question and it is a very good one,

considering the temple is thousands of years old," replied Amir, stroking his chin methodically. "Color pigments were mixed with different types of binders. For example, they used gum from the Acacia tree, egg yolk and they also created a casein glue, which is made from lime and milk. I am not exactly sure which type of binder was used in the priest's temples, however, you are correct that it is unusual for the color pigment to be so vivid in an above ground structure. This is typically the type of color we see in a pharaoh's tomb."

Davon nodded, enthusiastically. "Thank you for the explanation about the type of binders they used. I knew there was a reason why the colored reliefs had not faded." She gave him a glowing smile. "I don't think I need any more assistance right now, Amir, so why don't you enjoy the rest of the time down at the dock with the guard. I will go and find Baboo."

Amir lifted a cynical brow at the suggestion. "Alright, please come down to the dock when you are finished." He started down the hill, but then stopped and turned back. "Miss Marshall," he called, "just a quick reminder we must leave the island by four o'clock."

"We will be at the dock before four. Thanks Amir," she replied. She watched until he was well on his way. Davon dashed back inside the principle court and looked at Baboo, who was peering behind the wall side of the altar. "Another symbol of Ra, Baboo," she breathlessly informed him. "Did you find anything?"

"No. I have scanned the altar and the area all around here, but I have found nothing, but solid stone."

"Darn it, I thought we'd stumbled onto something." She stood still and frowned.

"Has Amir gone back down to the dock?"

"Yes," she replied in a worried tone. "I thought I would never get rid of him. We had better go check out the last two reliefs because it's almost four o'clock."

They left the entrance room and walked into a well-preserved rectangular space made out of enormous stone blocks. It held seven fat columns completely covered in hieroglyphics. This was the Birth House and the columns, which supported an elaborately engraved roof, helped to give the room a grand impression. Davon flicked on the flashlight and scanned the walls, finding the first relief of Isis on the wall above a large stone vessel. "The room is so ornate it somehow makes you believe the statue has to be here." However, when she compared the relief to Abdul's watch, her face fell. "It's not even close to a match. Can you see the second relief, Baboo?"

"Over here," he said, leaning in to examine the piece.

Davon shone the light on the carving. "This is a family relief of Isis, Osiris and Horus and it isn't even comparable," she exclaimed, moving the flashlight up and down the other walls with hopes of discovering a third relief of the goddess. "I can't believe it! I was so sure the relief would be here." A moment of sadness assaulted her and she leaned against a pillar and hung her head. "It just doesn't make sense. The Sanduu family owns the island. Abdul said the statue was near the water on the Sanduu...something. Everything is lining up except we cannot find the matching Isis relief." She let out a sorrowful wail. "What are we going to do now? It's too late! We don't have any more time!"

Baboo approached her. "I suggest we go back and look at the relief inside the main hall because it was the only one similar to the etching on the watch. Even though you think the statue would not be hidden there because there is no roof covering the carving, I think we should still examine the complete wall around the relief in case there happens to be something."

Nodding slowly, Davon stood erect. "You are right, Baboo. What have we got to lose?"

On the way to the main hall, they looked down to the dock to check on the whereabouts of Amir and the island guard. "They are both on the dock," Baboo confirmed. "Hopefully, Amir will not start to look for us again because I might need to use the hammer and crowbar."

As they entered the main hall, they gazed up again at the carvings on the giant pylons flanking the entranceway. Making their way to the relief, Davon compared it for a second time to the back of Abdul's watch. "The profile and the gown she is wearing are identical, but the angle of her arm is slightly different. And the plant she is holding in her left hand looks more like papyrus, whereas the plant on the watch is broader at the tip and similar to a lotus bud."

"I agree, but this relief is still very similar to the etching," replied Baboo as he inspected the stones at the base of the carving. He scraped at the mortar between two of the blocks. "The mortar here appears newer and here," he added, pointing to another joint. "It may seem ridiculous, but could I ask you to place your ear against this rock. I am going to put the end of the crowbar against it and tap it with the hammer to see if it rings hollow."

"What does a hollow stone block sound like?" asked Davon.

"I am not sure, but if there is a metal box hidden inside, you should hear something funny. Let's begin with a stone we know is solid. Could you please place your ear here?"

"I can do better than that," said Davon, pulling her stethoscope out of her bag. Baboo stared at the stethoscope and looked bewildered. "I never leave home without it," she explained as she got into position.

Baboo placed the end of the crowbar against the corner base stone and swiftly hit it with the hammer.

"Okay," said Davon, moving over to the stone block in question. "Hit this one." Baboo hit the block. "It sounds the same. Try the next one." They went along the bottom line of stones and then moved up to the next level, repeating the procedure. "I think the mortar was just replaced, Baboo. Maybe it was crumbling or rotten like the mortar in the priest's temple."

Baboo tossed the tools into his backpack. "We need to return to Luxor as soon as possible because it is time for Plan B. If we leave the minute we get back to the mainland, we could be there by midnight. Are you up to driving or do you want to check on flights?"

"When I was looking at flights to Cairo, I noticed there was a morning flight to Luxor. I don't know if there is a flight tonight. We can check when we get to the airport because we have to go there anyway to drop off the vehicle. If we choose to drive, we will still have to go to the airport to change the vehicle drop off location, so, I vote for whichever way is the fastest."

They gathered up their belongings and anxiously headed down the hill towards the dock. Amir stood when he saw them approaching and made his way towards them. "Good, right on time. Did you find everything you were looking for?"

"Everything, except the one Isis relief I was seeking," complained Davon, throwing her arms into the air.

Amir frowned. "And what does this relief look like?"

"It is almost identical to the relief inside the main hall, except Isis is holding what I think is a lotus flower," she answered, moving towards the dock. "And this is probably not pertinent, but she has a few stars above her head."

"Wait," called Amir just as Davon was about to step into the boat. "I know of the relief."

Davon slowly turned around. "Is it here on the island?" she asked, staring at him with meticulous concentration.

"The one you describe is on the island, but it is not a relief of Isis," replied Amir with a grin. "It is a relief of the goddess Nut, *(pronounced 'Noot')*. She is the goddess of the sky and protector of Ra."

Davon could not believe her ears! Although she felt ecstatic, she remained calm and explained how embarrassed she was at the blunder.

Amir laughed under his breath. "It is a common mistake to confuse Isis with Nut as they are depicted in a very similar way."

"Where is the relief? I would love to photograph it and include it in my thesis."

Pleased to know something this university student did not, he let her squirm for a few seconds before he answered. "The relief of Nut is carved on the Sanduu crypt, but unfortunately it is not open to the public."

"Please Amir, could you help me out. There are no other tourists on the island and no one has to know you showed the relief to me," begged Davon. She put her hands together as though she was about to pray and looked at him with pleading eyes.

"I am not sure. You see the Sanduu family owns Agilkia Island and the guard, who many think is guarding the temple, is actually guarding the tomb. The tomb, constructed in the ancient Egyptian way is hidden in that group of palm trees," he said, indicating an area to the side of the guard's hut, "and was built for the patriarch, who died in 1897. When the Sanduu family agreed to save Philae Temple and bring it to the island, they paid the complete cost of the restoration. Their only request was that the crypt remain off limits to the public."

Davon nodded in pretended understanding. Digging into her bag she pulled out a ten and a fifty dollar bill. "Amir, I promise you no one will ever find out I saw the relief of Nut. And I offer you and the guard another token of my incredible appreciation if you will only find it in your heart to show it to me," she said, humbly extending the money towards him.

Amir took the money. "Let me discuss it with Tarek," he replied, walking towards the guard, who was sitting in a white plastic chair in front of his home.

Davon waited until Amir was out of earshot and then looked at Baboo. "Oh Baboo, this is it! My gut instinct told me the relief was on the island. But how are we going to play this out? If he takes us inside the tomb is there a safe way you can knock him out until we find the statue?"

"Yes, I can apply pressure to the side of his neck and he will collapse."

"I hate to do that to Amir, but we have no choice," she whispered, as she watched the tour guide speak to the guard and then return to where they were waiting.

"You may see the relief, Miss Marshall, but your photographer must wait here. We will not allow any pictures."

Davon was suddenly flustered. "Oh, alright, that is fine," she mumbled, trying to think of a reason why she needed Baboo to accompany her. "I will not let him take any photographs however, would it be possible for him to also experience seeing the relief, which has been hidden from the public eye for over a hundred and twenty years?"

Amir pursed his lips in annoyance. "Only you may see the relief," he snapped, his manner cooling.

"Yes, I completely understand," replied Davon, wanting to appease him before he changed his mind about letting her see the carving.

Davon joined Amir and they walked to the back of the hut and then veered left for about one hundred feet towards a grove of palm trees. Nestled among them was a tall wrought iron fence, enclosing a large, undecorated tomb. Amir took a set of keys from his pocket and opened the padlock on the gate. He motioned Davon forward and as she made her way along the brick path, he followed her. There were no weeds or brush growing inside the fenced off area and Davon presumed the guard was also the groundskeeper. When they arrived at the entranceway, Davon stood to the side, expecting Amir to open the door to the tomb. She was surprised when he came and stood beside her.

"Look up, Miss Marshall, and behold the goddess Nut."

Davon leaned her head back and looked at the colorful relief carved into the ceiling of the tomb's overhang. The etching on the watch she held in her pocket was the exact replica. "It is exquisite, Amir!

Absolutely stunning!" she exclaimed, enthusiastically. "Can you tell me about the unique construction of the crypt? Is it possible to go inside?" she questioned, turning her gaze to the overly solid looking stone door.

"Tarek was very firm. You may only look at the relief and then we must leave. Besides, we could never enter the tomb as only the family holds the riddle to unlock the door."

"What do you mean?" asked Davon. A movement behind Amir caught her eye and she saw Baboo behind one of the palm trees. Oh no, she thought, shaking her head as she tried to warn him to stay away. When she noticed Amir watching her odd behaviour, she waved her hand and said, "Sorry, Amir, there was an insect buzzing around my face." She proceeded to brush away the imaginary bug, all the while hoping Baboo would understand her signal.

"As I told you at the dock, the tomb was built in the ancient Egyptian way. It has...what is the American word?" He thought for a moment and then his eyes lit up. "Booby trap, yes that is the word. It has a booby trap to discourage the unholy from trying to enter. Only the Sanduu family understands the secret to open the tomb," he explained, taking a step backwards. "Now, as it is after four o'clock, we must leave the island. Please come with me."

"One second, Amir," called Davon, moving around him. She dashed down a narrow dirt pathway to the back of the crypt. Amir let out an exasperated huff and then followed her. When he reached her, she was analyzing a very large protruding wedge-shaped stone in the rear archway. "I was half expecting to find another way into the tomb," she said with a half smile, moving her head from side to side. "It looks like that large stone might move. What do you think, Amir? Is it a weight that slides back to open the door?"

Amir was intrigued with this curious young American woman. However, he still shook his head in disbelief at her antics and let out a gruff grunt before answering the question. "I have never seen the door open, but once Tarek mentioned there is a stepping stone at the front of the tomb, which swings open the door when pressure is applied to a special place at the back of the tomb. But now, please, I must insist we leave."

"Alright," Davon replied with a devilish grin. "Can I just see if I can figure out which one of the stepping stones opens the door since we have to go by the front of the tomb to leave?" She did not wait for an answer, but as she started to jog back down the pathway she cast a glance at Amir and saw his expression sour. "I am leaving the island, don't worry," she called, trying to appease him. Reaching the front of the crypt, she got down on her hands and knees and examined the large paving stones, trying to manipulate some of the joints to see if one looked unusual. Although she tried applying full body weight to several stones, nothing happened.

When Amir caught up to her again, he raised his voice. "Miss Marshall, come with me right now! You are not only jeopardizing my job, but the job of Tarek!"

Davon slowly rose. "I apologize. Please forgive me," she said, wishing she could have just a few more minutes.

Amir did not reply. Instead he abruptly turned and marched towards the gate. Davon had no choice but to follow. Once they were on the other side of the fence, he closed the padlock and quickly walked to the dock, getting into the boat before Davon and Baboo. Starting the outboard motor, he angrily motioned for them to get in and sit. He then took them to the mainland wharf without saying a word.

When they arrived at the dock, Davon and Baboo exited the boat. "Thank you again, Amir. I really appreciate your help."

"My pleasure," he grunted, avoiding eye contact. Pushing off from the wharf, he motored away.

Davon waved a feeble goodbye and then looked at Baboo with a sly grin. "I'm positive the statue is hidden in the tomb! We have to get back to the island!" she whispered with excitement.

"We should talk about it in the car," replied Baboo, noticing that several fishermen on the shore were within listening distance.

As they walked quickly towards their vehicle, Davon noticed Amir's junker in the parking lot. "Is he coming back to get his car?"

"I don't know," replied Baboo, clicking open the doors to their vehicle. Getting inside, he started the engine and turned on the air conditioning. He waited for Davon to close her door. "So, you did find the relief?"

"Yes! The relief of Nut is on the outer ceiling of the tomb and it's an exact match! You probably noticed when you were behind the tree that we didn't go inside the tomb. Amir told me only the Sanduu family knows the secret or riddle to open the door, but he also said Tarek told him if you step on one of the stone blocks at the front of the tomb and then put pressure on a special place at the back of the crypt, the door will swing open. He said the tomb is booby trapped, but I bet that is just an old wife's tale to keep thieves away."

"How interesting," said Baboo, thinking for a moment. "I wonder if we can get one of the fishermen to take us over to the island. We will have to wait until it is dark before we go back so we can sneak past Tarek, unless you think we could bribe him to open the tomb."

Davon looked grim. "I don't think we will be able to bribe Tarek as he was only willing to let me have a quick look at the relief, but the problem in using a fisherman is he will wonder what we are up to. How difficult would it be to rent a boat?"

"The three motor boats at the dock this morning are gone and even if we went back into town to rent a boat, I think the distance in nautical miles from town to Agilkia Island is quite far, and do not forget we will be traveling at night. It might be smarter to pay off one of the fishermen. I saw a padlock on the gate, but it looks like the chain can be cut," said Baboo, as he continued to ask questions about the tomb.

Davon told him about the protruding wedge-shaped stone at the back of the crypt. "I examined the back wall of the tomb, which is made out of the same blocks of stones as the front and sides. They are rectangular in shape with no adornment. The only weird looking stone is the wedge-shaped one. I have a feeling it might be used as a counterweight to somehow open the door."

"Did you see any cables or hooks fastened to the stone?" he asked.

"No, I couldn't see the top because it is at least ten feet above the ground," replied Davon as she tried to visualize the tomb. "I just realized we are going to need a ladder if you have to get to the protruding stone." She paused for a second. "But, that doesn't make sense if the Sanduu family can open the door presumably without one. I mean, why would the architect make a ladder a requirement to open the door?"

"I saw a collapsible ladder at the hardware store this morning. Just in case we need to jump the fence or get to the protruding stone, I think we should go into town and buy it."

Things were getting too problematic! "It's going to be hard to hide a ladder. When we drag it into the boat, it will most certainly cause suspicion about the purpose of our excursion!"

"I don't think it can be helped," said Baboo as he reached for the door handle. "If you can give me fifty US dollars, I will go down to the beach and try to organize a boat for tonight." He looked at her objectively and noticed her white linen shirt, pants and headscarf. "While I am bribing a fisherman, you may want to change into some darker clothing for the mission."

"Yes, good idea," said Davon, pulling a fifty dollar bill from her bag and handing it to him.

Baboo turned off the ignition and tossed her the keys. "I will be back in a couple of minutes."

Getting out of the car with him, she went to the back of the vehicle and opened the trunk. Rooting through her suitcase, she selected a black T-shirt, black yoga pants and dark navy scarf. Returning with her clothes, she ducked down into the seat and changed. The heat of the day quickly penetrated the black garments and she groaned as she got out of the car for a second time. Putting her white clothing inside the suitcase, she zipped it up. As she slammed the trunk closed, she saw Baboo was already on his way back.

"All of the fishermen have gone out to fish. There is no one left on the beach. However, the good news is there is a small wooden boat pulled up past the high water mark. The problem is it does not look overly seaworthy."

"Oh great, how did I not realize the fishermen were going out on the water?" sighed Davon, rolling her eyes. "If we use the small wooden boat, do you think it will get us to the island?"

"Well, it is not full of holes, but it does look ancient," replied Baboo. "We still have an hour and a half before it gets dark. I am sure one of the fishermen will return by then. Let's go into town for the ladder and get something to eat because I have a feeling this is going to be a long, grueling night."

Frustrated, Davon got into the car. "I saw a restaurant across the street from the hardware store and it looked okay. I can go in and order for the both of us while you get the ladder."

"No," instructed Baboo, "You need to wait for me. It is not safe for you to go into the restaurant unescorted. I know you are trying to save precious minutes, but do not worry, we will be back here before the sun sets."

CHAPTER THIRTY-TWO

They arrived at the hardware store just as it was closing, but Baboo managed to get the aluminum ladder without any incident. It was neatly folded into three four-foot sections and easily fit into the backseat of the car with one or two inches to spare. There were many people milling about and several male bystanders hovered nearby, watching the loading procedure, which made Baboo a touch nervous.

Getting back into the driver's seat, he pulled out into the intersection. "There are too many eyes around here. I think it will be better to eat at the restaurant beside the internet cafe?"

"I think you are right," replied Davon, turning around to look out the rear window. "I'm amazed at how many locals just hang around."

Within minutes, they were seated in the almost empty cafe at a small table, overlooking Aswan Bay. Baboo ordered a local dish for both of them and two large bottles of water. The meal was a simple fare of rice, beans, and bread and was delicious. Between mouthfuls, they discussed their plans in hushed whispers. It was decided Davon would work the stepping-stones at the front of the tomb, while Baboo would attempt to put pressure on different sections of the back wall.

"What part do you think the protruding wedge-shaped stone plays?" asked Davon. "It is very odd looking and somehow doesn't fit in with the general architecture."

"When we get the ladder in place, I will take a look at it. The one thing I am concerned about is the flashlights. Both of mine have overly bright beams and I am worried that the guard, I believe Amir called him Tarek, will take notice of the light at the tomb. The last thing we need is for him to put in a call to the police."

"Well, hopefully he is early to bed and does not have a cell phone," Davon replied, quietly. "I have been thinking about the stepping-stones. Obviously, I need to put pressure on a stone or a sequence of stones to open the door, but because I pushed on several of the center stones with no results, before Amir dragged me away, I think Amir was mistaken when he mentioned that Tarek said you have to put pressure on one stone to open the door. Why would they make it so easy for grave robbers?" she questioned with a frown. "The other reason I believe the code has to be a sequence is because Amir said only the Sanduu family knows the riddle to open the door to the tomb. A riddle by definition is a puzzle, something you need to figure out."

"It does make more sense for the code to be a sequence," said Baboo, thoughtfully. "What do you think it could be?"

"I'm not sure. One would think it would be hard to figure out, yet simple, as it has been passed down by word of mouth for generations. I was thinking about something Egyptian: an outline of the all-seeing-eye, a pyramid, a scarab." A thought suddenly occurred to her when she looked out the window at the setting sun, flooding the horizon with brilliant colors of red, orange and purple. Ra was the Egyptian sun god and the myth stated he was born at dawn and sailed his boat across the heavens during the day. As the evening progressed, he weakened and died. Swallowed by Nut, he plunged into the underworld, leaving the moon and the stars to light the world. At dawn the following day, he was reborn, returning to the heavens to repeat the journey over and over again for all of eternity. How incredibly appropriate, thought Davon, night is approaching and we are looking for a statue of Ra in a tomb sheltered by the goddess Nut. "Perhaps the sequence is a sundial or clock, where you step on the hours where Ra is protected by Nut," she suggested excitedly, explaining her understanding of the myth of Ra to Baboo.

"I like that idea."

"Me too," replied Davon, taking a sip of water. She stood and put some Egyptian coins onto the table. Here is the money to pay the bill. We should probably get back to the bay and figure out our transportation to the island."

As Baboo started them on their way, he cast a glance in Davon's direction. "I just want to mention that the smallest sound travels quickly over water. It is crucial for us to remain silent during our trip to the island. Do not say anything to me or the driver once we are in the boat."

"Got it," replied Davon, pointing to the camel pen just ahead.

Baboo made the right hand turn and quickly approached the top of the incline just as the sun dipped below the horizon. Flicking on the car's headlights, he proceeded down the hill. Suddenly, he slammed on the brakes, coming to a complete stop in the middle of the road. "Do you see that?" he shouted. Maneuvering the vehicle towards the road's edge, he turned off the headlights. Stunned, they watched as bright lights moved in and around the temple on Agilkia Island.

"They have to be looking for the statue! Damn it, why else would they be there?" cursed Davon.

Baboo pulled out his binoculars and scanned the area. "They seem to be focusing around the temple. I do not see any lights in the direction of the tomb. There is a large motorboat parked at the island dock and some of them are heading towards it." Baboo and Davon observed the lights gathering at the front of the temple and then watched as one by one they appeared to float towards the dock. He handed the binoculars to her. "I know there is not much light, but these are high power lenses. See if you can recognize anyone." Baboo started the car and moved slowly forward, trying to give her a better view.

Davon looked through the binoculars. "They are all men, no surprise, and no one seems to be carrying anything but their flashlights. I cannot see their faces clearly. They must be Adin's men because if they were Abdul's, they would know to look for the statue in the tomb."

"Not necessarily. Maybe only the keeper of the statue knows its secrets."

"I hope you are right, Baboo, because we have come too far to leave without the statue." The roar of the motorboat starting up invaded the silence of the night. "They are piling into the boat," she said, "and it looks like they are heading towards Aswan." She continued to observe the retracting speedboat as Baboo stepped on the gas and drove down the hill towards the parking lot. "I wonder how Tarek dealt with the visit. They probably had some sort of documentation from Adin. When we motor over there, I think it would be best to go to the other side of the island, avoiding the dock. I don't want to risk a chance meeting with the tomb's guard."

Baboo shook his head. "Remember the crocs! Who knows where they sleep. To be on the safe side we need to use the dock. We will be as quiet as we can, but bring some cash with you in case he sees us. I know you think Tarek cannot be bought off, but I believe everyone has a price." He parked on the road behind a palm tree just beyond the parking lot. "The car is not totally hidden, but at least it is not overly obvious as the only vehicle parked in the lot," he said, adding, "It looks like Amir picked up his car."

Baboo opened the back door, removed the ladder and tools and then manually locked the doors not wanting to make any beeping noises. Davon picked up the larger of the two tool bags and Baboo slung the second over his shoulder and grabbed the ladder. They started off towards the water.

"Hang on," said Davon softly. "I forgot my jacket."

"The keys are in the pocket of your tool bag," he told her as he precariously held his cargo.

Putting the bag on the ground, Davon located the keys and ran back to the car, manually opening the passenger door. Snatching her jacket from the backseat, she put it on, relocked the door and then ran back to Baboo. Only the light from the moon guided them as they made their way down to the beach. Davon looked up and down the shore. "I guess this will have to do as our mode of transportation," she whispered, dropping the bag of tools next to the small wooden boat. "I can't see anyone, not even any fishing boats on the water."

Baboo nodded and put down his wares, silently removing the large nylon fishing net from the hull of the craft. He carefully replaced it with the ladder and bags of tools. "Help me push the boat into the water. I want to check for leaks," he said quietly .

The boat slid easily down the dry sandy bank, but made a loud splash as it entered the Nile. Davon made a face and turned around half expecting someone to rush onto the beach, accusing them of stealing, however no one appeared.

Hanging on to the side of the vessel, Baboo entered the water's edge and inspected it. He could see no evidence of leakage. "It seems okay. You get in first," he said in a hushed tone, pulling the stern of the craft towards the shore.

Davon placed one foot inside the boat and then the other. Maneuvering around the ladder and tools, she made her way to the bow and her seat. Once she was settled, Baboo pushed the craft away from the shore and jumped in. Sitting down on the middle seat, he adjusted the oars and began to row. The river was calm without a hint of a breeze and the bow of the boat created only a slight ripple as it parted the water. Zipping up her jacket, Davon was glad she had brought it along, for now that the blazing sun had set, it was quite cool. Save for the dip of the oars, they reached the island's dock in relative silence, although their arrival was somewhat announced when the bow of the boat accidently bumped into it. Davon winced as she grabbed the wharf. Quickly glancing towards Tarek's hut, she saw it lay in darkness. Grabbing the flashlight from the open bag, she pointed to its unlit light and then to the hut. She made a sleep gesture, trying to communicate that Tarek might be asleep. Davon then held up her hands and shrugged, pointing in the direction of Aswan, indicating that maybe he left the island with the previous intruders. Baboo nodded in understanding, but still placed his finger to his mouth before he indicated for her to get out of the boat. Crawling onto the dock, she kept low as she tied a meager looking rope from the craft to an iron ring. When Baboo handed her the ladder, she winced again as the bright shiny aluminum reflected the light from the moon as though it was a beacon. Carefully resting the ladder on the dock, she retrieved both tool bags and then held the boat as Baboo made his way onto the wharf. Together, they cautiously gathered up the items and silently moved towards land. It was darker on the island, and in the shadow cast by the hill and the temple, it was difficult to see.

Davon led the way and inched forward at a snail's pace, waiting for her eyes to adjust to the dim moonlight. She decided to skirt past Tarek's hut and stayed near the water's edge as close as she dare, all the while thinking about the possibility of crocodiles dozing along the shore. As she neared the hut, she paused for a moment, glancing at Tarek's white plastic chair, now tipped over. Turning around, she pointed out the discovery to Baboo. He nodded, but motioned her forward. Shrugging, she continued on her way, picking up her pace as she could now see the outline of the grove of palm trees, surrounding the tomb. She had taken no more than ten steps when all of a sudden she stumbled and fell. Rolling away from the object that tripped her, she quickly untangled herself from the tool bag, and jumped up, sprinting uphill as fast as she could. "Baboo, stop and turn on the flashlight! There's something awful there!"

Baboo sat the flashlight on the ground, flicked it on and then let out a gasp. The light illuminated the small body of Tarek face down in a pool of blood.

Davon's heart raced as she ran towards the figure to feel the side of his neck for the carotid artery. No pulse. She saw a long gash. "His throat was slit," she said with bitterness, quickly pulling her hand away. Standing up, she wiped the blood on her hand onto the victim's shirt. "We need to call the police." Turning her head from the scene, she pushed back her headscarf. She was revolted by the discovery and notably shaken by the second murder she had witnessed in less than two weeks.

"When we are safely off the island, I will make an anonymous call to the police. However, the person, who killed him means business. Right now we need to get to the tomb, look for the statue and then leave the island," Baboo calmly told her, reminding her of why they were here.

She gave no reply. Roughly yanking off her headscarf, she stuffed it into her pocket and grabbed the flashlight out of her bag. Flicking it on, she turned and marched down the pathway towards the crypt. When they approached the fence, she was relieved to see the gate was still securely shut. It seemed that the men they saw searching the temple had not come to the tomb. Baboo got out the wire cutters and easily cut the chain, letting the two sides of the gate swing open.

Davon led him to the front of the tomb. She illuminated the relief of Nut, and then turned the flashlight onto the stepping stones, mentally counting twenty stones running across the top and ten running down the sides. "There are two hundred stepping stones and as I told you I tried applying pressure to a couple of the middle ones, but nothing happened. Should I step on all of them individually to see if Amir was right about only one stone opening the door?" she asked quietly, her thoughts still lingering on the lifeless body only a few yards away.

Baboo did not say anything for a few minutes. Bending over, he began to examine the stones. "Not one of the stones seems to look particularly different from the others," he said, flashing the light on each one of the pavers. "I suggest you walk onto each stone and stand still for three to five seconds before you move on to the next. This will help determine if the code is indeed a sequence." Baboo moved off the stones and onto the pathway.

After taking a deep breath, Davon walked over to the top right hand corner and then stepped onto the first stone. She counted to three, moved to the next one and continued horizontally across the pavers until she was finished the first row. Without missing a beat, she walked across the second row, then the third and fourth, completing the sequence.

"Did you detect any movement?" asked Baboo, moving towards her.

She shook her head. "I don't think so. What do you want to do next? Should we try the clock sequence?"

"Are there any numbers on Abdul's watch other than on the dial?"

Davon pulled the watch off her wrist and examined it. "The only numbers are the ones on the face of the watch." She paused and thought for a moment. "I remember reading that during his daytime journey, Ra travels through the twelve provinces of Egypt, which represent the twelve hours of daylight. Perhaps the sequence is the hours of the day. I can start by drawing an imaginary clock, and put pressure on six o'clock, which will represent sunrise, and then go around the circle of stones applying pressure all the way to six o'clock again, which would now represent sunset. The beauty of this sequence is that the opposite is also true. If the code represents the time Ra is protected by Nut, six o'clock is now sunset, turning into sunrise when I get back to it."

Handing her a small lead pencil, Baboo looked her in the eye. "You should actually draw the circle, so you do not make a mistake. Make sure you pace evenly. The stone directly in front of the door should be midnight," he recommended, pointing to the only centered stone in the entranceway. "Good," he said as he watched her write the clock's corresponding numbers onto the flat surfaces. She started with the numbers 12, 3, 6, and 9 and quickly added the remaining numbers of the clock. It looked logical when it was completed. Baboo nodded his approval. "Yes, it makes sense. Now, before you start, we need to go to the back of the tomb and examine the wedge-shaped rock."

Again leading the way, Davon took him to the back of the crypt, shining her flashlight on the oddly shaped protruding stone. Baboo looked at it and then used his light to inspect the wall. Once that was completed he unfolded the ladder and clutching his flashlight, climbed upwards towards the peaked roof and extremely large wedge-shaped pediment. He shone his light through the narrow spaces on either side of the stone.

"Does it look like it moves?" asked Davon, watching him while she supported the bottom of the ladder.

"I think it pivots downward, pulling the stone door open. I can see two heavy duty latches drilled into both sides of the rock and they have two large hooks slipped through them. The hooks are attached to cables. If I push down on the top of the stone, it does move slightly, so you were correct in your assessment of its function," he said, as he returned to the ground. He proceeded to shine the flashlight around the base of the wall, applying pressure to several different places. "Use your flashlight to inspect that side of the wall. The pressure point should be no more than five feet off the ground."

Systematically running their fingers up, down, and across the back wall, they inspected every inch, finding nothing unusual. "Amir told me that pressure had to be applied to the stepping stones and at the same time to a place on the back wall, but maybe it isn't true," she said with an exasperated sigh as she glanced at the time. "It is already after seven! We have to get the door open! Why don't we work on the pattern of the stepping stones and see what happens."

They returned to the front of the crypt and while Baboo stood off to the side, Davon headed towards the marked six o'clock stone. "Take it slowly and put all of your weight onto one stone for perhaps ten seconds before moving to the next," said Baboo.

"Okay, here goes nothing." Davon, stepped onto six o'clock. She counted to ten and then moved to seven o'clock for ten seconds before moving to eight, and then nine. When she stepped onto the tenth stone, she felt it shifting slightly. "This stone is sinking a bit..."

"Don't stop the flow, Davon, keep moving," said Baboo, when he saw in her excitement she was hesitating.

"Is anything happening?" Davon questioned in between counts as she continued her way around the clock all the way back to six. As soon as she landed on six o'clock, she quickly glanced at the tomb's door. "Obviously, that's not the correct pattern, but I did feel some shifting at ten o'clock and maybe at one o'clock."

"I saw no movement of the door. I would suggest you now try starting at ten o'clock, jump to one o'clock, to four o'clock, and end at seven o'clock, skipping two stones all the way around," instructed Baboo.

Davon moved outside of the circle and approached ten o'clock. "Watch the door, Baboo," she said, feeling stirrings of excitement. She stepped onto the tenth stone, counting to ten before jumping to one o'clock, then to four, finishing on seven. "Weird," she mumbled. "Ten didn't move this time, but one shifted. Four and seven remained solid. I'm going to try the first arrangement again," she said, moving around the outside of the circle to six o'clock. She repeated the first sequence with the same results and placed a large X on the one o'clock and ten o'clock stones. This time, she stepped onto nine o'clock, then ten, followed by one. "When I step on nine, the ten o'clock stone shifts." She jogged back to nine o'clock and stepped onto every stone, making her way completely around circle and then repeated the sequence again. "Now, five o'clock is shifting as well as ten and one."

"I am going to the back of the tomb to see if the wedge-shaped rock is moving. Keep doing what you are doing. I will be back in a moment," said Baboo as he rushed off.

Davon continued to step her way around the clock, pausing for ten seconds on each stone before moving to the next. She had almost finished her fourth round when Baboo returned. "Did you see anything happening back there?"

"Not really. I went up the ladder to check the stone and re-examined the back wall. The rock is solidly in place and there does not appear to be any unusual or marked stones on the rear wall."

"Damn it!" cursed Davon, racking her brain for a solution.

Baboo sighed softly. "No one said this was going to be easy. Let's try again. This time I will climb the ladder and apply pressure to the rock with the crow bar. I will try to force it downward. As you are trying different sequences, keep an eye on the door."

"Okay," replied Davon, brushing off her feelings of discouragement. She examined the stones while she waited for Baboo to get to the back of the tomb, hoping to see some sort of pattern. "Ten moves when I have come from nine, one always moves and five sometimes moves. Think mathematically Davon! What is the relationship between one, five and ten? One is four stones away from five and five is five stones away from ten, but ten is only three stones away from one. Maybe if I start at one o'clock, move to five, move to ten and then try to jump six stones from ten, which would take me to four o'clock. But, if the pattern works that would mean I will have to jump seven stones from four, which would take me to eleven o'clock..." She calculated the last movement and wondered if the jump from five to stone ten was even possible. Shaking her head, she decided to see what happened when she started on one o'clock and only move to five and then ten. The one o'clock stone shifted as usual and after counting to ten, she moved to five, which did not budge. She counted to ten and then jumped to the ten o'clock stone, completely missing it. "Bloody hell! That is not the right sequence," she yelled. Standing up, she glanced at the solid tomb door and then jogged to the side of the crypt. "Are you seeing any movement, Baboo?"

"Nothing yet," he answered, "but I have had some success at shifting the wedge-shaped rock."

"Great! I'll try a few more sequences," she called, running back to the front of the tomb.

Abandoning the last pattern, she decided to start at one o'clock and step on every stone. The first round gave hope as two stones—one and ten o'clock both sunk. During the second round when she stepped on five o'clock, the stone unexpectedly sank three inches. As it dipped, Davon caught her running shoe along the edge and lost her footing. To maintain her balance, she was forced to step outside of the circle. The stone she stepped on, which was directly beside five o'clock, also began to sink, throwing Davon onto her hands and knees. The flashlight she was holding made a loud thud as it slipped out of her grip. Flipping gracefully onto its back, the flashlight illuminated the large relief of Nut, which gloriously hovered above. Davon glanced at the tomb's tightly closed door and began to rise. As she did so, she looked up at the beautifully painted relief. The artist had used only two colors to represent the goddess of the sky. Davon stared at Nut's midnight blue flowing gown and then at her translucent cream colored face. "That's it! The pattern is the stars in the relief!" she cried, suddenly realizing that some of the twelve white shimmering stars above Nut's head were in direct alignment with the shifting paving stones. Rushing to the side of the tomb, she called out to Baboo. "I think I have figured out the pattern, Baboo! Give me five minutes to mark the stones and then if you see any movement of the rock, apply pressure where you think it is necessary!"

She did not wait for a reply. Running back to the front of the tomb, she grabbed the pencil and began to mark the stones positioned under the twelve stars. Once that was completed, she returned to the eastside of Nut's head, figuring it should be the beginning of the pattern as the sun rises in the east and sets in the west. Taking a deep breath, she stepped onto the first stone. The stone immediately sank about two inches. She could feel her heart pounding as she counted aloud to ten. Raising her foot, she proceeded to the next stone, feeling ecstatic when it also sank the second she put weight onto it. Forcing herself to remain calm, she advanced through the pattern at an even pace, pausing for a count of ten each time before she moved to the next stone. When the stone would descend, she had to focus not only on the counting, but on her balance, because several times she felt as though she might fall. At the eighth stone, Davon risked a quick glance towards the tomb's door, agonizingly noticing it remained firmly shut. She pressed forward and when she stepped onto the eleventh stone, she heard a loud grinding noise. Choking back a smile, she carefully counted to ten and then stepped onto the twelfth and final stone, turning to look at the tomb's door.

With a deep, deafening rumble, the stone door rolled opened. Davon instantly yelled success to Baboo, asking him to join her as she rushed inside the cold and darkened crypt. Running the light around the room, she was surprised at its starkness. The interior was made of the same sandstone grey brick as the exterior, but was devoid of any decoration. A large stone sarcophagus lay in the center of the room, elevated on a stone slab.

"So, where is the statue of Ra?" she slyly whispered as she walked around and inspected the sides and base of the sarcophagus for any indication of a hidden panel or button. Not finding anything of interest, she turned her attention to the walls. Moving the flashlight slowly up and down, she studied every square inch of the first wall and then moved to the adjacent wall, continuing the same procedure. The walls were made up of large, plain sandstone blocks and in her investigation, she could see no indication of a hidden compartment. "But, what's this?" she asked, spying a small symbol on the east wall about three feet above the floor. "Ah ha, the eye of Ra," she said majestically, moving in for closer scrutiny.

The symbol was depressed into the middle of a stone block and had a decorative diameter of no more than one and a half inches. Davon shone the light close to the block and compared it to the ones beside it. Although it looked similar in color, the consistency of the stone appeared somewhat different. She pushed and prodded the symbol and then ran her fingers around the mortar, which seemed to be plastic-like. "Baboo, where are you? I need some tools," she called, suddenly recognizing the decorative diameter pressed into the stone. It was exactly the same as the outer ring of Abdul's watch. Pulling the timepiece out of her pocket, she compared the two and then grinning, pushed the face of the watch against the symbol. Hearing a click, the front of the block pivoted open and there inside a white silk-lined compartment sat the priceless statue of Ra.

She stood there for a moment in silence, admiring the exquisite gold sculpture of a man with a falcon's head, made entirely of casted gold. Staring first at the large sun disk resting upon his head, she leaned forward and examined the headdress, the eyes and the beak and then moved downward towards the accurately detailed image of a male body. She could actually identify the groups of muscles in the chest wall, arms and legs. He stood in a battle stance, holding a large sword and Davon came to understand why the statue represented power in the Sanduu Corporation.

Concerned about the whereabouts of Baboo, she reached into the vault and grasping the sculpture with both hands, she cradled it in her arms and quickly left the crypt to search for him. She wondered if he was maintaining pressure on the wedge-shaped rock to keep the door open. "Baboo," she yelled as she hurried to the pathway along the side of the tomb. "I have the statue. It doesn't matter now if the door closes. The statue is absolutely amazing..." she said with glee, stopping in mid-sentence the second she arrived at the back of the tomb. The first thing she saw was the one-ton wedge-shaped rock on the ground. It sat on top of the toppled, partially crushed ladder. "Oh My God!" she shrieked, racing around the obstruction. She discovered Baboo near the head of the stone, lying on his back. His lower body was trapped beneath the huge rock. Throwing the treasured object to the ground, she flew to his side.

"Did you get the statue?" he asked, his voice barely audible.

"Oh Baboo!" Tears clouded her vision as she struggled to control her emotions. "I'm going to have to go and get help. You have to be strong," she cried, frantically trying to think of what she needed to do. When she reached to check his pulse, he pushed her hand away.

"Listen to me. Both of my legs are completely crushed and I know I am going to die very soon. I have had a wonderful life and I am blessed to have met you in the final part of my journey. You were the daughter I never had. Make me proud, Davon, and finish the job. I am sorry you will have to complete it alone."

Davon let out a sob as she carefully bent over to hug him. She knew what he said was true. He was bleeding profusely and she could see the pool of blood around the bottom of the rock, increasing rapidly in size. There was no way to get to the injured area to apply pressure. "It's my fault," she whispered. "Amir said the tomb was booby trapped."

"It is no one's fault. The hook snapped and the one cable could not hold the rock in place," murmured Baboo, letting out a groan of pain. He was whispering now and Davon had to bend forward to hear him. "Davon, I spent my early life in Alexandria and the rest in Cairo, but I was born in India and am of the Hindu faith. We believe in rebirth and reincarnation." He paused for a moment, gasping for breath. "My parents were cremated and their ashes were placed in the sea off Alexandria." His voice grew ever fainter. "This is what I desire for my remains." Davon nodded, tears streaming down her face. "When I am gone, get to the airport. Do not tell anyone about my death or Tarek's. The police will hold you for questioning."

"I can't go and leave you here," Davon cried in anguish.

"Go. Call the police after you are safe in Vienna," he whispered, struggling to catch his breath. "Promise me."

She could not refuse him. "I promise to do as you ask, Baboo," she pledged, gripping his hand. A moment later, he was gone.

Davon let out a long excruciating wail before gently closing both of his eyes. Desperately trying to choke back the tears, pouring down her cheeks, she rose. The energy she had felt at the discovery of the statue had completely dissolved and her usual sharp, determined focus had disappeared. "Why did this have to happen? It's my fault. Forgive me Baboo, forgive me," she begged, staring at his lifeless body. She knew she had to pick up the statue, get into the boat and row herself to the mainland, but for some reason, she could not move. The stillness of the night seemed to be unbearably quiet. Averting her eyes from Baboo's mangled body, she forced herself to turn around, although she wanted nothing more than to lie down and scream in agony. Using the flashlight to scan the area, she found the statue and after picking it up, she slowly started to make her way to the front of the tomb where she had left her belongings. Remembering the car keys, she located them in the tool bag and after tossing it aside, she slipped the keys and the statue into her handbag, flinging it over her right shoulder.

"Goodbye my friend," she whispered, reluctantly leaving the fenced area. Carefully closing the two gates, she wrapped the cut chain around each side to keep them together. She needed to protect his body until she was able to contact the police.

Standing for some time beside the gate, she just tried to breathe. She was grieving, distressed and troubled about Baboo's gruesome death and could not get the picture of his mangled body out of her mind. "If only I could have done something to save him," she whimpered, berating herself as a physician. "I should have tried to find something to use as a tourniquet." Although she chastised herself, she truly knew there was nothing anyone could have done. She had no idea how long it would take to get to the airport once she reached the mainland and she still needed to purchase a ticket, but as hard as she tried, she could not seem to get her legs to move. Letting out a wounded sob, she forced herself to press forward. As she neared the site where she knew Tarek lay, she decided to walk up the hill closer to the hut to avoid seeing the body. She could not bear another ghastly scene, which she knew would haunt her forever.

A reprieve from the grisly events, however, was not to be. As she approached the area, the eerie silence was broken by a rustling sound a few feet from where she was standing. Turning the light towards the noise, she recoiled as if she had been struck, letting out a scream. "No, no, you horrible creature! Go away!" A large crocodile was slowly moving across the sand towards Tarek's corpse. She wanted to flee, run to the boat and get off the island as quickly as possible, but for some reason she was frozen, rooted to the ground, watching her worse nightmare come to life. Stooping to pick up a stone near her feet, she threw it at the grotesque beast. It bounced off his head, but did not thwart his advancement. Averting her eyes when she saw the animal grab Tarek by one of his legs and pull him towards the water, she began to retch. "Oh, please no!"

The peacefulness of the night was assaulted with the sound of splashing, thrashing and chomping. Unable to bear the repulsive racket, she plugged one ear, flashed the light along her route, and then sprinted towards the dock. Reaching the boat, she jumped inside and quickly untied it. With an oar in each hand, she pushed off and started to row, shaking and sobbing between each stroke.

The boat haphazardly inched its way towards the mainland as Davon fought to coordinate the thick bulky oars. She was making poor progress and several times the bow of the boat turned, propelling her in the wrong direction. By using one oar, she remedied the situation, but it seemed to be taking forever to reach the shore. She pushed each paddle deep into the water and then pulled back as she had seen Baboo do, but for some reason it wasn't working. Instead of gliding forcefully forward, the boat would abruptly turn one way or the other. Taking the oars out of the water, she rested them in the oarlocks and tried to breathe. Her heart was pounding and her eyes were clouded with tears. She blinked and then wiped away the moisture with the back of her hand. "You can do this," she silently whispered, attempting to empower herself. The sky was clear and the stars, now out in full force, twinkled above while the moon, much brighter than at dusk, glistened on the tranquil water. The rolling hills on either side of the River Nile folded themselves into dark shadows, creating an unnatural and eerie sight. What would have been magically breathtaking was totally lost on Davon, who was on the very edge of a breakdown. Wrapping her jacket around herself, she turned to see how far she was from the shore. Almost halfway, she told herself.

She gulped and pressed on, fighting the urge to lie down in the boat and let the current take her wherever it may. She discovered that by not pushing so deeply with the oars, but rather just lightly skimming the water, she was making progress. Finally, after what seemed like forever, she arrived at the beach. Jumping into the shallow water, she dragged the bow of the boat onto the dry sand as far as she was able, relieved to see the beach was still vacant of people and other crafts. Staggering up the hill to the car, she opened the driver's door, sat down and slumped over the steering wheel. She let herself cry uncontrollably for a few minutes. Although, still distraught, she dried her tears, started the vehicle and jamming it into gear, headed towards the main thoroughfare.

Almost at the turnoff near the camel's pen, she slowed the car and pulled over to the side of the road. Going into the trunk, she removed her wet shoes and socks and replaced them with sandals. She pushed the socks into the toes of the sneakers and tossed them into the ditch. Looking back into the trunk, she stared at Baboo's suitcase beside his electrical equipment. She knew she would not be able to take his belongings onto the plane, nor could she leave them in the rental car. After some deliberation, she hauled out all of his possessions and threw them down the embankment where they could not be seen from the road. She was well aware that the Egyptians living in this area were poor and knew if they found Baboo's things they would keep them to sell, not turn them over to the police. Returning to the vehicle, she flew by the camel pen and turned onto the main road.

CHAPTER THIRTY-THREE

Davon arrived at the very small airport and followed the two rectangular rental car signs, pointing the way to a tiny kiosk. Pulling up in front of it, she removed the papers from the glove compartment, grabbed her suitcase and got out of the car. "I am returning my rental car," she said to the middle-aged man, who exited the booth.

Taking the papers, he looked at her. "You are Baboo Bhat?" he asked her.

"Yes," replied Davon without blinking an eye.

"Okay. Sign here please."

Davon forged Baboo's name and handed him the keys. She then pulled up the handle on her suitcase and wheeled it towards the terminal. As she neared the glass door, she could see a group of men sitting at the one and only gate. Moving to the side of the glass, she peered around the rim and took another look, instantly recognizing one of them—the bodyguard of Adin who had accosted her in Luxor. A wave of rage rippled through her body and she felt her stomach lurch. These were the men responsible for Tarek's death! She heard them laugh as though they were on their way home from a great vacation and it made her feel physically ill.

"Would you like to enter?" asked the rental car agent, wondering

223

if she was having a problem with the door.

Startled, Davon spun around. "Oh, yes, in a moment," she answered. "Do you have any idea where those men are flying to?"

"A private plane will be taking them to Luxor."

"Thank you," she said, looking upset. "I need to buy a plane ticket, but I do not want to go into the terminal while those men are inside. Is there any other way to get to the ticket booth?"

The rental car fellow nodded, understanding that a single female would be nervous around a rowdy group of men. "Come with me, I will take you a different way." He led her to the side of the building and down a darkened alleyway. Stopping by a dimly lit lamppost, he used a key to open a metal door. He then indicated for Davon to step inside a storage room lined with all sorts of paper and equipment, and when she did, he followed her. "Maran, a woman is here to buy a plane ticket," he called in English. "Can you help her?"

A cleanly shaven, handsome young man appeared and smiled at Davon. "You need a ticket?"

"Yes, please," she replied.

With his hand on the door, the rental agent spoke to the young man in Arabic. Following the conversation, he looked at her and said, "My son will take care of you. Do not worry, you are safe with him."

"Thank you so much for your help," she replied as he exited. Turning towards Maran, she explained she needed to get to Vienna, Austria as soon as possible.

Maran thought for a moment. "The fastest way is through Cairo. There is a flight tonight, which leaves at 11:50. Wait here and I will check the computer for availability." He left and then returned a few seconds later with a stool. "Please sit here," he said with a grin.

Davon slumped down onto the stool, carefully placing her handbag onto the floor. She felt absolutely horrible and totally exhausted.

She knew she needed to block out the atrocities of the night, so that she could focus and make it to Vienna without breaking down. But, she couldn't do it. The memory of Baboo's last moments kept flooding back. She would never forgive herself for suggesting he put pressure on the wedged-shaped rock. Squeezing her eyes closed, she let out a soft sob. "I can't think about you until I get to Vienna or I won't make it, Baboo. I hope you understand," she said softly.

Maran poked his head around the corner. "I can get you to Cairo tonight. Then you will take a 6:00 am flight to Frankfurt and a 9:35 am flight to Vienna, arriving there at 10:40 am tomorrow morning. Are these flights suitable?" he asked.

"Yes, they are perfect," she answered with mustered strength, reaching into her purse for her passport and credit card. As she routed around for her wallet, the side of the handbag where she had hidden the statue started to collapse. Just as the top of the golden sun disk was about to be exposed, she somehow managed to grab the edge of the zipper, pulling up the side. That would have been disastrous, she thought, yelling at herself to be more careful as she handed Maran her documents. Zipping up the bag, she noticed a dirt smudge along the bottom of her pant leg. "Is there a restroom close by? I would like to change my clothes before the flight."

"The ladies room is in the main terminal. If you can wait another ten minutes the men you are concerned about will be gone. Their private plane has just arrived."

Davon nodded and forced a smile.

She stored her hand luggage and then settled into her seat at the very front of the plane. Thankfully, the flight was not fully booked. Maran had selected a seat for Davon with an empty seat beside it. Pressing her forehead against the window, Davon tried to identify her suitcase amongst the others on the cart, which the baggage handlers were now loading into the cargo hold. When she had exchanged her T-shirt and yoga pants for a pantsuit in the restroom, she had placed the statue into her suitcase, carefully wrapping it in clothes for protection. She was concerned about going through security with it in her carry-on luggage because the penalty for trying to remove an artifact from Egypt was prison for life with no chance of parole. She figured the Aswan airport was too small to have an x-ray machine for checked baggage and hoped Cairo did not have one either. Although the statue technically belonged to the Sanduu Corporation, she knew she would not have a leg to stand on if it was discovered in her possession.

The luggage was loaded and the ninety-minute flight took off on time. Pulling her headscarf across her face, Davon shut her eyes. Her anxiety level was high and she could feel her stomach churning. She would not relax until she was on her way to Vienna. She had checked her luggage from Aswan to Vienna with hopes it would be moved from plane to plane even though she herself would have to go through customs in Germany. If she had to collect her checked bag after each flight and take it with her through customs, the statue might be discovered. She thought about the inspection of checked suitcases at major airports where random bags were sometimes pulled from the conveyer belts and x-rayed, but convinced herself that even if Cairo did have an x-ray machine, her early morning arrival would probably mean it would not be running. Frankfurt was a different scenario. Ever since the escalation of terrorist attacks, security in Germany was tight. "Fretting about it is not going to help," she said quietly, "You are making yourself sick. Let it go, Davon and hope for the best." Pushing away all thought, she tried to focus on her yoga breath. Used to being able to snatch periods of thirty minutes here and there while doing long stretches of twelve to fourteen-hour shifts at the hospital, Davon somehow managed to fall asleep.

The loud and annoying dong, announcing the descent and urgency to buckle up and restore one's carry-on luggage, woke her. Readjusting her headscarf, Davon glanced out the window just in time to see the three pyramids of Giza, flooded in a ghostly bluish light. The image, beautifully haunting, seemed to call out, reminding her to be on guard. She was still in Egypt, traveling with contraband in her luggage.

The twin-engine plane pulled into the gate and she remained sitting until all of the other passengers deplaned. Then, tightening the knot on her scarf, she gathered her belongings and followed the line into the large open terminal. This was the last of the evening flights to arrive and once the passengers dispersed, she noticed there were very few people milling about. Making her way to the departure board, she located the Frankfurt gate. She had a four-hour wait. Tired and stressed, Davon sought out a private corner to clear her head and plan her next course of action. She sat down onto one of the dated hard plastic chairs and placed her carry-on bag on the chair beside her, knowing she had to come up with a scenario to get the statue to the hotel and into Abdul's hands. But as she attempted to strategically think of what she needed to do, her mind again started to detail and rehash the last moments of Baboo's life.

"Even though Baboo did not blame me, I know, it was my fault he died," she silently admitted, wiping away a tear. She felt as though someone was watching her and glancing up, she saw a lone male traveler on the other side of the room, staring. Standing up, she moved her possessions to a seating area behind a large column, which put her out of his line of view, and then without further adieu, continued with her one-way conversation. "Regardless of the facts, Davon," she told herself, "you cannot keep harping on this! You have to find the strength to move forward so you can finish the job. Remember, Abdul's life is now resting in your hands."

Davon looked at the time. It was 2:20 am. Making her way to a coffee machine near her seat, she selected two espressos and then downed the lukewarm, bitter tasting coffee. Within a few minutes, she started to feel more alert and spying an electrical outlet on the pillar near her row of seats, Davon pulled her computer and its adapter out of her bag and plugged it in. She needed to make a hotel reservation. Grabbing her cell phone, she removed the SIM card. The cell phone was completely dead, but she was concerned it might be traced to her or Baboo. She discretely tossed the card into one garbage can and the cell phone into another. Returning to the computer, she googled the Hotel Sacher Wien in Vienna and selected its webpage. Clicking on reservations, she booked one of the last mini-suites for a single night at nine hundred and forty Euros, guaranteeing it with her personal credit card.

"Expensive," she protested, as she finished the transaction, zooming in on the location of the hotel. "Now, I need to find a bodyguard firm."

She found several bodyguard agencies in Vienna and three in the general vicinity of the hotel. After exploring the home pages and reading the reviews, she emailed two of the three asking for evening appointments. Davon drummed her fingers on the keyboard, trying to decide how many bodyguards she would need to hire. She figured Adin would bring at least five or six of his men to the meeting, especially if Abdul accompanied him. So, to access Abdul, she would have to have more manpower than his brother.

She pushed her back into the seat, attempting to get comfortable and tried to picture the scenario. Abdul had mentioned the meeting was opened with the presence of the statue and a computer password, which meant he would probably be on a stage. She doubted Adin would allow his brother to go onto the platform alone. But, would he accompany Abdul or would Abdul be escorted by bodyguards? "If Adin knows Abdul does not have the statue with him; what is he planning?" she asked herself, wondering how the event tomorrow would play out. "Maybe he will just give up and let Abdul go because he can't keep him as a hostage forever or can he?" debated Davon, biting the inside of her cheek. She wished she knew more about the protocol of the meeting and wondered if she should check in as a delegate attending the day event or as a Sanduu Corporation employee. "That might not be a smart move," she argued, figuring she should attempt to stay under the radar until she was able to somehow get the statue to Abdul. "I'll just have to wait until I get to the hotel today. Hopefully, I can bribe a few people to give me the information I require."

Eventually, two employees arrived at the gate and announcements in Arabic and English were made. The boarding of her flight was about to commence. Shutting down the computer, she repacked it and headed to the restroom to freshen up. When she returned to the gate, she remained standing and stretched out her lower limbs with hopes of finding energy. She was mentally and physically drained and not sure how she was going to get through the next sixteen hours.

The flight was uneventful and Davon was able to doze for over an hour after the meal. She spent the rest of the time deliberating about what she was going to do when she arrived in Germany. She would be back in Western civilization, but would have to get through one of the tightest security systems in Europe, which used some of the most advanced screening technology anywhere. Frankfurt was a very large international airport and she had overheard her neighbouring traveler say the airport at present was on high alert. She prayed she would not have to claim her luggage before going through customs. If she made it through customs in Frankfurt, she would be safely in the Euro zone and would not have to go through customs again when she arrived in Vienna.

The plane landed at its snowy destination. Passengers donned heavy coats, scarves and gloves as they readied to deplane and Davon, following suit, pulled out her coat from her carry-on luggage. She wrapped her headscarf around her neck and followed the others out the door. An icy cold breeze blew past her as she walked along the jetway towards the terminal. She wore no gloves and although her hands should have been cold, she felt her palms becoming sweatier each time she looked up at the signs, directing the passengers towards customs. Don't appear nervous, she told herself, as she tried to flip into her stoic doctor mode. Wiping her hands on her pant legs, she readied her passport as she got into the custom's lineup and tried to think of anything, but the contraband in her suitcase.

Her face remained neutral as she handed the stern looking custom's officer her passport. He scanned the document and then looked her in the eye. "Miss Marshall, why are you visiting our country?"

"I am actually in transit and on my way to Vienna."

"May I see your boarding pass, please?" Davon gave him the boarding card. "It says here you have one piece of checked luggage. You need to collect your bag and go through security over there," he said, pointing to a screening area with at least one hundred passengers waiting to be processed.

"Oh dear," exclaimed Davon, ever so sweetly. "If I have to collect my bag, I will most likely miss my next flight. I checked it right through to Vienna because my connection was really tight. Is there any possible way you could excuse me, Sir. I am a physician and I need to get to Vienna this morning for an important meeting."

The custom's officer pursed his lips, looked at his screen and then back at her. "What type of medicine do you practice?"

"I work at Boston General Hospital in Emergency and Critical Care," she replied without hesitating.

He handed her back her documents. "My wife is in medical school. Have a good trip, Dr. Marshall."

"Thank you," she said as she moved through the kiosk. She could feel her heart pounding in her ears as she approached the departure board to check her next flight. She had received a free pass to move through German customs, but what about her luggage? Davon feared a customs official might check through it before it was placed onto the next flight. "I can't think about that now," she quietly reaffirmed as she followed the signs to the Vienna gate.

CHAPTER THIRTY-FOUR

Davon watched the snow settling on the tarmac as the plane pulled into the gate. The pilot had announced it was minus nine degrees Celsius, a dramatic difference from the thirty degrees plus temperatures she had experienced in Aswan. She hoped it would stop snowing because she didn't have boots, just a pair of black stilettos and her sandals, which she was now wearing. Planning to change into her shoes before she left the airport, Davon made her way to the baggage carousel to retrieve her luggage. She wondered if her bag had made it through Frankfurt and onto the Vienna plane. If her suitcase was detained in Germany, she would not be able to help Abdul. As she neared the baggage claim area, she noticed there seemed to be an unusual amount of security personal. Three officers with on-leash beagles were roaming in and around the large group of travelers, letting their animals sniff at pieces of luggage. Davon slowed her pace and observed the situation for a moment. They are looking for drugs and terrorists, not a golden statue of Ra, she reassured herself, as she proceeded towards the carousel with her flight number, flashing on a sign above it.

Diving behind a concrete pillar, Davon paled. "Shit, what is he doing here?" There standing at the very next carousel was Maxwell, casually waiting. The Boston contact was looking in her direction, but did not appear as though he had seen her. "Bastard," she muttered under her breath as she took another peek. "Obviously, he's attending the OPEC summit meeting. So, Abdul was right, he does work for an

American oil company!" When the carousel roared to life, she jumped at the noise, which startled the man beside her. "Sorry," she quietly squeaked. She gave the man an apologetic smile and stayed behind the post to keep an eye out for her suitcase while she watched Maxwell. She could not let him see her. The baggage from her flight as well as the baggage from Maxwell's flight started to make its way noisily down the chute and onto the rotating carousel. Can it get even more complicated, she thought, wondering where Maxwell was coming from and if he was staying at the same hotel. "What is he going to do if he discovers me at the event? I have to be careful," she whispered, thankful when she saw him reach for his bag and head towards the exit.

Letting out a big sigh of relief, she stepped away from the pillar, joining a small group of fellow travelers as they waited for their luggage. Although about forty suitcases had already come down the chute, her bag was nowhere to be seen. Davon made an effort to appear normal as a security fellow with a beagle passed by. His dog sniffed at several pieces of baggage and Davon realized this was at least the third time the officer had circled around. When he began to make his fourth loop around the carousel, her bag suddenly appeared at the top of the chute. "Thank goodness," she mouthed silently. She could hardly wait to grab her suitcase and get out of the airport.

As she waited for the bag to reach her, it was almost as if she could feel his eyes boring into the back of her head. She knew the officer and his dog were standing behind her. He spoke to her first in German, then in English when he realized she did not understand.

"Is that your luggage?" he asked.

Davon glanced at the bag before she turned around. "I think so," she answered. She failed to reach for it when it came near. With a shy half-smile, she observed the bag starting its second loop. Don't appear guilty, she warned herself, as she desperately tried not to look nervous. She smiled again and instead of openly chasing the suitcase, she discretely tried to inch her way towards it, distancing herself from the officer. To her horror, the officer continued to follow and when he was less than a foot away, he ordered the dog to sit. Davon stood rigidly, staring straight ahead. Her heart pounded and she feared the worst.

When her suitcase neared, the security officer suddenly reached for it. Placing it on the ground next to her, he extended the handle. "There you go, Miss," he said with a grin. "Welcome to Vienna."

Davon was flabbergasted, but somehow managed to say thank you. Taking the handle of the bag, she wheeled it towards the exit, wanting to get away from the security officer as quickly as possible. Not stopping to change out of her sandals, she left the secured area and headed right through the outside sliding glass doors.

Following the taxi signs, she came around a corner and saw there were about thirty people ahead of her. A cold wind nipped at her exposed skin and she yelled at herself for not getting out of her sandals when she had changed her clothes at the Aswan airport. I must look ridiculous, she thought, noticing that every other person was dressed appropriately. Spying several black limousines parked in a row across the roadway, she saw the chauffeur of the first vehicle, standing outside of his car as though he was waiting for business. Davon did not hesitate. Dashing across the street, she jogged right up to him. "Excuse me, are you for hire?"

"Yes Madame," he replied, popping open the hood of the trunk.

When he attempted to take her suitcase, she stopped him. "Please, I would like to have my bag in the back seat with me? I need to change my sandals. I just came from Egypt," she explained, feeling self-conscious about her bare toes, although the explanation was certainly not necessary.

The chauffeur nodded politely and opened the door to the backseat. Once she was inside, he placed the suitcase across from her and shut the door.

"Where are you going today?" he asked over the intercom as he started the vehicle.

"The Hotel Sacher Wien, please," answered Davon. Removing

her sandals, she massaged her cold feet and when the driver pulled into traffic, she unzipped her bag and pulled out a pair of tan knee-high nylons and the expensive black leather stilettos she had bought in Cairo. Putting them on, she discretely patted the statue to make sure it was still there, packed her sandals, closed the suitcase and then leaned back into the luxurious black leather. She was safe. At least for now.

CHAPTER THIRTY-FIVE

Within thirty minutes, she was at the hotel in the heart of Vienna's first district. The 1876 privately owned establishment was exceedingly grand. Definitely old world elegance, Davon thought, as the bellman took her suitcase and assisted her through the beautiful white marble lobby. She kept an eye out for Maxwell as she glanced at several of the charming rooms connected to the foyer. One in particular, the dark paneled library, seemed especially inviting.

As she approached the reception desk, she found herself fading. "I'm Davon Marshall. I have a suite booked for tonight," she said, straining to focus on the here and now.

The clerk gave her a welcoming smile. "Yes, good afternoon, Miss Marshall. Your suite is ready. May I please ask you for a credit card?"

Davon handed him her Visa. "There is an oil conference being held here tomorrow. I was wondering if I could get a copy of the agenda."

He glanced up from the computer and his expression was a look of disbelief. "A desk will be setup in front of the ballroom tonight for the delegates check-in. I believe the itinerary packages are given out then," he said, with a puzzled frown.

"I see," Davon replied. "I was just hoping the hotel might have a copy." She hesitated for a moment, wondering why he seemed shocked at the question. "Can I ask why you seemed surprised when I asked for an agenda?"

"I am sorry, Miss Marshall, I did not mean to insult you. I have worked at this hotel for nine years and have helped organize nine of the oil conferences. This is the very first time a female will be attending. I am actually pleased for you."

Davon laughed. "Well, don't be too glad. I am only here to help the male US delegate."

"Oh, so you are with Exxon Mobil. Shall I put your room on their account?"

"Thanks, but no. I have to pay for my own suite and then put it on my expenses." She looked at his nametag and then leaned closer as if she was about to share a secret. "I am going to level with you, Kurt. I'm brand new at this job and the boss does not even know who I am. I was told to get the agenda for the meeting and present it to him the minute he arrives. I really cannot wait until tonight to pick it up. You said you have organized nine of these meetings, are you sure you don't have tomorrow's agenda printed yet?" Davon smiled pleasantly.

Kurt returned the smile and his manner warmed. "Of course we have the basic agenda as we need to know what time to provide the beverages and food for the breaks, however, it does not have a list of speakers."

"I just need to present him with something when he gets here so it looks like I am doing my job. Please, can you help me?" she asked.

He pulled a sheet of paper from under the counter. "Give me a second. I will make you a copy." Turning around, he went through a doorway behind the desk.

In her suite, Davon lay on the bed, planning her next step. Although the oil barons started gathering sometime after eight-thirty, tomorrow morning, the actual meeting opened at nine o'clock. Kurt had confirmed her fear about female delegates, so trying to crash the meeting as a woman would fail. She realized there was no way she could sweet-talk or even bribe her way in. Middle Eastern men had strong convictions about women and business.

She wondered if the hotel used both sexes as waiters for the function. Picking up the phone, she called the front desk. "Kurt, I have looked through the agenda and I just want to thank you again for giving it to me. This is probably a silly question. I'm not quite sure about the protocol for the meeting. I know there are no female delegates but, am I allowed to be in the room while the meeting is taking place? I'm just thinking of a situation where I might have to get an important message to my boss."

"Unfortunately, Miss Marshall, I do not have an answer for you. I do know the organizers do not want any hotel personnel entering the ballroom during the meeting. Because the event is male dominated, we employ only male staff for the food service."

Davon cringed. "I see..."

Kurt sensed her frustration over the phone. "I did not tell you this Miss Marshall," he said, his voice becoming barely audible, "But, your boss, Mr. Templeton, has just checked in. He is on the seventh floor, suite 709."

"You are amazing! Thank you so much for helping me," said Davon, hanging up the phone. She flopped back down onto the bed and moaned. "What am I going to do now?"

CHAPTER THIRTY-SIX

Davon left the hotel and hurried down the street with the intention of flagging down a taxi once she was out of the doorman's sight. The hotel was a high-class establishment with several limousines for its patrons; it was not the type of place frequented by run-of-the-mill taxis. She had thought about ordering one of the limos, but she did not want anyone at the hotel knowing her destination. Although, it had stopped snowing, it was still cold. Pulling the collar of her jacket up, Davon clenched her fists and covered them with her sleeves. As she turned the first corner, she spotted what appeared to be a covered bus stop with a sign that looked like a taxi symbol. Only one person was standing under the canopy—a nicely dressed woman, wearing knee-high boots and a long winter coat.

Davon approached her. "Excuse me, do you speak English?"

"Yes," she promptly answered, "Can I help you?"

"I need a taxi and I am not sure how to get one."

"This is the right place and there is my taxi now." Davon glanced to where she was pointing. A white taxi was heading towards them. When it stopped, the woman opened the back door, said something to the driver in German and then motioned to Davon. "Please, take this taxi because you are not dressed for the cold. He will send another car for me."

Davon was amazed. "Thank you so much for your kindness!" she replied, jumping into the backseat of the toasty warm vehicle.

The driver dropped her at Wiener Leibwachter-Dienst, a bodyguard service in an exclusive part of the city. Davon entered the sleek-looking steel and glass building. After checking the directory, she took the elevator to the fifth floor. Locating the office, she walked in and approached the receptionist.

"I'm Davon Marshall. I have a meeting at four o'clock."

The receptionist stood. "Please come this way. Mrs. Schmidt is ready for you." Davon followed her into an office with an excellent view of the city.

The attractive, dark haired woman behind the desk stood and extended her hand. "Thank you for coming to see us, Ms. Marshall. I am Sabine Schmidt. Please have a seat and tell me what my company can do for you?"

Davon sat in one of the lime green leather chairs, taken aback that the owner was a woman. "I am attending a function tomorrow and will require seven male bodyguards for protection. At least one of them needs to be licensed to carry a firearm."

"All of our bodyguards are licensed to carry firearms," Sabine replied, jotting down the information. "At what time do you need them?"

"At eight o'clock tomorrow morning and I'll need them for at least twelve hours, perhaps longer. May I ask how your people are trained?"

Sabine handed her a brochure. "Every one of my bodyguards has martial arts training with a black belt or better. They are required to attend a shooting range on a weekly basis, which enables them to carry a registered semi-automatic pistol. I have never had a complaint from a customer and I have been in business for close to eight years. In the brochure you will see many positive reviews of the service."

Davon was very impressed with Sabine's professionalism. "Perfect. So, do you have seven men available for tomorrow morning?"

"Yes, I do. Where is the function being held?"

They discussed some of the basic logistics and Sabine suggested that one of the bodyguards be in charge of the team. "All of my bodyguards have some level of English, but Fritz speaks English very well. It might be best if you meet him right now to discuss your needs." When Davon agreed, she asked her assistant to call him in.

Davon glanced at her watch. "Not knowing how this meeting would go, I booked an appointment at five-thirty with Moz Bodyguard Service. Is it possible for your receptionist to cancel the appointment? I don't have a cell phone."

"Of course," said Sabine, buzzing her assistant for a second time.

A very buff young man with bulging biceps politely knocked on the door and then entered. "I heard you have an American client who needs to see me," said Fritz with a grin.

"Yes," replied Sabine. "This is Davon Marshall. She needs seven bodyguards for an event tomorrow morning."

Fritz held out his hand as he approached Davon, shaking hers with a firm grip. "I'm Fritz. I am pleased to meet you. With seven bodyguards, we need to discuss all of the particulars because it can be difficult to co-ordinate everyone," he advised.

"That is exactly why I called you," said Sabine, as Fritz sat down in the chair beside Davon. "Ms. Marshall, could you explain what you require from our service?"

Davon exhaled slowly. She wanted to give a simple explanation without too much background information. "I trust everything I tell you will remain between the three of us." She paused while they both affirmed strict confidentiality. "My story might sound a bit unusual," she started off, hoping to prepare them for the bizarre circumstances. "Tomorrow, there is a meeting of the oil barons at the Hotel Sacher Wien. The long time president of the group, Prince Abdul Sanduu, was apprehended five months ago. We suspect he will be brought to the event by the kidnappers because as the president, he needs to provide a computer password to open the meeting. I have been hired to grab him when he gets onto the stage and therefore require bodyguards to assist me."

"Okay," said Sabine, glancing at Fritz. "Just so you know, Ms. Marshall, I am required by law to report any crime that happens to come to my attention. Has the kidnapping been reported to the authorities?"

Throwing the 'simple explanation' idea out the window, Davon realized she was going to have to provide more information to get them to help her. "First of all, kidnapping is probably too strong of a word," she told Sabine, trying to lighten the situation, "and it occurred in Cairo, not Austria. The event came about because of a family squabble between two twin brothers. The younger sibling stupidly detained Abdul, with hopes of forcing him to relinquish power of their company. I have spoken to the Prince. He is content, has not been hurt and told me he will most likely be released once the meeting concludes. The problem is the younger brother, at this moment, is running the company and plans to complete the takeover of the organization at the meeting tomorrow. The only way for Abdul to regain control of his company is if I can help him."

"I know of the oil baron meeting. It is an all male affair. I do not mean to appear rude, but why were you, a female, hired to rescue him?" said Fritz, furrowing his brow.

Davon took no offence at the question. "I was hired because Abdul trusts me and only a few people can tell him apart from his twin brother," she answered. "I'm also very aware the meeting is an all male event and I have been toying with the idea of wearing some sort of disguise. All I need is a bit of assistance. Do you think you can help me without involving the authorities?"

"I guess your situation is in kind of a grey area. Will you or will Prince Abdul be paying the cost of hiring the bodyguards?" inquired Sabine.

"Prince Abdul will be paying," replied Davon assuredly.

"In that case there should be no problem taking you on. I will just put Prince Abdul's name on the invoice and you as the intermediary. Now in regards to the meeting, are you suggesting you might dress as a man to access it?" asked Sabine. "Because even if you are wearing men's clothing, I think seven bodyguards might attract attention. Do you know how many bodyguards an oil baron would typical have?"

"I don't know," answered Davon, feeling a sense of relief that Sabine was onboard. "I assume two or three per baron. The reason I asked for seven bodyguards is because I estimate the brother will personally have two and at least three to watch Abdul, and frankly, I want to have more bodyguards than him."

Fritz nodded in agreement and smiled. "The waiters at the Hotel Sacher Wien wear uniforms. We can put three of our team members in uniforms and they can pose as waiters along with you, Ms. Marshall. The rest of us can crash the party as bodyguards for...do you know the name of any of the attendees?"

"Yes, as a matter of fact I do. There is an American with Exxon Mobil attending. His name is Templeton. I have no idea if he will have a bodyguard. But, how are you going to get a hold of the hotel's uniforms?"

This time Sabine grinned. "My sister owns one of the largest clothing firms in Austria. I am certain she provides the uniforms for the hotel. Would you be willing to pose as a waiter, Ms. Marshall?"

"Please call me Davon. Posing as a waiter is fine, but I need something to cover my hair. I did notice the bellmen at the hotel wear hats," she replied, turning her head to show them her long ponytail.

"Even with a hat covering your hair, I fear you will still look very feminine," said Fritz. "We will have to sneak you into the ballroom though a back way. Sabine, can you pull up the floor plan of the Sacher Wien ballroom."

Sabine went onto the computer and within minutes was printing off the layout. She pulled her chair around the desk and sat between the two of them. "There are three main entrances to the front of the ballroom," she explained, pointing to the diagram. "And two emergency exits on each side, here and here, which would be alarmed, and it looks like this is the kitchen entrance on the left. The kitchen entrance would not be suitable to access the ballroom as it most likely would be heavily used by staff." She moved her finger to the stage area. This however, might be a back entranceway to the platform. It appears to come off of a wide hallway, which runs behind the kitchen."

"Do you think it will be alarmed?" asked Fritz.

"Probably," answered Sabine, nodding. "The hotel will turn off the alarm if the speakers want to access the stage that way. We just have to tell the hotel our speaker is entering through the platform doorway. In my opinion, this is the best way for Davon to get onto the stage unobserved."

Davon was fascinated by the discussion and stunned by Sabine's knowledge. "Can I ask how you were able to acquire a floor plan of the hotel?"

"Oh, I am sorry. I forgot to tell you I am also a licensed private investigator. I would have taken the time to let you know a little bit more about me if your event was not happening tomorrow," apologized Sabine.

"No worries, this is fantastic," said Davon, thoroughly impressed.

Sabine and Fritz continued talking and Davon listened to the discussion, thinking how fortunate she was to have found this agency.

"How will we know if the alarm to the platform door is turned on?" asked Fritz.

"The light above the door on both sides will be flashing red. When the alarm is disabled the light is off," Sabine informed him.

Fritz adjusted his position in the chair and thought for a moment. "When I get into the ballroom I will immediately check the alarm on the door. If it is on, I will have it disabled. Davon, dressed as a bellman, will have to find her way through the back hallway to the platform entranceway and I will meet her there, open the door and let her onto the stage," he said, turning from Sabine to Davon. "You will need to remain hidden somewhere behind the stage until the contact point. I suggest we also use the platform door to move the hostage. Now, at what time will the hostage be on the stage?"

Davon shook her head. "I really have no idea, but I assume it will be sometime between nine and nine-thirty as the meeting starts at nine o'clock," she said, realizing there might be another problem. "I just thought of something. The meeting will most likely be in Arabic. How are we going to understand when he is called onto the stage?"

"Sabine is there anyone at the company who speaks Arabic?" asked Fritz.

"I am afraid not. You will have to get Davon to a place where she can view the action and physically tell you when the target comes onto the stage. If we need to move the hostage, you will exit through the platform doorway and head here," she said, pointing to the route on the diagram. "You will leave through the kitchen's delivery entrance and I will have a van waiting for you." She looked at Davon. "If necessary we can bring the hostage to our office so you can make arrangements to move him out of the country?"

"Alright," Davon replied, anticipating that Abdul would probably want to immediately leave for the palace.

They discussed other particulars about the job, things Davon had not even thought of, and then while Sabine left to contact her sister about the uniforms, Fritz explained to Davon what she should say if she was challenged by anyone on her way to the platform doorway. "You must answer in German. Because you do not speak the language, I will make it simple. You will say I was told to come to the stage door and wait." He translated the phrase into German and asked Davon to repeat it, which she did almost perfectly.

"There is something I didn't mention," she said, feeling a touch guilty about the omission. "I have an object, a statue actually that I have to give to the president before we rescue him." Davon watched Fritz frown. "I know it sounds odd," she continued, determined not to give him any more information about the priceless artifact, "but Middle Eastern people have certain traditions and this is just one of them."

"In that case, I will change the phrase. You will say I was told to bring this package to the platform door." Davon practiced the new phrase and Fritz praised her accent. "Very good, you almost sound local."

Outwardly Davon appeared calm, but inside panic threatened. "Can I go over the plan one more time?" she asked. Fritz nodded. "Someone will bring the bellman's uniform to my suite tomorrow morning. At ten minutes to nine, I take the service elevator to the main floor, head towards the hallway behind the kitchen and then walk with purpose to the platform door. If the alarm is on, I will wait for you or one of the other bodyguards to disable it. If any hotel personnel detains me, I text you the number three on the cell phone that you will provide. Members of our team will have the number one printed on their left palm so I will know who to trust if pandemonium breaks out. If all goes well and I get through the door, I will meet you and two other members of the team, who will be dressed in black suits, backstage. We will wait there until the target is on the platform and then when I give the signal, we will move in, surround the target and immobilize the kidnapper's bodyguards. Our bodyguards dressed as waiters will cover us if we get into trouble. After I converse with the target, we will move him out of the ballroom and escort him back to the office." Davon took a deep breath. "It sounds so easy."

"We do things like this all of the time. It will be easy, don't worry," said Fritz, picking up on her nervousness.

"What if I can't find the right door? It is not like I can ask someone."

Fritz drew her attention to the floor plan. "The hallway behind the kitchen runs north, south and appears wider than the other auxiliary hallways coming off of it. The platform door should be distinctive, probably bigger than any of the other doors and it will have a light on the top of it. It is hard to tell from the diagram how far the doorway is from the kitchen, but it appears to be at least thirty meters away. These rooms here," he said, pointing to an area accessed from the hallway, "are most likely offices or dressing rooms, so be careful because there may be hotel personnel in the vicinity. Have you seen any females working at the hotel?"

"I just arrived in Vienna this afternoon. I only saw male employees at the hotel when I checked in."

"Well, the best advice I can give you is to act confident. People usually leave you alone if you look like you know what you are doing."

Just as Davon tried not to think of all of the things that could go wrong, Sabine proudly walked into the room. "Everything is set. Luckily, there are uniforms in stock. The hotel put in an order for ninety-five uniforms in various sizes. So, I can get the uniforms for the men, but there is nothing in a size four. She will have to make your uniform tonight, Davon. It will be delivered to your suite tomorrow morning at seven o'clock."

"Wonderful, thank you."

"Let's go over the final plans and I will give you a quick breakdown of costs," said Sabine as she handed Davon a preprogrammed cell phone.

CHAPTER THIRTY-SEVEN

Her heart raced as the service elevator zoomed downward. Trying to control her apprehension Davon focused on the blinking light on the control panel, flashing on and then off as the elevator passed between floors. Glancing at her reflection in the long wall mirrors on either side of the door, she wondered if she was going to be able to pull off the scheme. Her hair was twisted into a tight bun and she was dressed in the hotel's bellman's uniform, which was made out of a sturdy red serge. Gold piping ran down the sides of each pant leg and around the cuffs of the jacket. A matching red, pillbox hat with gold trim sat to the side of her head, its elastic strap securely fastening the odd-looking adornment under her chin. She bit the inside of her lip as she quickly scanned the outfit, stopping at the non-regulation black sandals upon her feet–the only suitable black footwear she had had in her suitcase. Although she wore the sandals with black socks, they looked completely out of place. Fritz had warned her to stand to the right and close to the elevator door with her gaze forward, so the camera, perched on the right side of the ceiling, could not get a clear view of her face. If anything went wrong, the first thing the police would do was look at the hotel's video surveillance footage.

As she clutched the hastily wrapped statue to her chest, she nervously clenched her teeth, trying not to make a sound. The elevator door opened and she stepped into a long hallway. Met by a cacophony of sounds coming from the dining room just off the main foyer, she skirted

247

the area, and headed towards the ballroom. She gave the ballroom entrance a wide berth, but glanced through the open doors as she passed. There were many white robed sheiks and men in black suits milling about.

"Abdul, you have to be here," she said under her breath, attempting to muster confidence. Swiftly turning left towards the kitchen's main hallway, she almost bumped into an elegantly dressed woman.

"Excuse me, do you speak English?" asked the woman, as Davon tried to pass.

"Pardon?"

"You do work here, don't you?" the woman snapped, as if to imply Davon was trying to get out of helping her.

"Of course," said Davon, taking a quick glance around. "What can I help you with?"

"Well," she replied, haughtily. "I have a number of complaints. We were promised a suite with a view and the view we were given is a parking lot! The suite, 1092, is certainly not up to my standards. My husband is a very important delegate attending the OPEC meeting. As he is presently at the meeting, he left me to deal with this outrageous oversight. I do not know what you were thinking, putting us in such a tiny suite at the back of the hotel. The room is just not suitable and I insist that you move us. I argued with the bellman who took me to the suite, but he pretended he did not speak English, so I set off to find someone who did!"

Positive she was an American, Davon felt embarrassed at the woman's arrogant attitude. "Thank you so much for bringing this matter to our attention, Madame. I assure you the other bellman did not understand your complaint. Not all of us speak English. I will notify Kurt at the front desk and if you proceed there immediately, he will move you to not only a larger suite, but to our best suite, which has a fantastic view." She smiled pleasantly and pointed her towards reception.

Satisfied with Davon's kowtowing, the woman quickly made her way there. "Sorry Kurt," Davon whispered. She knew the hotel was completely sold out.

Davon looked at her watch and cursed. It was almost nine o'clock. Glancing at the 'No Admittance' sign posted in several languages on the double door, she pushed down hard on the metal bar, opening one side. When she walked through the doorway, she was in a distinctly wider hall, but her dilemma was which way to go. The hallway was in the shape of a U and she was standing at the bottom of the curve. Choosing to move down the left side because the ballroom was on the left side of the kitchen, Davon realized she was going in the right direction when she passed three waiters moving large carts stacked with trays of food. She walked by them quickly, keeping her gaze forward. None of the men took any notice.

As she hurried past the kitchen's swinging doors, she took a peek through the glass. There were half a dozen yelling cooks and several waiters in smart navy uniforms—all too busy to notice a bellman in the hallway. Dashing in the direction of the platform door, Davon calculated the distance. "Fritz said thirty meters from the kitchen...about one hundred feet," she quietly said, pacing her way forward. As she passed the offices, they had seen on the floor plan, she saw they all had large viewing windows. This might not be good, she thought, when she saw some movement behind one of the desks. The door to the office opened and the occupant called out to her. Davon lowered her voice and repeated the phrase Fritz taught her, maintaining her speed. Looking up at the circular wall mirror, she observed the caller shrugging and returning to his office. "Good," she muttered, noticing the platform door was about ten feet ahead. Hurrying towards the oversized door with a non-flashing caged light above it, she twisted the handle. It was locked.

"What do I do now!" she cried, glancing at her watch. It was four minutes past nine. "The meeting has started and I don't have time to return to the ballroom's entrance." She pulled out the cell phone and was just about to dial when she heard a click.

The handle turned and when the door swung open, Fritz stood

before her. "Sorry, we had a problem turning off the alarm," he said as Davon stepped inside. "The meeting just started a minute ago and it is in English. A Prince Adin Sanduu is on the stage right now."

"The target is his identical twin," whispered Davon, as Fritz quietly directed her to the side of the stage. "Did you see another man in the room who looks like him?"

Shaking his head, Fritz pulled out his phone and texted the description to his men. "They can start scanning the crowd." He spoke softly and pointed for Davon to get closer to the edge of the curtain so that she could see the speaker and hear what he was saying.

"As Vice-president of our organization, I would like to welcome our guests from America, Russia and China. For your benefit, we will be holding the meeting in English. We are here to discuss the future of the oil industry, the dramatic fall in barrel price and the unbelievable suggestion from some world leaders that we should be limiting the production of our liquid gold," said Adin. "Our organization is based on tradition. For fifty-six years the president has opened the meeting by producing the statue of Ra and entering a seven digit code into the computer. As our members know, the statue of Ra is a sacred symbol to our tribes, representing not only power, but strength, ingenuity, and intelligence. The president must place the statue in the glass bulletproof case behind me," he explained, pausing for a moment to scan the crowd, "and not to do so," he said with emphasis, "means the instant loss of rank and title. Before I introduce my brother the President, I would like to let you know there will be an announcement later this morning about a long overdue change in the organization." Adin nodded and two bodyguards walked onto the stage with Abdul. "I now give you Abdul Sanduu, the President of OPEC," he said, stepping away from the microphone.

Davon's heart skipped a beat when she saw Abdul walk towards the podium. He was dressed in a black suit with a crisp white shirt and a light blue tie and although he looked handsome, his face appeared haggard as though he knew he had lost the battle. The bodyguards on either side of him stood rigidly at attention, very close to their captive.

"Whenever you are ready," whispered Fritz. "You and I will approach from here. Two of my men are stationed directly behind the target's bodyguards concealed by the curtain and a third is across the stage from us. When I give the signal, we will all walk onto the stage. Guns will be pressed into the backs of the abductor's bodyguards and they will be escorted off the stage and out of the hotel. I will remain with you and the Prince and my men on the floor will cover us if there is any trouble."

"The plan sounds good, but I want to wait until Abdul finishes the traditional opening of the meeting," answered Davon. She was positive Adin was planning to force Abdul out of the organization, thinking he did not have the statue. "Fritz, I might need you to call out Prince Abdul's name just before we walk onto the stage."

"No problem."

Abdul took his time adjusting the microphone and then slowly moved closer to the mouthpiece. "Welcome members and honored guests to our annual meeting in Vienna. It has been a challenging year. The impact of lower oil prices has affected every country worldwide and although some view it as a positive economic development, we know oil deflation causes instability in the stock market, devaluation of global currencies with the rise of the US dollar, and general deflation, which in turn can cause recessions. Commodities like copper, gold, iron and industrial metals decrease in value as the price of oil drops. Oil is our main export and revenues have been cut in half, yet our organization has chosen not to reduce the production of oil, which in turn would prop up prices. We have had this exact scenario in the past and cutting production stabilized the situation. Some members say not reducing production is a long-term strategy, which will weed out the small oil producers, thus assuring our place in the market for many years to come. But, while we wait for the small oil producers to fail, our revenues fall and our countrymen suffer—the poor, uneducated, and unemployed—all who depend on us to make sound decisions regarding our main export. We have always cooperated with other oil producing countries to maintain a fair market price. So what has changed? I fear my brother Adin has led you to believe that not reducing our oil production, as many other countries have already started to do, is the best option. Believe me it is not! I stand here today, as your President...

"To remain President," yelled Adin, abruptly standing, "you must produce the statue of Ra!"

"Please sit down, Adin," said Abdul, patiently.

Adin refused and leered at his twin. "You are not the president until you produce the statue of Ra and if you cannot produce the statue, I suggest you sit down, brother!" he loudly barked.

Abdul paled. "We are in the middle of an oil crisis. It is not the time to worry about traditions."

"Now," said Davon.

"Prince Abdul, one moment please," called Fritz from the side of the stage as he sent the texted takedown signal on his cell phone.

Abdul turned his head to the sound of the voice and watched as a man and bellman started to approach him. At the exact same time, a man moved forward from the opposite side of the stage and two heavily built men silently slipped through the curtain's opening and made their way to the bodyguards on either side of Abdul. Momentarily confused, Abdul frowned as he tried to understand what was going on. He glanced at the astonished audience and saw that their eyes, as well as the eyes of his now seated brother, were glued to the disruption on the stage.

"Get them out of here," said Fritz when he reached the hostage, motioning for his men to remove Adin's guards. He then stepped aside, so Abdul could see Davon.

"Abdul," she whispered excitedly. "I think this is something you need." She held open the brown paper parcel so he could see what was hidden inside.

Although his solemn face broke into a smile, he suddenly became teary-eyed. Davon understood he was completely overwhelmed with emotion. She wanted to reach out to him, comfort him, tell him everything was going to be okay, but she knew she could not, for a public act like this would embarrass him beyond redemption.

"Thank you," he said as he took the package. He refused to look Davon in the eye for fear of breaking down. Turning his back to the crowd, he struggled to compose himself as he carefully unwrapped the statue of Ra, opening the door to the glass cabinet to place it inside. Taking a deep breath, he then moved to a nearby side table where he entered a security code into a laptop. "Welcome, President Abdul Sanduu," voiced the computer, the sound amplified throughout the ballroom.

Abdul pulled a hanky from his pocket and dotted his eyes before returning to the microphone. Smiling at the crowd, he continued with his speech. "The meeting is now officially opened. Adin Sanduu mentioned that a long overdue change in the organization would be occurring this morning. As of today, I am officially announcing my brother's retirement as the Vice-President of Sanduu Corporation and CEO of OPEC." Abdul met the gaze of the scowling mirror image of himself. "He is now excused from attending this meeting." Fritz nodded to his men on the floor and they set upon Adin, jerking him roughly out of his chair.

Adin tried to shake off the hands gripping his arms. "Don't worry, I am leaving, but beware Abdul!" he said with a snarl, glaring hatefully at his brother as he was escorted to the exit.

Abdul pursed his lips as he watched his twin brother depart with the bodyguards Davon had hired. When the room broke into an uproar at the unforeseen event Abdul placed his hand over the microphone and turned to look at her. "How can I ever thank you? You have literally saved me once again, Davon. Please wait for me. The meeting will be over at four."

This time Davon looked confused. "I don't understand. Don't you want to get out of here?"

"It is my responsibility to run the meeting and rectify the damage Adin has done. Please, can you wait for me?" he pleaded.

"Of course I can wait for you, Abdul." She motioned towards Fritz. "This is Fritz, the team leader of the seven bodyguards I hired to protect you."

Abdul shook his hand and then smiled at the both of them. "Thank you so much for everything you have done. Now, I am sorry, but I need to run this meeting." He winked at her and then turned back to the microphone, saying something quickly in Arabic to calm the crowd before reverting to English. The audience responded with roaring laughter.

Davon and Fritz moved to the side of the stage. "I guess we will not be needing the getaway car. You should cancel it."

"Yes, I will call right away. Are you planning to stay on the sidelines for the rest of the meeting, Davon?"

"I don't think so. I refuse to be the only woman in the room. Besides, I think he is in good hands with you and your men. Guard him well and please let him know I am staying in room 603. Thanks Fritz, for implementing such a brilliant plan. It could not have gone any more smoothly!" She stuck out her hand and he shook it.

"It was my pleasure working with you," replied Fritz, walking with her as she headed towards the platform door. "I don't mean to sound forward, but if you are going to be here for a few more days I would love to show you around Vienna."

Davon gave him a smile. "Thanks, but I'm leaving town tomorrow. It was really nice working with you." Turning she made her way to the platform door and exited. Once the door clicked shut, Davon stopped in the empty, silent hallway and hung her head. Closing her eyes, she needed to make her peace. Instead of being ecstatic about her achievement in getting the statue to Abdul, all she felt was sadness. "You should have been here, Baboo. I'm sorry. I'm truly sorry about everything. I will call the police in Aswan the minute Abdul gets to my suite because I need his help. I just want you to know I haven't forgotten."

"Dr. Marshall!"

Davon snapped her head upright and turned toward the sound of her name. A grinning Maxwell was casually sauntering towards her. "What do you want?" she asked, curtly. She was tired and in no mood for playing games.

"What do I want? I want to know what the hell you are doing here. The American government trusted you and gave you a plane ticket, money and a Visa card to locate Prince Abdul. But, did you do that? No," he said with a huff, shaking his head. "Instead, you spent our money and sent us on a wild goose chase to Morocco. Now, you suddenly appear on the stage at the OPEC summit with Prince Abdul, and you have the statue of Ra in your possession! Tell me," he said with a sneer, "How did that come about?"

Davon was enraged. "Cut the bullshit, Maxwell, the American government, really? I know you work for an oil company." She wondered if he would try to stop her if she attempted to walk around him.

"You can't just take the perks, Davon, and ignore our deal. You have a lot of explaining to do." When Maxwell took a step forward, Davon took a step back. "Listen lady, you need to come with me. My boss wants to have a chat!" he roared, looking at her with contempt.

Her eyes locked with his. "I am not going anywhere with you. Back off, or there is going to be trouble," she threatened, trying to visualize how far the occupied office was down the hallway.

Maxwell's eyes went cold as he pulled a small revolver from his pocket. He aimed it at her. "I'm losing my patience. You had better come now. This way," he said, waving the gun in the direction he wanted her to head.

Davon felt nothing but raw fury. To have come this far, to have gone through what she had—all for this greedy imposter! There's no way he is going to shoot me, she told herself as she took a sideways glance at the platform door, which was about five feet away. Sprinting towards it, she lunged at the handle, yanking the door partially open. Maxwell, realizing she was attempting to escape, charged forward and slammed the door shut. A loud bang echoed down the hallway, but Davon did not even hear it. With a spark of rage in her eyes, she pounced upon him, wrestling him to the floor.

The gun dropped when they hit the ground. On his back with Davon straddling his chest, Maxwell fought her off, desperately struggling to reach for the weapon while Davon attacked his reaching arm with vigor. Stretching out a leg, she attempted to kick the gun further away; the only thought running through her mind was to gain control of the revolver. Recognizing he was dealing with a mad woman, Maxwell forgot about the gun and redirected his attention towards Davon. Reaching up, he slapped her with the back of his hand, hard, across the face. The blow stung and for a second Davon was stunned. Using the moment to his advantage, Maxwell shoved her backwards, hoping to smash her head against the wall. However, Davon did not fall backwards; she pivoted sideways, flipping off him, onto the side where the gun was lying. Scrambling up as quickly as she could, she tried to reach the gun before Maxwell, but he was already standing and running towards it.

"Freeze, or I will shoot!" yelled a male voice. "Hands up!"

Maxwell skidded to a standstill and raised his hands. "It was just a friendly squirmish," he said, slowly turning around to see who was reprimanding him.

"Are you alright, Davon?" Fritz asked, noticing from a sideways glance her crumpled hat, lying on the floor next to her, her disheveled hair, and ripped jacket.

"Thanks Fritz, I'm fine. Just a bit shook up," she answered. Walking over to Maxwell's gun, she picked it up. "Fritz meet Maxwell."

"What do you want me to do with him?"

"I'm not sure," replied Davon. Skirting around Maxwell to join Fritz, she handed him Maxwell's revolver and then whispered, "He was my contact in the States, but things went sour and he cancelled my contract. Just before you got here, he was trying to force me to go somewhere with him and that led to the struggle."

"If you need me to detain him for twenty-four hours without your involvement, I can have him locked up for carrying a weapon. I am sure it is not registered in Austria. My brother works for the local police department and he is on duty tonight."

Davon thought about the suggestion. "I think that might be for the best. It will give me time to get out of town. By the way, how did you know I was in trouble?"

"I heard the platform door slam a couple of minutes after I saw you leave. I thought I should investigate," Fritz said, pulling out his cell phone. Making a call, he spoke in German. "My brother will be at the backdoor of the hotel in three minutes. I will take Maxwell through the kitchen. Are you going to be alright or should I call one of my men?"

Davon smiled. "Really, I'm okay. Thank you, Fritz."

"This way Maxwell," Fritz said, ushering him towards the kitchen.

She watched them leave. Picking up her hat, she attempted to punch out the numerous indentations. Quickly straightening her hair, she shoved the hat onto the side of her head, pulling the string tight under her chin. "Now," she exclaimed, letting out a frustrated sigh, "Hopefully I can get to my room without any further interruptions." Brushing the dust off her uniform, she started to make her way down the long hallway.

CHAPTER THIRTY-EIGHT

Sitting in an ornate petit-point chair, Davon fidgeted. She had changed into the sleeveless black dress she had purchased in Cairo and because it was cool in the room, she had put on stockings, which felt uncomfortably tight across her upset stomach. Crossing and uncrossing her legs, Davon shifted her weight forward in the chair and back again, letting out a throaty sigh. It was not going to be easy to say what she planned, but she had made her decision. Glancing at the antique clock for the hundredth time, she jumped when the doorbell rang. She dashed to the door and then skidded to a stop, pausing for a second to take a slow deep breath. Pushing a piece of blonde hair behind her ear, she pulled the door open. There stood Abdul with three bodyguards standing beside him. In his hand was a large bouquet of pink roses.

Abdul handed Davon the flowers and then turned to look at the men. "Please wait here for me. I will not be long." Quickly entering the room, he closed the door. "My love, you are the most amazing woman!" he said with pride, softly kissing her cheek. He pulled her close and kissed her again, this time on the lips.

It was a soft, sensual kiss and Davon felt as though she was melting. "The roses are gorgeous, thank you," she said quietly.

"The flowers are nothing," he replied with a wave of his hand. "I have ordered the corporate jet to come and pick us up. When we get home I am buying you the largest diamond..."

"Abdul, stop, I cannot go home with you." Turning her gaze to the floor, she refused to look at him. She was tired, thoroughly spent and switching into doctor mode where there was no emotion, only facts, was at this moment a very difficult thing to do.

His vanishing smile was replaced with a look of concern. "Come and tell me about it," he said, instantly taking charge. Seizing the flowers, he placed them onto a nearby table and then ushered her towards a luxurious sofa positioned in front of the bay window. Lifting her chin, he looked into her cornflower blue eyes.

"I don't even know where to begin. Oh Abdul," she whispered, her lower lip quivering.

"Well, as you once told me, start at the beginning."

Davon sighed as she tried to systematically recall the events. "In Luxor, you told me we should find Jafar and get him to help us, but we could not find him anywhere. Our only hope in helping you was to search for the statue on our own."

Abdul wrinkled his forehead and stared at her in disbelief. "Do not tell me you found the statue on your own! How was that even possible?"

"Believe me, it was close to impossible. Finding the tomb and figuring out the riddle...I really don't even know how we did it, but somehow things just kind of fell into place. The horrible part is..." stuttered Davon. She suddenly felt as though she couldn't explain. Her chest was heavy and her throat tight. Tears streamed down her cheeks.

"It is okay, you can tell me what happened," said Abdul, gently. Reaching out, he pulled her towards him.

Davon leaned against his chest and fought to collect herself. She needed to tell the story to relieve the heavy burden of guilt she was carrying. "Oh Abdul, it was awful. There were two deaths on Agilkia

Island. Tarek, the guard of your great grandfather's tomb, was murdered by someone looking for the statue and my partner, Baboo, died when the wedge-shaped stone at the back of the tomb slipped out of place and fell on him." Once she started describing the details, it was as though the floodgates had opened. Her story came rushing out. "Baboo's death was my fault because I told him to put pressure on the rock so we could open the door, but the worst part is I had to leave his body there. I wanted to go to the police for help, but Baboo warned me before he died that they would hold me for questioning. I needed to get the statue to you and so I had to leave him, although it broke my heart. I will never get the picture of him lying there out of my mind. I should have phoned the police yesterday when I arrived in Vienna, but I didn't know if they would understand English and I still had to make the arrangements to get the statue to you." Her head dropped to her chest. "I'm such a horrible person!"

"Hold on. You are not a horrible person! You are wonderful and kind and loving and none of this is your fault—things happen," said Abdul, interrupting her. "I am sorry you had to go through this terrible incident, but try not to think about it anymore, my love. I will take care of everything. I will call the Aswan police right away. I know the Captain there."

"Wait!" she exclaimed, when he started to stand. "I need to tell you something else. I protected Baboo's body by closing the gate to the crypt, but Tarek was killed on the beach and I saw a crocodile pull his body into the water." She let out a small moan and shook her head as if to expel the memory from her mind.

Abdul could tell she was badly shaken. "You are going to be okay. I am here now," he said, hugging her tightly. "But, I have to call Aswan right away because it is getting late. Baboo's family also needs to be notified, do you have any contact information for him?" he gently asked as he pulled out a cell phone.

"Baboo doesn't have any family. He asked me to take his remains to Alexandria. His dying wish was to be cremated with his ashes sprinkled in the sea."

"You have been through quite a lot," said Abdul, stroking the top of her head. "But, please know I will take care of everything, including Baboo's funeral arrangements. You never have to go back to Egypt again."

Davon took a tissue and wiped her eyes. "I want to go to Alexandria and be there for Baboo's funeral. It is the least I can do for him."

Abdul carefully pushed back a golden strand of hair from her forehead and kissed the top of her head. "As you wish, my love," he said, transfixed on the beautiful woman in his arms. He knew he could never deny her anything.

The Police Captain in Aswan assured Abdul that he would personally take a boat to Agilkia Island and investigate the scene. Abdul explained the circumstances to Davon. "I think it will be a few hours before he can get back to me. We should eat. Are you hungry?"

"I can't even remember the last time I ate."

"Well then, I will order something for the both of us."

Abdul ordered room service and when the bellman arrived with the meal, he sent the bodyguards, stationed at the door, to the restaurant for dinner. As the bellman set up the table and chairs, Abdul could not help but smile. Moving towards Davon, he said quietly, "You looked much better in the hotel uniform than this fellow."

Giving him a quick smile for his attempt to lighten the situation, Davon chuckled softly. "You know darn well why I had to wear a uniform to your meeting," she replied, some of her old bravado returning. "The members of OPEC would have had a fit if I had shown up in this." She pointed to her black tailored dress.

"You are absolutely right and brilliant to have figured out a way

261

to personally get the statue to me!" Tipping the bellman, he closed the door. "Can I escort you to the table?" Davon took his arm and let him pull out her chair. After settling himself in his seat, he leaned forward. "While we eat dinner let's talk about something cheerful. You love working as a physician, tell me why it means so much to you."

Her eyes locked with his. "As long as I can remember I always wanted to be a doctor. One Christmas, my parents gave me a toy medical kit. I filled it to the brim with bandages and carried it everywhere, tending to the neighbourhood's skinned knees and elbows. I gave out candies as medicine and as you can imagine, I had no lack of patients. I went through elementary and high school, knowing what I wanted to be and worked hard to get good grades so that I could pick the university I wanted to attend. I finished my degree with honors and received a partial scholarship to attend medical school. When I graduated, I worked in Emergency and Critical Care, and found that being in the hospital is what I absolutely love," she said, cutting a small piece of chicken and taking a bite.

"Then how was it that you ended up at the palace?" asked Abdul, listening with interest.

Davon knew she had to tell him the truth. "It's bizarre really," she said with an embarrassed laugh. "I was dating a great guy, who I thought was going to ask me to marry him, but instead he broke it off. I was furious and immediately went onto the computer to look for a job as far away as possible. I applied for the position at the palace, Bedon hired me and the rest is history."

"If I ever meet this fool, I will have to remember to thank him," said Abdul, taking her hand. "You are not only extremely beautiful, you are intelligent, trustworthy, kind-hearted, adventurous, and the list goes on and on. It is my luck this fool broke up with you because now we are together."

"I feel the same way," said Davon, silently cursing fate for introducing her to another incredible man where a relationship was impossible!

The phone rang and Abdul stood to answer it. Unable to understand the Arabic conversation, Davon silently ate the rest of her dinner. Taking Abdul's empty plate, she tidied up the table and then grasping the handle of a glistening silver urn, she poured two steaming cups of coffee. With one cup in each hand, she moved the china mugs to the coffee table. Making herself comfortable on the sofa, she waited for Abdul to finish the call.

When the conversation ended Abdul hung up the receiver and turned to look at her. "The Police Captain boated to Agilkia Island to inspect the scene. They have to bring in special equipment to remove the rock covering Baboo's body. Until the equipment arrives, which should be later tonight or tomorrow morning, I have asked for a guard to remain onsite. I told the Captain to make arrangements to send Baboo's remains to Alexandria for cremation as quickly as they are able."

"Oh, thank you so much, Abdul!" Standing up, she went over and hugged him. "You have no idea what a relief it is to deal with this." She was thankful Baboo's body was found unmolested.

"Come and sit, there is more to tell you," said Abdul. Steering her back to the sofa, he took her hand. "I am sorry, but there was no trace of Tarek's corpse."

"I guess I didn't expect there to be," she whispered, her face becoming pale as she recalled the gruesome scene.

"Listen to me. After I arrive in Dubai, I will send the corporate jet back to Vienna to take you to Alexandria. Once you have taken care of Baboo's request, I will fly you back to the palace. We need to sort out our future, Davon."

Davon looked into his dark brown eyes and felt as though she couldn't breathe. He was gorgeous, charming, loving, understanding and incredibly rich, but he had nineteen wives and the volatile, erratic, and tense life he led, never stopped. She gently pulled her hand away and reached over to pick up her coffee cup. Fiddling with the handle, she attempted to find the right words. "Abdul, you are absolutely amazing. You are kind and thoughtful and I love being with you, but although I have explored every which way that we could make our relationship work, the reality is, a future together is just not possible."

"How can you say that? I love you and I know you love me. We have been through so much together. We belong together. I feel it deeply in my heart," replied Abdul.

The way he looked at her, she knew his heart was breaking, but there was no going back. Somehow, she had to explain. "You must understand. We were born and raised in different parts of the world. Our values may be similar, but our cultures are poles apart. Your life is unpredictable. I was with you in Cairo when there was an assassination attempt on your life and then the next thing I know—you are abducted by your insane twin brother. There were murders and deaths in the short time I worked on your side of the world, and frankly..."

"And that is precisely why I want you to come to the palace. I can protect you there. I will take care of you. I can give you anything you want. You will never have to work again."

"You really don't understand," Davon said, suddenly raising her voice. "What I want is to be free, free to make my own choices, free to work as a doctor. I do not want to be locked up with your other wives, waiting for the last Thursday of the month to go shopping in Dubai. Working as a physician in a hospital setting is what I was meant to do, it is extremely important to me and I will not give it up, for you or for anyone else. I am sorry, Abdul, because I really do love you," she said, wishing with all of her heart that the reality of the situation was different. "I will be returning home, to Boston, right after the funeral. I hope you understand why I must do this."

"Yes, you have clearly explained your reasoning," he said softly, his face full of sorrow. He looked at her with pleading eyes. "Davon, is there any way you would consider being friends? I could come to the States every so often and maybe we could plan to meet in Europe sometime."

Davon huffed. "No Abdul. I will never be a mistress! It is just not who I am."

"So marry me then. I have told you this before. I will make you my first wife and will promise to never sleep with the others again. Please, I beg you to consider my offer."

Davon crossed her arms and gave him an amused stare. "If I agreed, I would have to live somewhere in the Middle East where polygamy is legal. Thank you for asking, but my answer is still no. In my culture, you only have one wife and one husband. I'm not good at sharing, especially with someone like you," she said, as though she had been offended by the idea. "I think the best scenario is to just part ways. We must make a clean break and promise never to contact each other again." Although she was already dreading their last goodbye, she was determined to be steadfast in her decision.

Abdul realized she was serious. "I will not fight you on this issue because I know your mind is made up," he politely said, standing. "May I ask you for one last kiss?"

Davon jumped up and wrapped her arms tightly around him. Their lips met and the kiss was deeper, more passionate—an electrifying kiss she felt throughout her entire being, a kiss she knew she would never experience again.

Their lips slowly parted, but Abdul refused to release his grasp from her waist. "Keep the cell phone Fritz gave you in case there is a problem and you need to get a hold of me. My cell phone is also from Fritz and is linked to yours. I will cover all of the bills, including the cost of the funeral, the security company, your hotel in Alexandria and your flight home." He leaned back his head and looked directly into her eyes. "You have done so much for me, Davon, and I want desperately to give you something in return. Tell me your heart's desire and anything you want, is yours."

"Thank you for thinking of me, but you don't need to give me anything, Abdul. I did what I did because I wanted to help you."

"I will not take no as an answer. There must be something you want," he replied, unconvinced by her refusal.

She leaned her head against his shoulder and thought for a moment. "Well, actually, there may be two things you can do for me, now that I think about it." Standing up straight, she gave him a warm smile.

"Name them and they are done."

"To convince Baboo to switch alliances, I offered him ten thousand dollars. Without his help, I would have never found the statue. He had no family, but he did have a close friend in Luxor, who really could use the money. Would it be possible to give Baboo's pay to him?" she asked, cautiously. "I thought I would call and invite the friend and his wife to attend the funeral and I'm sure they will come. I could give the money to them in Alexandria."

Abdul smiled from ear to ear. "A wonderful idea. I will have a bank draft sent out. What is your second request?"

Davon became excited at the possibility of her second request being fulfilled. "Well, I'm not even sure if this is possible, but I had a servant at the palace named Bin, who was like a second mother to me. She was old, arthritic and absolutely wonderful. I loved her, Abdul. I really did," she said becoming teary-eyed. "One day, I came home from the clinic and she was gone. Raja had replaced her with another woman and refused to say where she had sent Bin. Every day, I think about her and worry she is having trouble surviving. My one regret about leaving the palace was not finding her and taking her with me to the United States. If you could find Bin and take care of her for the rest of her life, it will be the best gift you could ever give me."

"I will find her, Davon. But what about you? I want to give something to you," he insisted.

Davon stood on her tippy toes and kissed his cheek. "I do not want or need anything else."

CHAPTER THIRTY-NINE

The ringing phone woke her from a deep sleep. Sitting up, she reached across the king-size bed and picked up the receiver. It was her automated wakeup call. As the memory of the last twenty-four hours came rushing back, she let out a wounded groan and then threw her head against the padded headboard, getting a glimpse of her disheveled image in the full-length mirror. "Let it out, Davon! Get over him because you know marrying Abdul would never work. He has nineteen wives and you are not about to be number twenty! You could never be part of a harem, it is just not who you are. Besides, his life is too volatile and dangerous! You're a doctor and you get enough excitement in your life working in Emergency. You don't need this type of drama. Have a good cry and then put him out of your mind! You absolutely made the right decision to completely break off with him and you know it!" She slumped down in the bed and flung the bed sheets over her head. "But, I really love him and I love being with him. I need to talk to someone. I need to talk to Meg," she decided, looking at the digital clock on the bedside table.

She figured it would be around 3:00 am Boston time and it was a school night, but she knew her sister would forgive her for calling. Putting the call through the hotel switchboard, she finally heard the ring.

"Hello," said Meg sleepily.

"Sorry for waking you up, but I desperately need some

reassurance that I'm doing the right thing."

"Davon, is that you? Where are you?"

"In Vienna."

"Oh, so you weren't lying about the tour. Mom is convinced you are up to something," replied Meg with a yawn. "When are you coming home?"

"Soon, but I didn't call you about my flight arrangements. I'm in love."

"What! Who is he? Where did you meet him?"

"Mom was right, but don't tell her, I wasn't on a tour. I went back to Cairo to look for Prince Abdul."

"Okay, this is absolutely crazy. Tell me what is going on!"

"When I get home I'll fill you in on the details, but I did find him," she said with baited breath. "You see, I was sort of involved with Abdul before he disappeared. He wants to marry me, Meg!"

"What! Now, I'm awake! Have you said yes?" she exclaimed, sitting bolt upright in bed.

Davon hung her head. "I said no, but I'm having second thoughts. He left last night for the palace and I cried myself to sleep. I feel sick about the decision because I really do love him, Meg. He is an amazing man, the most wonderful, kind, and loving person I've ever known."

"Okay, settle down, Davon, and remember that you are an incredible and smart woman yourself. You need to trust your decision. I can't see you becoming part of a harem."

"I know. I just feel sad about the whole situation."

"What are you going to do about Matt? He called Mom and told her he was really worried about you."

"I'm going to call him right now and let him know our relationship is over. I can't string him along anymore. Sorry again for waking you up, but I really needed to hear your voice," Davon said with a sigh.

"You can call me anytime, Sis. Are you going to be okay?"

"Yeah, I feel better already. Please don't say anything to Mom and Dad. I should be home in a day or two. I'll email you my flight information."

"When I pick you up, we can talk more about it. Just remember, you will get through this. Love you," said Meg.

"Love you too," replied Davon, disconnecting the call.

Hearing her cell phone beep, she got out of bed and went into the living room. Picking up the phone, she noticed a text. It said the corporate jet was waiting for her at the Vienna airport. While she was reading the message, the cell phone rang.

"Hello."

"Davon, it's Fritz. I just sent you a text, but I wanted to let you know that Prince Abdul has asked me to accompany you to Alexandria. I will be coming to the hotel to pick you up. How much time do you need?"

"I need at least an hour, but really you don't need to come with me to Alexandria, Fritz. I can manage perfectly well on my own."

"I am sure you can, however, Prince Abdul gave me specific instructions and since we are using his jet and I am still on his payroll, I think we should do as he asked. Do you feel comfortable having me accompany you as your protection detail?"

"Yes, of course," she said, feeling a touch awkward at the news. "It will be nice to have company on the trip. I'll check out of the hotel and will meet you downstairs in the lobby."

"Alright then, see you at ten o'clock."

Davon put down the cell phone and frowned. She had planned to call Matt right after she had talked with her sister and knew she needed to do it before she chickened out, but now, within less than sixty minutes, she needed to shower, pack, grab something to eat, and get to the hotel lobby. It's probably best to call Matt when I get to Alexandria, she told herself, rationalizing she really did not want to wake him up at 3:30 in the morning. Going back into the bedroom, she threw her suitcase onto the bed and then hurried into the shower.

CHAPTER FORTY

When the corporate jet landed at the Alexandria airport, it stopped on the tarmac beside a customs official and a waiting limousine. Davon gazed up at the brilliant turquoise sky, dotted with large white cotton-ball clouds, as the official politely stamped their passports. The sun, which suddenly peeked out from behind an enormous ball of fluff, offered warmth, and Davon, glad she was away from the harsh weather in Austria, reveled in it. With the paperwork completed, the official helped them into the back seat of the vehicle and Davon, who had hardly spoken since their departure from Vienna, turned to look out the window.

Although Fritz had left her to her own thoughts during the flight, he now needed her attention. "We have reservations at the Sheraton. I have investigated the area and the hotel is near the Hindu Temple where the body is being sent," he remarked, glancing at her. "I have been asked to tell you that you have an appointment at 4:00 pm today with the Hindu priest, who is called a Pandit."

Davon nodded slowly, thankful, as Abdul had promised, all the arrangements for Baboo's funeral had been made. "I wonder when the body will get here," she said, hoping it would arrive this evening so she could organize the funeral for tomorrow. "I still have to notify some of his friends in Luxor about the accident and want to ask them if they would like to attend the funeral. If they do, I need to book flights for them."

"Is there anything I can help you with?" asked Fritz.

"Not really. I'm not even sure what I'm supposed to do. I hope the Pandit will let me know."

Fritz reached into his pocket. "The pilot handed me this when we landed and asked me to give it to you."

Recognizing Abdul's handwriting on the front of the crisp white envelope, Davon looked inside. Her sober face broke into a radiant smile. The envelope held a cheque, not for ten, but for fifty thousand US dollars made out to Fatar and Nasa Kazemde.

They arrived at the five star hotel and as Fritz and the driver managed the luggage, Davon went over to the reception desk to check in. She was functioning on autopilot and was having difficulty making sense of anything. In some respects, the last two and a half weeks were a blur, yet the death of Baboo was not only crystal clear in her mind, it remained at the forefront.

"Dr. Marshall, it is an honor to have you staying with us. Your suite is on the top floor of the hotel and is our best. If you can wait one moment, the manager is coming to take you up to the suite."

"Thank you," she answered politely, not really caring about her suite or where she was going to spend the night. Making her way towards the center of the lobby, she met Fritz.

"Wow, this is quite the place," he said, enamored by the spectacular facility. He put down the piece of carry-on luggage he was holding and looked at her. "Are you okay, Davon?" he asked in a tone of concern.

From a distance, she looked stunning. Dressed in an off-white suit with a high-buttoned jacket, which was simply adorned with an orange silk scarf, Davon could have easily fit in with the display of exotic flowers directly behind her. However, once close enough, one could not help but notice her deathly unhappy expression.

She eyed Fritz as though his concern was completely unfounded. "Yes, of course, I'm fine. I'm just waiting for the manager. He is going to show me to my suite," she quietly informed him.

"Alright," Fritz replied, convinced she was in a state of depression. "I have arranged for the driver to pick us up in forty-five minutes. Can you be back down in the lobby at three-fifty so we can get to your four o'clock appointment?"

"No problem," answered Davon in barely a whisper, just as a grey-haired gentleman, wearing a well-made navy suit, approached her with an outstretched hand.

CHAPTER FORTY-ONE

At precisely four o'clock, Davon paused at the entrance to the Hindu Temple to admire the interesting facade at the front of the building. Attached to a plain-looking brick structure were two extremely orate, cone-topped entranceways. She gazed up at the tall steeples and their five-tiers of intricately carved lacework, all intertwined with a unique display of carved figures. The figures appeared to depict the numerous aspects of human life and she noticed the same type of images were carved into the solid wooden door, she was now approaching. Pulling on the brass door handle, uniquely made in the likeness of a tree branch, she opened the door and walked into the foyer.

A pleasant looking woman, dressed in a lovely green sari, greeted her. "Welcome. May I help you?" she asked in perfect English.

"Yes, thank you. I have an appointment with the Pandit to discuss funeral arrangements."

"Miss Marshall?" she questioned. When Davon nodded, she smiled and pointed to a hallway, running along the side of the building. "This way, please. I will take you to his office."

The woman led her down the long hallway to a tranquil office at the back of the temple and offered her a chair. "Please be seated. The Pandit will be here momentarily."

Davon sat down and as she did so, she took a quick survey of the room. The furnishings were simple other than the elegant floor to ceiling bookcase located on the back wall. It was full of thick, leather bound books and had several statues of a chubby body with four arms, sporting the head of an elephant. I believe that is the image of one of their gods, she thought, as she heard someone enter the room.

"Miss Marshall, I am the Pandit of the temple," a short elderly man said, quietly shutting the door.

Davon rose to shake his hand. She looked at him and suddenly became emotional. He reminded her of Baboo with the same soft features, calm reassuring smile, and jovial twinkle in his eye. "Thank you for meeting with me," she answered, trying to stymie the urge to weep.

"It is my pleasure. Please be seated and when you are ready, tell me how you are related to the departed?" he said, offering her a moment to grieve. Walking around the desk, he took his seat and quietly waited.

Dabbing her eyes with a tissue, Davon composed herself. "Baboo has no family and although we are not biologically related, in some respects, he was like a father to me. He was the most wonderful, gracious, humble man," she said with a sigh. "As he was a Hindu, his dying wish was to be cremated with his ashes dispersed in the sea and since he was raised in Alexandria, I wanted his body to be brought here."

"Yes," said the Pandit, "it is only right. Are you also of the Hindu faith?" he asked politely.

"No, I am not a Hindu."

"Hmm," muttered the Pandit. "Are you aware of our traditions around death?" Davon looked at him and shook her head. "The body, which arrived at our Temple just moments ago, will be cleansed tomorrow according to tradition. Then the religious ceremony or funeral will be held on Sunday at 11:00 am followed by the cremation. The ashes will be collected afterwards and will be given to you the following day for dispersal in the Mediterranean Sea. I am very sorry to tell you this," he said gently, wanting to be as frank as possible, "as a non-Hindu, you will not be able to attend the ceremonies. On the morning of Monday, March 6th you may return to the temple for his ashes."

Davon was taken aback. "I understand the rational about not being able to attend the funeral service, but I was hoping it might be possible to have him cremated tonight," she said, wanting to return to the United States as soon as possible. The Pandit smiled, but did not immediately respond to the request and she suddenly realized her plan to have the cremation this evening, the dispersal of the ashes Saturday morning or afternoon and a flight home Saturday night, was not going to work. It is only an extra day or two, she told herself, trying not to be more disappointed than she already was about not being able to attend Baboo's funeral ceremony.

"I am afraid all of our ceremonies are usually held on Sunday. You see, my child, everything has a time and a place," he quietly said, standing. Realizing the meeting was over Davon slowly rose from her chair. The Pandit made his way to the door, opened it and began to escort her down the hallway. "I sense you are having difficulty dealing with Baboo's death."

"Yes, very much so," Davon said, feeling a deep sadness within. "It wasn't his time, he shouldn't have died." The guilt she felt was almost unbearable.

The Pandit stopped in front of the elegantly carved wooden door and then turned to look at her. "It was his time, Miss Marshall," he stated with great confidence, his words oddly comforting. "The gods in their wisdom have a plan for everyone in the circle of life. Death like birth is a part of the circle. This is not a time to judge or question, it is a time to celebrate, for in our faith, Baboo's faith, death is not the end, it is a new beginning."

CHAPTER FORTY-TWO

Davon sat in bed and gazed out the window. The sun had been up for over an hour and with her panoramic view of the ocean, she could see a large cruise ship making its way to port. She fiddled with her hair and glanced at the clock for the tenth time all the while debating, whether or not to phone Matt. She knew Alexandria was seven hours ahead, which meant it would be midnight in Boston. Matt was early to bed and early to rise and she chastised herself for not waking earlier to call him.

"It is probably better to call now because if I wait until this afternoon or evening it will be in the middle of his work day," she mumbled, as she picked up the bedside phone and placed the call.

"Hi Matt, it's me," she said, when she heard a grunting hello.

"Davon, where are you? I've been going crazy with worry. You said the end of February and it is now March the fourth," he dramatically pointed out. "I called your parents about five times and finally had to stop because I was upsetting your mom!"

"Sorry, but really Matt, I'm only a couple of days late."

He ignored the excuse. "Are you alright? When are you coming home?" he asked, anxiously.

"I'm fine and I will be home in a few days."

"What time does your flight arrive? I'll pick you up. Just let me get a pen."

"Matt, we need to talk," she said, calmly. She bit her lip, feeling her courage faltering.

Her words hung in the air for a few seconds before he softly replied, "Okay, I'm listening."

Davon gulped and then plunged right in. "Although I've tried to recapture the old me, the Davon you loved a year ago, it has been impossible. I've changed, Matt, and there is no going back. The nine months I spent at the palace were both wonderful and horrible and even though I did not share much of what went on there with you, it wasn't because I didn't want to, it was because some of the memories were just too painful to remember. I needed to take this trip to face those demons, to finally grow up, and figure out what I really want from life, and I am happy to say that now, I know what I must do." Her voice quivered and she worried about how to explain her position without crushing his spirit. "I realize this whole episode has been very hard on you and for that I'm sorry with all of my heart. Please believe me. When you broke up with me last year, I was devastated. It took me a long time to come to terms with not being with you, but now I finally understand what you did then was for the best. You were right, Matt, we do not belong together. We are two completely different people with different ideas and different dreams."

"Where is this coming from?" Matt asked with an exasperated sigh.

Davon paid no heed to the question. "What I am trying to tell you is that you are a great guy, Matt, but this time I want to end our relationship. You will always hold a special place in my heart and I hope one day we can be friends."

"Davon, please do not do this! Don't do something you are going to regret. You drive me insane sometimes, but I love you and I want to marry you. I was stupid to break up with you last year," he shouted. "Let me pick you up when you get home and we can sit down and talk, really talk. I can tell you are upset and I know you're not thinking clearly right now."

"You're wrong, Matt. I am thinking very clearly and I have never been so certain about a decision. I'm sorry I had to tell you about this over the phone, but I've made up my mind and nothing you say or do will change it. I wish you the best the world has to offer because you are a very special man. Goodbye Matt." Davon did not wait for a reply; she put down the receiver and then slowly made her way towards the window. The cruise ship had docked and as she watched the crew struggling to secure the boat to the pier, she brushed away her tears.

CHAPTER FORTY-THREE

Fritz sat across from Davon at the breakfast table. He watched her spread strawberry jam onto her toast, break off a small piece and politely raise it to her mouth. She chewed slowly and appeared to be enjoying the taste of her food, but it was hard to tell because she had barely spoken a word since they had been seated. Dressed in a white linen sleeveless top she looked like an angel with her perfect features and blonde curly hair. He tried not to stare. Taking a sip of coffee, he attempted again to start a conversation. Every time he broached a subject or asked a question, she would politely answer, but then would quickly return to her world of silence.

"Are you always this quiet?" he finally inquired, remembering she had been much more outspoken during the assignment at the Hotel Sacher Wien.

She looked at him, her deep blue eyes, assessing. "Forgive me, Fritz, I am not quite myself. The last few weeks have been horrendous. I'm really looking forward to going home."

"Were you close, I mean, the man, who passed away? Was he a relative?" he asked, thinking if she talked about his death, she might be able to come to terms with it.

"No, we were not related, we were business partners. I was with him when he died." She unconsciously shivered as she recalled the excruciating painful night. "I'm here because of his dying wish. He requested for his ashes to be sprinkled on the Mediterranean Sea, following his cremation." Fritz leaned forward and nodded, silently encouraging her to continue her story. "The Pandit told me I should not feel sad. In the Hindu religion, death is not the end, he said, it is a new beginning. Of course, this is because Hindus believe in reincarnation. The problem is I'm not sure if I do." She did not want to explain to Fritz. It was not just Baboo's death, for which she blamed herself, but that she had broken up with Matt only hours before, and the most heart wrenching fact—the one she was struggling desperately to come to terms with—was that she knew she would never see Abdul again.

Fritz nodded in understanding, his eyes locking with hers. "Hinduism is an interesting religion. I guess for those believers it is easier to accept death if you consider it is a new beginning."

Davon's solemn looking face transformed and for the first time Fritz saw an impish grin. "Only if you were a good person before you died," she said, breaking the tension in the air. "Because who knows what form you will come back as, if you were not."

"Well, I am sure your business partner will return as something wonderful," said Fritz, joining her with a chuckle. He was glad to see the light return to her eyes. It made her even more beautiful.

"Yes, he will. I know it!" she exclaimed, whole-heartedly. She picked up her fork and attacked her breakfast with a new surge of energy.

This time, Fritz laughed aloud, pleased his ruse had helped her open up. "You mentioned yesterday that you cannot acquire the ashes until Monday. I was wondering if you would like to do a bit of sightseeing this afternoon and tomorrow. I can order a car."

Her fleeting grin, once more, was replaced with a serious expression. "I don't know. I need to make a few phone calls and book my flight home. To be honest, I'm not really up to sightseeing right now," she said, noticing the response was not what he expected. "However, please feel free to do whatever you want this afternoon."

Concerned about her frame of mind, Fritz looked her in the eye. "It may not be my place to say anything, but I have noticed that you seem to be really depressed. Instead of isolating yourself in your suite all day and all night, stewing about your troubles, would it not be better to get outside to get your mind off things?" He could tell by the look on her face his words had an effect, however when she pursed her lips as though she was upset, he tried a different approach. "I am sure if you had a patient, who was isolating themselves because of a devastating event, you would advise them to make an effort to get back to a normal routine, get out and socialize with other people, would you not?"

Davon let out an agonizing sigh. She was well aware of the signs of post-traumatic stress. "You're absolutely right, Fritz," she said. "I can't let the events of my past ruin my future. Organize some sort of tour this afternoon and I promise I will be there."

Back in her suite, Davon pulled Fatar's business card out of her wallet. She tapped the card against a side table as she prepared herself for the conversation. Baboo's cause of death, she recognized, would open up a Pandora's Box full of questions. Although she did not want to lie to Fatar and Nasa about how he died, she realized she would face an interrogation if she told them the truth. She would have to alter the facts to soften the blow and as a doctor she knew just how, but the downside to the scenario was that the cards were stacked in their favor because they had known Baboo for many more years than she had. She would have to be careful. Picking up the cell phone, she dialed the number.

"Fatar, it is Davon, Baboo's niece. I am afraid I have some bad news," she said, instantly coming to the point of the phone call.

"Davon? What is it?" Fatar asked with a slight hesitation in his voice.

Davon understood the news would come as a complete shock. "Perhaps, you should sit down Fatar," she suggested.

She heard some shuffling noises in the background. "I am sitting now. What has happened?"

"I am so sorry to tell you this, but Uncle Baboo has passed away."

"Passed away? How can this be? What happened? Where are you?" he asked, breathing hard.

Davon looked at the floor and said the words she had intentionally planned. "His heart failed him, but I was with him as he was dying. He asked me to sprinkle his ashes on the sea in Alexandria and I am here, in Alexandria, now."

Fatar let out a worried gasp, said something in Arabic and then quickly reverted back to English. "Nasa and I will come right away. You cannot deal with this tragedy on your own, dear child," he said in a fatherly voice.

"Please do not worry. I am fine, Fatar. A friend has helped me make all of the arrangements. There is nothing left to do. I am just calling to ask if you and Nasa would like to attend the sprinkling of his ashes on the sea, which will occur on Monday morning. I can pay for your flights and for your hotel."

Fatar hotly dismissed the suggestion of a young woman shouldering the cost of their trip. "I cannot have you paying for us. We will drive and stay with Nasa's sister, who lives in Alexandria. I am able to get a rental car at a good price from my friend. Where will we find you?"

Davon sat down on the edge of the bed and frowned. Although she was worried about the long drive, she probably would not be able to convince him to fly. "I am staying at the Sheraton Hotel. But, please listen to me, Fatar, it certainly must be a very long drive. Will you not consider flying?"

"It is only 860 kilometers, which takes approximately ten hours. We have made the trip many times before. Sunday, we will leave at first light and God willing we should arrive in Alexandria by six or seven pm."

"Alright, I will expect you tomorrow. Would you please be my dinner guests at the hotel restaurant? I can make a reservation for eight or eight-thirty," she said, before adding, "Will that give you enough time to drop off your luggage at your sister-in-laws and get to the hotel?"

"Yes, yes. We will be at the hotel at eight o'clock Sunday night and are most anxious to see you. God bless."

"Drive safety," said Davon, grateful the conversation had gone better than she had anticipated. As she ended the call, her thoughts turned to the fifty thousand dollar money order Abdul had made out to them. She wondered if Fatar would refuse to take the money.

Scanning through the numerous flights leaving Alexandria on Monday afternoon, she finally found one that would get her to Paris, giving her an hour and a half to change planes for a direct flight home. Booking the flight, she filled in the required information and paid for it with her credit card. As she jotted down the reservation code, she felt the crushing weight of everything that had happened. She sat almost motionless, staring at the screen. "What exactly is going on with me?" she asked, thinking she should feel happy to return home, to a city and a job she loved. She refused to second-guess her decision about Matt because she knew that was not the problem and although Abdul was ever present in her mind, she prayed the pain of losing him would heal over time. "I think I'm afraid to face Mom and Dad," she said, feeling disheartened. "The best scenario will be to move in with Meg until I can get my own place because it will be impossible to live with Mom after she finds out I broke up with Matt. Dad will be supportive, but Mom, no way." She shook her head. Considering she would not be able to totally avoid her parents once she got home, she resigned herself to the fact that after the initial shock and the predictable interrogation, which she knew would quickly follow, her parents would settle down.

She entertained the thought of moving to another state. She was not running away from her problems this time, she just needed a fresh start. She thought about California and the offer she had received from UCLA Medical Center after she had graduated. If she had received that offer as a brand new physician, now with all of her experience, she was even more hireable. It would be nice to get away from Boston's harsh winters and the timing could not be more perfect.

Going to the UCLA Medical Center's website, she looked at the job postings. There were twenty-three positions she could apply for, but was this what she really wanted? Shutting down the computer, she decided to wait until she got home. She had money—lots of money—so there was no need to rush back to Boston General. Getting up, she told herself to get a grip and then reached for the phone.

"Yes, can you connect me to room 920, please?" She waited for him to answer. "Hi Fritz, I'm ready to go."

CHAPTER FORTY-FOUR

A driver and a young male guide picked them up at the hotel and escorted them to the famous library of Alexandria for a tour, and then to the Montazah Palace and gardens, Fort Qaitbey, Stanley Bridge, Pompey's Pillar and the Temple of Serpeum. It was a whirlwind of sightseeing and it was close to dark by the time they were taken back to the hotel.

"What time are you coming tomorrow morning, Karif?" Davon asked the guide as she got out of the air-conditioned vehicle.

"We will be at the hotel at 9:45 am. Tomorrow we will explore the Kom el Shoqafa catacombs, which open at ten o'clock and then we will go to see the Abu al-Abbas al-Mursi and El Qaed Ibrahim Mosque and the Deir Mar Mina Monastery," he explained. His face then flushed pink and he let out a small hum as though he was trying to search for the right words, before he suddenly blurted out, "All women entering a mosque must wear a head covering. Would it be possible to bring a headscarf for tomorrow?"

Davon realized he was embarrassed by the request. She knew female foreigners visiting the more popular touristy areas usually did not wear head coverings and that was the reason she had not worn a scarf today. "Yes, I can bring a scarf," she said to his apparent relief, not informing him that she already had a scarf in her bag. She smiled and tipped him with a US ten dollar bill. "I enjoyed the day very much, thank you."

"I did too, thanks," added Fritz, as they turned and walked into the lobby. "Are you planning to have dinner in your suite again tonight?"

Davon stopped and turned to look at him. "I actually was," she said with a guilty frown, "but since you pointed out the fact this morning that I have been acting like a hermit, I will do better. Would you like to have dinner with me in one of the hotel's restaurants?"

"That would be nice. Which restaurant would you like to go to?"

"Why don't you pick the restaurant and then I will eat at the other one with my friends tomorrow night. One serves Persian food and the other French."

Fritz smiled. "I'm not one for spicy foods, so I opt for the French restaurant."

"Great," replied Davon as she turned to get into her private elevator. "See you at the French restaurant at seven."

Davon inhaled the delicious aromas permeating the restaurant as she stood in the doorway and waited to be seated. She was glad she had had the forethought to make a reservation because the restaurant was extremely busy. Saturday night, she thought, making a mental note to make reservations for the following night. The maitre d' took her to a private table situated beside a window with an amazing view of the harbor.

She gave him a quick description of Fritz, as he pulled out her chair. "I'm ten minutes early, so he might not arrive until seven o'clock," she told him.

"May I offer you something to drink?" he asked, folding his hands neatly behind his back.

Davon shook her head. "I will wait for my guest, thank you."

As she stared at the lights dotting the coastline and at the large well-lit ships in the bay, an unexpected feeling of aloneness overcame her. It had been less than three weeks since she had left Boston, yet somehow it felt as though she had been away for much longer. She took in a deep breath and slowly exhaled. "So much has happened," she murmured to no one in particular, her world of despair returning. She thought about Baboo and desperately tried to let go of the guilt regarding his death. She considered what the Pandit said about the circle of life and remembered that even Baboo, in his final moments, had not blamed her for the accident. "Still, if it was Baboo's time, why did he have to die such a horrible death? He was a good person," she complained to the twinkling stars in the dark sky. "Life is so precious. You would think as a doctor I would be used to death, but I don't think I will ever get used to it."

"Used to what?" asked Fritz as he took a seat on the opposite side of the table.

Davon looked up. "Oh, nothing. Sometimes, I like to talk to myself—bad habit," she said, feeling somewhat foolish. She sat up straight, determined to be in good spirits while she was dining with him. "I was just thinking in less than forty-eight hours we will be home." It suddenly occurred to her that she wasn't aware if he had booked his flight. "Have you organized your flight to Vienna?" she asked.

"Everything has been arranged," replied Fritz, diverting his eyes. Picking up the menu, he offered no further comment about the time or date of his flight.

Receiving the message, loud and clear that he did not want to talk about his flight home, Davon lifted her eyebrows and then following his cue, picked up her menu. I guess his schedule is none of my business, she thought, realizing it was between his employer and him. Refusing to take umbrage at his briskness, she decided to change the subject. "I recall you have a brother in Vienna. Do you have any other family members there?" she asked.

288

"Only my brother and his family. He has three young children. My parents live in Salzburg, where we grew up," he replied in a more engaging manner, glancing up at her with a smile.

"I have heard Salzburg is a beautiful city," she said, just as the waiter came to take their order.

They decided to have the special—escargot and French onion soup to start, pan-fried sole as an entree, and crème brulee for dessert.

"And would you care for wine with dinner," questioned the waiter.

"I will have a glass of red, please," replied Davon.

"A glass of white for me, please," said Fritz. The waiter nodded and moved away from the table. "I am surprised they serve liquor in Egypt."

"Liquor is only allowed in the tourist areas," she informed him.

"Hmm. Where did you grow up, Davon?"

"We lived in a lot of different places around Washington DC and Virginia. My parents relocated to Boston when I was about ten years old and we have been there ever since," she explained, suddenly thinking she was glad Fritz had encouraged her to have dinner in the restaurant. "Before I forget, I would like to thank you for coming with me to Alexandria and for persuading me to get out of the hotel today."

"You don't have to thank me."

Davon waited until the waiter finished placing the glasses of wine onto the table. "I do have to thank you, because although you are getting paid for the assignment, you went above and beyond. I have been miserable ever since we got here," she admitted. "However, the tour this afternoon did take my mind off of things."

"Well then, from this point forward, I wish you better days," said Fritz, lifting his glass.

"To better days," echoed Davon, tapping her glass to his.

CHAPTER FORTY-FIVE

The catacombs were located in Alexandria's western necropolis. The driver pulled up to the side of a large courtyard and through the car window, Davon noticed a group of tourists, standing in front of a Roman-styled temple. "I guess we're not the first ones to arrive," she mentioned as they got out of the vehicle. They made their way towards the group and walked around several decorated and plain stone coffins. "Are these from the catacombs?" she asked, pausing to examine one of the more intricate looking ones.

"No, these stone vessels are from the Valley of the Kings. But, there are three coffins on the second level of the catacombs, which remain in the place where they were carved because they are extremely large," replied Karif. He turned his attention to the other tour guide, who had to raise his voice in an attempt to organize his rowdy group, and then stepped closer to Davon and Fritz so they could hear what he was saying. "While they are getting organized I will tell you about the tomb. It was built in the 2nd Century AD and was rediscovered in 1900 when a donkey hauling a cart full of stones fell through the entrance shaft. It is made up of three levels with a maze of rooms and hallways, however the bottom level is inaccessible due to flooding. The catacombs are carved out of solid rock and hold a mixture of Egyptian, Greek and Roman elements, which I will point out once inside. Archeologists believe it was used to intern the dead for over two hundred years and the remains of three hundred people were found upon its discovery," he explained. Glancing up, he watched the group ahead of them walk into the tomb. "We can now go inside."

Davon entered first, followed by Fritz and then Karif. Once her eyes adjusted to the dim light, she could see the opening of a wide round shaft tunneled down into the rock. A slender, unusual looking stone spiral staircase, running along the outer wall, led to the chamber below. There were a few tiny windows carved into the exterior sides of the upper walls to illuminate the area, albeit poorly. Davon peered over the edge of the shaft and saw the last few tourists from the previous group, venturing downwards.

Coming to stand beside her, Karif pointed into the shaft. "Historians believe the bodies of the deceased were lowered down through the middle by a pulley system as it would have been awkward to carry the corpses down the narrow spiral staircase." He motioned her forward. "Whenever you are ready, we will go all the way down to the second level and then make our way up, as the other group is already exploring the first level."

Slowly, Davon began to descend. The air smelt dusty and stagnant. When she reached the bottom of the ninety-ninth stair, Karif directed her to a small passageway and then towards a rather large underground temple. Pausing at the doorway, Davon examined the matching Egyptian-styled columns with capitals decorated in papyrus and lotus leaves. She then turned her attention to the walls on either side of the door with their carvings of two extremely well preserved cobras, balancing large sun disks on their heads. "The columns and the cobras are definitely Egyptian," she said, glancing into the chamber.

"Correct," answered Karif. "But, once you are inside the antechamber, I think you will be surprised to see the Greek and Roman influences incorporated into the Egyptian art."

Stepping inside, she saw two rectangular niches on either side of the room. They held carved figures of men and women with Greco-Roman styled heads and typical Roman fashioned hair from around the first Century.

Davon noticed and pointed it out to Fritz. "I would say the depiction of the face is Greek, while the hair, to me, looks Roman."

Karif laughed. "Very good, Dr. Marshall. Now, let us proceed into the main chamber," he suggested, pointing out the bearded serpents on either side of the doorway. "Here again, we have snakes, but these cobras represent a Greco-Roman divinity. They hold a caduceus—a symbol of death—and yet ironically, they wear the double crown of Upper and Lower Egypt." Davon stared at the caduceus, which was similar to the insignia of medicine. "Above them is a shield with the head of Medusa, a protector, based from Greek mythology. Its purpose was to discourage grave robbers."

They made their way inside the poorly lit chamber and Davon was surprised to see three large, highly decorated sarcophagi, taking up most of the space in the room. She glanced from the stone coffins to the walls, noticing they were completely covered in reliefs. The reliefs looked similar in style to the ones she had seen at Philae Temple and in Luxor. "These reliefs appear to be Egyptian, except..." She turned around. "...for the ones you see as you exit the room." Walking towards the doorway, she examined the relief on either side of the door. "I'm not sure who this represents, but he appears to be dressed as a Roman legionary."

"Correct again, Dr. Marshall. This is the Egyptian god Anubis, the protector of the death. In both reliefs he is depicted in Roman dress, however here, you can see he has the lower body of a serpent."

After they explored several of the hallways containing locili or small chambers where the bodies—mummies or cremated remains—had been placed, they made their way up to the first level, passing the tour guide and tourists from the other group.

"I have a question," said Fritz. "You mentioned that some of the bodies found had been cremated. Why were they not mummified?"

Karif stopped walking and looked at him. "Remember we talked about a meeting of three different cultures with three different religions. Alexander the Great in 331 BCE founded Alexandria and in 80 BCE the city was conquered by the Romans and held for close to seven hundred years. This produced a blending of the three cultures. The Greeks believed in inhumation or burial, the Romans cremation and the Egyptians mummification."

"Interesting," commented Fritz, "and we understand this from the art work in the tomb?"

"Precisely," replied Karif.

"The history of Egypt is so incredibly fascinating," said Davon, smiling. She felt good—almost her old self again.

Karif was pleased they were enjoying the day. "We are now going up to the first level of the catacombs. I will take you through the rotunda and into the triclinium or dining hall. This is where family members and friends of the deceased would gather to have meals, remembering the departed."

They continued to make small talk and were close to their destination when they heard a blood-curdling scream, followed by a crying plea for help. All three of them broke into a run. Jogging towards the voice, they headed to the triclinium area. When they entered the spacious chamber, they saw a woman frantically shaking a man, who was lying on the floor.

Davon skidded to a stop and fell to her hands and knees. "I'm a doctor. What happened?" she asked as she felt for the man's carotid pulse.

"My husband, Andy, didn't feel well so the guide told us to wait here and then he collapsed," blubbered the woman between hysterical sobs. She stood over top of Davon, hovering.

There were no signs of life or a pulse. Davon ripped open the man's shirt, sending buttons flying in all directions and then quickly gave him thirty chest compressions. Tilting back the man's head, she plugged his nose and gave two breaths. Immediately switching back to giving chest compressions, she calmly said, "Karif, call for an ambulance, please."

"I have to go outside for the cell phone to work," anxiously shouted Karif as he turned to leave.

"What can I do, Davon?" asked Fritz, wanting to help.

"Move the wife away, please, I need more room," she replied in a monotone, instantly returning to her count as though there had been no interruption.

Fritz tried to console the wife as they watched Davon continue CPR. Suddenly, the man took a breath and opened his eyes. Davon leaned back onto her heels and smiled. "Welcome back, Andy. You had a heart attack. I need you to remain still until the ambulance arrives."

"Where am I?" he asked in a groggy voice.

The wife pulled away from Fritz and rushed to his side. "We're in Egypt. Remember you weren't feeling well. You collapsed, love," she softly said, lifting his head to put her purse under it. "This doctor saved your life."

"Thank you," mumbled Andy, eyeing Davon.

Davon pulled her stethoscope out of her bag. "Let's have a listen to your heart and then we will cover you up until the ambulance arrives," she said, warming the end of the stethoscope with her hand before she placed it onto his chest. She took in his skin color as she listened, pleased to see a pinky tone returning to his cheeks. "Your heart sounds are pretty good, but you will need to be admitted to the hospital for a couple of days," she informed him, buttoning up his partially torn shirt. "Do you have travel medical insurance?"

"Yes," replied the wife. "I have the card in my wallet, but we are on a bus tour and have another week to go," she explained, as she placed her jacket over her husband, tucking it around his shoulders. "I hope that is not going to be a problem."

Davon frowned, not wanting to be the bearer of bad news. "I'm afraid you aren't going to be able to finish the tour. Your husband needs to be hospitalized for observation and tests and when he is discharged from the hospital in Alexandria you will need to get him home for a full medical checkup."

The wife looked shocked. "Do you know what the hospitals are like here?"

"That, I do not know," answered Davon, thinking about Egypt being a third-world country. "Where are you from?"

"Toronto, Canada."

"Oh, you are a long way from home. The most important thing is that Andy is stable before he gets onto the plane," she told her, now concerned about the care the Canadian would receive in an Egyptian hospital. Turning around, she looked at Fritz. "Can you please go and see what is happening about the ambulance?"

"Sure thing," he replied, dashing from the room.

Davon smiled at Andy and then reached under the jacket to take his wrist pulse. "If you like, I could go with you to the hospital, but just as a patient advocate. I'm an emergency room physician at Boston General, but I would not have any medical privileges here."

"That would be wonderful," exclaimed the wife, appearing somewhat relieved.

"Yes, it would be very reassuring to have you with me, Doctor...I don't even know your name," said Andy, attempting a smile.

He tried to sit up, but Davon stopped him. "Stay still, Andy. My name is Davon Marshall." The introduction was interrupted when Andy's tour guide casually strolled into the chamber.

"Is Andy alright, Mona?" the guide asked, looking surprised at the sight before him.

Mona glanced at Davon and waited for her to explain. "Andy

collapsed. An ambulance has been called to take him to the hospital."

The tour guide appeared distressed at the news. "I am afraid I cannot go with you to the hospital because I have to stay with the tour, but perhaps I can meet you there later tonight," he said, quickly adding, "Tomorrow morning, we leave for Cairo."

"Don't worry about coming to the hospital, Hamin," said Mona. "Dr. Marshall is coming with us, but you are going to have to take us off the tour. I will call you tonight when I get more information."

Hamin slowly nodded as he processed the information and then walking over to Andy, he squatted down beside him. "I wish you all the best and will pray for a quick recovery." After saying his goodbyes, Hamin left.

"Do you have any possessions on the bus?" asked Davon.

"I don't think so. All of our luggage is at the hotel," answered Mona.

A few seconds later Fritz jogged into the room. "The ambulance should be here in about five minutes, but I don't think they can get a stretcher down the spiral staircase. It is much too narrow." He grimaced as he made eye contact with Davon, hinting that they were going to have a huge problem getting Andy out of the catacombs.

Davon felt Andy pulling on her sleeve. "I can walk. I'm actually feeling pretty good."

"No," she quickly said. "Any physical exertion could trigger another heart attack." She looked Andy over. He was about 5'9" and was not overweight. "Could we carry him, Fritz, fireman style? How much do you weight, Andy?"

"I weight around 175 pounds."

They heard a racket in the hallway and Karif and two young ambulance attendants suddenly burst into the room. Davon noticed they did not have a stretcher, nor were they carrying any medical equipment.

"Karif, do they have an oxygen tank or any medical supplies? Andy needs aspirin and oxygen right away."

Speaking Arabic, he asked one of the attendants. He then looked at her. "The driver said they have no oxygen or medication. You will have to wait until you get to the hospital. They are concerned about getting the patient out of the tomb because of the narrow staircase. Can he walk?"

"Good grief," muttered Davon, under her breath, thinking an ambulance without medical supplies was close to useless. "No, he cannot walk. He will have to be carried."

"I can carry him on my back," offered Fritz, positive that neither one of the ambulance attendants would be strong enough.

"Are you sure?" asked Davon, racking her brain for an alternative. "Karif, please ask if they have a chair or a sling we can use." She waited for him to translate. When he shook his head, she realized they did not have much choice.

"I can bench-press 200 pounds, so I think I am your best bet," stated Fritz, making the decision without any consultation. "Andy, I am going to piggyback you up the stairs, but you will need to stand up."

CHAPTER FORTY-SIX

Andy clung to Fritz as the bodyguard slowly climbed the stairs. The two ambulance attendants walked behind—each gripping a thigh—attempting to take some of the weight off the bearer. It was a gruesome task, carrying a 175-pound male up the narrow passageway, yet somehow, Fritz managed to make headway, hunched over with the burden on his back, his eye level fixed to the ground. At the rear of the odd-looking band of seven, Davon listened to the huffing sound Fritz made with each step. She was concerned about his well-being and had to fight the urge to tell him to slow down, knowing she needed to trust him to stop when he felt tired. He had only stopped once for four to five minutes and was certainly due for another break. When they rounded a corner, a shaft of sunlight poured into the passageway from the small windows at the top of the staircase and Davon realized they were nearing ground level.

"I need to pause for a few minutes," Fritz said, letting Andy know he had to get off his back and stand. Sweat poured down Fritz's reddened face and he took a gulp of air.

Pushing past the attendants, Davon moved to his side. "Take as long as you need," she said, troubled by his panting. "The last thing I want is another cardiac arrest. We are almost at the top, ten maybe fifteen more stairs and we will be out in the open." She then turned her attention to Andy and encouraged him to lean on her while they waited for Fritz to recuperate.

Fritz bent over and took in a long deep breath. His legs felt heavy. It was as though they were made out of lead. "Well, I certainly won't need to do a workout tonight," he said, more to himself than anyone else, trying to gather strength.

"Honestly, we can't thank you enough," said Mona. "I don't know what we would have done if the two of you hadn't come along."

"Yes, we are very grateful," confirmed Andy, feeling embarrassed that he was not able to make his own way out of the catacombs.

"Not a problem," replied Fritz. "Now, let's get out of here." He took a deep inhale and squatted down. The attendants immediately hoisted Andy onto his back. With a loud grunt, he took the next step upward.

Fritz leaned against the wall of the temple and watched the ambulance attendants lift the stretcher Andy was on into the back of the ambulance. He looked at Davon, fussing over the patient like a mother hen and then smiled at her when she walked over to where he was standing.

"What you did was absolutely amazing, Fritz. I'm going to go to the hospital with Andy and I want you to go back to the hotel and get into a hot bath. Book a massage for tonight and bill it to my room."

Fritz shook his head. "First of all, you are the hero, not me and if you are going to the hospital, I am going to the hospital too."

Davon flushed at the compliment. "Thanks, but I was just doing my job, what you did literally took real strength and stamina. Are you sure your back is okay, because you really don't need to come to the hospital."

"Thank you for thinking about me, but my back is fine. You said your job is being a doctor, well my job, is to protect you. I am coming to the hospital and it is not up for discussion," he firmly told her.

"Alright," Davon replied, realizing there was no point in arguing. "I'm riding in the back of the ambulance with Andy. Can you get Karif to give you a ride? Also, could you pay him and the driver? I'll reimburse you later," she called as she went to the back of the ambulance and jumped inside.

Davon sat on a small pull-down seat beside Mona and took a look around the archaic transport vehicle. It was a simple metal box with three small windows on each one of the sidewalls. There was no piped in oxygen, resuscitation equipment or any way to contact the driver from the stretcher area in case of emergency. Although she noticed the stretcher was strapped to the floor, she could see no passenger seatbelts.

"I think we are going to have to hang on to our seats," she said to Mona, grabbing the base of her chair as the ambulance driver floored it and raced into the street, siren wailing.

Mona snatched the side of the stretcher to maintain her balance. She grimaced and then lowered her voice to a whisper. "I'm a bit worried. If this is the ambulance, what is the hospital going to be like?"

"Don't worry, Mona, I'll be there with you," replied Davon, reassuringly, even though she too was having second thoughts about the health care in this third world country.

CHAPTER FORTY-SEVEN

The hospital was a ten-minute ride away and during the trip, Davon took a medical history from Andy. When the attendants opened the back doors of the ambulance, they assisted Mona, then Davon out of the vehicle, before unhooking and pulling out the stretcher. Mona waited beside Davon in front of the sad-looking building with its mouldy, pealing plaster and looked as though she was about to cry.

"It's probably better inside," said Davon, patting her arm. "Most of the buildings in Alexandria have problems with mold. It's because of the salty air." Following the stretcher inside, they were met with a beehive of activity. "I would like to speak with the physician in charge, please," said Davon to an official looking man, wearing a white lab coat.

"Please wait," he replied, appearing to understand her request.

Ushering Mona forward, Davon advised her to go with Andy. "Stay with Andy and wherever they are taking him I will find you after I speak with the doctor." She waited beside an odd-looking table/reception desk and stared through the doorway into the large emergency room, watching the attendants wheel Andy towards the back. Counting the number of stretchers lined up against one wall, she managed to get to thirteen, when a handsome man, sporting a worried expression, approached her.

"I am Dr. Tuma, may I help you?" he asked in a brisk manner.

"Yes, I am Dr. Marshall, an emergency room physician from Boston General Hospital. I brought in a Canadian tourist, male, 59 years, past history of good health, who had a cardiac arrest in the Kom el Shoqafa catacombs at approximately 10:30 this morning. I resuscitated him and he came to after about six minutes of CPR. I have brought him here for assessment. At the moment he is relatively pain-free and appears stable, but of course, he will need the usual: ASA, Nitrates, Beta Blockers, O2, blood work, cardiac monitoring, angiogram..."

"Let me stop you right there, Dr. Marshall. As you can see, this," he said quickly with a wave of his hand, "is not a Canadian or US hospital and we have limited resources—I actually did some training at the Mayo Clinic and therefore know firsthand. I can do a basic cardiac workup, but I cannot offer him an angiogram. I will get to him as quickly as possible, but I am the only physician on duty, the emergency room is full and I am dealing with two other emergencies," he informed her, stating the facts without an inkling of remorse or concern.

Davon paled. She had no idea the hospital here would be in such dire straits. "How many patients do you have?"

"I have fifty-two, counting the stretchers in the hallway and as you can see the waiting room is also full, so if you will forgive me, I have to get back to work," he replied, turning to go.

"Wait, Dr. Tuma. I have my medical card and number with me. What would you say if I offered to help you out today?" She reached into her wallet and produced an ID card with her photograph.

Dr. Tuma stopped dead in his tracks and his somber expression faded. "I could sure use the help. You would have to wear a headscarf and you would not be able to attend to Egyptian males over the age of twelve. Is that agreeable?"

"It is not a problem. I worked at a clinic outside of Dubai, so I know all about the rules," she answered, feeling light-hearted and happy. "Would it be possible to find me a lab coat?" she suddenly added, glancing down at her unprofessional light blue cotton shirt and jeans.

"Yes and I will have Yaren, one of our clerks, act as a translator for you. Thank you, Dr. Marshall," replied Dr. Tuma as he dashed off.

Fritz, who was standing off to the side, walked over. He looked at Davon's smiling face and saw a dramatic change in her expression, her stance, her being. It was as though a huge burden had been lifted off her shoulders. The tiny wrinkles at her brow had vanished and the troubled expression, he had noticed from the first day he met her, was gone, replaced with a true glow. "Did I hear you say you are going to work here for the rest of the day?" he questioned.

Davon froze. She had completely forgotten Fritz was waiting for her. "I'm sorry. I didn't even think about you. I need to treat Andy and help Dr. Tuma get through some of these patients. You go back to the hotel and I promise I will call you when I am finished."

"You are a wonderful person, Davon Marshall," Fritz said with blatant admiration, understanding that for Davon, a hospital was like home, comforting and safe. "But, I think I should stick around for a bit to make sure you are okay here on your own before I venture off. I will sit over there and look through some of those interesting Egyptian brochures."

Davon removed her stethoscope, headscarf, cell phone and wallet from her purse, and then handed the bag to Fritz. "Can you take my bag back with you to the hotel? And when you feel I am safe enough, just go and please have a bit of fun on your last day in Egypt," she said with a small laugh. She noticed a young man walking towards her with a lab coat slung over his arm. "I think that is my translator," she told him. Nodding, Fritz took her bag. Davon quickly covered her hair with the scarf and then slipped the stethoscope around her neck.

"Dr. Marshall, I am Yaren. I will be your translator and will help you make your way around our emergency room. I am very familiar with all of the emergency procedures," he said, giving her the white coat.

"Thank you, Yaren. The first person I would like to see is the patient I brought to emergency," she replied. Slipping on the coat, she placed her phone and wallet into one of the pockets and then walked with him towards the emergency room doorway. "He needs oxygen, aspirin and ECG monitoring immediately. I would also like to give him some morphine, nitrates, a beta blocker, and get some blood work done as soon as possible and..." she said, glancing over to look at him, "insert a 'saline lock', if the hospital carries them."

Yaren listened intently. "I will get you an order sheet for the medication and will find you a portable ECG machine, and oxygen tank. You are responsible to draw blood work, start intravenous lines and IV locks. I can bring you an IV and blood kit. The patient is this way."

The emergency room was decrepit and gloomy. It had no windows and limited overhead lighting. The main light source, Davon noticed, came from the individual bedside lamps, which were wall-hung. Yaren explained that the room was divided into male and female sides, pointing out the over-sized, cloth partitions positioned down the center of the room. Emergencies, which had to be treated immediately, were placed closer to the reception desk, he explained, and those patients, who could wait, were situated at the back of the space. They made their way down the male side of the room and Davon averted her eyes to the floor, as they passed stretcher after stretcher on their way to Andy. Karif must not have told the ambulance attendants that Andy had had a heart attack because when they located him, he was at the very back of the emergency room in a small individual cubicle.

"Thanks, Yaren. If you could please bring me the things I need, I will assess the patient," she said, moving over to the side of the bed. "Any pain, Andy?" she asked, looking up briefly to acknowledge Mona.

"If I say no, will you let me out of here?" he answered, adjusting his position.

Davon grabbed her stethoscope. "I understand what you are saying, but unfortunately you will have to stay put until we figure out what went wrong. I spoke with the doctor in charge and he is allowing me to help him out for the day, which means I will be taking care of you. I want to assure you I will give you the best care I can, considering the

305

circumstances. Let me listen to your heart and then I want an honest answer about any discomfort." She put the earpieces into her ears, the end of the stethoscope below his left nipple and began to listen.

"Good news about Davon, right love?" said Mona, stroking Andy's arm.

Taking the blood pressure monitor from the bedside table, Davon took Andy's blood pressure and then felt for a pulse, just as Yaren and an aide came into the cubicle, wheeling a portable oxygen tank and ECG machine.

Yaren held out a chart with a large bottle of ASA and a blood work kit on top of it. "Dr. Marshall, if you could please write down the medication you require on this order sheet, I will pick it up for you. Dr. Tuma asked me to give you this bottle of aspirin."

Davon jotted down the medication she needed and then removed the sheet from the chart, giving it to Yaren. When he left to fill the order, she unscrewed the cap from the aspirin bottle and removed one. "Darn it. Is there any water around here?" she asked, glancing around the cubicle.

"I have a bottle of water in my purse," said Mona, reaching for it.

"Fantastic," replied Davon, popping the tablet into Andy's mouth. "Ideally, you should have had an aspirin in the catacombs, but it is better late than never," she told him, as Mona gave him a sip of water. Davon turned on the oxygen and readied the mask to place over his face. "Andy, I need you to point to where you are having pain or discomfort."

Andy moved his hand around his left upper chest. "It is not really a pain, just a constant achy feeling."

"I'm going to give you morphine to take that achy feeling away and then some other drugs to open up the blood flow to your heart. This is oxygen," she said as she placed the mask over his face. She pulled the older-looking ECG machine closer to the bedside and plugged it in. "I'm also going to do a cardiac reading of your heart and then poke you with a needle to get some blood," she informed him, placing the leads onto his chest and limbs. "When I took your history in the ambulance, you said there was no history of heart disease on your side of the family and that you have never had a heart attack before. You are on no medication, have no allergies, you are a non-smoker, non-diabetic and have no history of high blood pressure, correct?"

"Yes, that is correct," answered Mona. Andy nodded.

"That is very good news," she said, switching on the ECG machine, which quickly sprang to life. She then turned her attention to doing the blood work. Opening the kit, she spread the sterile disposable cloth onto the bedclothes and set up the vials. Placing the tourniquet tightly around his upper arm, she put on gloves, and then removed the needle from its safety cap. After swabbing the distended vein, she poked it, quickly attaching a vial to the end of the needle. She took five vials of blood before releasing the tourniquet and applying pressure to the site.

When Yaren returned, he brought along the drugs and the saline lock Davon had requested, as well as a printed sheet of paper. "Please select the blood work you want, Dr. Marshall," he said, politely offering her the page.

"Perfect timing, Yaren," she remarked, staring blankly at the printed Arabic figures.

Yaren blushed, took the sheet of paper and flipped it over. "I am sorry," he apologized. "English is on this side." He saw the stunned look on Davon's face. "We often have English speaking volunteer doctors."

"Wonderful," said Davon, realizing that was probably the reason Dr. Tuma had so readily agreed to let her work at the hospital. "I will indicate what blood work I would like. Can you please put Andy's name on the vials and take them to the lab?"

As Yaren gathered up the vials of blood, Davon ticked several boxes, denoting the tests she wanted done. Handing Yaren the request form, she glanced at the ECG strip and then started to get ready to insert the saline lock so she could give the IV medications. Moving around the bed, she positioned herself beside Andy's other arm, applied the tourniquet and inserted the cannula into the distended vein. When she saw the return of blood, she removed the tourniquet, and taped the saline lock into place. Checking the drug and dosage of the preloaded syringes first, she slowly gave each medication through the device.

"This is going to make you feel a little sleepy, Andy. Close your eyes and have a nap," said Davon, after she had given him the IV Morphine. She watched Andy drift off. Recapping the empty syringes, she placed them onto the bedside table.

"How are things looking?" inquired Mona, hoping her husband would get the all clear.

Davon picked up the pink colored ECG strip, coming out of the machine and looked at it. "Well, we know Andy has had a heart attack, but what we don't quite know, is the severity or cause and I still need to look at his blood work," she replied, keeping her facial expression neutral when she saw the ST-segment was elevated, indicating a portion of the heart muscle had died.

Mona nodded as though she understood. "Our flight leaves Cairo a week today. Is there any chance we will be able to make it?"

"Seven days might be a bit soon," answered Davon, knowing Andy would most likely have to be hospitalized for at least three weeks and would probably require surgery. "What I suggest is you contact your medical travel insurance provider and explain the situation. Your husband had a heart attack and has been admitted to Alexandria Hospital. Do you have a cell phone?"

"No, I will have to wait until I get back to the hotel," said Mona, looking fretful.

"Take my phone," said Davon, kindly offering it to her. "Things will be okay, Mona. I have heard insurance companies sometimes provide a medical person to travel home with you if the flight is over four hours. Make sure you tell them the doctor explained to you that Andy cannot make the scheduled flight home."

"I will," sighed Mona. "Thank you for your help."

Davon left Mona to her call, exiting the cubicle in search of Yaren. She found him at the nursing station in the center of the room. The nurses, she noticed were all male.

"Are you ready to see other patients?" he asked when she approached him.

"Yes. Is it possible to have one of the nurses check Andy's vital signs every fifteen minutes?"

Yaren turned to the nurse beside him and spoke rapidly in Arabic. "He will check on your patient. Dr. Tuma would like you to attend to the women and children."

"Alright, and Yaren, I want to be notified the minute Andy's blood work is completed," said Davon, adjusting her headscarf. "Give me a rundown on the patients Dr. Tuma would like me to see and I will start with the sickest person first."

There were fourteen women and eight children waiting to be seen. The first patient Davon saw was young woman, twenty-six weeks pregnant, threatening to miscarry. After doing an internal examination and ultrasound with an ancient-looking machine, Davon admitted her to the obstetrics ward for observation. Her next patient was a three-year-old boy with a fractured arm. Davon checked his x-ray and then applied a cast, using a type of old-fashioned plastering material she had only read about in medical journals. She discharged the boy and proceeded to treat an ear infection, several skin infections and a sprained ankle. When she completed an assessment or treatment, Davon would chart her patient notes in English and Yaren would take them from her and translate them into Arabic. This system appeared to be working well.

Just as she was about to go behind a curtain to change a wound dressing, Yaren waved her into the nursing station. "Here is the blood work you requested," he said, handing her two sheets of paper.

The results were printed in English and after Davon looked at them, she became concerned. "I need to speak with Dr. Tuma right away."

"Yes," said Yaren, "I will find him."

When Dr. Tuma came into the nursing station, Davon handed him the blood work and the printed strip of Andy's ECG. "His cardiac enzymes and ST-segment are elevated," she said. "He obviously has coronary obstruction and needs an angiogram, probably surgery. Is there another hospital in the vicinity where the test can be preformed?"

"Only in Cairo," said Dr. Tuma, thoroughly inspecting the results.

"Well then, we have no choice, but to transfer him as soon as possible," pointed out Davon. "I would however like him to go accompanied by a nurse and in a real ambulance. The ambulance that brought us to the hospital was in dire need of medical supplies."

Dr. Tuma explained that a private ambulance could be hired if the insurance company was willing to pay for it. "Yaren can make the arrangements, if you would like to inform the patient," he told her. Davon instantly agreed.

She set off down the corridor to discuss the situation with Andy and Mona. "How is he doing?" she asked as she stepped inside the curtain.

"He has been sleeping ever since you gave him the Morphine," whispered Mona, getting up from her small wooden chair.

"I'm afraid I am going to have to wake him to discuss the results of his tests." Davon called his name and gently touched his shoulder. Andy opened his eyes and blinked several times. "Sorry to wake you from your beauty sleep, but your test results are in. How are you feeling?"

Andy managed a weak smile. "No more pain. Am I doing okay,

Doc?"

"I have good news and bad news. What do you want first?"

"The good news, please," replied Andy, looking at his wife and then back towards Davon.

"The good news is you are basically in good health and that is the reason you did not die today. The bad news is you had a severe heart attack. I want you to have a special test called an angiogram, but the problem is they do not perform angiograms at this hospital. I am making arrangements for you to be transferred by ambulance to a hospital in Cairo where the angiogram can be done."

"Cairo is a few hours away. What if something happens on route? I'm worried about him traveling in that ancient ambulance," cried Mona.

"Not to worry, Mona. I am arranging for a private ambulance and nurse to accompany him. Did you get a hold of your insurance company?"

Mona nodded as she handed Davon back her cell phone. "Thanks for letting me use your phone. They said he is covered, but the hospital needs to fax them a medical report."

"Give me the fax number of the company and I will take care of it. Now, you will have to pay cash for the ambulance and nurse and then send the receipt to the insurance company for reimbursement. The cost is 2700 Egyptian pounds, which is about two hundred Canadian dollars. The doctor told me there is an ATM machine in the main lobby of the hospital. I have asked the clerk assisting me to organize a taxi for you, Mona. Go to your hotel before it gets dark, pack up your luggage and bring it to the hospital. By the time you get back here we should have the ambulance organized and be ready to go," instructed Davon.

"Are you coming with us to Cairo?" asked Andy, looking hopeful.

"I wish I could come with you, but unfortunately I have a prior commitment in Alexandria later today. That being said, your vital signs are now stable and I am confident you will have no problem making the trip. And don't forget, you will have a nurse with explicit instructions on what to do, if something should go wrong," explained Davon, contemplating whether she should tell them he would most likely require surgery if the angiogram showed a coronary occlusion. She noticed the depressed looks upon their faces and decided not to mention it. "It is always difficult when something like this happens away from home, but you will get through this," she said reassuringly. "Dr. Tuma said the hospital you are being transferred to is much larger than this one and more modern. And the fact that it does do angiograms proves it is where you need to be."

Yaren popped his head around the curtain. "The taxi is here."

"Okay, I'll go to the hotel and get our things," said Mona. She gave Andy a kiss on the cheek and then left with Yaren.

Davon patted his hand. "I will check on you in between my other patients. Try to go back to sleep."

CHAPTER FORTY-EIGHT

The cell phone in Davon's pocket began to vibrate and when she pulled it out to look at the text she had received, she noted the time. It was after 6:00 pm. The text was from Fritz, reminding her of her dinner date. He informed her, he would be coming to pick her up, using the hotel's limousine. Davon fired off a quick reply, stating she would not be done for another forty-five minutes. She had no idea where the time had gone.

The transfer of Andy to Cairo Hospital, as predicted, went smoothly. He was admitted to the cardiac unit and following his assessment there, Davon had an excellent phone conversation with the receiving physician. Breathing a sigh of relief, she was hopeful he would get good care at the Cairo facility. She turned her thoughts to the next patient on her list, a recent admission with breathing issues.

"Yaren," she called, "I need you to translate." She stepped around the curtain to find an eight-year-old boy with both parents hovering over him. The boy was agitated and kept trying to remove his oxygen mask and kick off his covers while his parents attempted as best they could to stop him. Davon smiled at the parents as she removed the mask and flipped off the blanket. The child settled somewhat. "Let the parents know, he has a temperature and that is why he is fidgeting," said Davon, looking at the child's sunken eyes and flushed cheeks. "Ask them how long he has been sick and if there is anyone else in the household with these symptoms." She pulled out her stethoscope, warmed it in the palm of her hand and then began to listen to his chest.

"He has only been sick for three days and no one else in the home is ill. They thought he had a cold, but this morning when he woke, he was having trouble breathing," said Yaren.

Davon finished her assessment. "Tell them he has pneumonia. He will have to be admitted to the hospital and I will need to start an intravenous to give him IV antibiotics. Does he have any allergies?"

Sitting in the nursing station, Davon quickly finished up her patient notes. She then glanced at the time and realized Fritz would be arriving in ten minutes. Standing up, she went in search of Dr. Tuma, finding him on the male side of the department.

"I have to be going," she informed him, removing the lab coat and then her possessions from the pockets.

Dr. Tuma smiled. "Thank you very much for your assistance. Is there any chance you can work again tomorrow?" he asked, leaning forward with hopes of receiving a positive answer.

"You know, I wish I could help you out because I really enjoyed working here today, but I actually leave for home tomorrow," she told him, returning the smile.

"Well then, Dr. Marshall, if you are ever in Alexandria again, you know where to find us. You are a very good physician and will always be welcome."

CHAPTER FORTY-NINE

The limousine, with its motor running, was waiting at the door of Emergency. Fritz ushered Davon inside. "How was your day?" he asked, sitting down on the seat beside her.

"It was extremely busy and I only had time for a quick coffee at about two o'clock, but, I loved it. The hospital is old and antiquated as you saw, however, they have basic equipment and I had no problem admitting a patient. At the hospital I work at, in Boston, there is always a shortage of beds and good luck if you need to admit someone. I probably saw around forty patients in total today, but the weird thing was, some of them were not really sick, I mean, to be seen in Emergency. When I mentioned this to Yaren, the clerk who was assisting me, he said these people don't have family doctors, so they have to come to the hospital," she remarked with a yawn, leaning her head on the back of the seat. "I guess that is the reason the emergency room is so incredibly busy, and to think they only have one doctor per shift. Crazy!"

"How is Andy?" Fritz inquired.

"He had to be transferred to a hospital in Cairo for a specialized test that was unavailable here," Davon replied. She offered no further details about Andy's condition because of doctor patient confidentiality, a premise, which had been thoroughly drummed into her head from day one of medical school. Fritz accepted the answer and did not probe any further.

When they arrived at the hotel, Fritz held open the car door. "Your handbag is on your bed. Call me if you need me tonight, otherwise I will see you at breakfast tomorrow morning. Enjoy your dinner with your friends."

"Thanks for coming to get me," said Davon, hurrying across the lobby and into the private elevator. She only had minutes to get ready.

Showered and dressed, Davon located the money order and placed it into her pocket. Grabbing her bag and slinging it over her shoulder, she stopped in front of the gilded full-length mirror and glanced at her reflection. She had pulled her hair back into a tight ponytail and was wearing a navy blue pantsuit with the blue silk shirt she had purchased at Cheri's boutique. The outfit looked more professional than dinner suitable, but she did not want to wear anything flashy, and had no energy or time to change. "Oh well," she sighed, as she pulled open the door to the suite. Taking the elevator to the lobby, she made herself comfortable on a white leather loveseat with a bird's eye view of the entranceway. Two minutes later, Fatar and Nasa came rushing through the sliding glass doors.

"We came as soon as we were able," Nasa said in a comforting tone, immediately embracing Davon. "How have you been managing since the tragedy? We have been so worried about you." When Nasa finally released her from the hug, Fatar took her hand and shook it.

"I'm alright. Of course, his death was a great shock and I have been struggling to come to terms with it, but I spoke with the Pandit at the Hindu Temple and he helped me feel somewhat better about things," she answered, trying to stop the flood of suppressed emotions, which were now rising to the surface. "I'm sure our table is ready, so why don't we go into the restaurant and once we are settled, I will tell you more about what happened."

The Persian restaurant with its dark wood paneling and ornate furniture had approximately twenty tables in the middle section as well as several booths running along each side. As they entered the premises, Davon quietly requested a booth, thinking it would give them a touch of privacy. They were given menus and a list of dinner specials.

Placing his menu to the side, Fatar looked at her. "You said Baboo's heart failed him. Did he have a heart attack? Was there any type of warning?"

When Davon had spent time at their home, she had not shared the fact that she was a physician. Better not to say anything, she thought, as she tried to think of some way to spin the truth about Baboo's death. "It was dark and Uncle Baboo fell down. I quickly realized how serious it was," she mumbled, tears coming to her eyes as she relived the event. "I was extremely upset because of the circumstances, yet Uncle Baboo was calm, almost serene. He accepted the reality that he did not have much time and told me of several requests, which he made me promise to fulfill. He then passed away and afterwards, his death was determined to be heart failure," she confided.

"You are a brave young woman to have dealt with this catastrophe on your own," said Nasa with sympathy. "What are the arrangements for the funeral tomorrow?"

"The funeral ceremony took place this morning at the Hindu Temple. As a non-Hindu, I was not permitted to attend." Both Nasa and Fatar nodded in understanding. "He will be cremated tonight and I will pick up his ashes tomorrow morning for dispersal in the sea. It will only be the three of us in attendance, wishing him farewell." The waiter approached to take their order and Davon waited for him to leave the table before she attempted to strike up a new conversation. Talking about Baboo's last moments was wreaking havoc with her emotions. "How is the tour guide business going? Have you been busy?" she questioned, hoping to find an opening to bring up the subject of the money order.

"Things are starting to pick up, now that the weather is improving. Spring and fall are always our busiest seasons," said Fatar.

"During the summer it is too hot and in the winter it is too cool for the tourists."

"It must be difficult to manage during the slower months," said Davon, thinking if Fatar mentioned cash issues, she would offer him the envelope from Abdul.

Although Davon could see concern in his eyes, Fatar shook his head not wanting to admit to money troubles. "No, no, it is not a problem. Nasa and I work long hours during our busy time and always put away enough money for the slower months."

With pride, Fatar informed her about a recently organized tour for the following month. Davon asked questions about some of the historical sites the group would visit and they had an interesting conversation about many of the highlights of Egypt. When Nasa explained that they were trying to encourage this group to supplement their tour with a Nile cruise, Davon enthusiastically talked about her visit to the Temple of Horus.

"I am so glad you suggested it, Nasa, because it was the highlight of the riverboat cruise. I had no idea it was such a well-preserved temple and its beauty, unbelievable! I definitely want to go back there one day," she excitedly told them, her mood lifting as she pictured the entrance to the temple.

The discussion paused for a moment when their meals arrived and then turned to the delightful presentation of the food.

"And what did you think about Philae Temple?" asked Nasa, taking a sample of the bean mixture on her plate. "I remember you were going on the trip specifically to see the temple of Isis."

Davon winced and put down her fork. "It was beautiful and everything I thought it would be, but going there will always be a painful memory. You see, that is the place where Uncle Baboo passed away."

"I am so sorry. I did not know." Nasa's hand flew to her mouth at the blunder.

Davon saw her exchange a worried look with Fatar. "Please, Nasa, don't feel bad. Besides, how could you have known?" The comment about Baboo's death on Agilkia Island stalled the conversation and the vibrant pre-dinner talk turned into a mundane discussion about the weather.

"It will be warm tomorrow and I have heard there will be little wind," said Fatar, alluding to the fact it would be a good day to disperse the ashes.

When they finished their meal Davon asked them if they would like dessert, but they politely declined. "Are you sure you won't consider something sweet to finish off the meal?"

"It is getting late," said Nasa. "We should be on our way. But, thank you for a lovely dinner."

Davon knew it was now or never. "Before you go, I have something I would like to give you," she said, reaching into her pocket. She took out the money order and placed it onto the table. "Uncle Baboo asked me to give you his last paycheck. I hope you will accept it." Pushing the envelope across the table, she offered it to them.

Looking puzzled, Fatar opened the envelope and removed the money order. His eyes widened when he took in the amount. "No, we cannot accept," he quickly said. "The money should go to you, Davon." He did not show the contents to Nasa. Replacing the money order into the envelope, he pushed it back towards her.

"Fatar, please listen to me. I do not need money and Uncle Baboo was well aware of that fact," said Davon, determined to find a way to convince him. "You and Nasa were like family to him. In his dying breath, he asked me to give this money to you. Please let me go home tomorrow, knowing I did what my uncle asked me to do," she convincingly pursued, feeling awful about the necessary lie. She would never forget how Fatar and Nasa had welcomed them the night they arrived unannounced on their doorstep and rationalized the fib by the memory of Baboo telling her he planned to share his bonus with his friends.

While Fatar sat almost motionless, Nasa took the envelope and looked at the contents. "So much money! Who knew Baboo made so much money!" she exclaimed in surprise.

Davon leaned forward and looked at her. "Please convince Fatar to take it, Nasa," she pleaded.

She listened to their conversation in Arabic and after several minutes of heated discussion, Fatar finally nodded. "I will take the money, but only because it was Baboo's dying wish. I cannot insult the memory of my wonderful friend."

"I know Uncle Baboo, wherever he is, is happy and smiling down at you," replied Davon, feeling thrilled.

CHAPTER FIFTY

Davon turned and slowly made her way to the rocky shore. Without a second thought about the water dripping off her calves and feet, she slipped on her sandals and walked towards Nasa and Fatar. She was thankful they had come. It would have been a lonely affair, had they not participated.

Nasa gave her a warm embrace. "So beautiful, your words brought tears to my eyes. I still cannot believe he is gone. Thank you for letting us share this with you," she whispered. They watched a wave push the ashes and the intricately woven wreath of white lilies towards the shore and then quickly back out to sea.

"I am proud you honored his wishes, giving him the type of burial he wanted. You did the right thing, Davon," said Fatar, wiping away a tear. "Baboo was a wonderful and generous man. He will be missed."

"Yes, he will be missed," replied Davon. She deeply regretted that she was not able to do something to prevent his death. Once more, gut retching anguish and despair filled her heart. *I hope you understand and forgive me, Baboo,* she silently prayed.

A gust of wind blew inland, stirring up the sand around them. Davon and Nasa clutched their headscarves as the strong breeze threatened to blow them away.

"It looks as though the weather is changing," said Nasa, looking up to the sky. "Thank goodness the wind did not come up until now."

They observed two small whirlwinds along the shoreline, close to where they were standing, twirling and dancing for a few moments, before they turned and veered out to sea. As quickly as the wind started, it oddly and abruptly settled. "Uncle Baboo told me those are whirlwinds of happiness," Davon said, her solemn face breaking into a radiant smile. A sudden sense of peacefulness came over her and she wondered if it was a sign that everything was going to be okay.

"They can also be a warning about an oncoming storm," Fatar stated matter-of-factly. "I think we should be getting on our way, Nasa."

"Of course, you should be going because you have a long drive ahead of you," said Davon. "I need to be leaving for the airport, anyway. Thank you so much for coming. It meant a lot to me."

"We can take you to the airport in our rental car," suggested Fatar.

"Thank you for the offer, but I have a car waiting for me. I really appreciate you taking care of Uncle Baboo's apartment in Cairo. Please take anything you like." Smiling, Davon gave Nasa a hug. "I hope I will see you again, sometime in the future."

"As we do you. Remember our home is your home. Come and stay with us anytime," said Nasa, as she and Fatar turned and walked up the path towards the parking lot.

Davon waved goodbye, and then looked back at the sea. The ashes had vanished and she could only catch a brief glimpse of the wreath as it rolled on the waves—floating now quite far from the shore. "I will never forget you, Baboo. I will carry the memory of you with me always," she whispered, determined not to cry. She bit her trembling lip and felt the sadness of the moment, the finality of death. It was only two hours before her scheduled flight and she knew she had to make her way to the airport. "Goodbye my dear friend." Turning in the direction of the main road where the car was waiting, she carefully made her way up the embankment. She felt tired, thoroughly spent, now that the funeral was over, but as she broached the top of the hill, the fatigue suddenly turned into annoyance. Fritz, for no reason, had moved the car farther along the road, several blocks away from the path where he knew she would be coming. "Why would he move the car way over there?" she grumbled, pulling off her headscarf. Marching towards the vehicle, she listened to the squishing water sounds coming from her wet sandals and let out an irritated huff.

When she reached the dark grey limousine, parked in exactly the same place where her black Lexus once had been, she suspiciously eyed it. "And why do you need to park in my parking space?" she muttered, nearing the rear door of the vehicle. Unexpectedly it opened. An Armani pant leg with a black, highly polished Italian shoe emerged. Davon stopped dead in her tracks and her heart began to pound. "It can't be," she gasped, not believing her eyes when Abdul stepped out of the vehicle. "What are you doing here?" she questioned him with a smile from ear to ear. "I thought we agreed..."

"You agreed, I did not," he said, walking towards her. "I came to bring you some gifts."

She gave him a quizzical look and a swift peck on the cheek. "I told you I didn't need anything."

"Yes, you did tell me that, however I think you might like this present," he replied with a playful grin. He handed her a legal-sized yellow manila envelope.

"What is it?" asked Davon, wrinkling her brow.

"Open it."

She tore the seal and pulled out a pad of papers, shaking her head in disbelief as she read the top page. "You bought me a private hospital in London, England! Are you crazy?"

Abdul laughed. "I thought you would like to run your own hospital. It is just a small one."

She scanned the first page and looked at him in amazement. "Nine hundred beds is not a small hospital, Abdul!" she said, throwing her arms around him. "You are unbelievable! I don't know what I am going to do with this, but I would love to give it a whirl! Britain has a national health system so I'm not sure how this is going to work." She was overwhelmed with excitement.

"You will figure it all out. Now, here is your next present," he said, offering her a second, especially fat manila envelope.

"I don't think I can handle two hospitals." Davon's hands were shaking as she ripped open the seal. She flipped through the contents and her cheerful disposition quickly became sober. "You are divorcing all of your wives!" she exclaimed, her tone suddenly cool.

"Yes, because I have never met a woman like you, Davon Marshall, and I want to spend the rest of my life with you and only you."

"I know I should be happy, but I feel terrible," she said, starting to tear. "I like all of your wives and your children...no, you can't do this, Abdul." She stepped away from him and shook her head.

Abdul reached out and took her into his arms. "It is already done, my love."

Davon looked him in the eye. "How can you get divorced so fast? It is because a man has all of the rights in your country, a woman is nothing!" she said in a quick flash of anger.

"What you say is true, but I am a fair man and I spoke with each of my wives individually. You have to understand, they do not love me, nor I them. Our marriages were arranged and the truth is I have only spent very little time with any of them over the years. I have promised to take care of them for the rest of their lives wherever they may choose to live—be it in the palace or somewhere else—and of course I will always provide for my children."

Taking a deep breath, Davon tried to calm herself. "When I left the palace in November, Lamna was pregnant. I know she loves and adores you!" The words came out quickly and ended with a muffled sob.

"She lost the baby in December," Abdul said softly. "Lamna told me she will never forgive me for not being there when she miscarried." He hung his head and closed his eyes, trying not to remember Lamna's hateful words when he explained he wanted a divorce.

Davon moved towards him and lifted his chin. "I'm sorry I lost my temper. I really do love you, Abdul and I know you are a kind and loving man. Please do not beat yourself up about Lamna. How could she have known you were abducted by your brother?"

"And that is exactly why I want you to be a part of my life, Davon, because you understand what my life is really about. You do not care about my money. You care about me and helping others and doing the right thing." Getting down on one knee, Abdul took her hand. "I love you more than anything in the world. Will you do me the honor of becoming my wife?"

Overcome with emotion, Davon looked into his incredible brown eyes, soft with love for her. She felt her heart racing as it did those many months ago. "Before I give you my answer, Abdul, I need to know where we will live. As much as I like your ex-wives and love your children, I could never live with them at the palace. Please do not ask me to."

"Of course not. I thought we would live in a small castle, one I own, on the outskirts of London. It is not far from your hospital. The castle has plenty of room for the children when they come to visit, that is, if you do not object," he replied, waiting for her response.

"You know I would never object to visits from your children! But a castle? Oh Abdul!" she said, laughing and weeping at the same time. "On that account, yes, I will do you the honor as long as I am forever more your only wife."

Reaching into his pocket, Abdul pulled out a black velvet box. Opening the lid, he presented her with a five-carat diamond ring. "I give you my solemn promise that you will be my one and only wife forever more." After slipping the ring onto her finger, he stood and embraced her. "I have never been so happy," he said as he gingerly lifted her chin and kissed her. It was a deep and passionate kiss and Davon felt herself melting into his arms. When Abdul slowly pulled away, she felt bereft. She wanted more. "I have one more gift to present to you," he said with a chuckle, "but this time you need to close your eyes."

Davon could not imagine what the next present would be and could barely contain her emotions as she did as she was bid. When Abdul told her to open her eyes, she burst into tears. There standing in front of her was her old servant, Bin.

Rushing forward, Davon bent over and hugged the tiny waif. "Bin, I cannot believe you're here! I missed you so much and I never got a chance to say goodbye!"

"It okay. I here. I never leave you again," said Bin, reaching up to wipe away Davon's tears.

Davon grasped both of her hands and then stood back to look at her. "You are beautiful," she said in Farsi, Bin's mother tongue.

"Because of you," Bin replied, her face aglow. She was dressed in a smart light woolen suit with a matching scarf and sandals, so unlike the cheap cotton uniform Davon had always remembered her wearing. Bin gave Abdul a quick sideways glance and grinned sheepishly.

"I had Raja find Bin," he explained to Davon. "I told her to buy Bin some decent clothes and get her a passport because I thought you might like it if she lived with us at the castle."

"Like it, I love it! Thank you." She walked over and tightly embraced him. "You have given me more than my heart's desire! I love you, Abdul."

"I love you too," he said with a smile. "We should probably be getting to the airport. The plane is waiting to take us to London." Abdul waved at the black Lexus, which immediately pulled away from the curb, driving away.

"Ah, my luggage is in that vehicle, Abdul."

"Yes, I know, my love. Fritz will take it to the airport. I asked him to come and work for us and he accepted. He will be flying with us to London."

"Don't tell me Fritz knew all along you were coming to Alexandria?"

"Yes, he did and I am afraid that is not all," replied Abdul, ushering the women into the backseat of the limousine. Bin sat beside Davon and Abdul took the seat across from them. "You have always said you want complete honesty..."

"I do," she confirmed, leaning forward to listen to the confession.

His expression became serious and he shifted awkwardly in his seat. "It was not necessary to hold Baboo's body for several days before his cremation. I requested it."

"Why!"

"Well, I needed the time to make all of the arrangements. I was worried if you left Egypt, I would never ever see you again."

Davon laughed as she took his hands in hers. "I forgive you, my darling, and love you even more because you told me."

Abdul tapped on the partition, which separated the driver and passengers, to indicate that they were ready to get on their way. "I like being honest with you," he said with a wide grin. "It gives me a very good feeling inside! Now, Davon, although this whole affair is a surprise for you, I actually have been planning our wedding since I left Vienna. If it is all right, I would like to get married as soon as possible—in London, perhaps"

"I..." Davon blanched when she thought about how she was going to tell her parents.

"But, if you would like to wait," he exclaimed, concerned about her reaction.

"No, Abdul, it's not like that," she said, understanding what he was thinking. "I want to get married as soon as possible too. I was just wondering how I'm going to tell my parents, because of course, I would like my family to attend the ceremony. I have never really talked about you and I'm sure it is going to come as a great shock to them."

Abdul leaned into the seat and rubbed his chin. "Maybe I should fly to Boston and ask your father for your hand. This is how you do things in the West, is it not?"

"Yes and no," she replied, smiling at the thought of Abdul and her father in the same room discussing her hand. She did not want to encourage him. Her thoughts were filled with uncertainties. If it had been Matt, asking to marry her, her parents would have whole-heartedly agreed, but Abdul? She had no idea how her father would respond to a request from a prince. However, the fact remained that no matter what her father or mother said she was going to marry this man. "I don't think a trip to Boston is necessary. It might be best if I break the news to them myself when we get to London and then once the proposal has had time to sink in, we can Skype them together. I do know, though, once my parents meet you, they will love you."

Abdul gave a nod of approval and Davon glowed. She could not believe how much she loved him. She glanced at her engagement ring and the struggles, the escapades, the highs and the lows of the last year came flooding back. Her life with Abdul was going to be an exciting journey—a dramatic curve on her road of life. She suddenly thought about Baboo and his words of wisdom because again, she had leapt right in, taking no time to meditate on the decision to marry. Closing her eyes, she asked herself the question. Should I marry Abdul? Her brain told her yes. Logically, he was the perfect mate. He was kind, supportive, generous, smart and hard working. Her heart told her yes. He was a loving man and a good father and she knew he would love her until his dying breath. Her gut instinct roared yes. He gave her a sense of security and she passionately felt he was her soulmate, her destiny. Opening her eyes, she smiled at the handsome man across from her. "Our life together is going to be one incredible journey," she said, thinking somehow, deep inside, she had always known they belonged together.

THE END

ABOUT THE AUTHOR

DP SCOTT, author of *The Riddle of Ra, Dance with the Harem, The Christmas Elf, A Wee Bit of Magic, Saturna and the Battle for Zard, Saturna and the Secrets of the Kingdom, There's a Monster in the Wall, and The Wedding Guidebook*, lives in Kelowna, BC with her husband Roy, and their cocker spaniel, Sophie. She is currently working on a new children's story set in Salem, Massachusetts. For updates and news, visit www.dpscott.ca.